THE FALL OF US

Praise for Rita A. Gordon

Praise for Rita A. Gordon

"Rita Gordon has proven to be a natural in the contemporary romance genre."

— Johanna McCloy, Editor, *Six Car Lengths Behind an Elephant* and *Dare to Be Fabulous*

Praise for **The Days With Rain:**

"The relationship between Rain and Parker was so deeply nuanced, packed with layers of frustration, annoyance, heartbreak, and sadness. When a book can evoke such a range of emotions, I know it's a winner."

— BookKraves, *Goodreads Reviewer (five star review)*

Praise for **Seven Days in Seattle:**

"Readers will connect with the realistic banter whose humor and subtlety is worthy of a Hollywood script."

— *BookLife Reviews, Editor's Pick*

"In Seven Days in Seattle, Rita Gordon weaves a swoon-worthy story that kept me riveted until the end."

— Kenya Goree-Bell, *Bestselling Author of The Blood Legacy Series*

"...intriguing story with a complex protagonist that flouts convention."

— *Kirkus Reviews*

"Seven Days in Seattle is a riveting fusion of passion, sightseeing, and coincidence with twists and turns every reader will wish to experience firsthand. To Rita A. Gordon: more, more, more, please!"

— Jacqueline Luckett, author of *Passing Love* and *Searching for Tina Turner*

"Beyond the hot and steamy romance, Gordon also takes you on a trip to Seattle (like a little travelogue) and beautifully weaves in references to African American literature, history, music, and art."

— Johanna McCloy, Editor, *Six Car Lengths Behind an Elephant* and *Dare to Be Fabulous*

Praise for **30 Days in Belfast:**

***Publishers Weekly* Indie Spotlight February 2023 (Romance & Relationships)**

"An addictive, rollicking tale of friendship, love, and lust."

— *Kirkus Reviews*

"Gordon's debut offers readers a winning combination of intrigue and romance, revealed slowly through the lens of opulent travel and luxurious living."

— *BookLife Reviews*

"I loved the relationships between the characters, the storyline was heartwarming and after a while, I couldn't put it down. Would definitely recommend!"

— *LoveReading, Indie Books We Love (starred review)*

"...It's the best book I've read, period."

— Sana Aubuliel, *Author of Letters to The Person I Was*

"A[n] easy, beautiful, knowledgeable read!"

— Brianna, *Goodreads Reviewer (five star review)*

"Have enough courage to trust love one more time and always one more time."

— Maya Angelou

THE FALL OF US

A Novel

RITA A. GORDON

12:56 a.m.
California

The Fall Of Us

www.ritaagordon.com

Cover & Interior Design by Rita A. Gordon

Author's photo by Abigail Huller

First Edition August 2024

Library of Congress Control Number: 2024911695

ISBN: 979-8-9899429-1-6 (hardcover)

ISBN: 979-8-9899429-2-3 (paperback)

ISBN: 979-8-9899429-3-0 (ebook)

Published in the USA by 12:56 a.m.

www.twelvefiftysixam.com

Contents

Dedication

This book is dedicated to all those who've found the forever type of love.

Author's Note

The Fall of Us is a story about passion and connection and how sometimes being friends simply isn't enough in matters of the heart. When we last saw Raven, Parker, and Noah, they were in the throes of self-discovery right before their worlds collided. This is the conclusion to their story.

Some passages in this work describe difficulties, including a condition that is similar to hyperthymesia, cases of dissociation, sleep terrors, and a miscarriage. Additionally, some passages allude to improprieties in the form of abuse. With that in mind, I advise you to consider your health and well-being before diving into Raven, Parker, and Noah's story.

I also want to take a moment to thank you for following me on this journey of passion, friendship, and unconditional love.

Prologue

I Know What I Want

Raven

BEHIND CLOSED EYELIDS, I'M overcome with memories of the past week with Nik. For seven days in Seattle, I belonged to a powerful man whose last name I never knew. Left behind are traces of him. Every loving glance, each lingering kiss, the long list of precious moments he created...just for me. Even now, the scent of amber, musk, and spice steeped in my clothes surrounds me. The soreness between my thighs reminds me that for one week...he was mine.

But I need to forget. I have to shut it all out and stop the reel running in my head. What we had is over. I need to sleep. In less than five hours, I have the largest deal of my career and I need a clear head.

I reach for my phone. The only thing that can stop the reel from running rampant in my mind is the sound of his voice...my former lover, my best friend, the man who, with one word, can calm my nerves. Parker. I replay the voicemail he sent me the day after I broke up with him.

"Rain, I love you. I hope hearing my voice helps you get through the day knowing you are loved. Knowing that every breath I take reminds me that you are my life force. And I want to be that for you. I love you so much. Have a good day, babe. I'm waiting for you."

He's still waiting. When I return from Seattle, he'll be waiting for me at the airport. Years ago, Parker and I made a series of promises to each other. We would keep each other informed of our whereabouts. Regardless of the discussion's difficulty, we would always tell each other everything. Lastly, we would never deny each other anything.

My eyes flutter closed when I think about Parker, the curve of his smile, the sparkle in his aquamarine eyes when I walk into a room, his deep woodsy, sweet scent, and the smooth, loving sound of his voice when he says, "Talk to me, babe. Tell me what you want."

I whisper to myself in the darkness. *I want to go home. I want to heal. I want....*

Chapter 1

Let's Make a Deal

Noah

If you could rewrite one moment in your life, would you?

I would.

The second I opened my eyes this morning to find Rain sitting beside me, set to walk out of my life—I should have begged her to stay. She told me once that *"Begging seems to be your default setting."* She was right—at least when it came to her. Right now, I'd make a deal with the devil to regain the chance I lost.

Standing at the wall of windows in my office, looking out over the city, I grab my wrist, rolling my fingers along the bracelet Rain gave me, wondering where she is. Is she thinking about how good it was between us? How we spent our time tangled together until we became one? How our breaths and heartbeats were so in sync, I don't know where I started and she ended? I'm not sure what spell she put on me, but something about *this* woman got to me, and I started to fall for her. But that's over now. She'll never know I was seconds away from telling her, "Don't go."

"Here's the man of the hour." I turn around when I hear Mak's voice as my brothers file into my office.

My brothers have been on this journey with me, watching from the sidelines as what was supposed to be a one-night stand turned into something that felt like...more. I listen as they do their best to convince me to find Rain and make it work between us. They are understandably disappointed in me for letting Rain go. But there's no time to discuss that now, so I redirect the conversation to why we're here today, Ross Enterprises.

I usher my brothers out of my office and down the hall. We have a meeting to attend, yet I can't stop thinking about Rain.

"I'm impressed with June Ross. She's what, less than six months into the role, and she's already leading one of their largest expansion efforts. She's a powerhouse," Rok says.

"Remember, we're going to deal, not date," Mak says. Rok shakes his head.

"Thanks for the clarification, Casanova," Rok deadpans.

Mak was instrumental in uncovering some potential issues with the client that could invalidate their ability to sign our ethics clause. This real estate development deal is worth millions and will add thousands of square feet to our portfolio if we can close the deal. Ross Enterprises will build office space in Seattle and several other US cities and then venture into other countries.

"I want this deal to go our way. Brian says their attorney, Miss Nichols, is a powerhouse. We need to be on our toes," I say, giving them the low-down from our head counsel before we reach the conference room.

I take a deep breath, pull myself together, and try to forget the past week I spent enjoying days with Rain. She got up this morning to prepare for her meeting, which I hope goes well for her. It took every fiber of my being to hold my shit together and not pull her back into my arms this morning before she left. Letting her go was the hardest thing I had to do. She is the one woman that I've found myself falling for. I've never felt this way for any woman. But I need to let all that go. I have a meeting to run, clients to impress, and a deal to close.

I touch my brother's shoulder. "Rok, you good man?"

"Ready."

"Mak?"

"Ready."

"Great. Then let's make this deal."

"They're ready for you in the conference room," Jewel says.

I walk past Jewel toward the conference room. From the partially open door, I spot Jake Ross sitting with his back to the window, and June Ross, his sister, directly to his right. Pushing the door open, I step beyond the threshold and am stunned by the woman sitting to Jake's left. *Rain?* What the actual fuck?

Jake stands, and June and Rain follow suit. My eyes lock on Rain. The luscious lips I crave are slightly parted, and I sense we feel the same: surprised. She's the last person I would expect to attend this meeting. My brothers Rok and Mak step past me, and it's obvious where their eyes land. I can almost hear Rok say, "Lil Sis." What a cruel joke life is playing on me. But is it? I take a deep breath and pull myself together.

"Ms. Ross. Mr. Ross. Good to see you again," I start. "And Ms. Nichols. It's good to meet you." I offer my hand to her. She takes it. The delicate hand that so lovingly roamed my body for the past week gives me a firm grip. The kinetic energy between us is still there, and I pull back as my body responds to her touch. Fuck. I shake hands with Jake and June, and my brothers follow behind, shaking hands with our clients. Then we all take our seats. I sit directly across from Rain. The sight of her has me transfixed. Rok clears his throat—my signal to begin.

"Let's begin with introductions. I'm Noah Knight. This is Roman Knight, our CEO, and to his left is Mark Knight." As my eyes sweep past my brothers, they have a "did you know about this look" on their faces. I had no idea. I would have never touched Rain if I did. I don't believe in mixing business with pleasure. It can go all kinds of sideways. I must navigate one of our largest deals with the woman I want most. *Keep a clear head, man.* I tell myself.

June introduces her team. "I'm June Ross, COO. This is Jake Ross, our CFO, and our counsel on this contract, Raven Nichols, Esquire, is with us today. We've thoroughly reviewed the contract and have a few questions, but we look forward to getting this deal done," June says. I feel relief knowing she wants to make this work.

If this deal goes through and we sign this agreement, we will have a partnership to secure property on their behalf and build their office spaces for multiple locations around the globe. That's the tricky part. If Rain is their lead counsel, she'll review every agreement or legal document we have with them over the next several years until all projects are completed. This means I'll work directly with Rain for at least two years. As it stands, I can't look at this woman without wanting to reach out and touch her. My body responds to the sight of her. What the fuck am I going to do?

"That's great. We're looking forward to closing this deal as well."

Chapter 2

You Don't Look Like a Nik

Raven

"Right this way, Miss Nichols. Your colleagues are waiting for you in the conference room." The executive assistant I've been conversing with gestures to the open conference door. I step in, and my clients greet me.

The conference room is modern and spacious. Two sides are bordered by a wall of windows overlooking the Seattle skyline. A narrow wall is clad in horizontal wood slats where a large monitor hangs. Around the long wooden conference table in the center of the room are twelve chairs, but only six places set, three on either side of the table with water glasses strategically placed in front of each chair. I walk to where my clients stand near the wall of windows.

"Miss Ross. It's good to see you again." I extend my hand to June Ross, the new COO of Ross Enterprises. She greets me and then hugs me like we're old friends. Standing next to her with one hand held out to me and the other in his pocket is her handsome brother, Jake Ross, the CFO.

"Mister Ross. It's a pleasure to meet you, sir." I place my hand in his.

"Good to have you on the team, Miss Nichols. Alejandro and my sister sing your praises." I nod and smile. "The development team should be here in a minute. Have a seat," he says, then gestures for me to sit beside him. I take a seat. "We're excited to get started," he adds.

Reaching into my bag, I take out my iPad, open the case, and hear the secretary say, "They're ready for you in the conference room," followed by footsteps.

I glance at my watch briefly. It's nine on the dot. Good, they're on time. Looking up, I lock eyes with the man standing at the threshold....

Nik?

He's the last person I expect to see, looking as sexy as sin in a dark blue suit and grey tie. Nik, who I now know as Noah Knight, is the man I'll be working alongside for this project.

When I walked away from Nik this morning, I was resigned to never see him again. I was reconciled to the fact that the memories of the seven days we spent together would eventually fade, albeit not completely. But I could move on. I could swallow the feeling like a large lunch and allow that to satisfy my hunger until my next meal—whenever that would be.

My plan was to ace this meeting and take Parker up on his offer to help me talk through my personal issues and find a solution to help me finally get my act together. Then he walked in...Nik, or Noah, whatever he calls himself, is my new partner. How will I ever be in a room with him and not be taken in by the scent of amber and musk and that damn spice I still can't place? How can I shake his hand and not want him to pull me close and devour me?

And then there's Rok, Roman Knight, the man I drooled in front of at our first meeting. Next to him is the man I dubbed Baby Mak, otherwise known as Casanova. Throughout today's meeting, I heard hints of the silky-smooth tone he used on me when he saved me from dealing with

Blake. *"I got you, beautiful,"* he had whispered in my ear, sending me straight into a Casanova haze. Oh, God...this is going to be complicated.

"That's it." June stands, as do Nik and his two brothers, who lovingly referred to me this past week as Lil Sis. Jake and I stand, too. "We're looking forward to working with you."

I gather the executed agreement and put it in my bag. I look down at my watch—ten o'clock. I have a few minutes before I need to be downstairs to meet my driver and head to the airport. Jake Ross turns to me.

"Great job, Raven. I'm looking forward to working more closely with you. I'll have our coordinator get time on the calendar to follow up with June and me."

June walks over to her brother. "We'll assemble a team to work with you. Awesome job, Raven," she says before walking past us to talk with Roman. Noah breaks away from his brothers and walks toward me, sending my heart racing. What do I say to the man who, for one week, I've come beneath repeatedly screaming his name? Nik.

"Rain." My name rolls off his tongue, smooth and sultry, so only I can hear. "I suppose I should call you Ms. Nichols."

He doesn't want to hear this, but I say, "Raven or Rae for short is fine."

"Raven." I hear the reluctance in his voice. He's remembering our conversation. *"Please tell me you go by something other than Rae."* He refused to call me by my nickname and looked so relieved when I told him he could call me Rain. I never told him that only Parker calls me Rain. After today—that will remain the case.

This has to be difficult for him, too. Only yesterday, this man gave me the key to his heart. *"I need you to take it and protect it because honestly, Rain, I never met anyone like you, and I'm sure I never will again. Maybe one day, when I'm ready for it, it will find its way back to me—when I'm ready to open that door, we could do it together."*

"I suppose I should call you Noah."

"Some people call me Nik, without a C."

"Noah's better. I told you...you don't look like a Nik."

"You were right."

I look around the room. Jake and June are talking to Rok and Mak. Rok peers over June's shoulder and catches my gaze, giving me a warm smile. I remember dancing with him at his cousin Chase's birthday party. He was fun, thoughtful, protective—everything I could want in a big brother. Seeing the three of them together...I'm struggling to deal with all the emotions flooding me. The beautiful memories I tricked myself into believing weren't real are back, and I can't breathe. I need to leave. I promised Parker I'd come back whole. I can't do this. All I want to do is get home to Parker. I fucked up. This is all too much, and I feel myself spiraling. *Breathe.*

"Listen, Noah. I have to go. Great job making this deal seamless."

"Seems you're the winner here. We've agreed to your terms and conditions," he tells me.

"Thank you. But I really need to leave." I rush past him toward Rok and Mak.

"Ms. Nichols, great job." Rok's sentiments are warm and welcoming, and I feel the sting of tears welling in my eyes. I'll lose it if I don't get out of here soon.

"Congratulations," Mak says.

"Thank you. If you'll excuse me, I have a flight to catch. I'm looking forward to working with you," I say. Picking up my stride, I reach the elevator and push the button. It opens, and I step in. Nik tries to break away from June and Jake, but they're his priority.

As soon as the elevator doors close, I shut my eyes and try to push out what just happened. The meeting was a success. I met all of their objections to my revisions to the contract. But the entire meeting, I held my breath, remembering every touch, kiss, and moment with Nik. Everything about him is so fresh in my mind.

On our last night, he held me while he fed me cake. "Anything for you," he said, feeding me a few more bites before returning the plate to the counter and getting our champagne flutes. "Toast. To all my days with Rain lived and imagined."

I toasted him. "To the man I've come to know. Cheers." I looked at my watch. It was past midnight. "Take me to bed, Nik," I told him, and he did because we had a lifetime of living to fit into a few hours, and neither of us wanted the day to begin or end.

Nik took me repeatedly, making good use of every surface: the wall, the bed, the shower, until we fell asleep, content, consumed, and clinging to one another like fresh clothes from the dryer.

When it was all over, I opened my eyes and crawled out of bed. I put on my clothes, gathered my things, and looked around the house to see if I'd missed anything. This was the part where I usually evoked my first experience in detachment, letting decades-old memories wash over me until I couldn't take it anymore. Instead, I went back into the bedroom.

Nik looked so peaceful, lying on his back, one arm resting on the pillow above his head. Watching him, I thought about how the past week with this man had been amazing, and I didn't want it to end. Neither of us did. But it had to, even though it hurt. Not only was I leaving him, but the brothers I never had, a loving family I so desperately desired. A family I have to begin again with my sister.

I reached for my purse and removed the phone that tied me to them. I walked over to the bed and placed it on the nightstand beside his head. I couldn't leave without saying goodbye. Bending, I sat on the side of the bed. When it dipped, Nik stirred, and his arm instinctively reached out and wrapped around my waist.

"Hey," I whispered.

"Hey." His eyes opened and locked on mine. "You're dressed."

"Yeah. I gotta get ready for work. I wanted to say goodbye."

"Let me get the driver."

"My car should be here by now."

He sat up, and I gave him room to get out of bed. He put on his robe and reached out a hand to me. I stood and took it, and he pulled me close. I was consumed by his warmth and the lingering hint of amber, musk, and spice I couldn't recognize.

He held me tight and inhaled. "Rain, you're so beautiful." He pushed my hair over my shoulders. "You made me remember there are things more rewarding than power and status. Thank you." He kissed me. It was soft and quick.

"I need to go before your sexy accent talks me out of my clothes," I told him, and we both laughed.

"Okay," he breathed against my lips.

He took my hand and led me to the door. The driver took my things, and I turned to Nik before I left.

"Thank you for being the man I knew you could be."

Then I turned, got in the car, and left.

I never expected to see him again.

Sitting in the meeting, recalling those moments, my heart pounded the entire time, and I wondered what he was going through in his head. God, does he think I planned this all? Neither of us knew, or it wouldn't have gone as far. We would have had a pleasant conversation at the bar and walked away until we met again on Monday. It's too late. For one week, Nik was mine. Now it's over. I need to pull myself together because regardless of whether we wanted more—there can be no more. Although I strongly desire Nik, my feelings for him differ from those for Parker. Maybe that would have come with time—it's too late for that now.

I came to Seattle to close this deal. I accomplished that. I told Parker I'd come home to fix myself. I'm doing that. I have to forget Nik without a C, and find a new normal with the businessman, Noah Knight.

The elevator dings, signaling I've reached the ground floor. I open my eyes, force back the tears, and head toward the door. I'm reclaiming my life. I'm going home. Home to Parker.

Chapter 3
Time to Go Home

Parker

I'm patiently waiting for Rain when the front doors of the building glide open, and she emerges, power walking toward the car. She hesitates when she sees me, but only a second until her brain registers that I'm in Seattle for her. Rain is stunning. She's wearing a three-piece black suit with spiked heels, and her fitted vest doubles as her shirt.

"Parker," she calls to me over the sounds of the bustling city. My heart skips a beat. Her heels click-clack as she runs across the sidewalk toward me. I brace myself as she rushes into my open arms. Hugging her tight, I lift her off her feet. She wraps her arm around my neck, squeezing me like she hasn't seen me in years. I take it all in, enjoying the feel of her in my arms with her head buried in my neck. She lifts her head and then crashes her lips to mine, giving me a lovely hello kiss that's more than chaste.

Seeing Rain is like stepping outside to breathe fresh air after being closed in a stale room. I can exhale a sigh of relief, knowing I'm bringing her home. I hold her briefly, then lower her feet to the ground.

"Parker," she repeats.

I brush the hair off her face. Her cheeks are damp from crying. "Ah, Rain. What's this?" I wipe away a fresh tear.

"What are you doing here?"

I kiss her forehead. "I'm here to take you home." As soon as the words leave my mouth, the building doors slide open again. A man about my height with short black hair, wearing a dark blue suit, emerges with his hand up like he's about to say something. I recognize him immediately—Noah Knight. The man with whom Rain had a week-long fling—the person leading her straight into my arms.

He stops the second he sees us. I catch his gaze. He lowers his hand and steps back; the door slides open, and he retreats inside. I'll deal with him another day.

Rain is unaware that he followed her outside. Or maybe she is and was trying to get away. She doesn't know I know everything about Noah Knight. When she sent me the lake house address, I gave it to my friend Niall King. He and his brother, Aedan King, are co-founders of King Enterprise security company. He provided me with all the information I needed on Noah. When I discovered Noah was the developer for Rain's project—I knew I had to fly to Seattle to get her.

Noah likely assumes they're on solid footing because he and Rain spent so much time together. It's not enough time to get to know her. He doesn't know that the slightest upset can be triggering for her. Because of her inability to stop her brain from replaying experiences, they collide and then spin out of control like a snowball rolling downhill, blowing them out of proportion until they become something more than they are...until they become too overwhelming. Finding out she and Noah work together and all its implications would have the same impact. Leaving is her attempt to walk away from him and the affair—but that's no longer an option. She'll have to see him regularly if she lands the deal. I can only imagine her face when she discovered Noah was the developer she'd been negotiating with. Even now, she pulls at my neck, attempting to find asylum—sending me a signal that she wants to silence the stream of thoughts in her head.

"Rain, honey, it's time to go home," I tell her.

The driver holds the door open for us. I untangle Rain from my neck, help her into the car, and then slide in beside her. The door shuts. As if on cue, concealed from the world behind darkened car windows, the emotions she's been suppressing burst through. I've seen this before when she gets overwhelmed. But it's a side of her others never witness. On the surface, it may seem she's overreacting. In actuality, her mind is reliving a culmination of past events layered over her circumstances with Noah—like watching hundreds of movies simultaneously. She puts her hand to her face and cries. Rain is inconsolable now as the tears stream down her cheeks. My heart hurts. Dropping her head behind my arm, she tries in vain to hide her distress. I pull her onto my lap, and she rests her head on my shoulder. I grab a few tissues from the console and dry her face.

"Ah, honey. It's okay. I'm here now. We're heading to the airport." She sniffles, and I can tell she's struggling to get her breathing under control. I'd do anything to take the stress away and make her smile. "Rain, lift your head a little and take this." I hand her a tissue. "I wore your favorite suit and tie, and you're getting snot all over it." She takes the tissue and tries to laugh, but it comes out as a wet, snot-laden snort. "Come on, babe. Blow your nose." She blows her nose and then hands me the tissue. As miserable as she may feel, my wild Rain is still there.

"Thank you, Parker," she says in a barely audible voice as she tightens her arms around my neck. I'm surrounded by jasmine, honey, and her, and I wouldn't want to be anywhere else.

I take in her essence as the low hum of the city noises fills the silence during the ride. She doesn't need my words. I tighten my grip on her, and she raises her face and kisses my chin. I swipe my thumb across her lips, then lick my thumb.

"You taste like salted caramel babe." Although she's still clinging to me, I feel her smile against my skin. Relief washes over me, knowing I can help her through this.

Rain is quietly nestled into me when I feel the vibration of her phone. I reach between us and into her suit pocket to retrieve it.

"Rain, lift your chin," I tell her, and hold the phone to her face to unlock it and retrieve the message. "It's Alejandro. He says congratulations. June called him to say the deal is on, and they confirmed you'll be the lead attorney on the project. I'll text him your thanks and tell him you'll take the lead. You okay with that?"

Rain doesn't say anything, but I feel the slight movement of her head in my neck, nodding in agreement. I want to kiss her so badly and make it all better.

Her phone sounds again. It's Alejandro.

Alejandro: Awesome. Get some rest today. We have a lot to cover tomorrow. We'll talk soon.

He doesn't have to worry. Once I get Rain home, I'll ensure she gets all the rest she needs.

I put her phone in my suit pocket and hold the woman I've loved all my adult life. Because at this moment, all she needs to know is that I've got her, she's safe, and we'll figure our way through this. We're heading home.

Chapter 4

Gone Again

Noah

My brothers, as usual, have my back. They know I'm just as shocked as they were to see Rain in the meeting. All this time, I knew she was bright. However, I didn't realize she was the lead counsel for one of the largest companies in the world. If I had to dial back the clock, would I have done anything different had I known we would be working together? I would never have slept with her—*or would I?*

Despite our unusual circumstances, she handled herself beautifully in the meeting. She kept me on my toes to the point where I thought I'd lost control of the discussion.

Returning to the executive floor, I head straight to my brother Rok's office. I don't bother to knock; I go right in.

"Nik. What was that about?" Rok asks, cutting to the chase.

I shake my head. "I had no idea Rain was on this deal."

"How could you not?" Mak jumps in.

"You know we both kept everything on the surface. No names. No talk about business. We both agreed."

"If we do this, we'll go by Nik and Rain, no last names. No talk about work," Rain pressed that morning at the restaurant.

"But she knew about the meeting in San Francisco with Wade Wallace and Jude in Seattle."

"We never talked about Wade. She might have heard Jude's first name but nothing more. He left the party following our discussion. They never met. Like I said, we kept everything anonymous," I remind them. I roll my thumb across the beaded bracelet Rain gave me.

"And this is where it lands you. What are you going to do, man? We just inked our second-largest deal. Rae's hand will be in all contracts between us and Ross Enterprises for the next few years as counsel for their project team," Mak says.

"Unless she decides to remove herself from the project," I say.

"What are you talking about? Who would do that? Certainly not someone as smart and ambitious as her. This is a mega deal for her—I wouldn't walk away, and she won't either," Rok asserts.

"You're right. This is huge." I blow air in my cheeks. "I tried to get time with her before she left..."

"What happened?" Mak asks.

"Her ride was waiting. She had a plane to catch," I say.

Rok's eyebrows are furrowed. "We could have flown her back on our jet."

"I think someone else already has that covered," I hate to admit.

"English, please." Baby Mak's British accent is pronounced even to my ear when he's irritated.

"Her friend was downstairs waiting for her." My brothers' piercing look, mixed with shock, jolts my heart. Rain said she'd just gotten out of a bad relationship and that she'd never cheat. That can't be what I saw. *Can it?*

There's no way she would do that to me. Blake was the one she had been dating before she arrived in Seattle. The man I saw wasn't Blake.

"She has another man. What are you saying, Nik? You got played?" Mak's voice is stern. He's concerned about me, but I need him to back off.

"She wouldn't do that. This is something else."

Rok picks up his phone, looks at the screen, then flips it over. "What then?"

"Friend. We didn't discuss her personal life, Rok. I need to talk to her. I think we both need time to process what just happened."

"You're right," Rok concedes. If anyone can understand the predicament I'm in, he does. He's the most level head of the three of us.

"We just landed a deal. We should be celebrating," I say, lightening the mood.

"Who would have thought our Sis turned out to be one of the top players in this space? She's tough. You have to give her credit for her work on this contract. Brian was right. She gave us a run for our money," Mak admits.

"Listen, we have a small window to provide June and her team with our first draft plans for review. Mak, make sure our subcontractor agreements are airtight because Raven will be all over that."

Mak's eyebrow raises. "Raven?"

"You know what I mean."

"Her name is Raven Nichols, Esquire. Get used to it," Rok asserts.

"Sorry, man," Mak says.

"This is going to be rough," I add.

Rok purses his lips. "Tell me about it. Our Sis is fine, fierce, and now...our client."

Chapter 5
This Is Not the Way

Raven

Even with my eyes squeezed shut, counting Parker's breaths as his chest rises and falls against me, I sense the moment we arrive at the airport. The slow roll of the car tires. The sound of jet engines roaring. The muted voice of security clocking the time in the distance above all the noise. "Ten minutes," the nameless voice says. That's all the time it will take for Parker and me to get from the car to the plane and for the crew to be ready to go. It's a far cry from the fifty-five minutes or more required to fly commercial.

Lifting my head from his shoulder, I drag my nose against his neck. Inhaling, I let his sweet, woodsy scent envelop my senses and consume me, not wanting my mind to wander to what I am leaving behind. Tracing a line up his jaw across his ear, I bury my nose behind his ear. He smells good...like home. Everything about this man is so familiar because, for five years, he was my man. His arms tighten around my waist.

Years ago, Parker warned me against going down this path of dating other men. He detailed what would happen if I did and gave me a choice. He could have put his foot down that day, but he taught me a lesson instead. Still, I ignored his warning. I can see that day as if it were yesterday.

We were at the park in London—the last time Parker gave me an orgasm. That was before I chose to go on this destructive path with other men.

"I want to talk about what you said back there," I told him after he gave me an ultimatum about dating other men.

"We can talk about anything you want." His voice was strangely calm.

I told him, "I won't agree to do what you said."

He didn't respond right away. Instead, he watched the people coming and going in the park. It was the second time that day his anger caused him to look away from me. Purposely, I pushed his limits.

"I know you heard me, Parker."

"I heard what you said. And know what it implies."

"I'm not yours, Parker," I said in defiance.

"Hold my hand, Rain." He held out his hand, and I put my hand in his without saying a word. "Come sit here." He patted his lap. I stood, then sat on his lap. I remember him brushing my hair over my shoulders. His touch was loving...gentle. The look in his eyes like I was his life force was so compelling. Even though I fought it, I felt his love at that moment. Then he asked, "Do you love me, Rain?"

"Yes, Parker. I never stopped."

"I love you too. You are everything to me." Even after all we'd been through, he sounded so sure.

"I know."

"Do you trust me?"

"With my life."

"Have I ever hurt you?"

"No. You never would." And that's the truth. Parker would never do anything to hurt me.

"Straddle me," he said, shocking me because we weren't dating. Still, I did what he asked. "Kiss me."

"We're not that way, Parker."

"It wasn't a question. You don't have to be here. The car's across the street."

He locked eyes with me, and I recall our promise never to deny each other anything. I lowered my mouth to his and kissed him, taking full advantage of the fact that it had been a long time since I last kissed him that way. He let me control the kiss. It was gentle at first, then I parted his lips with my tongue greedily, wanting more—I licked into him. It felt so good kissing him after ten months apart, like returning home after a long trip. Safe. Familiar. Home.

Then Parker reached his hand between us and unzipped my pants. I was straddling him in the park, and no one could see his hand between us. Soon after, he broke the kiss.

"Lift your body for me," he whispered.

Initially, I was surprised, but on instinct and desire, I lifted. Then I crashed my lips to his, wanting more of everything he offered. He put his hand in my underwear and his fingers between my wet folds that were pulsing for him. I subtly rocked my hips in time with the rhythm of his hands, craving more friction. I sucked his tongue, desperate for more. I longed to have his length inside me. He worked my body with his fingers until my walls began to squeeze his hand.

"Come for me, Rain. Give it all to me," he commanded. I did. I came. He captured my groans in a kiss as he stroked me, pulling my climax from me until the pulsing subsided.

"Parker. What are you doing?" My words came out, rushed, breathless.

He removed his fingers, put them in his mouth, and licked them clean. Then he zipped my pants. He brushed my hair over my shoulders and looked me in the eyes admiringly, but only briefly.

"Proving a point." His voice came out calm but stern.

"What?"

"Rain. If you want to see other men, you'll do what I asked. Don't challenge me again unless you mean it. I know you well enough to know you're toying with me, and I don't like it. You got what you wanted. It's time to go." And he was absolutely right. I wanted him. And I would do whatever he asked.

He was teaching me a much-needed lesson because I hurt him in the worst way by telling him we both had to move on. That I would eventually start dating someone else. I can't explain why I did what I did. I was so stubborn back then. Perhaps I thought I was doing the right thing—I see now that I was wrong. Still, almost two years later, I persisted, telling him about a man I wanted to date. *"My god, woman. What have you done? This is not a game. Why are you gambling with someone's life by bringing them into this? This is not the way,"* he had said to me back then. He was right. And now...there's Nik. What have I done?

Shame washes over me thinking about what I told the man whose promise ring I still wear on my right hand. We committed our bodies to each other. That day in the park, I rebelled against his expectations of what I could and couldn't do if I dated other men. That he would ruin any man who dared slight me. He should have said—who touched me.

To this day, no man has claimed me like Parker. Only his seed has run down my legs. Yet, knowingly, I put other men at risk of having to deal with Parker—no more.

"Rain. We're here."

"Parker," I whisper in his ear. "Thank you." I kiss his neck, cheek, and ear and squeeze him tight because I love him that much—I never stopped. But he's not mine, not now. Crisp air sweeps through the car when the driver opens the door.

"You need help with Ms. Nichols, sir?"

"No. I got her." Even now, with a million thoughts running through my head, the deep timber of Parker's voice cuts through it all, comforting me.

Parker's body shifts beneath me as we prepare to exit the car. He slides his hand beneath me and lifts me. He's so strong. He leaves the vehicle with me in his arms and carries me to his plane. As we move forward, I concentrate on the pound of his weighted steps as he ascends the metal stairs before the temperature changes, signaling when we enter the cabin.

"Babe, I'm going to put you in your seat. I'll be right beside you."

I don't look up. "No," I whisper, not wanting to abandon the comfort his arms provide.

"I got this," he tells someone. "Prepare the plane. Take us home."

Parker continues holding me in his lap. He brushes my hair from my face. "Rain, look at me. It's just us. I got you. We're heading home." He places a hand beneath my chin and lifts my face. "Honey. I need to know you're okay. Open your eyes for me." His thumb brushes my eyebrow on one side and the other. I open my eyes. His aquamarine eyes are full of concern, watching me—willing my worries away.

My brain is reeling. That's what stress does—it brings every negative thought to the surface.

"Honey, it'll be okay. I'm here," he assures me.

Focus on his voice. I tell myself. *Breathe his essence. The sweet, woodsy scent. Feel his heartbeat. Count his breaths.* I take a few minutes to concentrate on everything that's him. The warmth of this body against mine. His strong arms surrounding me. He's here. I blink and push past all the memories.

"There she is. Hey, beautiful. I promise we'll be home soon. How are you feeling? You want to talk to me?"

I release a heavy sigh. "Parker, I'm sorry about everything. I'm just so sorry." And I am. Sorry for the list of loveless names leaving behind a trail of destruction in their wake over the years. What was I trying to prove, that another man could love me more than Parker? Is that even possible? Did Nik?

"You don't have to apologize. Are you okay?"

"I will be. I need time to process the week." My head feels heavy, weighed down by completing the most important meeting of my career. It's all too much, layered with the revelation about Nik and the shame of what I did to Parker.

I don't know how much Parker knows about today's meeting between Ross Enterprises and Knight Development Corporation other than what Alejandro texted, but I need to tell him about Nik. There are no secrets between us—never have been.

"I'm with you. I'll be okay. But the meeting, it was..."

Parker brushes his thumb across my lips. "You don't have to talk about that now if you don't want to. I want to know you'll be okay."

He has to know.

"Parker. Nik is Noah Knight."

Chapter 6

Home

Parker

Rain says she's okay. However, I don't recall a time in our twelve-year history when she clung to me for this long unless we were making love all day. It's been almost five years since we've shared a moment like this.

When Rain disclosed that Nik was Noah Knight, I didn't share that I already knew that fact. It won't help her. She's hurting. I had no doubt she'd be devastated when she learned about Nik's true identity, but I didn't anticipate this. Maybe in the back of my mind, I did. Unexpectedly, it triggered something else in her. Her sudden desire to be close to me in ways we haven't in years is overwhelming. Every touch and kiss she gives me has ignited the fire I've been suppressing. I can't handle it anymore. This year, I will get my woman back. She wants to be whole, to find her way back to me—I'll get her there. It'll take time, but we'll get her there...together.

The car pulls up at her house, but Rain doesn't move. Her head is on my lap as I stroke her hair. She's exhausted. I've ensured everything is prepared for her arrival, so she won't have to do anything when she goes inside. The rooms are filled with flowers, and dinner is taken care of.

"Rain, we're home."

Slowly, she lifts her head. Taking her hand, I help her from the car, wrapping my arms around her shoulder to keep her warm. The driver takes her things inside and then leaves.

"You want something to eat? I had the cook prepare something. Everything should be ready."

"Let me freshen up." She turns in my arm, stands on her toes, places her arm around my neck, and gently kisses me. "You're the best," she says before disappearing to her room.

The undercurrent of sadness in her voice tugs at my heart. Rain can't continue like this. This thing with Noah is the last straw. I haven't seen her truly happy since before our breakup. Even her time in Seattle was wrought with highs and lows wrapped in stress and confusion, and God only knows what else. I go to the guest room, grab my laptop, take it to her office, set it up, and then return to the kitchen.

"I'll serve tonight. I'll let you know the schedule in the morning. Thank you, Jeeves," I tell the cook, and he leaves.

I plate our meal and pour some wine. When Rain returns, she has on her black oversized sweatpants that sit just below her waist and a cropped t-shirt. She walks over to stand beside me and rubs a hand down the center of my back. I'm overcome with the urge to turn in her arms and hug her, but I resist.

"You need me to help with anything?"

"All good. Have a seat."

Rain goes to the other side of the counter and sits in front of one of the plates I prepared. I grab a bottle of sparkling water from the fridge, pour her a glass, and sit beside her. I watch as she twirls her pasta around her fork. It's her favorite meal, and I get a kick from watching her enjoy it. The way she closes her eyes after the first taste hits her tongue and pulls the fork from her mouth is sensual. A slight hum escapes, and I don't even think she's aware she's doing it.

She puts the fork down and turns to me. "This is the hard part where I say you were right all those years ago."

"I don't want to be right, Rain. I want you to be healthy. Happy. Whole."

"Yeah, it took almost five years, but I've come to the same conclusion. You said whatever I was going through, we could work it out together."

"We still can."

"Parker, we need to discuss Nik." My jaw ticks when she says his name. I nod, hoping this is the last man I hear her talking about that she's been with. "I felt something for him but don't understand those feelings. It's nothing like what I feel for you. I don't feel...." She pauses, seemingly searching for the right word. But that's not it. She doesn't want to say the words aloud.

After all these years, there isn't a side of this woman I haven't seen. I understand what she's trying to say. There's no connection like she has with me. And because she can't feel it—whatever *it* is that she feels for him isn't enough for her to chase. It's fleeting. It'll pass, just like all the others. This thing she had with Noah is the one relationship that got under her skin. But I know Rain better than she knows herself. It didn't get deep enough. She doesn't love him. She can't.

"You don't have to explain it to me. You do, however, need to discuss it with Noah. You two will be working together. You need to determine how to move forward without giving up what you worked hard to get at the firm."

As much as I want to, I won't push her on this. It almost broke me in two, but I committed to stepping aside to let her explore relationships outside us. I take a deep breath. *God, I want my woman back.* I'll trust her to resolve her feelings for Noah. I trust Rain never stopped loving me. I see it in her eyes every time she looks at me. Every touch tells me she longs to be held tight in my arms.

"Right. June will take a few weeks to assemble the rest of the team I'll be working with. Then we'll meet with Noah and his team."

"I suggest you talk to him before that."

"I will. Seeing him unexpectedly enter the room and then trying to concentrate on the business at hand was bad enough. And his brothers..."

"What about his brothers?"

"They were beginning to feel like family. Like the brothers I never had."

"That doesn't have to change, but just like with Noah, you have to find a new normal around them."

I give her words to help provide perspective. If this were my former self, I'd tell her to request that he offer her a different point of contact from his company. Or worse yet, I'd make the call to have it taken care of by now. But I don't do that. I'm here to listen and help her navigate this dilemma in the way that works best for her.

"They're good people."

"I'm not indicating anything different. You're not alone in this. You've been building a family. You're working things out with your sister. Remember, you also have Josh, Ethan, Jade...my parents. They all love you and would do anything for you." She nods. She stares past me, getting lost in her thoughts. I stand and swivel her chair to face me. "Hey, I realize it's early, but you should get some rest. I imagine you were up late last night. I have some work to do. I'll be in your office working if you want to nap."

Rain wraps her arms around my waist, pulls me to her, and presses her face to my stomach.

"Leaving here on the heels of my ordeal with Blake was a mistake. My emotions were too raw. I should have flown in this morning to Seattle. This thing with Nik would never have happened. I would have been with you last week. I could have managed this better, Parker."

"I told you, there's nothing to apologize for. You set out years ago to find yourself. You're doing that. I'm not pretending it hasn't been tough for me. At first, I thought about my feelings and what you were doing to us. Over the years, I watched you make decisions I disagreed with but realized it was not my business to step in. You needed to find your own way. Watching you grow into yourself has been hard yet beautiful. Thinking back, I would have only stood in your way. I didn't want to do that." I step back. "Look at me, Rain." She looks up. "The day you broke up with me, you promised to find your way back. You're almost there. I'll be here, waiting. I love you."

Rain stands, throws her arms around my neck, and hugs me. I hold her tight, giving her what she needs, once again disregarding my own needs. Because right now, Rain is in a space where she needs me to be her best friend. And despite my need to destroy the last man that will ever touch her and claim my woman by burying myself deep within her, I need to hold my shit together.

"I love you too, Parker. Will you sit with me while I take a nap? If I snore while you're on a call, nudge me. After I get up, we can have a snack or something." Rain leans into me, reminding me how perfectly our bodies fit together. She dusts her lips along my jaw.

"You don't snore, babe. But no. I'll be in your office. If you wake, I'll be by your side before you know it," I say, telling her the only thing that will keep me from re-claiming what's mine.

"I understand." She kisses me. It's brief, loving, and then she leaves.

Chapter 7

Two O'Clock

Raven

The sound of something hitting the floor jolts me out of my sleep. I jump up and look around. A sliver of light from the moon casts enough light, revealing the culprit—my phone. The last thing I remember was reading the message Parker relayed to Alejandro on my behalf. Shoot, I need to debrief with Alejandro. I pop up, retrieve my phone from the floor, and flip it over. Ugh, it's two in the morning. That means instead of taking a nap, I slept eight hours.

I get out of bed and look for Parker. The lights are off in my office, so he must have gone to bed. I go to the guest room, and he's there sleeping. I walk over to the bed, slide beside him, and wrap my arms around him. Like always, his hand instinctively reaches for mine. I listen to him breathing. *One, two, three, four.*

"Parker."

There's a noticeable change in his breath as he wakes.

"You okay?" His arm tightens around me.

"Yeah. But you know..."

"I do." And he does.

Like all the times before, Parker knows I can't stay away from him. I can't be in the same house as him and not be near him. My body instinctively craves his heat. I don't understand it even after all these years of being apart. I've been fighting this, trying to find what I have with him in others. It's impossible. Nothing feels as right as when I'm beside him. When I was with Nik, I was craving the things I had with Parker. I was attracted to the power and his commanding nature—all the things I see in Parker. But at the end of the day—no one can compete. God, does that make me a monster mindlessly chasing other men? Being with Parker is as natural as breathing. Why do I resist?

"What am I going to do?"

"Babe, what time is it?" There's a slight irritation in his voice, and rightfully so. He's exhausted. Once again, he spent his day saving me from myself. Who else would do that?

"Two something."

"Ah, babe. You have to work in a few hours. Are you rested?"

"Somewhat."

"Rain, I need to get a few more hours of sleep. I'll hold you until you fall asleep, but I can't stay up, babe." His strong arms pull me into him.

"Parker, I want to make it work with my family. I want to get my head together."

"I get it, babe."

"No, you don't."

"What am I missing, Rain?" His voice is low and groggy.

"I want to make it work between you and me. But I can't until I do those things."

"You will," he says with such confidence. But his words are layered with frustration because our relationship is on pause.

He's been more than patient with me. With two words, Parker could have ended this; whatever *this* is, I'm putting him through—us through. Two simple yet powerful words. "Marry me," is all he had to say. He could hold his hand out to me, and I would walk over to him like I always do. Like he proved that day in the park. I would place my hand in his. He could have said those words, and I wouldn't have hesitated to say yes because I had promised never to deny Parker anything. Still, despite everything we've been through, he's never said the words. He would never ask me for anything I wouldn't be willing to give. Had he asked, I'd be prepared to live with him for the rest of my life. He wanted that. I never told him, but we want the same things. We could have had a family by now. I exhale.

I crawl up his body until half of me is covering him, conforming to his muscles beneath me. God, I want my man back. "Promise," I tell him.

"Will you go see the therapist?" he asks.

"Only if you go with me."

"We'll be fine." He smiles sleepily.

I kiss him, then snuggle into his neck. We'll be fine.

Chapter 8

Housewarming

Noah

"Turn the music up," my cousin Drew calls out to no one in particular. He's holding a beer in one hand and popping his fingers with the other as *No Diggity* booms from the speakers. I grab a beer and look over the deck, enjoying the sight of my family enjoying themselves by the pool.

"Man, you did good getting this place." Rok pats me on the shoulder.

"Thanks, man." I tip my chin forward. "I think we better go save the baby. I don't want burnt steak," I say, heading downstairs to where Mak is minding the grill. Rok follows me.

"Beautiful home, son," my dad says from the lounger beside Mum.

"Yeah, baby. You did good," Mum adds.

"Thanks, Mum and Dad. Do you need anything?"

"Not yet. We're waiting to see how your brother does." Dad smirks.

"Eli, be nice. You know he can cook," my Mum scolds. My Dad won't disagree. He knows how to keep her happy.

"We're on our way to save him now."

I walk to the grill, which, I hate to admit, smells good. It smells like he used hickory wood chips to give it a robust smoking flavor. "So, Baby Mak. What's cooking?"

"Only you would invite your brother to a barbecue and have me cook."

"You volunteered to show off your culinary skills." I grab a cooking utensil, cut a slice of the steak, and taste it. I turn to Rok, whose eyebrow is raised, waiting for the verdict.

"Well, do we add chef to his list of monikers?" Rok asks.

Setting the utensils down, I raise both my hands and step back. "I'm going to let you do you, brother. I'm not gonna lie. That's good. Where'd you learn to cook, man?"

"He has a mother," my mum interjects.

"No offense," I say.

"Kathrine Johnson brilliant, Casanova, Chef. You really are husband material," Rok teases. He knows baby Mak is allergic to the words husband, wife, marriage, commitment, or anything that appears domestic. He's the love 'em then leave 'em type.

"I wouldn't go that far. Let's chalk it up to me being the most talented among the three of us." Mak beams.

I shake my head. "We'll leave you to it. Mum's hungry, so hurry up."

"So, have you heard from our girl?" Rok asks.

This is not a subject I want to broach right now. Thinking about Rain, where she is, or who she's with is a sore subject. When I last saw her, she was in the arms of another man. I don't know him, but I suspect it was Parker, the friend she constantly communicated with during her week with me. Rain and I are meeting in a few weeks, and I need to get my head straight before we do. I take a deep breath.

"I haven't talked to her. I need to do something before we get in front of the team together."

"Yeah, you don't want it to be awkward."

"I know, man."

"Then arrange a time to meet her."

"She's in San Francisco."

"Get on the damn jet, Nik, and have an adult conversation with the woman. I don't want this deal to get messy because of this."

"It won't get messy. But it's good we didn't make plans beyond one week."

"That's not what I'm talking about. You could have made a relationship work. Couples work together all the time. Now, you two are in limbo. That's the messy part. You need to fix this."

"I will."

My cousins Chase and Drew walk over and join us.

I turn to Drew to take the attention off me and say, "You had some moves going on over there. Too bad there's not a bunch of women, like at your brother's birthday party."

"Yeah, we had a good time. But this is family. It's all good," Drew says.

"You have a nice place here. I'm proud of you," Chase jumps in.

"Thanks, just trying to slow down a bit," I tell them.

"I noticed. You were going steady for a minute with Rae. I thought my girl had you on lock." Of course, Chase had to go there.

Mak walks over to join us. "That's what I thought. But my brother here...I don't know what's got into his head."

"KDC. That's my focus."

"This," Chase opens his hands like a gameshow host presenting a car prize, "is what it's all about—living life to its fullest. Enjoying the things you worked hard to get. Hanging with family. Now you need to get married and fill this house with—."

"Whoa. Slow your roll, Chase. Anyway, what are you talking about? You don't have a steady woman," Mak says.

"Cause our girl Rae was supposed to fix me up with one like she did you. Where is Melanie, anyway?" Chase asks.

"We're still getting to know each other. You know me," Mak admits.

"Casanova." I shake my head.

"Naw, it's not like that. It's early in the relationship."

"You got a good one, Mak. Don't let her go this time," I advise him. What I should have said is: don't make the same mistake as I did.

Chapter 9
We Need To Talk

Raven

It was only a matter of time before I heard from Nik. He didn't bother going through my office to contact me. He located my personal number and texted me directly.

Noah: Raven, I'm excited to work together. We need to talk. I'll be in SF next week doing business. Are you available?

That was his message. I've looked at my phone a hundred times, thinking about how to respond. I can't answer without talking to Parker. He was there to pick up the pieces after my affair with Nik, Noah, or whatever I'm supposed to call him.

Our therapist asked what the catalyst was for me to finally meet with her. Sitting beside Parker, holding his hand, I told her the truth: Nik.

My week in Seattle threw me into such a tailspin that I didn't think I would find my way out. Never in a million years would I have expected Nik to walk into the conference room that morning. I had resigned myself to what we had being over. But there he was, sitting across the table. His presence reminding me of every second I spent in his arms—the man who went from fling to fellow overnight. When I walked out the door of the Knight Development building and saw Parker standing there, it was like an epiphany. I couldn't be more broken than I was at that moment. Walking into Parker's arms made me feel safe. It always has. I knew then that I needed to get my shit together.

I text Parker.

Me: Parker, where are you?

He's likely heading home. We've maintained our regular routine as friends, except I've yet to spend a day away from him. My first week back from Seattle, Parker stayed at my place to ensure I was all right. I wasn't. I'm glad he was there for me. My sleep terrors were amplified, triggered by the stress of knowing I had to face Nik...Noah, again. I still haven't come to terms with my feelings for him. How can I feel so strongly about two men? But is it the same?

My phone buzzes. It's Parker.

Parker: Just arrived home. You good?

Me: I need to talk to you about something.

Parker: My place or yours?

Me: Yours.

Parker: I'll send the car.

That's it. It doesn't take long for the driver to arrive. It's Thursday. I don't need to bring an overnight bag when staying with Parker. I have personal belongings at his house already. It's the same for him at my house. A section of my closet contains Parker's clothes. It's been that way since we started dating in college. One of the first things I adjusted to was his lifestyle. There were times when we needed a break from what was happening and would simply get on a plane and go to one of his properties around the world. We don't worry about packing bags. I have things at his homes around the globe, and he has belongings at mine, including the complex we own together in London.

Parker is waiting outside when we pull into his driveway. He opens my door, helps me out, and hugs me like he hasn't seen me in years. He's been doing that a lot lately, but I don't mind. I've also found myself needing to be closer to him since returning from Seattle.

"Hey, how was your day?" he asks, walking me inside.

"Good. I received an email with the list of team members I'll work with for Ross Enterprises. The first meeting is already scheduled."

"That's great. This is what you've always wanted."

In the foyer, Parker takes my coat and puts it away. I drop my things in one of the guest rooms even though I'll end up in Parker's room. When I'm done, I find him in the kitchen. I sit on the opposite side of the counter while Parker plates our meal. He pours me a glass of wine and brings it with my plate. After he gets his plate, he sits next to me.

"You said you wanted to talk. I sense that whatever it is might be serious. We can wait if you want," he says.

Parker knows me so well. After all these years, my modus operandi hasn't changed much. I need to be close to him—to touch him while I talk about the hard things. It's more manageable when I feel his energy. It's times like this when I'm convinced something is wrong with me. Yet, it doesn't seem to faze Parker. He accepts me as I am, quirks and all.

"Let's do that."

"How'd the fitting go with Mom?"

Two months from now, we'll celebrate Parker's birthday. Janis, the perfect socialite and proxy mom extraordinaire, had a lovely platinum-colored dress designed for me. She took it to heart when I told her years ago that figuring out what to wear to the various functions I attended on their behalf was stressful. Sometimes I can get away with wearing the same outfit styled differently. Then, there are events like Parker's birthday bash, where key elites will attend to honor him. That's a thing—celebrating the life of the children of the elite, especially the only son. This is important for the family, and I need to mentally prepare myself. It'll be the first major event I've attended since celebrating the establishment of Josh's first private school. That was the first time Parker and I attended a major elite event subsequent to our break up. Although we were no longer dating, everyone embraced me as part of their society.

"Good. The dress is lovely. You know your mom. Only the best will do."

"You look spectacular in everything you wear."

"Will Josh be there to eat all your cake?" I laugh before I can finish the question.

Parker and Josh act like children when it comes to cake. Josh is a huge cake lover but can never have the first slice unless it's his birthday. So, I eat from Parker's plate and hand my cake plate to Josh. It's silly, but it keeps poor Josh from falling so far in line behind what seems to be a ridiculous protocol. Josh, like Nik's brothers, has become like my brother, leaving me longing to get my real family life together.

He tips his head and holds my gaze, searching for signs that I'm still in the conversation. "Of course he will. But that's not all that's on your mind."

"Can we talk about what you learned about my dad? You mentioned you received a file."

"I was going to wait to talk to you this weekend. You're just getting your footing back on things."

"You're right, but I'm anxious to hear what you uncovered."

"After dinner." He reaches out and rubs my hand. "You okay with that?"

"Of course." It's okay because, after all these years, I've finally learned to trust his judgment. There's a method to everything he does, and I realize I also need to let him do what he does best.

During dinner, I occasionally glance at Parker. His phone buzzes. He looks down but doesn't pick it up. Thinking about it, he is rarely preoccupied with his phone around me. In the car, he won't take a call unless he has to or if he knows the person calling might want to talk to me, like his parents or Josh. In those instances, he'll pick up the call but immediately make them aware of my presence by putting me on screen or telling them they're on speaker.

"You can get that if you need to." He looks at me curiously but ignores the call. You'd think I would have learned by now that the man gives me his undivided attention.

Parker finishes eating before me and begins putting things away. When I'm done, I take my plate to the sink. I help him by wiping down the counter. When I'm done, I wash my hands, hold them out over the sink, and look over my shoulder at Parker. He rolls his eyes and dries my hands with a towel.

"Funny," he says.

"I am, aren't I?"

"You missed your calling," he deadpans.

When we're done tidying up, he grabs our wine glasses, and we head into the family room. Parker typically sits on the chaise lounge and I join him, but he sits on the couch instead. I sit beside him, and he hands me my glass.

"You want to go first, or should I?" he asks.

"Sure. I'm trying to be good sitting beside you instead of on your lap, but I might need to switch it up after what you tell me about my dad."

Parker doesn't respond. He places his drink on the coffee table, raises his eyebrow, and waits for me. Swinging my legs over his, I put an arm around his shoulder. I can't help myself. This is how we've talked about serious topics for years.

I take a deep breath and dive in. "I got a text from Nik."

"Noah," he corrects me.

"Noah. He has a meeting in the city and wants to clear the air before we meet with the project team."

"So that things won't be awkward? Or is there another agenda?"

"Here." I pull up the text message from Nik and then hand my phone to Parker.

"This message is vague. What do you want to do?" he asks, laying the phone down.

"I want the project to go smoothly. Like you said, I worked too hard to get to this point to let what happened between Nik...Noah and I get in the way of my success."

"That's not what I'm asking. Do you want to continue the relationship you started with Noah? I guarantee it will come up." Parker adjusts a curl near my forehead. I sip my drink and then hold it to his lips. He drinks.

This is the twenty-four million-dollar question. How do I feel about a man I spent one week with compared to a lifetime of loving Parker? My life is such a mess. I bite my lip.

"No. I've been thinking about it since I returned, trying to reconcile my feelings for him. I admit initially, something was there. My answer would have been different if you had asked me that on Monday. Everything was happening so fast."

"During our calls, you seemed sure you'd developed real feelings for him in Seattle. Are you saying it's nothing more than you getting caught up in the moment?"

"Thinking back, I'd say that was the case."

"Rain, I need to understand what this means."

"I don't love him, Parker. I like him, but I don't love him. Even if I had more time with him, I couldn't love him. Not like...not like you."

"The other men. What about them? If they hadn't done the things they did, would there have been a chance with them?"

"Never."

"Are you saying what I think?"

I stare at Parker, trying to read his expression. He's changed so much over the years. There was a time when he wanted to ensure every aspect of my life was easy. Some would call it the soft life. His love was so consuming that I didn't know how to handle it. I got so wrapped up in him that I didn't know who I was. I was losing myself.

Then I got pregnant. I was confused and scared, but I was still happy to have created something with the man I love. When we lost our child, something snapped in me. I needed to break free—I needed to breathe. I needed to find my way back to myself. The way I handled it was wrong, but it was all I knew to do at the time. I used the best example I had: to walk away like my father did to us.

In all that time, Parker's love and commitment to me never wavered. However, he learned how to balance how he showed it. He accepted that hovering over me was not helping and that I had to make my own mistakes.

Consequently, I was able to grow in ways I didn't think possible. I made a lot of mistakes, more than necessary, but they were mine to make. Part of growing meant I had to come to terms with the fact that I needed to compromise with Parker—there are things that he can handle on my behalf, and I can do some things to help him. It took an encounter with my cheating ex, Blake, at a party to realize that I had learned from Parker's lessons. It felt good when I contacted Wade Wallace and told him about his nephew, Blake. I did it for Parker. That was the first time I thought I was contributing to our friendship. Up until then, I felt too inadequate to be more than friends. I ran away from Parker because I thought I had nothing to offer a man like him. I was wrong. I was scared.

"Rain?" he prompts me. What do I say to this man? How do I tell him I made a mistake? How do I tell him I've been seeking men who don't remind me of him, and when one man came close, it knocked me to my senses. How do I tell him I could never be happy until I have the one thing I want most?

When I told Parker I was falling for Nik, I felt I had something to offer Nik. That he needed me. He did, but he didn't need *me* per se. Nik needs a woman who loves him and whom he can cherish. Nik didn't believe he was capable of being a thoughtful partner. I showed him he was. However, I mistook what we had as him needing me. He doesn't. Nik and I have a lot in common because of our culture, but he doesn't complete me. Parker needs me. I'm his other half—together, we're whole.

"For once, Parker, I can't read your face. You've protected your heart from my mess for so long—I don't know what you're asking me. What I can tell you is that I am not pursuing Nik. What we had was over when I left."

"So, you're saying you're done trying to find whatever you were searching for in other men?" I nod. "I need to hear the word Rain. Talk to me."

"Yes, Parker. I'm done. I don't know what I was looking for or whether I was even searching for anything. I was acting out. I was pissed at you for what you said in London. For what you did. I was mad at myself for wanting you in a way I didn't deserve. Pissed I can't be with you the way I want without getting lost in you."

Parker's eyes become dark, and frustration, desire, and relief all pass in his expression.

"Do I dare ask what that look is about?" I ask, not really wanting to know the answer. "I'm sorry Parker. I said it before, but it's true." He takes my drink, sips it, and hands it to me. He sighs. "This is usually when you tell me to get off you. Talk to me, Parker. Say something."

"What do you want me to say, Rain? That I love you? I tell you that every day. I have been for the past ten years. The only reason I can't say twelve years is that you might have thought I was a creep if I'd told you during those first two years when we became friends. I've always been in love with you—since the moment we locked eyes. I've never stopped. Do you want me to tell you that I crushed every man who hurt you to keep me from killing them? Is that what you want to hear? Do you want me to spell out the depths of how far my love for you goes? Do you not understand the restraint I've exhibited whenever you walk into a room? *You* are all I've ever wanted, Rain. Nothing and no one else can ever satisfy that need. The reason I told you to get off me in the past is to keep from taking you upstairs, stripping you naked, and claiming what's mine."

When he says that, my sex throbs, wanting him.

"You don't feel that way now?"

"You're not ready."

I close my eyes. This is the first time I'm on the verge of offering myself to Parker after more than four years. *You're not ready.* The words sting more than he knows, or maybe he said them because he knew they would. Perhaps they sting because they're true. If I'm honest with myself, Parker has never done anything to hurt me. I wish I could say the same about me. I hurt him. I hurt us both. I told him we couldn't be together because I couldn't receive his love. Fear had me in a vice. I was so lost in him. I gave up my man because I felt I was too messed up for someone as good as him. Because I had nothing to offer him. *Am I ready?* My face grows warm. I need to fight back the tears because I'm tired of crying over crises I've caused. Parker's only doing what I asked. My stomach churns, thinking about what I did.

"Babe. Don't go," he said as I was heading toward the door. I only stopped because he asked. "Rain, look at me." Turning, I looked at him. "You, Rain, are the one true love of my life. I don't plan to live a life without you in it. Honey, I hear what you're saying. You need time to fix yourself. I believe we can both work through this together. We are connected, Rain. There is no me without you. There is only us."

"I know, Parker, but you must let me do this. Please let me fix me. Maybe our love will bring me back to you when it's time, when I'm ready, when I'm whole—when my head is not a mess. I promise to try and find my way back—to us...to love. But now, you need to let me go, Parker. Please."

He did. I own this.

I open my eyes. Parker studies my face, waiting for a response. "You're right." I put my drink on the table. I hold my palm up across my lap. He places his hand in mine. I lift it to my lips, and I kiss his fingers like he's done to me a thousand times before. "Okay. I understand."

My announcement earns me a small smile as he tightens his arm around my waist. Parker is rarely short on words. He's big on commands and teaching me lessons. Sometimes, he can be wild and funny, but right now, his mood is quiet. I hug him, burying my head in the warmth of his neck.

This is where I belong.

Chapter 10

Room to Breathe

Parker

I live a good life. I do what I love, have a great family and amazing friends, serve the community, and only want one thing...Rain.

When Rain asked me about claiming what was mine, I released the breath that I felt like I'd been holding for four years. For four years, I've been denied what I want most. For her, I would have waited a lifetime. We've both grown a lot in those years. I learned I can't control things when it comes to Rain—that she has to do things in her own way and time. I also learned that if I push her buttons, she'll obliterate mine. We're two people so much alike that it feels great and grating simultaneously.

But now is not the time for reminiscing.

"Rain, I need you to sit up and look at me." I hold her waist, which fits perfectly in my arms, reminding me that her body was designed for me. She lifts her head from my shoulder and looks at me. "You're lovely to look at, you know that, right?"

She smiles. "Thank you."

"We need to talk about your dad. Are you ready for that?" She nods. "Rain, I need your words. Please."

"I'm ready. What did you find out?"

"Your father still lives in the Bay Area."

"What? Oh. My. God." Her mouth hangs open in shock.

"He's a corporate attorney specializing in employment law. He's worked for various technology companies in Silicon Valley. Your parents are legally divorced—have been for years." Rain looks away. I cup her cheek and turn her face back toward me. She shuts her eyes. I give her a minute before I continue. "I need you to look at me." She pulls my hand away, lays it across her lap, and subconsciously presses my fingers one by one as if counting them. "Hey, it's okay. Talk to me."

"Did you see him?"

"He had lunch with colleagues near his office one day. I arranged to have lunch at the same place. He has a distinguished reputation."

Rain looks at me wide-eyed. "He's here. He's an attorney. For god's sake, what could keep him away from his kids all these years? Why couldn't I find him when I searched for him?"

"He goes by a hyphenated last name."

Her eyebrows furrow. "That makes no sense. Why would he do that, Parker? Why?" she pleads.

"He remarried. He took on his wife's last name. He goes by Sweet-Nichols. Maybe he didn't want to be found. Perhaps it's as simple as sharing names with the one you love."

"Remarried? Do they have children?"

"No."

"Do you know where he lives?"

"I have all his contact information. I don't know the circumstances behind him not contacting you. This is something you should talk with your mom about before reaching out. See if this leads to her finally opening up to you."

Rain sighs. "This is hard to digest. In the back of my mind, I suspected he was around, but I...." She pauses.

"Tell me what you're thinking."

"He's been gone so long without attempting to reach out. At some point, I assumed he was dead."

"Dead?"

"Yeah, I guess it was just easier to imagine he was. What other reason would he have?" She stares at her lap and brushes invisible lint from her leg.

"Oh, God, Rain. Is that how you thought of him all these years?"

I can't imagine not having my parents in my life. Rain felt her life was normal up until her dad left. After that, she indicated that things fell apart. Her mom and sister became distant. She felt like she was fending for herself. I'm an only child, but my parents ensured I knew they were there for me. I didn't feel alone because I also had Josh, who is like a brother, and other members of our community our age.

"Not the whole time. When I got older, yeah. I was just trying to rationalize it all." Rain tries to remove her hand from mine. I lace my fingers in hers.

"He's not dead. Are you going to talk to your mom?"

"I'm so pissed at her. But that seems like the best place to start. Now that I know he's local, and you have his contact information, she'll be less likely to dance around the topic if she knows I can access him."

"If you need me to be there when you talk to her, I can."

"What did he look like, Parker?"

"I imagine an older version of what you remember?"

"I mean, did he look happy?"

"Rain, honey, he was engaged in conversation. He looked like whatever he meant to convey to his colleagues. It wasn't evident whether he was happy."

"This must have been what Mr. Kane meant when he said I looked familiar. Remember at the party?"

"I'm sure he knows your father. Kane's a prominent figure in the legal field, so it wouldn't be that far-fetched."

"At the time, I thought maybe he saw my picture associated with my scholarship application. Now, it makes sense. He's seen my dad."

"So, how do you want to handle this? After all these years, would you want to see him?"

"I'm not sure. I think so. Seeing him again seemed so unlikely. Now that it's a potential reality, I...I don't know what to do."

"You don't have to do anything you don't want. I'll give you his information when you're ready."

"I wonder why he didn't have any more children."

"If you decide to meet him, that could be a question you ask. When you're ready, I can help you with a list. In the meantime, I'll tell you what I know."

"What do you think about it all?"

"From what you described about your youth, you two were close. You felt loved by him. I can't imagine what would compel me to leave my children. I also know from experience you can't turn love off like a light switch." She squeezes my hand.

When I say, "my children," my chest feels tight, and it's hard to breathe. I remember holding Rain in my arms at the hospital when she woke up. Having to explain to the love of my life that we'd lost our child is not something I want to remember or experience again. The second I knew Rain was carrying our baby, I felt a level of love for my child that to this day I can't comprehend. I felt an even deeper love for Rain. Within weeks, I lost them both.

This is the part when I usually get up and leave the room to keep Rain from witnessing my grief. Instead, I grip her chin and hold her gaze. She feels it, too. Residual pain from the sting of death. Soon after, the crumbling of our world. My heart is racing. I inhale.

Rain senses my distress. "I'm sorry, Parker. It was all too much, and I didn't know how to cope with the loss of my father...our child. Your love. It was too intense."

"It wasn't all you. I didn't give you room to breathe. I was so desperate to have what my parents had. I see now that I was smothering you."

"Don't say that. You've shown me nothing but unconditional love. I didn't know how to accept it. I'm the one who's been out here acting out." She tries to lift her hand to cover her mouth, but I don't let her. "I'm so embarrassed. Oh god. Nik." I try to control myself at the sound of his name.

I gently squeeze her hand. "You have to talk to him. What's the plan?"

Chapter II
Call Me Raven

Noah

The last time I was in San Francisco, I met with Wade Wallace and his team to bid on purchasing his business, including all the Wade commercial properties. Two other developers were also in attendance, vying to secure this deal. I heard about a fourth bidder but have yet to uncover their identity. That's an important piece of this puzzle if I want to stay ahead of the competition. At one point eight million square feet, this property will be our largest if Knight Development can close the deal. I never thought KDC would be one deal away from becoming the top development firm this fast. This is my dream.

The meeting with Wade Wallace is a big deal. I could win the bid if he likes my proposal to enhance his current business model.

The nickel-colored granite building with cutouts resembling corrugated cardboard stands tall against the sunny San Francisco skyline. I take the elevator straight to the executive floor. I'm not surprised that the ride is swift and smooth. Upon arrival, an executive assistant meets me and takes me to Wade's office.

"Mr. Wallace, it's good to see you again." Wade stands and walks around his desk. He extends his hand, gesturing for me to sit at a table near the wall of windows overlooking the city, then sits on the other side.

"Mr. Knight, it's good to have you here. I'm interested in discussing the proposal you sent. Your ideas about a complete remodel are impressive."

"Thank you. The Wade Building is an icon and one of the tallest in the city. My proposal will modernize it, returning it to its previous glory, and attract tenants back to this area of the city. As it stands, you're currently at fifty percent capacity. The remodel will take two years. We can work in stages to ensure the current tenants experience minimal disruption."

"What about the potential tenants you want to attract?"

"That's where remodeling comes in. I'd bring in a top designer to reimagine the space. We can reserve the upper levels for elite tenants with private club memberships. Once the designer provides renderings and a timeline for occupancy, we can begin selling units."

"It's ambitious."

"You've seen an example of what we're capable of doing. The Knight building is an example of how successful this can be. We've been at one hundred percent occupancy since opening, and there's a five-year wait list."

"What about the community?"

"Local schools would have free access to come tour. We'd also arrange art classes and projects for children to learn architecture and celebrate this building and its importance to the city. We can showcase their art on rotation in the lobby."

"I saw the announcement of the recent deals you landed. How does the timeline of those projects impact this one?"

"It wouldn't. If your concern is our resources, we've already started adding staff. We have some of the most brilliant minds wanting to join our firm."

"What about you? This is no life for a young man such as yourself."

He's testing me to see if I have what it takes to take this on. His son Jude prepared me for this when I met him at Chase's birthday party.

"You and your brothers and a few others made the shortlist because of how you manage your business. He's been watching you," Jude said before suggesting I "stay the course and jump through the hoops."

"I'm fine. I'm dedicated to my work. KDC is my blood."

"I know your father. He's a family man. Don't you want to follow in his footsteps?"

"When I find the right person, I will."

I immediately think of Rain when he talks about being a family man. She was the one woman that made me think about settling down. It'll be good to see her again. The vibration of my phone buzzing in my pocket brings me back to the conversation at hand.

"I trust you will," Wade says. We wrap up the conversation, say our goodbyes, and I head to the elevator.

On the way down I check my messages. It's her.

Rain: I'll see you in fifteen.

***

Following my meeting with Wade, I head straight to the restaurant to meet Rain. It's been a few weeks since I've seen her. The irony of being back in her city isn't lost on me. She was the reason I hesitated to come here to meet

Wade the first time. In less than a week, I had become so attached that I didn't want to leave her side. Since then, our circumstances have drastically changed. We're colleagues.

I reserved a private room so we wouldn't have to talk over the noise of other patrons. I arrive a little early so she won't be waiting for me. I'm leaning against the wall, scrolling through my email, when the manager brings Rain in.

"Madam, your table," he says. I push off the wall. Rain walks in, looking stunning, wearing a lavender sheath dress that emphasizes her beautiful curves and spiked heels. She's more beautiful than ever. God, this woman. Our eyes lock.

My mind wanders to the first time we were together, and I have to catch myself from growling her name. "Rain," I say, extending a hand to her. "How are you?"

"I'm good, Noah."

I help her to her seat and sit across from her. This is going to be complicated. My attraction to her is overwhelming. I would have dipped my head and kissed her by now if we weren't working together.

"Thank you for meeting me today. I know this might seem awkward, which is why I wanted to see you. Since we'll be working together, I expect we'll see each other often."

"Seems that way. You're right, it's surreal to think we were...." Her voice trails off. She doesn't want to admit what we were to each other. That for one week, she was mine.

"I understand, Rain. I wanted to discuss that and something else that came up recently."

"Raven."

I blow out air. This isn't easy. She's always been Rain to me. Heaven help me. "Raven. Everything I told you in Seattle was true. Everything you experienced—." She holds up her hand, stopping me.

"I'm not under the impression you lied to me. Is that what you think I did?"

"No, I don't. I don't want you to think I was pretending to be someone else in order to get what I wanted. Walking away was difficult. Even after you left, I questioned myself. Did I do the right thing? Could I have made it work? Would she have wanted more with me?"

"Don't, Noah. It's over. We're colleagues."

"We can be both." The words are out of my mouth before I realize. That's how it is with her—I can't help but tell her what's in my head. I let my words hang in the air between us as the server comes to take our order. "Do you want me to order for you?"

"I'll have a shrimp Ceasar and sparkling water. I have a meeting following this one."

"Two, please," I tell the server, and she disappears. I look at Rain, who's studying my face. I wonder what she's thinking. Is she mulling over my question? Is she recalling our week together? "If you don't want to talk about it—."

"Noah, we can't continue what we had in Seattle. Besides, that's why we're here: to talk about our future working together. You and I spent a week living like we were a couple. I'm sure we can handle a conversation about how we move forward as colleagues."

"Rain, I was wrong to let you leave. I thought I couldn't be the man you wanted, but looking back, it felt so natural with you. I tricked myself into believing I had to be a certain way to succeed in business. To dominate the commercial development space. I thought I couldn't be the hard-driving developer and have a woman at my side. In actuality, I hadn't found the right woman. Then I met you. All those things I did while we were together were natural because of you. Tell me you felt something for me."

"You have to call me Raven."

What the hell? "Why?"

"Only one person calls me Rain. His name is Parker. He's my best friend, and we used to date years ago."

My stomach turns when she finishes. Parker. Fuck. What is this? He's the one from the calls that she had every morning.

"You didn't answer my question," I press.

"I craved everything about you. Every touch, kiss, lingering glance...everything. For those seven days in Seattle, I was caught up in *you*. I would have agreed to something more if you had asked me...then."

"Why not now?"

"Because, Noah, I was wrapped up in a fantasy. A beautiful, sweet, sex-filled fantasy. You're a dream. Just not mine. Yes, my emotions for you were running high."

"It was more than that. Remember that day at the restaurant when I asked you to recite what I did before you left the first night?"

"You know I remember everything. I proved it then." And she did. She recalled the moment that was the turning point for me where it felt like...more.

Rain inhaled, unsure whether to tell me, but she did. She detailed my every move that night. "The aftershock of your release passed from you to me. Your breath was labored, then you growled and said, 'Oh fuck, Rain.' You slid out of me and rolled on your back. Your face was wet with sweat. Your scent, a mix of sweat, amber, musk, and me, lingered in the air around us. Then you looked at the ceiling and rubbed your head like you were trying to wring water out. It seemed like you were trying to figure something out. I don't know what. But then you reached over and pulled me on top of you. I dusted your lips with mine because I love kissing you. You're right—I do it because it drives you wild. You held me and stared at me like you were trying to memorize my face, then—."

I interrupted her because the truth was, I fell for her that night.

"It wasn't a dream. Not just a high. It was real. I am real, Rain. I'm here right now. I want this—I want us."

"I know what it's like to be with someone and be high on them. I also know what true love feels like. I'm not falling in love with you if that's what you're asking."

"That's not what I'm asking. I want to know if we can make it work, to get there...to love."

"No."

I mask my reaction to hearing that word. "Just like that. You know?"

"I know."

"How is that possible?"

"Because, Noah, I'm already in love. I never fell out."

"In love? What?"

"I love Parker. He's the reason this can't work."

Her admission kicks the wind out of me. This beautiful woman, the one I crave, the one I envision having a family with, is in love with someone else. I straighten. I need to keep it together. "Does he know you love him?"

Her face softens. "Yes. He's always known."

"Rain. I find this all hard to believe. We experienced what we did—."

"Please, call me Raven."

"Raven," I say, attempting to mask my frustration. "Are you and Parker dating?"

"What Parker and I have is between us."

"You were with someone who cheated. I think you can understand the reason for my question."

"You're right. It's a fair question. When I met you, I had just ended my relationship with Blake. You know that. You witnessed the aftermath of that relationship. There was no one else."

"But I saw you with a tall blond. I assume that was Parker."

Her eyebrows raise. "I don't know what you're talking about."

"When you left my building Monday morning following the meeting. I tried to talk with you."

"I told you I had a plane to catch."

"I followed you outside. You were in the arms of another man. Kissing."

"Parker. His name is Parker Page. I was surprised to see him. He was supposed to meet me at the airport in San Francisco. He came to take me home. I didn't know he planned to fly to Seattle to get me. He's my best friend."

He may be her best friend, but it's clear now why Rain was comfortable in my world—her friend Parker likely flew in on his own jet to retrieve her. He must be the one who took Blake down. It takes someone of significant means and influence to bring Blake to his knees in less than twenty-four hours. Still, they're not together.

"You seem close."

"We are close."

"You love him, but you're not together? You were with me. How does—?"

"Noah, please stop. I didn't cheat on you. I don't have a man. Being in love and having a man isn't synonymous. You said you wanted to clear the air before we head into our business dealings. There is no us. We said one week. It's done. You and I are colleagues. I'm known as Raven Nichols, Esquire in business. You were my world for one week. I'll always have that. But, Noah, we have to work together. There has to be a common ground where we can move past our time in Seattle. Can we be friends, colleagues, anything but...?"

The way this woman looks at me, with sincerity wrapped in pleading in her eyes. I know she's torn. Her honesty is refreshing and a reminder we weren't supposed to happen. It was an unexpected chance encounter on her path to the top. One I'll never regret. For me, Rain is the fire that ignited my soul. I won't give up on getting what I want. We'll see how it goes working together. This is not the end of us.

"Sure, Raven. For now, we can be friends." For now.

"You mentioned we had other business to discuss."

"CNBC wants to interview me about the current state of the commercial real estate market. They also want to talk about the press release on the Ross Enterprises deal. We haven't finalized some elements that they may want to discuss."

"Then don't discuss any deal not inked."

"I have a meeting in New York to finalize and sign the terms. You and I need to be there on Thursday before the interview."

Chapter 12

Our Woman Is Coming Home

Parker

"Josh, man, I can't believe you have time for lunch."

"I'm in town this week. So, if you need anything, you have me through the weekend before I head out again. How's it going with Raven?"

"Better. I feel like we're getting back on track." I sigh, releasing the weight of years of longing for my woman. This sigh enables me to have conversations about the future. The hurdles ahead no longer seem so insurmountable. But still, there are some mountains to climb.

"You should be happy. What's up?"

"Remember the guy from Seattle?"

"Yeah. Noah."

"The contract she worked on for Ross Enterprises was with his company, Knight Development Corporation."

"The deal she landed?"

"They'll be working together for the duration of the build-out."

"That could be two or more years. What is Raven going to do? Does she still want to see him?"

"Rain said they're done."

"Done with him or done with this thing, whatever she was doing?"

"The break from me? Per Rain, that's done. She wants to work on rebuilding our relationship."

"Man, wow. That's great. Our woman is coming home. That's what you want."

"She's not ready, man."

"Then help her get ready. She's your world." Josh knows. For twelve years, he's been there watching me as I fell in love with Rain. He's witnessed every milestone and setback in our lives.

"I am. We're working on it."

Josh pats me on the shoulder. "Give her a little more time. The reward will be greater than you expected. It's been difficult to watch from the sidelines."

"You're a good friend. You looked out for my girl when I couldn't see straight. Man, I was so messed up."

"You're always there for me. We're brothers, and Raven is my sister. Now, I need her to find me a wife." He smirks.

"You ready for that, man?"

"When have you known me to play the field?"

"Yeah, I guess you're right."

"Are you and Raven going to have me over for dinner? I need to talk to her about finding me someone."

"Let it rest. You'll get there soon enough. When the right one comes along, you'll know it. The first time I saw Rain, I knew she was the one." All those years ago. I was right. Rain is the love of my life. One day, she'll be my wife.

Chapter 13

A New York Minute

Raven

When Nik told me I needed to be in New York this week, it sounded like a ploy to get more time with me, coming on the heels of our discussion about relationships. Additionally, he offered to fly me out on his private jet and let me stay at one of his properties while I was in town. I opted to arrange my own transportation and stay where I typically do in New York. Subsequent to reviewing over sixty pages of legal documents, I understand why he wanted me here.

"If they ask about the thirteen hundred street location," Noah says, pointing to a line on the page, "I can say we've secured the property—."

"But you can't name the designer. We haven't locked that deal down. You've narrowed it down to two—it's time you decided. This is going to come up again. But for this interview, I'd avoid discussing how you plan to increase rent value across the board at this location."

"I'll have that hashed out by next week. But you're right. The valuation could change based on who I choose. I'll take your advice and steer clear of this for now," he says.

"Well, seems you're ready. We should head to the studio."

"Raven, thank you for doing this on short notice. Sometimes, this is how the media works."

"So I've been told." By Parker, I don't add, because I don't want to delve into a conversation about relationships.

The television station is around the corner from our meeting, so Noah and I walk. Upon arrival, we go through the standard security protocol, and Noah is rushed into makeup. I sit across the room, watching as he gets ready and reviewing the details he'll need to remember if the interviewer asks him. He holds my gaze in the mirror whenever he addresses me. Despite my best efforts to push the thoughts of our week in Seattle from my head, they flood in. I see flashes of the look on his face as he stares at me while standing in the mirror the day we went shopping—the day he bought me the green silk dress.

"What about this one?" I asked, turning to show him the strapless green dress. He had a look of desire in his eyes I'd seen before—right before he devoured me in bed.

"Not that one," he said.

"Seriously? Why?"

"Because you look absolutely fuckable in that. And I might just take you right here in this dressing room." He walked over to where I stood on the raised platform surrounded by mirrors. When I turned to look at my reflection from all sides in the mirrors bordering the small room's walls, he stood behind me; he kissed my neck as we stared at our reflection in the mirror. At that moment, I knew he was lost in his thoughts.

"You wouldn't dare."

Not a man to back down from a challenge, he unzipped my dress, which pooled around my feet on the floor. "Nik, what are you doing?" I feigned protest.

"Showing you how much I appreciate seeing you in that dress." He turned me to face him, pulled me close, and kissed me. It was slow and sensual, and everything it shouldn't have been in the dressing room. We both got caught up in the kiss, and he slid his hand between us and down my underwear. He worked my body until my body contracted around his fingers. He masked my groans with a kiss until I came on his hand in the middle of the dressing room. His sly smile told me he was satisfied with his work. His look gave me the "I have everything you need" vibes.

He has that look now.

The studio team has their production down pat. Within seconds, Nik is seated near the interviewer, Jill VanHeart, one of the top daytime anchors on TV. The buzzing of people moving and doing their jobs goes from a soft lull to silence. I watch the monitor from the control room. This man is so damn fine both on and off camera. I think that was part of the attraction. His quiet confidence resonates on the screen as I look through the monitor. Three. Two. One.

"We're here on set this afternoon with Noah Knight, President of Capital Markets for Knight Development Corporation, a multi-sector commercial realty developer with sixty-five million square feet under construction. We've invited him here today to help shed light on the current situation, or looming crash, as some refer to it, which is threatening the commercial real estate market. And as we know, NY is a microcosm for what we see in the overall market."

"Thanks for having me, Jill. It's good to be here," Nik responds.

"Noah, there's been a lot of talk about a crash. What's interesting is we haven't seen the downfall that everyone predicted. Why not, and what should we expect?"

"That's a great question. We need to look at the current situation in the market. We're at a twenty percent real estate vacancy rate, which is quite a high number for New York, which typically hovers around twelve percent."

"That seems high."

"Twenty percent sounds high, but the system is absorbing the vacancy. The more important thing is to understand the reasons behind the vacancies."

"Over the past few years, most industries have been impacted by the pandemic. I suspect that has something to do with it," Jill says.

"Some are Covid-related, but there are other factors. Pre-pandemic, about seven out of ten people were coming into the office. Now we're at about six. This means we are almost at peak numbers of people in the office to where we were prior. So, the vacancy numbers we see appear driven by other factors, specifically obsolete space. Manhattan has about four hundred and sixty million square feet of office space. For comparison, Seattle is just a hair under one hundred eighty million. Manhattan also has a vacant office space of over ninety million square feet. One hundred million is obsolete."

"Obsolete."

"Yes. There's a lot of non-usable space. Over time, that space will need to be demolished. It could take anywhere between two to ten years to demolish and replace. So basically, a lot of vacant space will sit on the market for a while."

"Seems like a lot of dry powder sitting around establishing a natural floor for what pricing for buildings are once they start trading."

"Not really. That depends on what type of assets. Since Covid, we've seen a flight to quality in class A building. As far as office space is concerned, the C and B buildings are dead. They're not at the correct value. They will need to reach land value to be transactionable. If they don't, they'll get digested through the banking system, but banks don't act quickly."

"Do you think banks will let these go into default? I hear commercial mortgage-backed securities aren't lending on a commercial real estate basis. Are you experiencing this?"

"That's not true. CMBS is open—they're just on a lower valuation. If someone is refinancing, where you saw rates were at three percent, now they're five to six percent—but at New World rates. CMBS has opened up, but there's no way to get the refinance without interjecting a lot of capital. Class A rent rates have gone up. CMBS is alive. The valuation is lower. Cap rates have gone up because of where we are with the treasury. That impacts the volume. Higher interest rates lead to fewer deals. Thus, our current situation."

"For it to return to where it was, does the fed have to cut rates?"

This is a point we covered. Nik's eyes instinctively shift from Jill's to the monitor. At that moment, I know it's my attention he's seeking. We talked about grand sweeping statements criticizing the government.

"I can't comment on that. Commercial real estate has been one of the most affected by fed action. However, cutting rates is a number one booster–it's not happening fast enough. The question is, what happens when all these loans expire this year? The bust didn't happen because banks don't know what to do with the properties. They'll figure it out before it's too late."

"So you think this will work itself out."

"I do."

"Speaking of class A properties, you bought a well-known building in Seattle. The Knight Development Corporation is receiving the second highest rents in the country. Can we talk about that and what's next on the horizon for your company?" she asks, and I watch, mesmerized, as the handsome man I knew as Nik, without a C, discusses the success of his company and his brothers' efforts.

***

"You had to stop off where?" Parker asks, confused.

"To one of those over-stuffed tiny souvenir shops," I say, clutching my prized possession. On my quest to see how close the replica is to the actual building, I walk over to the wall of windows. Parker walks up behind me, grabs my waist, and pulls me into him.

"What are you doing? What's in your hand?" He looks over my shoulder while trying to pry my prize from my fingers. "Babe, let go. Let me see." Parker manages to lift one of my fingers. I clamp my finger back down as soon as he lets it go.

"No. Go stand over there. I'm doing something." I point to a spot across the room.

He kisses down my neck. When that doesn't work to distract me, he nibbles on my ear. I reach back to run my finger through his hair, taking in the moment.

"Damnit," I say when he takes the pewter from my hand. The tricksters. He still has one hand around my waist, holding me tight against his body. He examines the miniature metal Empire State Building in his hand.

"Babe, is this what you went to get?"

"Yeah."

"I could have taken you to the Empire State Building while we were here."

"I just wanted this," I tell him, taking back my trinket and pressing it against the window so it overlays the structure in the backdrop. "See, it looks just like the real one."

"It does, honey. Next time, tell me what you want, and I'll get it for you. I know you like iconic buildings. If you want, we can take time off next year to visit the ones in each state."

"Parker, you don't have to do that."

"Anything for you, honey." He holds me as we stare out the window, taking in the view a while before he says, "Hey, let's get ready for dinner. Cook should be done by now."

I turn in his arms and look up at him. "Okay, handsome." Then the doorbell rings. Parker releases me to go answer it.

I turn back toward the view, taking it in. It's been a while since we've been in New York together. The last time we attended a fundraiser hosted at the Met. We weren't together then. I was dating someone else at the time. My flying out with Parker was the catalyst for the breakup with the guy I was with then. Parker warned me about dating these insecure men who couldn't handle the fact that he and I were best friends. I should have listened. It wasn't until I returned from Seattle that it all finally clicked—I was running.

"Rain's in here. We were about to have dinner. Would you like a drink?" Parker tells someone.

"No, thanks."

I know that voice. Nik?

"Rain, babe, you have company," Parker maintains a neutral voice when he calls me, even though I know he feels the opposite.

I walk into the adjacent room. Noah is standing next to Parker, wearing an *I didn't plan on this look*. Neither was I.

"Hey, Noah. We weren't expecting you. Is everything okay?"

"I was headed to dinner and stopped to see if you wanted to dine with me, but it seems you already have plans."

I look at Parker, whose eyes shift between me and Noah.

"Let me introduce you to Parker Page, the man I told you about. He's an attorney and philanthropist, amongst other things." Nik nods. "Parker, this is Noah Knight, the developer I'm working with."

"Noah, I remember you from Seattle," he says, and I sense irritation wrapped around the power in his timbre. Nik mentioned seeing Parker kiss me, which confirms Parker also saw Nik. He never told me, not that it matters.

"Our chef has prepared our dinner." My eyes shift to Parker. I purse my lips and slightly squint, giving him my most subtle, *forgive me for what I'm about to do* look. "I'm sure our cook made enough for three if you want to have dinner with us. Parker doesn't flinch. I should know better. As an accomplished attorney, he's used to the unexpected.

"No, that's alright. I have reservations. I'll be heading out. Thanks again for the quick work on the contract and helping me prep for the interview," Nik says.

"No problem."

"It was an impressive interview. Your take on the market was spot on," Parker says. His voice is uncannily neutral. If this was the Parker from six years ago, I would expect my possessive giant to haul me to bed and fuck me senseless following this intrusion. But he's different. He's more sure of himself and us than he's ever been before. Now, as it stands, if we were together that way, I'd initiate sex because watching Parker Page at this moment has me all in my feelings.

"Thank you."

"I'll show you out," I tell Noah, walking past him to the door. Parker doesn't follow.

Noah opens the door and enters the private hallway where our elevator and emergency stairwell are housed.

"I didn't mean to intrude, but I can't say I regret it—I got to see you again."

"What are you doing, Noah? We spent most of the day together. You could have said something earlier about dinner. I would have told you Parker and I came to New York together."

"You mentioned this is where you'd be. I thought—."

"It wasn't an open invitation. But by now, you know that—I don't hide things. I told you where I was so you knew how close I was to the meeting location. This is Parker's New York home. I stay here when I'm in town. You can't do this type of stuff, Noah."

The elevator opens. "I didn't intend to upset you. Dinner was all I wanted." I give him my best *you've got to be kidding me* look. "Seriously, I get it—I could have called first. I'll see you in a few weeks."

"See you then," I tell him as I watch him enter the elevator. When the door closes, I rejoin Parker.

"Babe, are you okay?"

"Yeah. I don't know what Noah was thinking showing up like that."

"You know exactly what he was thinking."

"I'm just surprised he did that."

"He's a man that wants what he wants. You need to rein him in before I do."

"Come on, Parker."

"Rain, babe, we talked about this. You asked me to let you handle him."

"I know."

Parker puts his arm around my shoulder and pulls me to his side. He's said his peace—handling Noah is up to me.

Chapter 14
Rip the Band-Aid

Raven

"Raven Rain Nichols, Esquire, are you ready?" Parker calls to me from the bedroom. I take one more look at myself in the mirror and blow out a breath. I can do this. I've met with some of the most influential people on this planet. I can argue a case in front of a jury. I can have the hardest conversation I'll ever have with my mom.

"Yeah. I'm ready." The bathroom door flies open, and Parker steps in.

"Hey, you'll be fine." He stands behind me, snakes his arms around my waist, and rests his chin on my head. His closeness calms me. He's always had that effect on me.

I stare at our reflection. I got this. "Okay. Let's go."

Parker steps back and gestures to the door. I leave the bathroom, grab my purse, and head to the car.

"You have everything?" he asks, opening the back door. I get in. Parker slides in beside me.

"Yup. The only thing I really need is for my mom to give me some answers."

"You'll have some soon enough."

"This is another part of the healing process."

"Remember, this is your journey, not your mom's. I don't want you to have high expectations of anything she offers. This is about how you respond to what you learn about your dad. How you move forward and find yourself."

I nod. "Will you stay close by until I'm done?"

"Of course. I'm never far away." It's true. He never has been, even when I fled to London to escape the heartbreak I had caused. The day I fainted in front of my CEO and refused to go to the doctor, he was there, too.

"Rain." I hear my name. I can't hold back the tears because it's Parker's voice, but it's not real. He's not here. He's home or at work in San Francisco. But he keeps calling me, and I don't want to answer. I don't want to fall further into the void. I can't let Alex see me like this. I need to pull my shit together. Like we practiced, I think about Parker's voice and let that pull me out of the fog. That's it. I can hear him just like he's here with me.

"I'm here, Rain. This is real. I'm here in London."

"It can't be." I open my eyes. God, I see his beautiful face. It seems so real. I can feel his hand on mine.

"Rain, babe. I'm really here. You fainted, hon," I hear him say, and I touch his hand and squeeze it.

"Parker?"

"Yes."

"You're really here. In London."

"Yes, Rain." He laces his fingers in mine and kisses them. "I'm here. I've come to take you home."

"But I don't understand." He rises and sits beside me, and although I try to pull away, he doesn't let go of my hand. It's really Parker.

"AJ called me. I'm your emergency contact. He said you wouldn't let him call a doctor. I'll take you home."

That day, I didn't know whether I wanted to kiss him or kill him for not telling me he had been in London the entire time. But that's Parker—always there for me.

The car stops in front of my mom's house. The last big confrontation I had with her, she basically told me she didn't know anything about my dad and refused to discuss him with me. I left feeling angry and frustrated.

I look past Parker, out the window and across the lawn to the house. I had more bad days than good days at this house. I look at Parker. "Can you do something for me?"

"Anything."

"Will you kiss me?"

I don't have to wait for an answer. Parker cups my cheek, leans in, and kisses me. It's soft and sweet as he presses his lips to mine. He licks my lips, but he doesn't open my mouth. He pulls back.

"You good?"

"Yeah. Thank you."

The driver opens the door. Parker gets out and then helps me. He pulls me into a hug.

"Signal me as soon as you're ready to leave. This is the first step. You got this."

I turn and head to the front door. It opens as soon as I reach it.

The first thing out of my mom's mouth is, "Parker has somewhere to be?" which surprises me. For someone disinterested in their daughter's life, she seems preoccupied with what Parker's doing.

"He just dropped me off," I say, heading to the kitchen. I open a cupboard, grab a glass, fill it with water, then sit at her counter.

I look around the kitchen. It's different than when we lived here with Dad. I dust my fingers across the smooth brown granite counter that was added years after my father left. There used to be a table and chairs here. We used to sit around it and have breakfast as a family. That was before he left.

My mom's voice brings me back to why I'm here. "Seems like you're here for business. To what do I owe this visit?"

"You might want to sit for this."

To my surprise, she sits. Okay—that was easy.

"You have my full attention."

Rip the Band-Aid, Rain, rip it. "I want to talk about Dad."

"You can leave if that's all you're here for."

"I'm not leaving this time without you talking to me. I know where Dad is. I know he's remarried. I want *you* to tell me why he hasn't contacted his kids all these years. What would make a man behave that way?"

The look of shock on her face is telling. She did something. I sense it.

"Where did you get your information?"

"It doesn't matter. What does matter is what you say next. The contemptuous look on your face tells me his leaving has something to do with you."

My mom stares at me as if she's trying to determine whether I'm bluffing. She purses her lips.

"He left because I wasn't in love with him."

"Why did he marry you if you weren't in love? This is America. You both had a choice in the matter."

"I was pregnant."

"That's not a reason."

"It's reason enough."

"There's more that you're not saying. Be honest for once. The alternative is I walk out of here and ask him myself. Is that what you want? This is your chance to tell your side of the story." I don't hesitate to get straight to the point—it's the only way I know.

"I loved Bill. At the time, he didn't want me—or was confused. I don't know. Our relationship was complicated. We were on and off again. Somewhere during the off time, I met your dad. He said he loved me."

"But you didn't love him. You were in love with someone else. Why'd you continue to see him?"

"I told you. I got pregnant."

"And like I said, that's not a reason to get married."

"It was for him. He's an honorable guy. He wanted to get married. I wanted security. I married him."

"This part I know. I want to know why he left and never looked back."

"I don't know."

I look at her like she has three heads. She's got to be fucking kidding me. "Mom, we both know that's a lie."

She fidgets in her chair, pulling at her clothes. "I told him I was in love with Bill. Bill wanted me back. Bill said he'd made a mistake ever letting me go."

"What the hell? So, he just left? Why did Dad leave his children? This makes no sense."

There's a long pause. She looks past me like she's remembering the moment. Her brown eyes grow black and shift to me, and her face hardens.

"I told him you all were not his."

I gasp. "What the fuck? Why would you do that? Is that true? Is he not my father? I look like him, don't I? What the hell?"

"Raven. Enough already."

"Don't Raven me. He would have returned even if he thought I wasn't his kid. What did you do?" My voice raises an octave.

"This discussion is over. I told you. I wasn't in love with him. I asked him to leave. He left."

"You left out the part where you told him we weren't his children," I say, my voice laced with anger. I take out my phone and text Parker.

Me: Come get me.

"There's nothing more to tell. I shouldn't have told you this much. Let him be. Let him live his life wherever he is. Forget about him."

"Forget about him? He's my father, for Christ's sake. You have no empathy for the man. You manipulated him. I'm certain you're not telling me the whole story because you lied to him. There's a word for people like you."

"You wouldn't dare call your mom out of her name."

"Oh, so you know what I'm about to say. You know exactly what you are."

"I'm your mother."

"No. You're the person who incubated me. I don't have a mother, and if this is your subtle attempt to tell me that Bill is my dad—don't. My dad may have believed your lies—I don't. Bill can't even look me in the eye. I don't feel any connection to him. He's not my father." My phone buzzes. I flip it over. Parker is waiting for me. "So, are you done, or do you want to tell me the whole truth?"

"You should leave."

I slide my chair back, get up, and leave.

Chapter 15

She Dropped a Bomb on Me

Raven

When I leave the house, Parker is waiting for me on the doorstep. He takes my hand, leads me to the car, and we get in. I don't say anything when I get in the car. I just want to get out of the neighborhood. To put as much distance between me and my mom, her house, her world, her words—anything that resembles her. What kind of a mother does this? No wonder I can't get my head together. All this time, I thought there was something I could have done to prevent Dad from leaving or that maybe I somehow caused his continued absence. Now I know. The man thinks I'm someone else's child—at least, that's what he was told. I have no idea what he believes. All I know is that he hasn't been around since that morning, and my head has been messed up ever since.

I want to scream. Parker must sense my irritation. He reaches across the seat and touches my hand.

"You want to talk about it?"

"Sure. At home. But first, I need something strong to drink." I turn to look at him. He pulls me to his side. I exhale and allow the comfort of his arms to calm me.

"I got you."

I lace my fingers in his. "You always do."

It's the weekend. It doesn't take us long to return to Parker's house. With the stress of having this conversation, I can't handle being alone. Therapy is helping, but something about being with Parker makes me feel I can tackle the world. Parker collects my things and puts them in the foyer closet when we arrive. I head straight to the kitchen. He follows me.

"What's your poison? Wine, cocktail, or whiskey?"

"You'll need some, too, with what I'm about to tell you. Whiskey."

"Macallan coming up unless you want something else."

"That's fine," I say, watching Parker leave the room and return with a bottle of whiskey and two tumblers. He pours us both a glass. I don't bother toasting or clicking his glass or anything. As much as I want to guzzle it, I don't. I take a sip. Parker taught me years ago that you don't guzzle or do shots with the good stuff. You sip and enjoy the flavor. It goes down smoothly, like everything he buys. He watches me curiously.

"You sure you're okay?"

"As well as can be after the bomb she dropped on me."

"Ready to talk about it?"

"This is one for the chaise lounge."

He shakes his head at my admission. "Okay, let's do it."

Parker collects our glasses, and I follow him into his family room to his oversized chaise. I suspect it's gotten more use than he'd thought it would when he first purchased it. He places our glasses on the table nearby and then sits. I sit with my butt on the chaise, my legs draped across his, and my arm wrapped around his shoulder.

He swipes his thumb across my cheek. "Do you want me to ask questions, or do you want to tell me as it comes to you?"

"I'll just tell you." He hands me my drink. I take a sip. "My..." I can't even make my mouth say the word mom. "She told my dad she was in love with Bill and that Robin and I weren't his kids. I think the last part is a lie. But that's what she told him, and he left."

"That's a lot to digest."

"You're telling me."

"A DNA test will validate parentage. That's simple to sort out. I'm sure there's more to this."

"That's what I said. She wouldn't tell me anything even after I threatened to go to Dad and get the full story."

"Your dad's an esteemed attorney. He would not walk away from his children without a fight. Unless—."

"She did or said something to ensure he'd never see us again. I know she lied to him. I just don't know about what or why."

"What do you want to do?"

The fact that he asked the question and didn't pick up his phone and make a call to solve my problem shows me how much Parker has changed. If this had been ten years ago, he would have called my mom or had investigators dig up everything about her, Bill, and my dad. He would already have had a meeting scheduled to talk to my dad. I would have had the entire story by morning if I asked. He hasn't done that. He wants to know what I want to do.

"Go talk to my dad. Tell him I think about him every day. Let him know what she told me. Have him fill in the blanks. Tell him I want my dad back. There's no way he just left us. I feel it in my gut."

"Then we'll have to coordinate a meeting between you and your dad. Do you want me to be present?"

"Nearby."

"Okay. I'll help you write a note to him."

"Now I need to decide what and when to tell my sister."

Chapter 16

How Do We Fix This?

Parker

After Rain told me about her mom, she finished her glass of whiskey. We talked a bit more, and then she wanted to sit and relax with me before I convinced her to eat dinner early. I knew her discussion with her mother was weighing on her when she insisted on having a second glass of whiskey. Then, like I knew she would, she fell asleep in my arms.

It doesn't matter that I put her in the guest room bed to sleep. Rain got up thirty minutes later and crawled into bed beside me. Even now, her face is buried in my side, hair splayed wild across my chest, while her arm is wrapped tight around me. I should have covered her hair in her silk-lined cap, but I didn't. I anticipated she'd come to me. I love it when her hair is wild and unruly. I love that it's on me—that she's on me. I love everything about her, especially her heat radiating through me...penetrating my soul.

I stroke her curly locks. She shifts beside me.

"What time is it?" she asks.

I reach for my phone. "Nine forty-five."

"God. I never go to bed this early." I chuckle at her comment. There were times when we were younger that I couldn't get her out of bed. Rain reaches up and touches my lips with her fingers.

"You're laughing at me."

"Always with you. Never at you." I nibble on one of her fingers. She pulls her hand away.

"How do we fix this?"

"We already are. Give it some time." I pull her close.

Chapter 17

Charcuterie of Things

Noah

"Man, I need to know how you're going to navigate this thing with Rae," Rok says, grabbing some cheese and whatever else he can find in my fridge. By the time he's done reaching for things, there's a charcuterie board of items laid out nicely on a platter. Since the housewarming party, my home has become the go-to place for my family, randomly dropping in.

"Christ, man. You and Baby Mak have a lot of hidden kitchen talents. What the...."

"I'm serious about eventually settling down. The ladies love this stuff. Besides, I'm good at it. Look at this," he says, showing off his charcuterie platter. Rows of cheese, sliced baguettes, baby pickles, cured meats, and a hand full of grapes and strawberries are neatly laid out in rows on an oversized slate platter.

"You're the CEO of one of the largest real estate development companies. The ladies are going to love you no matter what."

"They'll love me because I'm the best-looking of the three of us. Besides, I'm looking for the real thing."

Ignoring his, *I'm the best-looking* comment, I say, "I get it, but don't tell Baby Mak. He might get hives."

"What am I getting hives from?" I hear Baby Mak before he comes through the foyer into the kitchen.

"I swear, does anyone ring first?" I ask, feigning annoyance.

"You shouldn't have shared the door code," Rok says. "I was telling your brother that I'm ready to find the right woman and settle down."

Baby Mak reaches into the platter Rok made, puts some prosciutto on his cheese, and then pops it into his mouth.

"Settle down at your own risk. No one told me there was a party today. This is good."

"Thanks," Rok says.

"There is no party," I say, getting some beer out of the fridge. "But if we're eating this, we need drinks." I shake my head and smile at how my brothers easily rope me into making this a get-together.

"We should have wine with this," Rok says.

"Whatever." I reach into the wine fridge, grab a bottle of red wine, and hand it to him. "You can open it since this is your party." I smirk.

"At least you didn't have to cook the meat. Where are the olives?" Baby Mak asks.

"Get over it. Why are you all here anyway?" I know they're up to something.

"I prefer pickles. Nik, get the baby some olives. We want to know what's going on with our Sis."

"Raven," I state, retrieving olives from the fridge.

"Yeah," Baby Mak continues to press. "How'd your conversation go?"

I hand him the olives.

“What do you want to hear?” I ask.

“We want to know if our deal stays solid,” Rok says.

“It’s solid.”

“So, you worked things out with her?” Mak inquires, popping an olive in his mouth.

“If by working things out, you mean, are we together as a couple? No. Do we agree to work together as colleagues? Sure. You saw how smoothly the interview on CNBC went. For now, it’s fine,” I say, knowing I haven’t fully come to terms with the agreement. Nor do I tell them I stopped by to take her to dinner. I had no idea how close she was to this Parker dude. My jaw ticks thinking about it.

“Talk to me, Nik. I want to know everything that went down,” Rok presses in his *I’m the boss* tone.

“What are you doing, Mak?” I ask as he makes a neat row of olives on the platter next to the pickles.

“Don’t get sidetracked. Rok asked you a question.”

I want to tell them to piss off, but that’s not how we are with each other. These are my brothers. We ride or die, and we run KDC. “I told Rain....” I shake my head. I can’t get used to this. “*Raven*, what we had in Seattle didn’t have to end; we could have both.”

“Both meaning you’d maintain a relationship and be colleagues,” Rok clarifies.

“Yeah.”

“The look on your face says she didn’t go for it.” My baby brother is brilliant in more ways than one.

“She said we can be friends and colleagues.”

“Wow, man, I’m sorry. That had to be hard to hear,” Rok says earnestly.

“I thought we could make it work. I know we can.”

“Hold up. You said Sis wasn’t in on being both. You gotta respect that,” Mak says.

“I am. That doesn’t mean I can’t continue to show her what she’s missing.”

Rok walks to the patio door to look out at the view. It’s the contemplative side of him I’ve seen my whole life. He turns around, locks eyes with me and says, “Don’t cross the line. Respect her wishes. I don’t want my Lil Sis to ever be uncomfortable.”

“Never. That’s not what I’m talking about.”

“Then what is this, Nik? If Lil Sis is not interested, let it go. This is not an agenda you can push because you didn’t like the answer you received. Contrary to how it feels, it’s not a business deal you’re negotiating.”

“I suggest you find someone who is the right person for you. I thought it was her, but it appears I’m wrong about something,” Mak admits.

“The jury’s still out. The door’s not closed yet,” I tell them.

“We feel you, brother. Remember what I said. Let time do its thing,” Rok says.

“Can I get a Manhattan in this place?” Baby Mak asks. I roll my eyes, and we all laugh.

Chapter 18

It's the Little Things

Parker

"Honey, open that before the kids get here," my mom tells Dad.

"We're already here. I can take care of it," I say, entering the kitchen with Rain beside me. My dad looks down to where my hand is laced with Rain's, then back at me. He winks.

He doesn't miss a thing. He was the one who taught me that it's the little things, not grand sweeping gestures, that tell you everything you need to know about the person you're with. It's been years since Rain walked in anywhere randomly holding my hand. I usually reach for her, pull her to my side, or pine for her attention while trying to maintain the boundaries of friendship. But when we got out of the car, she grabbed my hand. Since I met her in front of the Knight building in Seattle, she's given me something. A light kiss, a lingering glance, the touch of a hand, a snuggle, a hug. Hope. I think the nibble on my ear almost sent me over the edge, but I need to wait until she's fully ready for what's next in our relationship.

"Perfect timing," Mom says. Dad grabs Mom by the waist and turns her toward us.

"Raven, you look lovely." My dad kisses Rain's cheek.

"Darling, I can't wait to see you in that dress with your heels and everything," my mom says, pulling Rain into a hug.

"Thank you. I can't wait. It's a beautiful dress. You have impeccable taste. Now, what can I help with?" Rain lets go of my hand, goes to the sink, washes her hands, and begins helping my mom.

"Mom, you could have brought in Cook for that stuff."

"Parker Page, don't make me banish you from the kitchen. Didn't you say you were going to open this?" She hands me a bottle of wine. I set it down on the counter, then pick up my mom and twirl her around.

"Put me down. What in the world are you doing?"

"Getting my hug. You gave Rain one."

"Between you and your friends, it's too much."

"My friends? Who's been here?"

"The usual suspects," my dad pipes in, leaning against the counter where he's been quietly observing my shenanigans.

"Josh and Ethan stopped by yesterday morning. They came to recruit your dad to go golfing."

"Is Josh going to be in town for the party?"

"They both will."

"Wow. It's been a while since all three of us were together at an event."

"They're your best friends, Parker. Of course, they'll be there. And who would miss one of Mrs. Page's themed parties?" Rain asks.

"That's right, Darling. This is a big deal. Preston, do you want to eat here or in the dining room?"

"Dining room," I say, still a little traumatized from seeing my parents doing it on the kitchen counter over a month ago.

"Parker Page, when did your name change?"

Rain's eyebrows furrow, giving me a *what are you doing* look.

"Sorry, Mom."

"The dining room is fine, honey," my dad says, helping my mom take dishes into the dining room.

It doesn't take us long to get settled around the table. I help Mom plate the salad and lasagna she made. Dad pours us all a glass of wine.

"Raven, I told Preston about your impressive win for Ross Enterprises. We're so proud of you."

"Thanks. It was a lot of hard work, but it paid off. Parker helped me with a hurdle I needed to jump over."

"Nothing compared to the months of work you put in on the deal. You did great work, Rain. Everyone is impressed."

"So impressive. Word got back to Kane. He mentioned it last week. You remember meeting him, Raven?" my dad says.

"I remember Mr. Kane. Should I be worried? He thought he recognized me. I'd never met him before."

"Hmm. Nothing to be worried about. His memory is not as impressive as yours, but I believe he has something like a photographic memory. He could have seen a picture or something," my dad says.

Rain looks at me questioningly. "Like if he saw a picture of her on someone's desk?" I ask, seeking clarification.

"Possibly, why?"

I don't want to discuss Rain's business. If she wants to say something, she will. "Just asking."

"Mr. Page," Rain says.

"Preston."

"Preston, sir. I recently discovered that my dad, whom I haven't seen since I was eight, is an attorney."

My mom puts down her fork and looks at Rain. Her face is soft and sympathetic.

"Oh, darling. I can only imagine how learning about him feels after all these years. Have you seen him?"

"No, not yet, but I plan to." Rain looks at me.

"She just found out. She talked to her mom but didn't get anything more to help."

"I'm sorry, honey," my dad pipes in. "Please let me know if there's something I can do. Our resources are at your disposal. I imagine my son is doing whatever he can to help you through this."

"He is, sir. He's been amazing. The Kane connection made me think of it."

"If you want time with Kane, I can arrange it," my dad offers.

"It's okay. Maybe after I talk with my dad, I'll have Mr. Kane fill in the final pieces if there are any. I'd love to know how he knows my face."

"Fair enough. We're here for you. You're part of us. Never forget that."

My dad reaches across the table and touches Mom's hand, then Rain's.

Chapter 19
Confessions

Raven

Okay, I can do this. Parker and Ethan are next door having coffee and waiting for me. I have an emergency text message ready to send if I need to signal them. One tap and *its time* will appear on Parker's phone, and they'll come to my rescue. The seat I chose gives me a good view of the restaurant. My back is not at the door, nor am I facing it, but a simple sideways glance gives me a view of everything. I don't know why I feel compelled to take these precautions. It's unlikely my dad would do anything unsavory. I just don't understand why he stayed away from us. I'll soon find out.

The server brings me a glass of water.

"Would you like anything before your guest arrives?"

"No. Thank you." I look past the server. A tall, handsome gentleman wearing a dark grey micro-pinstriped suit enters. His warm honey-brown skin color mirrors mine. His short, curly hair is sprinkled with grey. I recognize him. *Dad.* He remembers me and heads toward the table. "My guest is here. Bring another water, please," I manage to say, allowing the breath I'd been holding to escape.

He sits. Like me—it takes him a moment to pull it together. He inhales and scans my face quickly. I wonder if he's searching for familiarity from the past.

"Hello, Raven." The deep, rich timbre of his voice sounds more imposing than I remember.

"Hi..." God, I sound silly. Like an eight-year-old version of myself. *Hi.* I mimic it in my head. How do I talk to this man?

"I'll give you two some time to review the menu," our server says, then leaves.

My father's eyes haven't left me. "I followed your career. You're everything I imagined you'd become and more. Beautiful, brilliant, bold. I figured it was only a matter of time before you pinned me down. Seems you found the one way in...Kane."

"Sounds like you might know more about me than I know about you."

"I suppose I've had an advantage over the years."

"I've been informed you're a distinguished attorney...pretty high up on the food chain, if I have my facts correct." He presses his lips together in a typical *I'm not showing my cards* lawyer move, waiting for me to finish my point. "I happen to know the man at the top of the chain. It took me over twenty years, but I finally gained some advantage."

"Yes. That's one of the reasons I'm here today. But you didn't come here to talk about your powerful friends."

"I came here to talk about you."

"There's not much to talk about. Since you went through Kane, you know I'm an attorney."

"Listen, Dad. God, what do I even call you? Dad, Rhett, Sir, Mr. Sweet-Nichols?" What do I call the man I've only ever known as *Dad*? God, what am I doing here?

"Depends on what you came here for."

"Answers. Closure. Confessions."

"I have nothing to confess," he says. His body stiffens, and I sense a twinge of something beneath the surface. I struck a nerve.

"I do. My world was turned upside down the day you left. I spent years blaming myself. Did I do something wrong? Was there anything I could have done to make you stay?" As usual, I jump right into the hard stuff.

"You did nothing wrong. Why would you even think that?"

The server returns. We haven't looked at the menu, but I've been here many times with Parker and his friend Ethan because they work nearby. Ethan's building is directly adjacent to the restaurant. After all these years, it still seems strange to have friends whose names are on skyscrapers, like the twenty-story Whitmark Building, named after Ethan Whitmark, one of many wealthy African American tech entrepreneurs I've come to know, like the Ross'.

I look at my dad. "You need time to decide?"

He opens the menu and scans it briefly.

"Start with the lady." He tips his head in my direction.

"I'll have a shrimp Caesar salad. I'm good with water for now."

The waiter looks at Dad.

"Chicken Caesar salad. Nothing else. Thanks." The server nods and then leaves. "Raven, why would you think you had done something?"

"I saw you when you left. I was there. I called to you. I don't know. I thought you didn't respond because you were upset with me or something."

His eyes lock with mine, revealing something that looks like surprise mixed with fear or confusion—I don't know which. "I thought I heard a sound. I wasn't sure. I thought your mom was about to...."

The words die on his tongue. He swallows. He's revealed more than he wants.

This is hard for me, too. I want to say so many things, but I don't know what's going on in his head. He's guarded. Does he want to be here to figure this out? Is he afraid of me? I'm certainly not afraid of him. I am scared of what not having him in my life means. Regardless of how difficult this conversation gets, I need to do this to heal. Like what I have with Parker, my relationship with my dad can only move forward with honesty.

"The day you walked out, you took everything from me. I was only eight. I didn't have much. You provided everything I had up until that point. Then you took it all away—my love, my confidence, my power. When you walked out that door, you broke me," I say. I look at him with conviction—finally able to speak the words aloud.

"That wasn't my intention."

"But it is my reality. So, tell me...tell me why you left. Tell me why I had to find you."

"You must have talked to your mother. She would have told you something." I laugh sardonically, but he continues. "Raven, you must know, I'm surprised you're here. You shouldn't be here."

"What? Why?" I'm sure he hears the shock and panic in my tone.

The server returns with our meals, serving me first, then Dad.

"You need anything else. Parmesan, more water?"

"Nothing. Thanks," I say, attempting to get him to move on.

Our conversation was getting deep. I need to eat something. With my history of fainting, I might pass out. I cut into my shrimp and eat. I watch as my dad begins eating his meal. I study the color of his skin, how his hands move, and how, like me, he separates the chicken away from the leafy greens before he cuts into it. His movements, how he holds his fork and tips his head slightly right before he takes a bite, mirror mine. I wonder how many more similarities we share.

As I'm watching him, he pauses and looks around the restaurant. I suppose my staring is a bit unsettling. I wonder if it makes him uncomfortable. Does a man like him get embarrassed? He looks so much like the man I remember but slightly different. He's still handsome. I remember when we used to go places when we were younger, and women would turn, stare, and comment—staring like I am now. I can't help it. After all these years...he's here.

Something catches his eye, but I'm so focused on how familiar he seems. He reaches into his suit pocket and retrieves his phone. He swipes the screen. Is he going to take a call while with me? Seriously. What the hell? I look around in frustration. I lock eyes with those of a man standing at the reservation desk—a man I haven't seen in what? Almost ten years? What the fuck?

Kevin?

From where I'm sitting, I can hear him provide the receptionist with his information. "Kevin for one."

Before I realize what's happening, my father stands. Within seconds, he is at the door, standing near Kevin. Kevin looks at me, then back to my dad. I have no idea what's going on. Why is Kevin here?

"You need to leave. The order against you is still in effect."

I'm stunned to hear the words come from my dad. What in the world is going on? How does Dad know him?

"I have a reservation. I had no idea *she* was here," Kevin says in his defense. His voice is laced with disdain. Ignoring my dad, he steps forward.

"Now you know. Leave," my dad commands.

The door opens. Parker and Ethan walk into the restaurant, dwarfing everyone standing near their six-four and six-five frames.

"Kevin, all these years, and you still haven't learned how to behave. I'll have to fix that," Parker says.

Kevin recognizes Parker and holds his hands up, signaling he's innocent. My face is warm, and my mouth hangs open as the scene unfolds before me like a movie. What the ever-loving fuck is happening?

Kevin steps past Parker and Ethan, pushes the door open abruptly, and leaves without another word. Ethan tells the receptionist something. Parker locks eyes with me and mouths, "You good?" I nod. Instead of leaving, he and Ethan take in the scene for a second. My dad looks at them, then at me, seeking silent confirmation from across the room that no further action is needed. I shake my head, and he returns to the table.

"Friends of yours." It's not a question. He knows they are.

The hostess seats Parker and Ethan on the other side of the restaurant.

"Sounds like you know the answer already."

"Just confirming." He drinks his water.

"How did you know about Kevin? I can't believe you recognized him. I haven't seen him in years. Just how much do you know about me?"

"I know who Kevin is because I get a copy of any police report filed with your name."

"What in the hell?"

"I may have been gone, but I do some things instinctively."

"Like the need to protect a daughter you haven't talked to in over twenty years? I don't need you for that. That man over there has been the only protection I've needed." I nod in the direction of Parker. "He's the reason I haven't seen Kevin since college—the only reason Kevin didn't defy you and walk over here. Because the look in his eyes indicated he was headed my way."

After all these years, Kevin is still stewing about what happened at the party off-campus.

"Get the fuck out of my face. You have no idea what you're doing," I screamed at Kevin even though I was too sick to stand without the support of the wall.

"I know exactly what I'm doing. You're leaving with me," Kevin demanded. He reached for me but was snatched away before his hand could make contact.

I wonder if he still recalls the impact of Parker's fist smashing into his face. I still remember the cracking sound of Parker's knuckles coming in contact with Kevin's face before I saw blood shoot from his mouth. He should never have tried to take someone else's woman.

"As I said earlier, you have powerful friends," he tells me.

My eyes shift to where Parker and Ethan are seated. Ethan shows Parker something on his phone. Parker feels my gaze. He looks up and winks at me. I smile. He lifts his chin, signaling me to focus on my conversation.

"Yeah, there are a lot of benefits to knowing people with their level of power. But at the end of the day, it doesn't help me clear my head of nightmares about the day you left."

"I had no idea it would impact you this way. I'm sorry."

"Sorry doesn't solve this. Why are you shocked that I'm here? And don't ask me to talk to my emotionally immature mom, who you left us with. Before I came to see you, I gave her an ultimatum. Either she tells me the full story, or I'll get answers from you. I'm here. I want answers."

"Your mother wanted someone else."

"That part she admitted. I also know she told you we weren't yours. Anybody looking at me and you would beg to differ. Tell me why you believed her. Tell me why you left. Tell me why you never came back for me."

"I couldn't."

"You could have. I'm here. We could have done this years ago."

"No."

"Why? This is your chance to tell your side of the story."

I sense hesitation, but he opens his mouth to speak.

"She threatened me. She wanted to be with Bill so bad that she resorted to threats."

"You're an esteemed attorney. You know your way around the law. You, by your own admission, have access to records of a man who attempted to assault me years ago. Isn't that what you were looking at on your phone just now? What in the world could my mom have said to you to make you leave your children behind?"

"She never told you anything?"

"Dad, for God's sake. No. What the hell did she do?"

The server returns to check in on us. I ask him to take my plate because I'm not in the mood to eat after everything that has transpired. I let him know we don't require anything else at the moment. He clears the table and then leaves. I raise an eyebrow. My dad takes a deep breath. He blinks. His face is unreadable. He doesn't want to tell me. Silence screams between us.

"Your mom said she would tell the authorities I abused my children." His words come out slow and methodical. His eyes don't flinch as he focuses on me, waiting for my response. But I don't have one. I never expected this. My face is hot. I need air.

Until the day my dad left, our life with him was everything a child could want from their father. To know my carefree life with a loving parent was shattered by my mom makes me ill. My mom threatened my dad to get what she wanted...Bill. I didn't expect something this evil. I feel sick to my stomach because what she told him isn't true. I feel disgusted because I lived with a woman who I've come to realize I don't recognize...a monster. I've been suffering all these years not knowing why my dad was gone. Why he stopped loving us. All the suffering, the years of sleep terrors, all this to discover it was because of her. Because my mom wanted another man and was a coward. She lied and took away our lives. She destroyed everything she was designed to protect.

"You never did anything like that to us. Why would she...how can she get away with this?"

"I didn't know if she fed you all stories to make you say something to support her lies."

"Never. I couldn't even get her to talk about you. She refused to mention your name." I see a sigh of relief wash over him, and rightfully so. All these years, my sister and I had no idea why he left. We loved our dad. To know that all this time, he'd been thinking we'd turned against him because of some lie my mother threatened him with to keep him away. Oh my god. The burn of bile is fighting its way to the surface. "I'm sorry. I need to.... Give me a minute. I can't believe she did that." I stand and rush to the restroom at the back of the restaurant. I hear footsteps behind me. Parker.

I lean over the sink and look in the mirror; my color is drained. My face is ashen. I'm dizzy. I rest my elbows on the sink and hold my head in my hands. The bite of bile rises, and before I realize it, I'm hurling the contents of my stomach into the sink.

"Don't let anyone in," Parker commands.

He pulls my hair away from my face. I hurl again. And again. Then again, until there's nothing left but the sound of air forcing its way from my gut.

"Use the men's room." The muted sound of Ethan's voice carries from the hallway.

Parker turns on the water, washing my mess down the drain. He runs paper towels under the faucet and then uses them to clean my face.

"Ethan."

The door creaks. "Yeah, man."

"Can you get her sparkling water?"

"On it."

"Hold on, babe." Parker pulls me into his chest. "I got you. Just breathe. Listen to my heartbeat. Count." I listen and count. One. Two. Three.

Within moments, Ethan returns with a glass and bottle of sparkling water. Parker fills the glass with tap water.

"Babe, use this to rinse your mouth." I do what he says: rinse my mouth with water and spit it in the sink. He rinses the glass and fills it with sparkling water for me to drink. I drink the entire thing. He watches me like he always does, making sure I'm okay.

"Thank you. My dad...."

"Ethan."

"Right here, man."

"You want him gone?" Parker asks me.

"Raven, say the word. I'll take care of it," Ethan assures me.

"No. Just let him know I need a minute." Ethan leaves to talk to my dad.

"Parker. My mom is a monster. I can't do this."

"You can. You're doing great so far. Whatever happens, I'm here, Rain. I understand the conversation may be hard, but you are tougher than anything thrown your way. You've proven that. You have nothing else to prove. Everyone else has to demonstrate they deserve you. Even me. Remember that."

He has a point. I take a deep breath. Okay, I can do this.

"Parker, I'm going to need whiskey, therapy, and god only knows what after this." I give him a tentative smile to shake off my dread, knowing I need to go back out and finish the conversation.

"We'll have all of the above." He wraps his arms around me and squeezes me until some of the stress leaves my body.

"Okay. I'm ready to go back out."

Parker and I head toward the table. Ethan is sitting with my dad. They both stand when Parker and I arrive.

"Parker, this is my dad, Mr. Sweet-Nichols. Dad, this is Parker Page, the man I love, and his friend Ethan Whitmark, whom you've already met."

"Mr. Page, Mr. Whitmark, I'm sorry we had to meet under these circumstances. Thank you for everything you've done for Raven."

"Sir, good to meet you," Parker says.

"We'll let you finish your conversation, Raven," Ethan says, placing a hand on Parker's shoulder.

"Rain, let me know if you need me," Parker says before kissing my cheek. Then he and Ethan walk away. I sit back down.

"Sorry about that."

"I understand. I unloaded a mountain on you. You have good friends that don't hesitate to help you."

"They're incredible. But..."

"I digressed."

"What you said—it just seemed too farfetched. I've never had anything other than fond memories of you until the day you left. For mom to taint those few years and sever our ties with a lie wrapped in a threat is...unconscionable. Yet, I can't believe you left us with *her*."

"I told you. I didn't have a choice. You were already being needlessly ripped away from one parent. Your mother is many things, but even I know she has her limits. Except when it came to me—she wanted me permanently out of her life so she could focus on Bill. But she wouldn't do anything to you all."

"Dad. Everything she said was a lie. She's a sociopath. I don't even think she loves Bill. You know they're not married, right?"

"I'm aware."

"This is a lot to take in."

"Telling you was as difficult as leaving."

I blow out air. "Okay. Now I know why you flinched when I told you why I was here."

"I didn't think I'd ever have to talk about this."

"Until I asked to meet you. God, I can only imagine what was going through your head when you sat down."

"It's okay. We got through it, didn't we?"

"You did better than me." I tip my head toward the hallway leading to the restroom.

"Are you okay?"

I nod and give him a reassuring smile. "So, I'm told you remarried, thus the name Sweet. Why didn't you have kids?" I ask. My dad looks around the restaurant and then back at me. He's not surprised I know about him and his family situation.

"You mentioned you had your traumas since that day. I had mine."

"Was it what she said or the fact we were essentially ripped away from you?"

"The latter. You said I took your power when I left. Your mother took mine. I wasn't about to let anyone else have that much control over me again."

Oh my god. My mom blew up our family, leaving shards of shrapnel in everyone. I close my eyes. *Breathe.* I reopen them. "How do we move forward? Mom has no more power. She lied to keep you away from us. She lied about me not being your daughter. I recognize every gesture you've made since we sat down because I make the same ones. I'll take a DNA test." I blurt out the last part.

"You'd do that?"

"Yes. If you will."

"I don't have an issue taking one. What about your sister?"

"Robin. You mean your daughter."

"Robin."

"She doesn't know I found you, but I can easily get her to give me a sample. Do you still think Mom can threaten you?"

"No. Not after what you told me. I imagine she knew it was over the second you told her you would come to me for answers. That's why she didn't tell you. The moment you confronted her, she lost her power over us."

"But you didn't know what she'd told us, so you couldn't reach out."

"That's right."

"This is too much to take in. My life is a mess because of a lie."

"Your life is not a mess."

"It is. You need to understand that everything I tell you is the raw truth. That's the commitment I made to that man over there. It's my commitment to you. It's the only way I know to live—truthfully, out loud...exposed."

"Your friend Parker is the one who filed the report against Kevin on your behalf. That was ten years ago. Yet you two never married."

"Because my brain has been so messed up since you left. I refused to give anyone the power you had over me. To take my love away. So, I walked away before anything could happen. I broke his heart."

"He's still here."

"Thank God. Somehow, he knew I was struggling to receive his love because I was scared. Every morning, Parker has to relive with me the day you walked out. You couldn't have forgotten I have perfect recall."

"I remember."

"Dad, you must have known that moment would replay in my head daily."

"I tried to leave without waking anyone. I had no idea you were there watching."

"I told you, I didn't know that then. I thought you heard me call to you."

"Oh god, Raven. I'm so sorry. Maybe now...knowing the truth will help." On the surface, what he's saying sounds simple. Maybe I'll find some peace—and the sleep terrors will end. Maybe I can finally live a normal life...that I can forget. There is no forgetting.

"I can only hope. But that day has colored everything I do. I'm so lucky Parker never left my side. He saw past my pain to the real me."

"He sounds like a good man."

"He found you for me."

"I'm grateful. I wish things could have been different."

"Listen. I've had enough of turmoil and bitterness in my life. I'm on the path to fixing myself. This is part of that. I've spent much of my life being angry at you and confused about why you left. Now that I know the truth, I need to try and let that go. If you want to be a part of my life, we can work on that. Just let me know. I'm going to take some time to process our conversation. In the meantime, I'll arrange for DNA testing."

"What about what I told you about your mom? Are you going to talk to her?"

"I already told her that I don't have a mom."

"That wasn't my purpose in telling you what she did."

I ignore his comment. The topic of my mother is a moot point. "Robin is planning a trip out here. I'll talk to her and have her do the testing."

"You don't want me to call her?"

"If that's what you want. You have nothing to fear now. But I suggest you let me talk to her. You see, all these years, she thought I had something to do with you leaving. We finally talked about that. What happened between you and Mom impacted us all."

"I'm sorry to hear it caused your rift."

"We're working through it."

"Still, Raven, thank you for finding me. I don't think I could have done anything different."

"It's too late. The damage is done. We can only pick up the pieces we want. Toss the rest out with yesterday's leftovers." I stand. My dad stands and extends his hand. I shake it. "I'll call you."

"I'd like that," he says.

I go to the door where Parker and Ethan are waiting for me.

Chapter 20
In Sync

Parker

Rain is doing well for someone who just faced their father for the first time in over twenty years. After we left the restaurant, Rain said she wanted to go to my house and drink something strong. Although she said she wanted something strong to drink, she only wanted wine because we both know she's a lightweight.

I lean against the kitchen counter watching Rain. She's settled on a barstool on the other side. She stares into her drink like it holds the answers to her questions. She takes a sip, then looks up.

"Hopefully, I didn't get vomit on you." I can tell by the uncertainty in her voice that she's nervous. Still, she's worried about me.

"I'm fine, babe. What about you? You want to talk?"

"She did this, Parker. That...that thing which calls herself a mother. She did this. She ruined our lives. She made him leave and ensured he wouldn't return because she wanted someone else."

"Bill."

"Yeah. Bill. What a cruel fucking joke." Her words come out in a sardonic laugh.

"He didn't want to leave, but he did, and he never came back. How did she manage that? Your dad is a man who wields a lot of power."

"She told him that we weren't his children and that she loved Bill. She gave him an ultimatum to leave and stay away, or she would tell the authorities he did something to us."

My heart is pounding like it's trying to leave my chest. I push away from the counter to go to Rain. "Rain, honey, is it true? I'll kill him if he touched you."

She raises her hand in a stop gesture. "No, Parker. My mom lied. My dad never did anything like that. That's not who he is. It was a threat so she could get what she wanted. She's the monster."

I go to Rain anyway and swivel her chair to face me. Pulling her toward me, I wrap my arms around her shoulders. Holding Rain feels right. I absorb her warmth. "I'm sorry, Rain. Tell me what you need."

"Being here with you is all I need."

"What about your dad? What's next? Do you want to build a relationship with him?"

She pulls away from me and looks up. "Yeah, but first, I want to set the record straight and squash all the lies. We can't move forward with uncertainty hanging over our heads. He knows now my mom didn't taint me with her lie. I sensed that was a huge relief, but I want him to have proof of parentage."

I listen intently, but I don't share my true feelings about her mother and how cruel she is to destroy so many lives—lives she was supposed to nourish and protect. It's unforgivable. I spent the past twelve years trying to protect Rain from people like her mother.

"I can only imagine that hanging over his head all these years."

"That's why I believe he needs confirmation that I'm his daughter. I'll give him that. I need to arrange DNA testing."

"I can have someone come to you and your dad to collect samples."

"And Robin?"

"Robin, too. Are you going to tell her everything you learned today?"

"Yeah, although I think I should talk to her face to face," Rain says, staring off to the side as if contemplating her next move.

"You mentioned before that she has a trip planned. You could wait until then."

"I suppose Dad and I can provide our samples first. Then I'll talk to Robin about it when I see her. Then, we can collect her sample while she's here."

"She may not agree."

"That's on her. I want proof that he's my father." She drinks the last of her wine. I get the bottle, refill her glass, and top off mine.

"Are you hungry now? I noticed you didn't eat at the restaurant."

Rain hops down from her stool and goes to the pantry. "Ready to eat all my feelings. You got any sweets in here?"

"I'll order something before you get all in your feelings eating snacks."

"I just want cake. A whole one. I could eat it with a serving spoon."

I laugh. "I'll order dessert with our meal unless you want to help me make something sweet." I take out my phone and place an order from her favorite restaurant. "Are we making dessert, or am I ordering?"

"Order. I'm not feeling that ambitious. Maybe we can try to make something together tomorrow. Oh, we should try that recipe for the cake Josh likes. I'll freeze a piece to save for him for when he's back in town."

After ordering, I lay my phone on the counter and walk up behind Rain, who's busy searching the pantry shelves for anything to satisfy her craving. I snake my arm around her. She continues rifling through the cupboard. She reaches for the flour, but I step back, bringing her with me.

"No. We're not making Josh's favorite dessert. Haven't you heard the saying that cooking is a way to a man's heart? I can't have my best friend falling in love with you." I turn her around in my arms. "Don't think it got past me when you introduced me to your dad as the man you love." I pull her into me and rest my chin on her head, burying her face in my chest. "Thank you. You'll always be the love of my life."

Rain and I take in this rare moment when it feels like we're rebuilding our world together in sync. It's not her on her own path with me chasing, and it's also not me resignedly watching from the sidelines. This moment, this second, we're in sync. We're gradually finding our way back to each other...to love. She writhes in my arms until I let her go.

"Tired of me hugging you already?" I tease.

"More like having one of those moments where I tell you to get off me because I'm ready to haul you off upstairs."

I bark out a laugh when she uses my words. "Welcome to my world, babe. Give it time." The doorbell rings. Our food is here. Rain starts toward the door. "What are you doing? I'll get that. You can grab plates."

I go to the door, retrieve our meal, and return to the kitchen. Rain has the plates and silverware out waiting. I unpack the containers, and together, we plate the meal. Rain sits.

"Sometimes, it's a pain that I'm so stubborn, and it makes admitting you were right much more difficult," she confesses.

"What was I right about, babe?"

"That day, you told me that I wasn't ready. I understand what you meant. Not just about that but a lot of things."

"You also taught me about patience. As much as I wanted to rush your process and claim you as mine, I couldn't," I admit.

"You mean, take back what was yours, as I recall. You always said I was yours."

"I stand corrected. As much as I want to take back what's mine, I realize it could be so much better as we mature. I've always loved you, but I'm overwhelmed with how much more intense it is now. Watching you come into yourself—babe, it's so beautiful."

"Well, what I wanted to say is I get it. If this had happened two weeks ago, I would not have been able to have this conversation without clinging to you in a chair. That conversation I had with Dad would have crushed me to the point where you'd be pulling me out of your arms, trying to get me to focus and breathe."

"You had a moment at the restaurant. You handled it, then went back out and handled your business."

"You know what I mean."

"I know exactly what you mean. You're doing great, honey. We both are. I'll take back what's mine soon enough," I say with a smirk.

Chapter 21

Page Twenty, Line Six

Noah

There are two reasons I love being in San Francisco. One is that I can count on most days being sunny. The other is Rain. When I think of her, I think of the best week of my life. I think about what our future could be like. I think about what I can do or say to get her to reconsider us.

I walk into the conference room, where core team members will meet us. As I enter, I hold my breath. Rain is already here. She stands.

"Hi, Noah. Good to see you again." She holds out her hand. Fuck, this is going to be hard. I take it. The same kinetic energy I felt between us over a month ago still exists. Being with her in Seattle was so natural that standing here inhaling her essence, I need to fight the urge to pull her into me and kiss her.

"Raven. I'm excited to meet the team."

She removes her hand from mine and sits. "They'll be here shortly. I'm usually early."

"I noticed. How've you been since I last saw you?"

"Good. Great. Working hard."

"How does it work now that you're lead counsel for this project? Do you still manage other projects of a similar size?"

"I lead several projects, but this is the largest. I have associates under me who serve as the point of contact for my other projects."

"All that time, I knew you were brilliant. I didn't realize..."

"Noah, please don't."

"I was just going to point out that seeing you was a pleasant surprise. My brothers and I are quite impressed with your work."

"That's nice to hear."

One by one, people begin filing into the conference room. As they do, Rain says their name under her breath.

"Paul. Page twenty, line six. Jane. Mark."

"Raven," I say, keeping my voice low so only she hears me. "Have you met them all before?"

"No."

"Then how do you know Paul, Jane, and Mark?"

"I read their files."

"What's on page twenty, line six?'

"You need to talk to Paul about construction; the contingency timeline is off by thirty days. It doesn't match our original agreement, which impacts the project's pricing. There may be a reason for the change, but it wasn't noted."

"This is you in action. Smart. Beautiful. I wish others had your talent. I'm still waiting for Jane's response to an email I sent yesterday."

"Recheck your email. It's there."

"How do you know?"

"Jane does all her email responses once a day, early in the morning."

I pull out my phone and check my email. She's right. An email arrived while I was on my way here. "You've received pictures of everyone? You seem to know them by sight."

"I don't plan to make the same mistake I made in Seattle."

"We weren't a mistake."

She doesn't respond. She blinks and then scans the room. And as if a switch turns on, she begins the meeting.

"Hi, everyone. I believe we're all here. Let's get started. I'm Raven Nichols, Esquire, and to my right is Noah Knight. I'm excited to say we'll be leading this team over the next few years. In that time, we'll get to know each other better. We'll get to introductions in a minute. I want to remind you that I sent an agenda before the meeting. I hope everyone had a chance to review it." There are nods around the room. "Great, if anyone has anything to add, we'll have time for that. First up, I'll give my partner, Noah, the floor to introduce himself."

"Hi, all. As Ms. Nichols alluded, we'll spend several years bringing over one million square feet of property space to fruition in multiple cities across two countries. All of us on this project were chosen for our niche capabilities to make this project a success. Out of the gate, there will be a lot of things that may seem tedious at the moment, but in the end, the hard work we do now helps us get to the good part. So, if Ms. Nichols and I poke holes in things, it's with the end goal in mind. I look forward to working with you all. Ms. Nichols."

"Thank you, Mr. Knight."

"Noah."

"Thank you, Noah," she says, leading the team through all the agenda items.

I watch, mesmerized at how smooth she is. Now I see how her recall ability shows up at work. She's laser-focused on each person she talks to, like they're the only ones in the room. She's likely the only one in the room that remembers everyone's name. She moves efficiently through each agenda item she addresses. She doesn't forget a question or get sidetracked. She doesn't need to reference her notes. It's as if she pulls her talking points from thin air.

"Paul, can you provide more details on page twenty, line six?" she says, looking directly at him. Even Paul has to look at his computer to see what she's referring to as she asks him specifics about his work.

The team is in awe of her. So am I. I can't get enough of this woman. When all the agenda items are addressed, the meeting ends, and I wait for everyone to leave. Rain slips her iPad into her tote. She stands.

"You know you're fucking brilliant, right?"

"You mentioned it."

"That's because you are."

"Like your brother Mark?"

"Him plus one. Or two. You get the gist."

"Thanks."

"Seriously. Great meeting."

"You're not so bad yourself. Now I see why you were such a master at planning all my events. And you're very motivational. You have this team eating out of your hands. They'll follow you anywhere. Likely do whatever you ask."

"What about you?" I take her hand.

She looks at where our hands are joined. "I did that already," she says, removing her hand from mine.

"Have dinner with me."

"Don't you have a jet to catch?"

"I leave tomorrow. Have dinner with me."

"No."

I groan to myself. She knows what that word does to me. "You're goading me."

"Not this time."

"Not goading me? Or dinner another time?"

"I'm not goading you, Noah, and I won't be having dinner with you tonight or anytime soon." She slides her arm through her tote.

"What about team dinners?"

"Is that what tonight is?"

"No. I'm asking Rain out to dinner."

"My name is—."

"Raven. I know. Raven, I'd love to take you out to dinner. Yes, it's for my own selfish reasons: to have time with you. I miss you. Just dinner. Nothing more." And here I go again, feeling more like I'm negotiating a deal rather than a date. Rain does that to me. She constantly has me doing things I've never done with another woman.

"Thank you for asking, but no."

"I get it."

"Noah."

"Don't say it."

"Please, let me finish." I nod. "I'm really excited to work with you. I can learn a lot from you, and I plan to absorb every ounce of knowledge I can extract as we work together."

"I willingly give it."

She gives me an acknowledging smile. "Noah, meeting you changed my life in a way you can't possibly comprehend. I can honestly look back and say that each moment we shared was magical. You did that. We had our time together—it was great. Perfect. Then, as we agreed, we ended it to return to reality. Since then, a lot has happened. This is our reality—two people living separate lives."

"It doesn't have to be separate."

"Noah, there is no us."

"But there can be."

"That's not possible. You're building a life in Seattle, and I'm building one in San Francisco. I'm part of an us that doesn't include you."

"Not Blake?"

"God, no. How could you think...?"

"I know it's not him. You mean us, as in you and your friend?"

"That's right. Me and Parker."

"I don't understand. You said you're not dating him. You and I can be more. I'm asking you to give us a chance. We started something beautiful. I should have never told you I wouldn't come to claim you like I'm your man. Because that's exactly what I want to do."

She looks down at her watch and then back at me. She smiles. "I knew you would. It's who you are. I have to go, Noah. I'll see you in a few weeks." She touches my hand and turns to leave. She stops, walks back to me, and kisses my cheek. I want to turn and capture her lips so badly, but I don't. She's not mine. Not yet.

Within seconds, she's gone.

Chapter 22

Three Guys at a Bar

Parker

It's been a while since Josh, Ethan, and I had the chance to grab a drink and chill. Ethan's secret product development project has kept him tied up until recently. He finally got it to the greenlight stage, which was the only reason he could be with me when Rain met her father. On the other hand, Josh is always on a plane, so we coordinate around his schedule.

"Hey, man. How's it going?" Ethan asks, extending his hand and locking arms with me.

"Good. No court today."

"You know you live for that stuff. Speaking of living for...how's your girl?"

Ethan has been a part of Rain and my life almost as long as Josh. He began his technology company before we graduated university. When he found out painting was her side hobby, he commissioned several pieces and now Rain's artwork graces the walls of his office and executive conference room.

"Good. Still processing her meeting with her father."

"Yeah, that had to be hard for her. Her dad seems like a decent guy. I spoke with him briefly, but he was cordial. Is she going to see him again?"

"She's trying to figure out timing on all that."

"I'm there if she needs my help again." He raises his chin. "Our boy's here," he says as Josh heads toward us.

"Gentlemen. What are we drinking?" Josh stands between us and puts one hand on my shoulder, the other on Ethan's.

"Just getting started. I have a whiskey coming." The bartender arrives and places a drink in front of me.

"I'll have the same," Ethan says.

"Make that two," Josh adds, he takes a seat beside me then turns to me. "Man, congratulations on that settlement with Dalton Media. You play for keeps when you go after the big guns. Five hundred million." He shakes his head. "I suppose drinks are on you."

"Thanks, drinks should be on Ethan. He just got government approval on his new flame-retardant technology. How does that stuff work anyway, Ethan? I think you're in cahoots with NASA. That's some other-worldly technology you're creating."

"Man, I'm just trying to save lives. Anyway, your case hit the headlines on CNN. I saw it online. How do you avoid being in those pictures when all the attorneys walk out of the building following the judgment? I swear you're stealth."

He's right. Although I have plenty of security, I still don't take the risk of having my face plastered in the media associated with high-profile cases. People don't like losing that type of money. It could put a target on my back. I have myself and Rain to think about.

"I exit via the back of the building as soon as the decision is reached," I admit.

"I need to take my cue from you. I can't keep my name and picture out of the media," Ethan faux whines.

"Your name is on the damn building, man. It's too late for that. Anyway, I'm sure the ladies love you," I tell him.

"Get over it, man," Ethan shoots back.

The bartender puts one drink in front of Ethan and the other in front of Josh. I raise my glass. They do the same.

"Cheers," I say, and they repeat.

"Speaking of love, how's my girl?" Josh asks with a wry grin.

"Your girl now? Our girl is good," I say.

"We were just talking about her," Ethan adds.

"Fill me in. Last I talked to you, Rae was going to meet her dad." He swirls his drink as he awaits my response.

"Ethan and I were there when she met him."

"Tag-teamed by the likes of you two. That must have been intimidating."

"Not intentionally. We were on the sidelines at the shop next door," Ethan adds. "Then some creep from her past rolled in."

My jaw tightens just thinking about it.

"What? How's our girl? What happened?" Josh asks, voice laced with concern.

"I handled it. He's the guy I put an order against when we were in college. He didn't know Ethan and I were next door. We saw him go into the restaurant, so we followed him. Get this. Her father has been keeping tabs on her and knew the guy by sight—had a picture of him."

"Not Kevin? What the fuck?" Josh says and I'm shocked because he has rarely cursed in all my years of knowing him.

"Yeah, man. Her dad's been keeping up with her. He recognized Kevin when he walked in and immediately tried to sideline him. Kevin wouldn't leave until I walked in and threatened him."

"This woman has too much going on to have this go down on top of everything. I'm sorry this happened to Rae."

"Just a freak coincidence."

"I'm sure you have it under control."

"Yeah. He won't press his luck again."

"Remind me to stay on your good side." Josh laughs and then takes a sip of his drink.

"Rain would kill me if I looked at you sideways. I think she's more protective of you than me. I'm jealous," I tell Josh.

Both Josh and Ethan laugh. "Right. I'm not the one you should be worried about. What's happening with that Noah dude? After what you told me about him showing up at your house in New York, even I feel a little overly protective, so I imagine you might be unhinged about now."

"I promised Rain that I would rein myself in on this one and let her handle her business with him."

"What business is she handling?"

"That's my question," Ethan jumps in. "There should be no business."

"She has to work with him. She said she established what that should look like."

"Which is?"

"Professional. Rain told him that she is in love with me."

"Seriously?'

"That's what she said."

"Dude won't stop going after what he wants," Josh says.

"Would you?" Ethan asks.

"No. I'm not giving up on my woman."

"And what does this guy think about that?" Josh asks.

"It doesn't matter. He'll have me to deal with if he doesn't back off. If he crosses me, it won't end well for him."

"Cheers to that." Ethan holds up his glass, and we all tap it.

Chapter 23
Looking for Mr. Right

Raven

Sometimes, you meet people in this world whom you click with and feel like you've known all your life. For me, that's Parker and my friend Jade. I met Jade in an evening painting class during my second year in college. She was creating a painting of what she considered her dream garden. It was so captivating that I stopped what I was doing and watched, mesmerized, as she crafted each flower. I remember she caught me staring.

"If you record yourself and put music to it, I bet you'd get millions of views on social media. Your work is stunning and fascinating to watch."

"Thank you..." She paused, waiting for me to say my name.

"Raven. People call me Rae."

"Thank you, Rae."

And that's how it started. Every two weeks for the next three months, we sat next to each other, talked about life, and got to know each other. We've been friends ever since. Now, we're grabbing a drink after leaving the school where we volunteer, teaching children art in their afterschool program. I look around the quaint space, which feels like a secret hideaway tucked away in an alley in downtown San Francisco.

Jade kisses me on the cheek, takes a seat next to me and says, "You seem to have a continuous string of cool spots to try in the Bay Area."

"I suppose. How's the dating going? You mentioned a new guy you were thinking about talking to if he called. Did he call?"

"Aamon. Yes, he called the other day. I let it go to voicemail."

"Why?"

"Still debating."

"Did he leave a message?"

"It was brief, but I'm not sure. He sounded too—."

A member of the wait staff comes to us to take our order. We're sitting in brown leather wingback chairs near the fireplace. Conditioned by her church background, Jade opts for sparkling water. I do the same. When the waiter leaves, my eyes shift back to Jade. She sighs heavily because she's perplexed about something. She tends to get this way when talking about men.

"Talk to me, Jade. He sounded too what?"

"I don't know. I'm just not sure."

"Well, you can block him if you don't want to talk to him. Or, if you want to see what happens, you can return the call and talk on the phone. But if you sense he's a dud, then don't bother calling. Trust your gut."

"Yeah. I'll think about it."

"Or you can let me hook you up with someone."

"Let me see how this goes. Besides, I'm focused on work and volunteering. My life is full. If I put my energy into a man, I want it to be the right man. I don't want to kiss a bunch of frogs. I'm out if it doesn't feel right within a few weeks."

"Just like that?"

"Yeah. Life is short. It's rare for people to meet *the one*. When you meet that one person, you have to grab hold and not let go. Tomorrow is not promised to us."

"You're right."

The waiter returns. He opens a bottle of sparkling water and pours two glasses full.

"Will there be anything else?"

"Not at the moment. Thank you," I say, then he leaves.

"So, what's happening with you, Parker, and Noah?"

Now it's my turn to sigh. "Noah is a work colleague."

"Wait, what? You two talked?"

"Yeah. He flew out ahead of our big meeting and wanted to clear the air. He says he wants to continue what we had in Seattle."

"By the look on your face, that's not what you want."

"When I was in Seattle, I thought I did. I felt this overwhelming desire for him."

"But?"

I take a sip of my water before responding. "It was likely the afterglow of sex. Don't get me wrong, the man is fine as hell, brilliant, commanding, and amazing in bed, but..."

"He's not Parker."

"No. He's not."

"Did you talk to Parker about it?"

"He's known everything since day one. I always tell him everything. He sensed I was spiraling in Seattle, met me there, and brought me home."

"Yeah, you told me he came and scooped you up. That's your signal—he's the one."

"Sometimes I think Parker knows me better than I know myself. He knows exactly what I need."

"You love him."

"I never stopped."

There's a moment of silence as we drink our water and ponder my revelation. A couple comes in, fingers laced, looking in love. I smile. Loving Parker has been my life. Like Parker, Jade has lived through the years of my transition to who I am today.

"Then you need to get your man."

"He knows I'm his."

"I don't understand. Why aren't you back together?"

"He says I'm not ready."

"And you agree?"

"Once again, he's right. I need to resolve this thing with my family. It's eating away at me."

"You're working on that. You texted me that you met your dad. What else is there?"

"I still need to talk to my sister. And we all need to complete DNA testing."

"What for?"

"Because my mom told my dad that Robin and I aren't his children."

Jade gasps. I haven't told her the whole story yet. She only knew I was meeting my dad. I fill her in and tell her everything that happened the day I met my dad, including how Parker and Ethan helped.

"Holy hell, Rae. That's insane. I hate this happened to you, but glad you found your dad."

"I'm going to try and build something with him. Not pick up the pieces, more like start over from scratch."

"What about your mom?"

"I can't talk to her. I can't even stand to look at her."

"So that's it with her?"

"Pretty much. What mom does this crap to their children? She needs professional help. Something's wrong with her, but it's not my responsibility to solve her problems. I have enough on my own. I'm finally feeling more like myself." I drink the last of my water and set the glass on the table. The waiter notices and returns to fill my glass. "Thank you," I tell him, then as quickly as he appeared, he's gone.

"So, the therapy is working?"

"Humph, I should have listened to Parker years ago. But I suppose there's a time and place for everything and a reason I'm only getting to this point now. Everything that happened over my lifetime prepared me for a better version of myself—one that is ready to accept love."

"Like Parker's been giving you all these years."

"Unconditional. He's been there through everything, even though I couldn't appreciate it."

"Twelve years."

She's right. For twelve years Parker's love and commitment to me has never wavered, even when I did the unthinkable. He never left my side.

I smile. "I told my dad I loved Parker."

"Really?"

"It came out so naturally. It was out of my mouth before I realized, almost like it had to be put into the universe."

"That's beautiful. I want a love like that."

"You just put it out in the universe, so it's bound to happen."

"Well, if that's the case, I'm putting out that soon I will find the love of my life and marry him."

"I'm putting into the universe that the love of my life will take back what's his and put a ring on it," I say.

We clink our glasses together and laugh.

Chapter 24

What Seemed Right At the Time

Raven

Holding Parker's hand, staring into his eyes, I inhale and do my best not to cry. These sessions, the questions, the discussions are all about healing myself and finding my way back to him. *Focus. Say the words. It's okay. Parker loves me unconditionally.*

"Rain. Did you hear the question? When conflicts arise between you and Parker, do you tend to pursue working through it right away or withdraw and need your space before talking?"

"My initial tendency is fight-or-flight. Parker..." I take another breath before beginning again. "Parker recognizes that in me immediately, then pauses to check in with me. He says let's talk about it."

"Then what do you do?"

"If it's something I want and I sense resistance—I fight. I reiterate what I want because I know he'll give it to me." My eyes shift from Parker to our therapist. She's expressionless.

"Parker, is what she is describing what you experienced?"

"I love Rain. I would never deny her anything."

"Rain, you mentioned fight-or-flight. What did you mean by that? Is it always a fight scenario?"

"No. Most times when he wants to talk it out, if I feel I can handle it, I do. We'll sit down and talk. That was until...well, when we lost our child, I fell into a stupor and Parker tried to talk to me, but I refused. Early on he knew something was wrong. He tried to get me to talk about it, but I wouldn't open up. It was then that I started the process of mentally withdrawing from him. I was going through the motions like we were a couple when all along I was scared."

"What were you afraid of?"

"Getting lost in his love. No matter how I behaved before we broke up, Parker was there trying to make it work, and I felt I didn't deserve him. So, I broke up with him, but he didn't want that. He said we could work it out. I ran. I didn't give him a chance to talk about it. All these years I've been living with the fact that he offered a way for us to get through it together, but I refused. I used his love for me against him and forced his hand. I made him stick to his promise to give me what I wanted."

"That's a definitive commitment. What other promises did you make to each other?" she asks.

"Years ago, Parker and I made a series of promises to each other. We would keep each other informed of our whereabouts. Regardless of the discussion's difficulty, we would always tell each other everything. Lastly, we would never deny each other anything."

"And whatever we told each other would be the truth," Parker adds.

The therapist places her pen down and looks between Parker and me. "So, in essence you stacked the deck. Parker how did that make you feel?"

"I lost my child and my woman in less than a few weeks. They were my family. For ten months I felt like I was on life support waiting to die. Then she responded to the message I sent her, and I felt like I could breathe on my own again. This was my opportunity to continue to show her how much I loved and supported her. I watched and listened to everything she was telling me, trying to accept the bits of her she offered. You see, I spent my adult life with Rain. I knew she was running scared, however, there was no way I could give up despite her decision to live a life without me. I spent months in therapy. It was soul crushing, but I waited until she was ready to talk it through. When she ran to my arms in Seattle, I felt in my soul that Rain had come home to me. That's why we're here. I would wait a lifetime for his woman."

"And I'm done running. I love him more than ever."

Parker squeezes my hand and says, "We love each other and that's enough."

***

"Parker Page, what in the world are you doing?" I ask as he slides closer and positions his phone for a selfie.

He's been smiling goofily at me since we left our therapist's office. We usually go home after our appointment, but I wanted to go out and have lunch with him.

"You look beautiful and happy. I want a picture of us together." Okay, I didn't expect that.

"That's lovely," I say, looking at his phone screen and smiling. He taps the screen. I turn to look at him. He's a beautiful man, so caring and good to me, even when doing something to irk me—he's doing it out of love.

"Oh, I like this one," he says.

"What?"

"The way you were looking at me." He taps his phone screen and shows me the picture of me looking at him lovingly. He's right. I look like a woman in love. "I'm glad you decided we'd go to our appointments together," he says.

"Why? Because you get to hear all my deepest feelings and darkest fears?"

"You've always shared most of that with me. But yeah, now I feel I know you even better."

"That doesn't scare you." It's not a question because I already know the answer. Nothing scares Parker. Especially not hearing the truth. We vowed always to tell each other the truth no matter how hard it is to hear.

It was great to clear the air about this during our therapy session. Admitting that even though over the years we've been open in our discussions, we didn't allow ourselves the space to work through what we were telling each other. It's not just about saying the words. I admitted during the session that despite how I conducted myself over the years, my love for him only grew stronger. Still, I fought it. But now he knows I'm no longer fighting his love and it feels freeing to finally move forward...together.

"No, Rain. I love you. Hearing about your feelings, what you did while trying to find yourself, doesn't scare me. It helps me," he admits.

I want to cry. He understands me so well.

The waiter comes to check in on us.

"Can I get you two anything else? Perhaps another drink?"

Parker looks at me.

"I'd like to see the dessert menu," I say, meaning Parker will review the menu for me since I don't intend to memorize another one.

"And you, sir?"

"Nothing now. Let's give her a chance to review the menu." Parker says, holding out his hand for the menu. The server passes it to him and then leaves. "You feel like cheesecake or something chocolaty?"

"Cheesecake sounds good," I say. He lifts his chin, and the server returns. Parker relays our order, and we're alone again.

"I meant what I said about how you look. How do you feel?"

"I feel good. Thank you for being there for me."

"I wouldn't want to be anywhere else. Your sister will be here soon. Are you ready for that?"

My sister still doesn't know about our father and our conversation. Parker had a person come collect DNA from my father and me. Next is my sister. But first, I have to tell her why I need her to take a DNA test. I blow air in my cheek and release it.

"Ready as I'll ever be. I'm just not sure how she'll handle a conversation with Mom."

"How she navigates that is on her. She and you had very different relationships with your mom following your dad's departure. Try not to let her reaction impact what you two are building."

"Well, first, let's see how she responds to me."

"Did you decide on a date to see your dad again?"

"Yeah. We're going to open our results together."

"I'm proud of you. Working through this with him is the start of you two building your new life, whatever that looks like. I'm glad to see you facing this head-on."

"Something I should've been doing all along instead of running from my problems and procrastinating."

"You were only doing what seemed right at the time."

The waiter returns with a cheesecake and two forks. I dig in right away, and Parker does the same. I tap my fork against his.

"Cheers," I say, and then take a bite. "Um, god, Parker. This is so good." He reaches out to touch my lip.

"Well, my two favorite people." I freeze mid-chew when I hear a familiar woman's voice.

Tina?

Chapter 25

That's All Folks

Parker

Rain eats a forkful of cheesecake, and I swipe a bit from the side of her lip with my thumb. I lick the cheesecake from my thumb before I hear the last woman I expect to interrupt us. Tina. Although I've seen her at events, I haven't been with her in months.

"I didn't realize you had favorites. Are you coming or going, Tina?" I ask.

"Coming," she says with a smirk.

"Tina." Rain nods to her. "Don't let us stop you."

"I haven't seen you in a while, Parker. What's up with that?" I need to rein this woman in. This is not behavior representative of someone from our society. Tina has always been rebellious against our social etiquette. Over the years, Josh and I would always have to remind her of her status.

"Tina, you haven't seen me because there hasn't been a reason. The next social event isn't for a while. Was there something else we could help with? Rain and I are having a meal."

"Will I see you soon?"

"No, Tina. I recall telling you I'm with Rain. You need to respect that. Unless we happen to be at the same event, you won't see me."

"So, that's it."

"Don't make this difficult. Show some decorum. Remember who you are and what we represent."

"Tina. I think Parker is trying to tell you that 'that's all, folks.' The *arrangement* is over."

For the first time since I've known her, Tina's face goes red. She gets it. She got it when I told her but didn't expect Rain to confirm it. After all these years, Tina knows how determined Rain can get.

"Well, I guess the dynamic duo is together again."

"If you don't mind, we would like to finish our meal," Rain says, and I want to kiss her.

"Have a good evening," I say.

"Well," Tina says under her breath, walking away.

"You should have never let her touch you." Rain's eyes narrow at me. She's upset but not pissed. She got over that a long time ago. She learned how to handle Tina. It gives Rain a sense of pride and control to put Tina in her place when she's acting out of character, so I don't interfere.

"You're right. I should have never done it, but I did, and it's done. You know I love you. Eat your cheesecake."

"Parker Page, Esquire."

"You want to talk about it here or at home?" Usually, Rain wants to have all her serious conversations at home on my lap. Lately, she's grown into her own and can handle the most challenging conversation wherever she is. I love this about her—seeing her grow. It's good for her.

"Here. I can't stand that woman, and I can't stand that she put her mouth on you."

"You had a choice in the matter. Also, you went through—." She cuts me off before I discuss the list of men she's been with.

"Don't remind me."

"But I have to. That's what we do, honey. We talk it out. You had a choice back then. We could have navigated our lives differently and figured it out as a couple, but you wanted to do that alone and—."

"I said I wanted to see other men."

"That's right. I waited. I'm still waiting. Although Tina has put her mouth on me as you describe, I never laid with her. You are the last woman I've been with that way. You're the last woman I kissed. The only woman I will allow to kiss me."

"You don't have to remind me. I believe you. I know how you are. I'm not as strong as you, but I've learned my lesson."

"But you're still upset about Tina, and I understand. I promise she won't behave this way around us ever again. Tina received confirmation that our arrangement was over the second she saw us. What you witnessed was Tina pushing the envelope. You confirmed you're with me. Tina knows your word is binding and won't challenge you."

"I still want to kick her ass," she says and laughs, and I slide my arms around her waist and pull her to me.

"Will you settle for a kiss from me instead?"

"I'll take it," she says, and I kiss Rain. It's soft, warm, and loving but not overly sensual. Just enough to let her know we're making our way to the other side. Soon, we'll be there.

Chapter 26

The Messenger

Raven

I DECIDED TO MEET my sister at her hotel. She was initially going to stay with our mom. I suggested she use this as a mini vacation since it's been a while since she's been back in San Francisco. I don't know how she'll respond to my news about Dad and how that will impact her relationship with Mom. With her go-with-the-flow attitude, it didn't take much convincing.

I see her across the room from where I sit at the hotel restaurant table.

"Hey, Rae," Robin says like she's out of breath. She sits.

"Hi. How was the flight?"

"Good. Uneventful. How's Parker?"

"Good."

"Work?"

"They put me on as lead counsel after I returned from Seattle."

"That's great. Does that mean you'll spend more time in Seattle?"

"Not at the moment. The core team is here. The developer is there. I expect I'll fly out once or twice per quarter."

"That's something."

"I suppose."

"You mentioned you had a conversation with Mom. What was it about?"

"Her and dad."

My sister's eyes widen. "Did she say anything more than in the past?"

"A little. Enough to make me take action."

"Action? This sounds serious. What happened?"

The server comes to take our order. As usual, we order the same thing. Ceasar salad and iced tea. Once the server leaves, I respond.

"Mom told Dad she didn't love him, that she loved Bill, and asked him to leave."

"He wouldn't just leave because of that. What's the rest of the story?"

"She told him we weren't his."

Her eyes widen, and her mouth is gaping open. "What?"

"She told him we weren't his kids and that we were Bill's, and threatened him if he didn't leave."

"Get out of here. What are you saying? That can't be true. Did she tell you how she threatened him? Why would she do that? We're not Bill's kids."

I don't respond right away. My eyes shift over Robin's shoulder when I see the server coming with our salads. The server places a plate in front of each of us.

"Can I get you anything else? Parmesan?"

I look at my sister. She holds my gaze. Gone is her rolling-with-the-flow attitude. She wants answers.

"That's all," she says. When the server leaves, she continues. "Well, Rae. Why would she do that?"

This is the part that sucks. I have to be the bad guy—the messenger. Once again, I have to be the one to divulge our family's dirty secrets. All because my mom isn't adult enough to handle this discussion with her children. This is another blip in my life that will leave an indelible mark on my brain. I take a sip of my drink. I can do this.

"She wouldn't tell me. So, I had someone find Dad, and I asked him myself."

"What? You saw Dad?" I nod. "When? Why didn't you tell me? What did he have to say for himself after all these years?" Her voice is laced with shock, wrapped in anger.

"I saw him two weeks ago. I went to him after I couldn't get answers from Mom. I wanted to know everything before I talked to you. I didn't want you to get the information piecemeal like I received it. I wanted to gather all the facts."

"Did you find out everything you wanted?"

"Most of it."

"I want to know why mom did what she did." She closes her eyes and then opens them again, bracing herself for whatever comes next.

I rest my arm on the table, inhale, and tell her, "She never loved Dad. She's always loved Bill. They weren't together when she met Dad. She got pregnant. Dad wanted to marry her, so she married him. At some point, she and Bill got back together while she and Dad were married."

"She was cheating on him."

"I suppose."

"I want to know why she threatened Dad. How did she make him abandon us?"

"She wanted to ensure he wouldn't interfere with her and Bill's life, so she told him we weren't his kids and that she'd tell the authorities he touched us if he tried to see us." I lower my voice when I say the last part, but like my dad delivered the message to me, my eyes don't leave hers, and I don't flinch. I deliver the news like I'm citing facts to the jury. Robin bites the inside of her lip.

"That can't be true."

"It is."

"Is this some kind of scam by Dad? What's he getting out of telling you this?"

"He's a highly regarded attorney—his career and life would have been destroyed if he came after us. He'd be in jail. This is not his doing—it's Mom's. She destroyed all our lives, Robin, for a fuck."

"This is too much to believe. What the hell, Raven."

"There's more."

"What more can there be?"

"Dad and I took a DNA test. I want him to be certain I'm his child. I want to squash Mom's lies and start again with Dad."

"Have you received the results yet?"

"No. They should be here soon. That's what I want to talk to you about. I would love for you to provide a sample, too, so we can begin to live again without stuff from the past hanging over our heads."

"What? You don't believe we're Dad's kids?"

"I'm certain I am after having shared a meal with him after all these years. Every move, every gesture he made, I've seen them all before in...me. The test is to bring closure to the worst day in my life."

"It was my worst day, too. I'll take one. How do I do this?"

"You don't have to do anything. I'll send someone to your hotel before you fly out."

"What about Mom?"

"What about her? I'm not talking to her anymore. This is between Dad and us. If you want to talk with her—that's on you. I'm done with her deceit."

"She's our mother."

"No real mom would do what she did. Robin, my brain is so fucked up because of what she did. I'm done with her."

"I'm going to talk with her."

"Do what you need. You know where I stand."

Chapter 27
Context

Parker

Standing at the wall of windows in my office, my eyes shift from the screen of my phone to the cityscape beyond the window. I love San Francisco. I love Rain even more.

"Rain, I'm sure it'll be fine. Stick to what you want to say. You know how to do this," I tell Rain. She's worried about her meeting with Noah today. He said he's bringing contracts. I have a suspicion it's a ruse to see her.

"He's made it clear that he wants to be more than colleagues. I'm reminding you what I'm about to walk into."

"You've provided context for your request. You've established that you don't want the same things. He has to accept that. If he can't accept what you're telling him, I'll step in. He won't like that." I look at Rain on the screen.

My jaw ticks. I'm irritated that she has to deal with this when I can squash it in seconds. But I promised I wouldn't interfere with their business. If she wants to make their business relationship work, she needs to convince Noah to back down and respect her wishes.

"I'll make him understand."

"If he respects you, he'll do what you tell him."

My phone buzzes while Rain talks. It's Wade Wallace.

"Babe. I need to take this call. I'll pick you up at your office later, and then we'll go to dinner."

"Okay. See you later." I hear the hesitation in her voice.

"Hey."

"Yeah?"

"I love you, Rain. Call me if you need me."

"I love you, too. Thanks," she says and disconnects the call. I answer Wade's call.

"Mr. Wallace, how's it going?"

"Things are good, Parker. However, I'm calling because Noah is on his way to see me this morning."

"I'm aware. He's in town for another business meeting."

"And, of course, while he's here—."

"He wants to meet with you."

"He's in the lead with his proposal. I told you I wouldn't make you pull rank on me. What's the timeline on your business with him?"

"Where are you at with your other bidders?"

"A month out from completing everything."

"We're fine on time, but I have first right of refusal."

"You mean you're the decision maker." He's right. My family owns a majority share. I can take everything now and pay someone to run his business. But that's not what I want. I want Noah to walk away from Rain like she asked. Then I don't have to kill his dream of closing this deal.

"I mean, this will be over soon. Tell him the truth—you're not done meeting with the others. And call me if he contacts you again."

"Listen, Parker. I respect you, but one thing is for sure."

"What's that?"

"I never want to be on your bad side. Whatever Noah has done—should I be concerned?"

"No. His track record shows he'll deliver results if he wins the bid. My issue is not business-related. It's personal."

"I understand. I appreciate the context."

"Thank you for trusting me."

Chapter 28
The New Deal

Noah

When I had Jewel arrange for me to fly to San Francisco to meet with Rain, I also had her schedule time for me to see Wade Wallace. I've kept in contact with Wade's son Jude, who, like me, still hasn't figured out the identity of the fourth bidder on his property. The best I can do to keep my name ahead of the others is to give him as much time as possible.

"Noah, it's good to see you again," Wade greets me as I take a seat at his table near the window.

"Mr. Wallace. It's great to be back in your lovely city."

"Well, I'm glad you let us know you were in town. My team thoroughly reviewed your proposal and was impressed with your five-year projections."

"As I mentioned a few weeks ago, we have a proven track record for success, and with the updates we made specific to this market, we can easily hit those numbers."

"I don't doubt you."

Okay. He's impressed. The numbers look good. He doesn't hesitate to meet with me. What's the hold-up? There's something else going on here. I just don't know what.

"Should we expect word soon on your decision or next steps? Knight Development Corporation can provide additional information to help you understand how we'll execute against that model."

"I have what I need. I'm still meeting with the others to discuss their proposals. Once that's completed, I can make a decision."

"You'll let me know if you have any questions?" I want to close this deal so bad I can taste it. This will put KDC on top. This will make all the sacrifices I made worth it. Our legacy will be secure.

"Absolutely. By the way, how's your father doing?"

"He's great. Enjoying retirement."

"Soon I'll be in his position."

Wade wanted to leave sooner and turn his business over to his sons. They're focused on their media firm, so he's forced to seek outside bidders to sell his company to.

"It's a good position to be in, and in your case—I'm sure it's well deserved."

"My boys tell me they're doing business with you."

"Yes, they met with our PR team. Everyone is impressed with their portfolio."

"That's great. They're good kids. They do great work. Listen, next time you're in town, get on my calendar. I hope to have a decision soon, but just in case—keep up the good work."

Next time, I hope we'll be inking a deal to acquire this building.

"Thanks, I will." Next time.

***

The restaurant where I arranged to meet Rain is near her office, not far from Wade's building. Rain wanted to meet at the office, but if I'm being honest with myself, I don't know if I can handle meeting her in private. My desire for her is too intense, and I'm fighting a constant battle about telling her just how much. When she arrives, the manager brings her to my table.

I stand. "Good to see you again, Raven." Reining my desire to kiss her cheek, I help her to her seat. Her scent makes my mouth water, and I want to dip my head into her neck and inhale her. I wonder if I have the same effect on her.

"Thank you. It's good to be seen, Noah. Did you bring the documents?" That's Rain—straight to business. This is what makes her so good at what she does. I respect her for that.

"Can I order you a drink?"

"Sparkling water."

I lift my chin. The server comes to the table and asks, "Are you ready to order, Mr. Knight?"

"Two glasses of sparkling water and charcuterie board for now. Thank you," I tell the server, and he retreats to the kitchen.

"I believe you have six documents for me."

This woman.

"I have them here." I reach beside me and hand the contracts folder to Rain. She asked me to send them digitally, but I told her I preferred to hand deliver them. I'd do anything to be near this woman, including getting on my private jet to bring her contracts. "You need to look them over?"

"You wouldn't modify a document we've already agreed was sound. But yes, I will review them." She gives me a hint of a smile. I'll take it. "Why did you ask me here today, Noah?"

"To talk. Seeing you on video calls and packed meetings in conference rooms is not enough for me." As usual, I give her the truth.

"It has to be, Noah. I understand a man like you is used to getting what he wants, but—."

I cut to the chase. "I got what I want. I want more."

"It doesn't work that way. Don't you care about what I want?"

"Tell me what you want."

"I want us to be okay."

"We are okay."

"You know what I mean. We have to find common ground, Noah. This is just as hard for me as it is for you. Whenever our eyes lock, whether on video or in a conference room, I see the seven days we spent together." Her voice is steady but low. "I recall every touch, every kiss, every time we called out to each other. I remember the weight of your body on mine." I close my eyes briefly, imagining her beneath me. "It will always be there, Noah. We'll always have those moments."

"I want more of that."

"But I don't. Yet it's there. Every time I see you. It's there whether I want it to be or not. I'm not saying what we had wasn't beautiful. It was. But it wasn't real. It was only supposed to be one night. What we had was fleeting. We got caught up. You don't need me."

"I do."

The server returns with our sparkling water and a wooden board neatly arranged with various items. I hold Rain's gaze as the server opens the bottle and pours us each a glass. My heart races knowing that whenever she sees me, she recalls every moment we shared. That's the part that I don't understand—how can she not give into the emotions that go along with that? I don't have her abilities and even I can't un-feel what we had. The week we shared challenged every perception I had about relationships. Looking into her eyes, I know she's pondering my response. I do need her. *Don't I?*

The server leaves. Rain takes a sip, then says, "You need someone who can give you more. That's not me."

"Rain."

"Raven."

"Raven. Tell me how we fix this."

"You can't fix something that's not broken. What we had was perfect...for seven days...seven beautiful days in Seattle. There is no more."

I sigh. "What do you need from me?"

"Be your powerful, bold, I don't take no for an answer self. But let me be that one woman who can still handle you. Let me be that across the boardroom as your friend. We will always have Seattle. We can't change that. You know for a fact—it will always be at the forefront of my mind...whenever you're around. But don't take advantage of that."

"I'm not. I promise. I'm having a hard time letting go because *you* are what I want. I understand what you're saying, but it's difficult to accept."

"You need to accept I'm not yours—that I'm promised to someone else."

"Are you saying you're dating now?"

"I'm saying the same thing I told you before. I love someone else. I'm saying if you let me go, we can still be great friends and kick-ass colleagues because I don't want to lose you. I actually like you as a person—you know that. Those are the two things I have to offer."

I sit back and study Rain. She's a wonderful mix of beauty and brilliance that I can't get enough of. She puts a slice of cheese and prosciutto on a cracker and eats the whole thing. The week we were together, she was always snacking. She was always at ease around me, like we'd been together all our lives. Even now she seems at ease negotiating with me. She's all business right now and I love every bit of it. Am I misinterpreting her? I can't be.

"Are we making another deal? Because I don't know if I can stick to this one. You see what happened with our first deal." I laugh at the fact that I'm constantly negotiating and losing to this woman.

"How about you take time to think about it? I'll give you that much."

"What if I say no?"

"You're a smart man. I trust you'll make the right decision."

"Are you going to eat? I can take you to dinner tonight if you're not hungry now. I don't fly out until in the morning."

"No, I already have plans. I'm saving my appetite for dinner. But thanks."

"Is there a deadline for this decision I need to make?"

Rain puts the folder I gave her into her tote. "You'll know the right time to tell me."

Chapter 29

Suits

Parker

"Parker Page, Esquire, let me see," Rain demands, reaching inside my suit jacket and searching for my phone.

The car stops in front of the restaurant. The driver opens my door. I exit and extend my hand to help Rain out of the vehicle.

"If you show me yours, I'll show you mine," I smirk.

"You're so cheeky. Hand it over." She pats me down and then reaches into my front pant pocket. My body craves her. I slide my hand around her waist and pull her into me.

"You're trying to get fucked." Ignoring me, she takes my phone out. I dip my head and surprise her with a kiss. While she's lost in the moment, I take my phone back. I break the kiss. "Are you going to show *me*?" I ask.

"Ugh, Parker, that's not fair. You'll have to wait until your birthday to see me in my dress."

"It's not a wedding dress."

"Doesn't matter. It's your special day. You have to wait to see me in it. However, it's not my birthday, so I want to see the picture of your suit." Ever since I told her I took a picture while getting fitted for my suit, she's been dying to see it. I think my woman has a suit fetish.

I raise my hand, holding the phone in the air. "If you can get it before we go in for dinner, I'll show you." Rain stands on her toes and tries to reach the phone. I'm sure we look like two teenagers standing on the street fooling around. I look down at her. She has no chance of getting my phone, but watching her try is sexy. I dip my head into her neck and inhale.

"You smell good. We can just stand out here and make out," I tease.

"Parker."

"Rain, babe, I had a long day. I'm hungry. Let's go in and eat."

"I'll exchange," she blurts out.

"Okay, what you got?"

"This." She wraps her arms around my waist and tips her head back. "Kiss me." She doesn't need to ask twice. I dip my head and claim her lips again. This time, she opens her mouth to me, and I take her all in. This is our first deep kiss in almost five years. God, I love this woman. I'm ready to devour her, but we haven't reached that stage yet. She pulls back...breathless. "Parker," she whispers.

"I know, hon. Let's go in." I take her hand and lead her inside. We're quiet as we settle at our usual table, hidden away from prying eyes.

The server automatically brings out our drinks. Since Rain doesn't like dealing with menus, I started arranging our meals before our visit. No one has to take our order. They already have it. That provides me with uninterrupted time with her—precious moments, as I told her when I gave her the watch for her birthday all those years ago. She's worn it every day since then.

"Toast?" I raise my glass, and Rain does the same. "To love." I smile at her.

"To love." She takes a sip but never breaks eye contact. "Hopefully, I wasn't being too forward."

I laugh. "Your kiss was everything it was supposed to be. Thank you." I reach into my pocket and hand her my phone. She takes it, holds it to my face to unlock it, then scrolls through my pictures. Her eyes widen when she finds what she's looking for.

"Oh, Parker, wow. This is going to be my new favorite suit," she says about the grey-colored silk suit that coordinates with the color of her dress for my birthday.

"Don't get excited. I'm not putting that suit in rotation."

"Come on, Parker. Please."

"Not happening. It's too flashy. I know you're not making a serious request."

"What if it is?" She knows what would happen if she was serious. I give her a, *please tell me you're not serious* look.

"Rain," I growl.

"Okay. The black suit with red tie is still my all-time favorite, only because I can get you to wear it more often."

"What are you saying?"

"It won't be the last time you wear your birthday suit," she says, unable to resist laughing at the double entendre. I laugh, too.

"Cute. You and the joke."

"Glad you like us."

"I like the joke. I love you. There's a big difference." I put my finger under her chin and look into her eyes. She smiles at me. This woman is the only thing I've ever wanted. I wish she knew how beautiful she is. How brilliant her mind is. How caring her soul is. I tell her every day. I know she hears me and remembers. I want her to believe it for herself. "You still trust me?"

"Yes, Parker. Of course."

"I love you. I promise you'll never want for anything in this lifetime nor the next."

"I believe you."

I press my lips to her and kiss her. It's soft and loving—everything it should be at this moment. I break the kiss, and she rests her head on my shoulder. Although we're still working through the details of our relationship, I have confidence everything will be fine. Over the past few weeks, she hasn't given me any indication to think differently.

The server comes with our meal. I ordered Rain a combination of salmon and pasta, both her favorites. My order consists of lobster and mashed potatoes because I know she'll also eat from my plate. Rain eats her meal. She makes that sexy humming sound I love when she's enjoying something. I can't wait for the day she's making that same sound beneath me again.

"So, I'm meeting Dad in a few days to review our results."

"He finally agreed on a time?"

"His schedule is apparently busy."

"That's understandable. No different than yours or mine. How are you feeling about all this?"

"Confident. Anxious."

"Anxious about what?"

"I'm certain I'm his daughter."

"So, this is not about the test results."

"No. I'm worried about what comes next. Do we have regular father-daughter dates? Do we spend time together for holidays? Do I meet his wife? What's she like? Does she hold animosity toward me?"

"Babe, why would she not like you? You haven't done anything to anyone. This situation is not your doing."

"I know, but those are the things I've been contemplating. I could be overthinking this, but I can't help myself. I don't want to continue my normal routine without him as part of my life."

"Then tell him that. I'm sure he wants the same."

"I will," she assures me.

"Eat up. We still have dessert coming. One of your favorites."

Her eyes widen. "Chocolate mousse? Please tell me you ordered that. I've been craving it all week."

"Yes. Now finish that." I raise my chin, gesturing to her plate.

Rain and I eat and discuss navigating her next visit with her father. I'm sure she'll be fine, but I sense she needs to talk it through. It feels good to see her more confident in handling her family issues. They used to hold her back. Now, she can manage complicated discussions with as much confidence and grace as she does legal matters, without relying on me to guide her. This is what Rain meant when she said she wanted to find herself. She has accomplished so much, and I'm in awe of how far she's come.

The server reappears to clear our dinner plates.

"Ready for dessert?" he asks.

"Definitely," Rain responds. The server disappears again. But another person walks up behind him. This is not a server. This man is in a suit.

Noah?

Chapter 30

Dessert Is Served

Raven

When the server leaves, the last person I expect to see standing in his place is Nik.

"Hi, Raven. It's good to see you again. You didn't get very far," he says in his deep British-accented voice. His comment is intentionally reminiscent of the day he interrupted my breakfast in Seattle the morning following our one-night stand. I'm not playing his game.

"Noah, good to see you. Parker, you met Noah at the house."

Parker stands and shakes Noah's hand. "I recall," he says, attempting to control his irritation. This seems to be a theme: Nik popping up unexpectedly when I'm with Parker. "Rain mentioned your lunch meeting today. Did you forget something?"

"No. I happened to have reservations. I'm sitting over there." He tips his head to a table slightly out of our view. "I heard R-Raven's voice and thought I'd come to say something."

"Thank you for the acknowledgment. Rain and I had our dinner. I hope you enjoy yours." I notice the tic in Nik's jaw whenever Parker says my name. Nik started to call me Rain, but he couldn't. He thinks Parker is competition. There is none. In a room full of choices, there's only one man for me...Parker.

Parker sits back down next to me. He places an arm on the table near where Nik stands and the other on my lap. He's establishing boundaries. A sudden wave of anxiety washes over me. What are these two men going to do? I need to do something.

"That was nice of you, Noah. Parker is right; please don't let us keep you from enjoying dinner. If you're up for it, try the salmon. It's great. We're about to have dessert. I'll be in the office tomorrow if you need anything else. Have a good evening."

The server returns with our dessert while Nik is still there. Parker lifts his chin. The server places the crystal dish of mousse on the table with two spoons.

"Thanks, I'll take your suggestion," Nik finally says.

"Enjoy your meal. Good night, Noah," Parker says. Nik looks at me. I have nothing else to add to this awkward encounter. I raise an eyebrow. Nik nods and goes to his table.

"Rain, honey. Handle him." Parker picks up a spoonful of mousse and feeds me. What do I do with this man? He's changed. If this had been a year ago, Nik would not be sitting across the restaurant from us. Parker would have had him escorted out. Nik doesn't run San Francisco or Seattle—the elites do. Yet Parker didn't apply his rank. I eat a few more scoops of mousse that Parker feeds me while contemplating his comment.

"That's it? That's all you got? Handle him," I say in jest but with an undertone of surprise.

Parker smiles confidently at me. He's so freaking fine. "Babe, you're sitting next to me, moaning to every spoonful of chocolate I feed you." He caresses my cheek with his thumb. Then he dips his head like he's going to kiss me but licks my lips. "I get to lick chocolate from your lips." He holds my chin and looks into my eyes. "For the past two months, you have awakened in my arms. Do you expect that to change anytime soon?"

"I don't."

"Neither do I. I don't need to say more because I'm operating from perspective and experience. I spent almost half my life being with you—loving you and learning everything about you. Noah's few hours of, dare I say, lust can't touch that. You asked me to step aside on this matter. I trust you to manage him. Like I told you, if he doesn't listen, let me know."

Ugh, I have to admit he's right. Parker knows me inside out. How I think and react to things—none of it's new to him. Our closeness means something more than it has the past few years. Since we left Seattle, I haven't left his side. We haven't made love, but we are together at one of our homes every night. We have moved beyond the confines of friendship. We're on the path to becoming something...more.

"Not lacking in hubris, are you?"

"Never. That's one of the things you love about me."

I'm attracted to his power and confidence. I love that he doesn't consider Nik a threat. I also realize Parker is always five steps ahead of any man I've ever met, which means although he hasn't mentioned it, he's keeping tabs on Nik. He said he'd step in if Nik didn't listen to me, and he meant it.

"I told him we could be friends and colleagues."

"You're trying to make it work. That's all you can ask for. If he respects you and is serious about making this business relationship work, he will meet you where you are—as colleagues. Are you going to eat the rest of this?" He positions the spoon for me to eat more. I wrap my lips around the spoon and eat my dessert. Then I lick around my lips, getting the extra chocolate.

"You're so smart," Parker says, pressing his thumb to my bottom lip and opening my mouth. He presses his lips to mine and licks into my mouth. He sucks my tongue and my sex clenches. Oh my god, this kiss. I groan into his mouth. He pulls back. "There she is. I like it when you moan for me."

"Parker," I say, breathless.

"We're sharing, remember? I prefer my chocolate on you."

Chapter 31

Who's Your Daddy

Raven

It's been a few weeks since I've seen my dad, but I've texted him a few times to update him on what's happening. He knows Robin submitted her sample, so her results should be ready next week. Although he and I received our results in the mail a few days ago, we want to open them together. I don't want to deal with the pressure of being in public when we uncover our findings. Also, I'm not ready to meet his wife yet, so I asked if he would spend the afternoon at my house with me and Parker.

I thought about how my dad would feel about reviewing the results with Parker present, but it doesn't matter. I want Parker there. He's been the only person in my corner for most of my life. Like he told me before—people have to earn the right to be with me. Parker earned a spot by my side.

The bell rings.

"I feel like I'm on one of those reality shows where they have two men backstage, and you have to guess who's your daddy," I tell Parker.

He shakes his head, stifling a laugh. "It's not that bad."

"Sort of."

"You ready, babe?"

As I walk past Parker, he pulls me into his side. "Ready."

He turns me, dips his head, and kisses me softly and sweetly, just enough to let me know he's got me. "I'll be in here," he says, letting me go. I leave Parker standing in the kitchen and go to the door.

I open the door. My dad stands tall and handsome, filling the frame while smiling at me. After years of thinking I'd never see him again, it feels surreal yet good to have him back in my life. I want to tell him so much, but we have to get the purpose of today's visit behind us.

"Hi, Dad. Come in." I gesture for him to enter. He's wearing a blue sweater over his white shirt, along with dark-wash jeans. It seems strange seeing him dressed so casually compared to our first meeting. He has an unopened envelope in his hands.

"Hi Raven. Is Parker with you?"

"Yeah, follow me. We set up snacks in the kitchen. It's the room that gets the most use when we have company. We're pretty casual."

"Despite what you may think, I'm casual, too. You have a lovely home," he says as we step into the kitchen.

"Mr. Sweet-Nichols, it's nice to see you again." Parker extends a hand to my dad. They shake.

"Good to see you too. Mr. Page."

"Call me Parker, please."

"You can call me Rhett."

"Dad, have a seat. Would you like something to drink?"

My dad sits at the counter. "Sparkling water if you have it."

"Rain got me hooked on it, so we always have it on hand," Parker says, going to the refrigerator. He retrieves the water and pours us all a glass.

I slide a plate in front of Dad.

"I didn't know what you liked, so Parker and I improvised. This plate has prosciutto, salami, and ham. I hope you don't have any allergies," I say, pointing to one of the many plates lined up on the counter.

"No."

"Good, because this one has like five varieties of nuts. If you don't see one there you like, I'm sure I have some in the cupboard."

"This is fine."

I point to another dish. "These are hard, mild, and soft cheeses. All this is fruit, crackers, and those tiny bowls contain jellies, marmalades, and things like that. One of them is spicy. And if none of that suits you, there's empanadas, shrimp cornbread, and my favorite, salmon cakes. I just made those."

"You cook?"

"Sometimes," I say. My dad looks at Parker and raises his eyebrow.

"Sometimes," Parker repeats. He winks at me.

I hand my dad a fork. We all fill our plates with our personal selections.

"You two have similar tastes, it seems." Parker lifts his chin toward my plate, where I have all but one item different from Dad's.

"So, Raven how did Robin handle the discussion?" My dad eats while waiting for my response.

"She was as shocked as I was, but she handled it okay under the circumstances. Robin and I aren't that close, but we have talked more since I returned from Seattle than we have in years."

"What was your trip to Seattle for?" He takes a bite of the salmon cake. "Oh, this is good."

"Thanks. Initially, I went for business, but she and I had also planned to spend time together. That went a little sideways, but we eventually reconnected and met for lunch." I shove food in my mouth, not wanting to say more about the trip. Heat washes over my face thinking about it. I hate how I handled myself. I hate what I did to Parker and our relationship. However, through therapy, I'm learning to deal with all of my emotions and heal.

"How was business?"

"Great. That's the deal that made me lead counsel."

"You're a big shot in this profession. I'm proud of you."

"I am, too," Parker says.

"I never thought of myself that way. I only see the project in front of me. Then the next and the next. But thank you. I never knew you were an attorney back then."

"When you were younger?"

"Yeah. I don't recall ever thinking about what you did for a living. We never talked about that. You were always focused on us and what we were doing. I remember all the pictures I drew of buildings in San Francisco and how you took me to see every one of them."

"You were fascinated by architecture. You had an eye for iconic structures."

"She still does. The Transamerica Center is her favorite."

"It was back then."

"That's what I'm saying. You embraced every detail about our lives as children, and I just remember how *seen* I felt. It was a long time after you left before I felt that way again."

"I'm sorry, Raven."

"It's okay. I have Parker. He's made me feel seen ever since the day I met him." I look at Parker. He smiles at me. I know he wants to hug me. He winks.

"Thank you, Parker," my dad says.

"Well, are we going to do this?" I say, holding up my envelope.

"Let's," my dad says.

"Parker, count to three," I tell him.

"Okay, hon. Here goes. One. Two. Three."

The room is quiet except for the sound of paper ripping as my dad and I open our envelopes and unfold our results. Then it goes quiet again. I read my results.

My mind rewinds to that morning when I was eight and woke up early because I heard a noise. I didn't know where it came from, so I went downstairs and listened in the living room. It was quiet for a while; then I heard rustling. I was sitting in an oversized lounge chair with my feet and knees tucked close to my chest. The noise got closer, and I saw my dad heading toward the door. He had a bunch of things with him, like a duffle bag and a piece of luggage. I didn't know what was happening because he didn't travel much for work. *"Dad,"* I called out. But I don't know if he heard me because I don't know if I was thinking the word or if I actually called out to him. He hesitated a second, then continued out the door. He turned back after all his belongings were on the other side of the threshold. I thought our eyes locked briefly. At the time, I was unsure if he saw me. It was so dark. It looked like he shook his head, turned, closed the door, and left. That was the last time I saw him until a few weeks ago. When I learned from our recent conversation that he didn't know it was me, I felt free of the burden of thinking I could have done something to prevent him from leaving. And the veil that had been coloring my view of the world since I was eight fell away.

For twenty years, that memory has haunted me. It's shaped who I am—how I react to people. It's the same terror I wake up to every day. It's the memory that grips me like a vice and won't let go. The only thing that keeps me from being consumed by the memory is the sound of Parker's voice. The man at the center of my sleep terror and the one who saved me from them are with me now, waiting to see what comes next. Here to help me reclaim my life and move forward.

My eyes shift to Parker. He's trying to read my eyes, which are filled with tears. I turn and look at my dad. He gives me a small smile. My dad opens his arms. I go to him.

"Dad."

"Yes, baby girl. That's me."

Chapter 32

New Beginnings

Raven

I've been carrying what felt like the weight of the world on my shoulders since the day my father left. Now, locked in his embrace, soaking his shoulder with my sobbing, the stress of everything I've been harboring falls away. Filled is the abyss associated with his absence. Gone is the penance of believing I could have prevented him from leaving, the unanswered questions now uncovered. I'm finally free.

"Hey, it's okay," my dad assures me, rubbing my back. "I never doubted you were mine," he whispers.

I lift my head. "Me neither. But I wanted proof...for you."

My dad swipes his thumb under my eye, wiping a tear away. "Now we have it. You and I are too alike for the results to have said anything different."

I half laugh, half cry. "Is it that obvious?"

"Like staring in a mirror. Parker, please get my daughter some tissue."

"Right here, sir." I listen to the sound of the box sliding across the counter like a curtain closing. Finally cutting me off from nightmares of the past.

My dad pulls a handful of tissues from the box and hands them to me. "It's been a long time since I've seen you cry. I think the last time was when you fell on your skates."

I dry my eyes and nose with the tissue. "I was trying a dance move," I say beneath the wad of tissue.

"You needed to learn the basics of skating first." My dad chuckles.

I kiss my dad on the cheek and say, "Thank you for agreeing to this." Then I walk over to Parker, who's been quietly observing us. He wraps his arms around my shoulders and pulls me into an embrace.

"You good?"

"Yeah."

He kisses my forehead. "You want some champagne?"

"Dad? Should we celebrate?"

"Why not?"

"Okay, champagne coming up," Parker says, releasing me. He retrieves a bottle from the refrigerator. I return to my seat, and Dad and I pile our plates with more food in our way of eating our feelings.

"Parker, congratulations on your big win recently." In the brief time I've been reacquainted with my dad, he continues to surprise me with how updated he is on our lives.

Parker fills three glasses with champagne and puts one in front of each of us. "Thank you, sir. It was a tough case, but we got through it." He lifts his glass. "Sir, would you like to do the honors?"

"Raven, are you okay with that?" I nod. "To new beginnings. May today be the first day for the rest of our lives...together."

"Together," I say.

"Together," Parker echoes. We all drink.

"So does that mean I can schedule father-daughter dates with you?" I ask.

My dad smiles so wide it lights up the room and warms my heart. I sense we're on the same wavelength. "Yes, Raven. I'd like that. Of course, I'd like to get to know you better too, Parker."

"Absolutely," Parker says. I smile at Parker, whose gaze rarely leaves me. I know this man loves me so much. I don't know what I was thinking to ever leave him. My eyes shift to Dad.

"You have questions for me," he says, like he's reading my mind.

"Lots, but this one's been lingering. When I first met Mr. Kane at an event, he said he recognized me. I never met him before then. He doesn't have recall abilities like I do, but he has a photographic memory based on what Parker says. At first, I thought he recognized me because he saw you. I look like I could be your daughter."

"You are."

"But that's not how it works. Why does he know my face?"

"Because he's seen you before. He's been to my office. I have a picture of you and Robin with me on my credenza—one was when you were younger. I also have a graduation picture. I hinted at the restaurant that I was watching from afar."

His words wrap around my heart, thinking we were always on his mind. I swallow and say, "Dad, thank you. I had hoped that might be the case. I told Parker there's no way you could just walk away and forget us."

"Being away was hard. I wish I could have seen you grow up. I tried to attend as many of your school events as possible."

I inhale at his confession and the thought that my dad was nearby. "Really?"

"Yes. It was difficult trying to stay at a distance."

"Because of her?"

"But that's over. I'm sorry I missed so many years with you."

"She left you no choice. I don't want to talk about her. I just want to move forward. It's been difficult enough all these years without you. The sleep terrors."

"What was that like?"

"Like a horrible movie reel playing every day. But they seem to have subsided since you told me at the restaurant that you didn't know I was there."

"You've been doing good, Rain," Parker adds. Dad's eyes shift to Parker.

"Parker helps me get through the distress associated with my sleep terrors. I don't understand it, but he calms me."

"If there's anything I can do, let me know."

"Don't ever leave me again."

"I don't plan on it."

Chapter 33

Not So Subtle

Parker

Spending the afternoon with Rain's father went better than I expected. Rain looks more relaxed than I've seen her in a while. It was nice to see how natural they seemed in each other's presence, even after all the time and trauma had passed due to his absence.

After he leaves, Rain is exhausted and wants to chill in front of the TV and watch classic movies. I'm okay with that. Our lives have been so consumed with events and family matters that settling down for the rest of the day is a welcome change.

"Rain, babe, you want more champagne or red wine?" I call her from the kitchen. She's on the couch in the family room.

"Wine is fine, and bring some of those leftovers. Actually, I'll get the snacks. You get the wine," she says, coming into the kitchen. She pulls a grape off the bunch and pops it into her mouth.

"How do you feel?" I ask.

She eats another grape. I watch her as she chews. She has such kissable lips. I can't wait for the day to have them all over me again.

"I don't know...different."

I walk over to her and wrap an arm around her waist. "Different good or bad?"

"Good. Just...I don't know. I feel like a new person...like I've been wandering around with tinted glasses, now they're gone, and I see clearer."

"I'm so sorry you had to go through what you did."

"It's done. I feel like I'm on the other side of that now." She slides her hands under my shirt and around my waist. Her fingers are warm and smooth, and her touch crackles against my skin. I dip my head and cover her lips with mine. I part her lips with my tongue, lick into her, capturing her tongue, and suck. Her sweetness and lingering hint of grapes make me want to bury myself deep in her. But it's not our time yet. Rain mingles her tongue with mine. I know she feels my desire rise against her. I pull back.

"Rain, babe—."

"I know. We have a movie to watch." Her voice comes out rushed, breathless as she finishes my statement.

I give her a chaste kiss. "We do." I grab the wine. Rain gets a large plate of snacks for us to share, and we return to the family room.

I set our wine on the side table near the chaise lounge. I take my usual spot. Rain grabs a throw to put over us and sits next to me. She flips through the screen until she finds a movie to watch.

"We're not watching your favorite tonight?"

"I figured we'd watch something else. So, what do you think of Dad knowing about your court case?"

"We researched him. It makes sense he studied us. You are his daughter. He wants to know everything about you and who you're with. It sounds like he's been watching you from afar."

"It reminds me of you."

"Me?"

"Yeah. I didn't know you were there when you followed me to London."

"I told you I'll never be far from you. I'll always protect you. You'll never want for anything."

"You've been so good to me."

"I love you. I don't know any other way to be with you."

"I screwed up so bad."

This is the part that's hard for me: when she turns on herself for things that aren't entirely in her control. This is when I sense she's still healing. I have to walk that delicate line of being her confidant and set aside those moments when we're stepping into her being my woman, and I'm her man. This straddling the line is difficult—but I'll wait until she's ready. Today, she's in her feelings following a breakthrough with her dad.

"Rain, we both have equal roles to play in how our relationship develops."

"You're right."

"Then, babe, stop beating yourself up over it."

"I'm working on it. Establishing a new normal with Dad is part of it."

"And an important part. I've really seen a change in your morning activity since you first met him. Have you noticed?"

"When I recall the day he left, the feeling isn't as intense as before. I don't feel the bile rise in my throat, and I don't get lost in my thoughts. It's like I have more control over my memory of that day."

"You're no longer afraid of your thoughts of that day."

"Seems that way. I didn't dream about it or think about it this morning."

"I noticed. I was counting your breaths this morning."

"You were?" She turns to me in surprise.

I cup her cheek. “Watching you sleep uninterrupted was the highlight of my day. You’re beautiful—you know that?”

“I know what you tell me, and you’ve never lied to me. Although I would have expected our kiss to be a highlight.”

“That should go without saying. Is that your subtle way of telling me you want a kiss?”

“Not so subtle.”

I pull Rain into my lap, wrap my arms around her, and kiss her hard. She opens her mouth to receive me, and I swallow her groans. Our kiss is hot, urgent, and needy. My body responds to her, but I pull back. Rain is in her feelings—high from a good day, but she’s not ready for the next stage in our relationship. I know what she feels now is only physical. This is not a kiss that locks in her commitment to us. This is her wanting me inside her. I close my eyes and take in her essence. I want her, but I also want more than she’s ready to give...her commitment to a life together. I want her to be my wife.

“What are you doing, Parker?” Her fingers slide through my hair. I give into another equally heated kiss. My woman is hard to resist. I pull away slightly and lick evidence of our kiss from her lips.

“You’re trying to get fucked. That’s not happening. You have to get off me now.”

“Parker.”

“Now.”

Chapter 34

Defining Lose

Noah

Standing in front of a conference room full of people in San Francisco with Rain by my side is not how I imagined my life two months ago. Since then, I met a beautiful woman at a bar one Tuesday afternoon that changed my life forever. Before I met Rain, I was all about the business of gaining power. Making multi-million-dollar deals before most people had breakfast was my life. I never had the same woman twice...until I met Rain.

"Well, that's it for today. If anyone has more questions following the meeting, you can catch me in my office. Noah is in the office next door until tomorrow. Right, Noah?"

"Correct. Thanks everyone for the great work. The project is moving forward smoothly. I'll see you tomorrow," I say, and a few people linger to catch up with me and Rain separately.

When everyone leaves, I check my phone briefly to ensure I haven't missed anything from Rok or Mak. There's a group text from them checking in on the Wade deal. I really want to close that deal soon.

"Thanks for flying out this week, Noah. We accomplished a lot today."

"Not a problem."

"I'll be in my office if you need me. I have a few calls to make."

"Hold up a minute. I've been thinking about our last discussion. You know, our deal."

"Is that what we're doing? Negotiating a deal?"

"Well, that is the way you positioned it with me."

"I stand corrected. What about it?"

"I was surprised when you said you didn't want to lose me."

"I don't, Noah."

"That's what makes this all so hard. I don't want to lose you either. Somehow, I feel like our definitions of that term are different."

"They don't have to be," she says.

"They are. When I say I don't want to lose you, I mean everything. The closeness, the intimacy, being colleagues, all of it, all of you."

"It doesn't have to be all or nothing. I know that's how we were in Seattle. But our circumstances have changed. We're colleagues. We will likely see or talk to each other every other week, if not more, for the next two years. We can use that time to work on our friendship. What we had in Seattle wasn't supposed to happen."

"But it did."

"And like I told you before. Our time together was amazing. You rediscovered who you really are."

"What's that?"

"A kind, caring family man who wants to build a life with the right woman."

"How do you know that's not you?"

"I just do."

"How can you be so sure?

"Because you're here trying too hard to convince me you need me. You don't need me—you need your person—the one designed for you. I only showed you that you don't have to hide behind your all-I-need-is-power façade."

"And I recall you asked me to let you be the one woman that can handle me."

"How am I doing so far?"

"I haven't pulled you into my arms and kissed you, so I guess good so far."

"I'm not yours. Don't pull me into your arms."

"I'm trying not to."

My phone buzzes. It's Jewel, my executive assistant. She only calls while I'm in a meeting if something important comes up.

"Rain, it's Jewel. Sinclair, the designer, is ready to talk," I tell her. We've been waiting to hear whether the designer will agree to sign on for the multi-year project. If she does, we can move the Ross Enterprises project to the next stage.

"Take the call," she says.

"Put her through, Jewel." Jewel confirms the connection. "I'm here," I say. "Sinclair, how are you?"

"Good, Noah. I reviewed the proposal you sent and it looks good with one exception." This is good news. If I can close this deal, it'll create more value for both KDC and Ross Enterprises since they'll likely rent out some of the office spaces in their buildings to retailers and restaurateurs. With Sinclair's notoriety for high-end design, the rents these finished buildings could command would be top tier, increasing KDC's bonus related to the project.

"What's that?"

"Being associated with this development deal is lucrative because of the visibility behind the two companies involved. If you don't hire me for future projects, this can be seen as a one-off for me. I don't want to be seen as a one hit wonder."

"What are you suggesting?"

"Bring me into design Knight Development Corporation's next build as well."

I put the phone on mute and explain the ask to Rain. She'll have to agree to and negotiate any terms related to this on behalf of Ross Enterprises.

"What do you think Rain? Can we make this work without any risk to Ross Enterprises?"

"You'll have to decide on behalf of KDC, but yes, I can work out the terms so there's no liability to Ross. We'll build something into the agreement that factors in a timeline between projects, and confidentiality. We'll also need to consider how we handle PR. I'll draft the terms."

I unmute the call. "Okay, Sinclair, I'll ensure you're signed for a future Knight Development project if you sign on to this project. I'll send you the numbers to consider associated with this change." When Sinclair agrees, I nod to Rain. She gives me a silent high five and I lace my fingers with hers. This woman—the things we could do together, I think to myself. I end the call. "Thank you," I tell Rain.

"It's what I'm here for, Noah."

"Yeah, but I know your brilliant brain ran through every scenario within seconds to give me that definitive decision."

Holding Rain's hand, feeling her warmth again, my brain cries out for me to pull her into me, but I don't. I don't dare take anything she hasn't given me. I brush my thumb across hers.

"Yeah, I suppose that's why people hire me."

"Rain." I lock gazes with her. "It's also a reason I don't want to lose you. Everything about you is amazing."

Rain pulls her hand away.

"Listen, Noah. When I say I don't want to lose you—that's the truth. But if I have to...if we can't make this work as friends and colleagues, I will. Are you willing to walk away from this? The incredible things we can do together in business? To disregard how in sync we are on this deal?"

"How we work together is exactly what I want. But I also want so much more. I'm not trying to pressure you, but you said you only want to hear the truth from me. This is it. I like this feeling. I like you." I touch my heart.

"I like you as a person. I like your standard of work and commitment to our community. You are honest and giving, and all the things I mentioned before when we were in Seattle. I like your brothers and cousins. I feel like we all get along so well. It feels natural. I miss our time together. But for different reasons than you think. I want to be in a room again with you all, laughing, partying, and working, not feeling the pressure to do or be anything more. That's the part I don't want to lose. But I can't see myself being part of all that as your life partner. I want forever with someone else. I understand that's hard to hear, but you have no idea the journey I've been on for the past decade to get to this point. Someone else does. I feel grounded to that person."

"We can be grounded. We have two years. We can try."

"No, we don't. You need to decide."

Her phone rings. She swipes the screen. "Noah, please excuse me. I need to take this call," she says. "I'll be in my office."

"I'll check back in before I leave," I tell her. She nods and leaves.

Chapter 35

The Call

Raven

I WALK INTO MY office and stare out the window while I talk with Parker on a video call.

"Hey, handsome. Miss me?"

"Always." His eyes shift. He looks around my office and then back to me.

"Who are you looking for? It's just me here."

"You didn't eat your fruit, babe. The bowl is full. At least have one piece before I get there."

"I will. Is that why you called?"

"I was calling to let you know I'll be a little early to pick you up. My last meeting was canceled."

"Perfect. Gives me extra time to make out with you."

"Yeah, I know what you're trying to do."

"What?" I smile wryly.

"That reminds me of something else I want to discuss with you."

"We can talk now, I have time. I just finished a meeting with Noah and the team."

"How's it going with him?"

"I'm trying to handle my business."

"He has a choice. Deal with you or me."

"I know."

"Well, our discussion and make-out session can wait until I see you. I love you, Rain."

"I love you, too. I'll see you soon," I tell him and end the call, but my phone buzzes. It's my sister.

"Hey, Robin. How's it going?"

I look down at the people dodging between cars as they jaywalk across the street to avoid going to the corner. It's a move I've done many times myself. Not anymore. Not after Parker caught me trying do that once. He immediately latched onto my waist and pulled me toward him, telling me that my life is too important for a risky move like that. I smile thinking about the man I love.

"You free to talk?" Her voice is rushed like she's fast walking somewhere.

"Yeah. What's up?"

"I just got my results. Dad is not *my* dad. Oh, God, Rae..." Robin cries. It's the first time I've experienced her in distress since we were kids.

"What?" I place my hand on my desk to keep my balance. "What are you talking about?" Robin tries to mask her crying on the other end.

"The DNA results. There's no possibility that he's my dad. That means—."

"That Bill is your father?"

"I don't know. I hate this. I hate it. I can't take this." She sobs uncontrollably. Oh, God, why do I have to be so strong? Okay. I can do this. I can help her get through this.

"Breathe. It'll be all right. I got you."

Robin blows out a breath, inhales, and then breathes out another. “Do you know if mom was with anyone else?”

“Someone else? I’m only aware of Dad and Bill.”

“Oh my god, Raven. What does this mean?”

“It means you’re still my sister. No one can take that away from us.”

“I need to talk to mom.” Her voice is panicked.

“What are you going to say?”

“I don’t know. I need to...oh my god, Raven. I wasn’t expecting this. This is too much.”

“You want me there?”

“Would you?”

“Yeah. I’ll get a flight tonight.” My phone buzzes again. It’s my dad. “I’ll call you after I make arrangements, okay?”

“Okay,” she says. I end the call and connect to my dad.

“Dad.”

“Raven. I just opened the results for Robin.”

“I know she just called me. She’s upset. I need to go see her.”

“Oh, baby girl. I didn’t want you to get the news from her. I called as soon as I read it.”

“Dad, what does this mean? How is this possible? I don’t feel so good.” I close my eyes briefly.

“Are you at work?”

“Yeah.”

“You need to sit down. Take a deep breath.”

“I can’t. I need to go. I have to get to Robin.”

“Then please call me as soon as you can.”

“Raven? Are you available to talk?” Nik’s voice comes from behind me.

I hang up my call and turn around. I don't have time to talk to Nik. This is the last fucking straw with my mom. I need to call Parker.

"Nik, I can't do this right now...I..." The room spins. I feel weightless.

Chapter 36

Collecting Rain

Parker

Rain said she was done with her meetings for the day. I ring her phone once more as I ride up the elevator. It goes to voicemail. The only time she doesn't take my calls is if she falls into a dissociative state or is in a meeting. She hasn't experienced a dissociative episode in a while. Hopefully, she's preoccupied with a meeting.

I step out of the elevator. As I near her office, I hear my special ringtone come through on her phone. I hang up and walk into her office. My phone buzzes. It's her dad. I called him earlier to discuss Rain and seek his approval to marry her. He can't be calling me about that—he was ecstatic. I don't pick it up because I see Noah's back, and in his arms is...Rain. He lifts her. What the hell?

I rush to her. "Rain," I say, but she doesn't respond. I can't see her face. "Noah, what are you doing?"

He lays her on the couch and fans her with his hand.

"She fainted."

"Step away. Go get her some water," I command. He steps back. I sit beside Rain. "Noah. She needs water. If you want to help. Help. Or get me an admin." I lock eyes with him. He leaves the room.

I pull Rain into me so she's resting on my arm.

"Rain, babe. It's me, honey." She shifts. I lift her slightly and remove her jacket. My girl is burning up. I hate it when this happens to her. Something must have happened to trigger this episode. If I find out it was Noah, all hell will break loose. I caress Rain's cheek. "Honey, it's me. Parker. Can you hear me? Can you talk to me, babe?" Noah walks in and hands me a glass of water. I take it.

"Thank you," I tell him. "What happened to her?"

"I came in to see if she was finished with her calls. She indicated she didn't have time to talk but didn't finish what she had to say. Right before you walked in, she fainted. What is this? What's happening to her? I'll call a doctor."

"She doesn't need a doctor. Did she have lunch?"

"She worked through it."

"She can't do that."

I push the hair away from her face. I put my cheek to her forehead to gauge her temperature. Good, she's cooling down.

"Rain, honey, can you talk to me?" She nods. I whisper. "Honey, use your words. I need to know you're here. It's Parker. I got you."

"I'm here, Parker." Her voice is shallow.

"Do we need to count?" I ask, taking her through our routine.

"No."

"Okay. Can you tell me what you see?"

"My desk. Noah. He's watching me." She strokes my arm. "Your arm is wrapped around me." Rain maneuvers herself so she's sitting up.

"That's good, babe. Can you drink this for me?" She nods.

I place the rim of the glass to her lips and help her drink. I sigh, relieved that she is coming back to herself.

"Can you hand me that banana?" I ask Noah. He retrieves one from the fruit bowl on her desk and hands it to me. Since the incident in London four years ago, I have always ensured Rain has fresh fruit on her desk. I peel it, break off a piece of fruit, and put it to Rain's lips. "Babe, you have to eat something."

She eats the piece. I feel the moisture from her tongue as she eats from my fingers. I feed her until half the banana is gone. I brush the residue from her lips with my thumb. I lick my thumb. I can tell by how she narrows her eyes that she's protesting my public display of affection. That's a good sign.

"Better?" She nods. "Rain, can you tell me what happened?"

"We need to leave. I need to get on a plane."

"What are you talking about? To where?"

"Seattle. Tonight."

I look up at Noah. He shakes his head. "It's not work-related. But I can take her if she needs to go to Seattle tonight."

I don't respond. I pull out my phone and press the contact for my pilot. He picks up immediately. "Perry, ready the plane. We need to go to Seattle. We'll be there in ninety minutes. Yes. Two. Ms. Nichols and me. Right. See you soon." I end the call and dial my executive assistant. "Cate. Yes. She's with me. I'm at her office. Have our overnight bags downstairs in the car in twenty. I'll keep you posted. Yes, cancel my meetings. Yes. Coordinate with her EA and clear her calendar. One more thing. Arrange a conference call for Mr. Sweet-Nichols while we're in flight. Thank you."

Rain reaches for my hand. I look at her and wink.

"Noah. I won't be here tomorrow—," she starts before he interrupts her. I'd almost forgotten he's here. I'm so focused on Rain.

"It's okay, Raven. I got this. Is there anything I can do?" Noah asks.

"No," she says, then looks at me. She gives me a small smile, and I want to dust my lips across hers, but I don't.

This is a defining moment when Noah sees Rain in her most vulnerable state, but he can't help her. He hasn't experienced the years of understanding every aspect of her health, life, needs...her desires. Ever since I met Rain, I've been in tune with every breath she takes. I've been there for every good day and not-so-good moment. In times like these, we'll get through it together—we always do. Instinctively, I lift her hand and kiss her fingers.

"How are you feeling?" Noah asks.

"I'm okay. Thank you for catching me."

"I wouldn't let anything happen to you," he says earnestly. But I know he's making a play for Rain.

"Noah, if you'll excuse us. I need to talk to Parker. Thank you again."

"I'm glad I was here."

"Noah. Thank you," I tell him. He leaves, closing the door behind him.

I pull Rain onto my lap. I hug her. She wants to bury her head in my neck, but I cup her face in my hand. Looking into her eyes, I search for signs that everything is okay with her. She blinks.

"Babe, are you ready to talk?" She turns her head and kisses the palm of my hand. I turn her face back toward me and say, "Whatever it is, I got you. We'll talk when you're ready."

I dust my lips across hers. I watch her watching me, wondering what's going on behind those eyes. She's so beautiful. I didn't know what to think when I saw her in Noah's arms. He's been persistent in pursuing her, and it's hard to know how far he'll take it. I trust Rain knows how to handle him. All I know is that she wasn't responding when I walked in. Something triggered her attack.

I map the situation in my head. Someone called her. She needs to be in Seattle. It's not work. Why would her dad call me? Robin. Fuck. They got the results. I stare at Rain. She shuts her eyes briefly when she realizes I put it together.

"Oh, honey."

Chapter 37

A Seed of Doubt

Raven

My mind is reeling. What do I say to my sister to help her get through learning our dad is not her biological father? I need to talk to my dad. I look down at where my fingers are linked with Parker's. Before leaving the office, he realized Robin had received her results. I didn't think the stress of what was happening would cause me to pass out. I close my eyes.

Noah witnessed everything. I wonder what he feels about me now. He seemed out of his element, as I suspected he would. This incident confirms that I'm not his person. What comes so instinctively to Parker doesn't for Noah. I've learned that if you're truly connected to someone, every fiber of your being shifts to safeguard them. Noah wanted to help me, but he couldn't. There are no signals passing between us guiding him on how to.

I'm Parker's person. He instinctually knows what to do to stabilize me, no matter the circumstances. When I fell ill at the college party, he didn't hesitate to find me and have a doctor on standby to treat me. The first time he witnessed me having a sleep terror, he knew precisely how to calm me down and get me to focus. In London, he helped me so many times. Like tonight, Parker knows something is wrong if I don't answer his call or the door. There's no pause. He's prepared to act. He's always there.

I'm always amazed at how he efficiently employs these techniques and resources whenever needed. Like tonight, he arranged everything within minutes of me saying I needed to be in Seattle. There's no question, no hesitation, only action. So here I sit beside him on his jet, going to see my sister.

"Rain, honey. I had the crew prepare dinner. Do you want to eat before or after we talk with your dad?"

I turn to Parker. We haven't said much since we left the office. He held me close the entire ride to the airport. I'm still shocked at fainting in front of Noah and learning about Robin's DNA results.

"They can serve now. We can eat and talk."

Parker gestures to the staff. They lay linen on the table before us in preparation for our meal. Soon, the table is covered with dishes.

"How are you feeling?" he asks.

"I feel okay, same as when we left, but Parker, I can't imagine what Robin is going through. Even while waiting for my results, I never imagined they would come back differently. I felt in my heart that he was my father. We're so much alike. I suspect Robin would have felt the same about her and Dad. I never really thought about the similarities that Robin shared with him. I saw so much of Mom in her."

"You're sisters. Now you know you have different fathers. That doesn't take away who she is to you."

"How do I help her through this?"

"We need to talk to your dad and understand the full story."

I eat my meal, and in between bites, I glance at Parker. He's lost in thought. He has so much going on with the mega cases he tackles, a foundation that disperses billions a year, and me. He's been helping me find my way to becoming whole. Whenever I'm with him, it's as if nothing else exists in his world but me. Sitting beside him, I feel complete. I touch his hand. He caresses my cheek, dips his head, and kisses me. It's soft and lovely. I smile against his lips.

"Better?" I ask him.

"So much."

"What time is our call with Dad?"

Parker looks at his watch. "We should dial in now." He sets his device on the table in its stand. He flips through the screen and connects with my dad through a video call.

"Raven, how are you?" My dad asks.

"I'm stunned."

"That's expected. Parker?"

"I'm good, sir. What can you tell us about these results?"

"I know what you know. I'm not Robin's biological father."

"Do you think Bill is?" I ask.

"Yes."

"What makes you certain?" Parker presses.

"Bill's the only other man I've known she was with."

"Dad, how long were you two together before mom got pregnant with Robin?"

"Raven, honey."

"Dad?"

"The answer to the question behind your question is that your mom cheated on me. That's the only explanation for the results. We were together four months before she got pregnant."

I gasp. Parker grabs my hand and gives it a shake. "Did you suspect it at the time? Did you have any idea the baby wasn't yours?"

"No."

"Sir, when she asked you to leave and told you that Robin and Rain weren't yours, did you suspect anything then?"

"I thought she was lying to get what she wanted—me gone. It planted a seed of doubt, but I love my girls. I didn't want to believe it."

"Doubt. Something was there then?"

"Yes and no."

"You mean you had doubts about Robin," I say. "You and I are so alike—it's uncanny. But you didn't doubt I was your child, did you?"

"Never."

"But Robin. She was so much like Mom, yet unlike you. I even questioned how she and I could be so drastically different coming from the same parents. Oh, god, Dad. How do I help her?"

"Be there for her. Reinforce that she's your sister no matter what, and I still love her like my daughter because she is. For twelve years, she was. She always will be."

"Oh, Dad."

"I'm sorry you have to go through this, baby girl. Let her know I'm available to talk."

"Is there anything else you haven't told me that she and I need to know?"

"Yes."

"Rain. Are you okay? You want to continue this?" Parker asks.

"I'm okay. Go on, Dad."

"I established a Trust—one for you and one for your sister. The year after I left, I found out your mom was giving the money I sent for you and

Robin to Bill. He was putting it in his account but wasn't using it for you and your sister."

"What the hell? They can't be that low."

"You'll be receiving the account information next week."

"But Robin—."

"Is still my daughter no matter what the paper says."

"Sir, you should be the one to tell Robin about the Trust. I think she'd appreciate hearing it from you."

"I agree. What if I hadn't found you?" I ask.

"It was always set to go to you within thirty days of my death, your mother's, or the day you made contact with me, whichever came first."

"You knew I'd find you first."

"I did. You're a part of me. Nothing can change that."

Chapter 38

The Secret's Out

Raven

When we reach my sister's house, it's after ten o'clock at night. Parker helps me out of the car. He snakes an arm around me and pulls me into him. It's chilly outside, but his body warms me like a blanket. Parker lowers his head to mine and kisses me. I open my mouth and take him in. His kiss is full of power, passion, and everything that tells me he's mine.

"Text me when you're ready. I'll come get you."

"Just send the driver. You need your rest."

He smacks me on the butt. "Text me. Now help your sister."

I walk to the door. Bram, her husband, opens it. He's about six feet tall, shorter than Parker by four inches. He is wearing jeans and a grey T-shirt that I expect he put on at this late hour because I was coming over.

"Raven. How are you?" he greets me.

"Hi, Bram. I've had better days." I look past him as my sister heads toward us.

"Rae." She calls to me as I step into the foyer. Not usually one for hugging, she surprises me by pulling me into a tight embrace. "We can talk in the living room. Did you want anything to drink?"

Bram closes the door. "I'll let you two talk," he says and retreats to some other part of the house.

"I had dinner on the flight."

"How's Parker?" she asks. I follow her to the living room, which is an eclectic mix of midcentury meets seventies vibe. I take a seat on an occasional chair. Robin sits opposite me on her couch.

"Good. He's headed to the hotel."

"You could have stayed here."

"It's okay. How have you been doing since we talked earlier?"

"Still processing everything." Her eyes are swollen like she's been crying.

"Did you call her?"

"No. I think any further discussions I have with Mom should be face-to-face. And Bill..."

"What about Bill? Do you think he knows?"

"I have no idea. This is so surreal. This is not the conversation I thought I would have at this age. I'm supposed to be enjoying life, not trying to figure out who my parents are. This is the crap you see on reality shows."

"A testament to our mom."

"This means she had to have cheated on him."

"She's capable of anything."

"I never thought for a second that Dad wasn't our dad. Now I know he's not *my* dad. Did you talk to him?"

Robin gets up, goes to her makeshift bar, which is on a brass and glass rolling cart. She picks up a beveled crystal decanter and pours herself a glass of brown liquid which I suspect is whiskey. She holds up her glass, gesturing to me. I shake my head. The last thing I need to do is start drinking. Robin takes a sip and begins pacing the room, glass in hand. I track her movements.

"On the plane."

"And?"

"He says he loves you. That no matter what, you're still his daughter."

"Are you serious?"

"He doesn't care what the paper said. For twelve years, he raised you as his. He never thought anything different. You two should talk. He's a lovely man. He keeps a picture of us with him on his desk."

"You saw it?"

"No. Someone I trust did. How do you want to handle this?"

"I need to talk to Mom."

"How can I help you?"

Robin stops pacing and turns to me.

"Go with me."

Go with her? What the hell? That's the last thing I want to do. I thought I was done dealing with my mother.

"Robin, are you sure? I swear I might strangle that woman if I see her again."

"There's no way Parker will let that happen. I have to do this, Raven. You have to go with me. She can't get away with this bullshit. Why wouldn't she tell me Bill is my father? Unless..."

"Unless what? You don't think Bill is your father?"

"I don't know. Anything is possible now. What if he's not? I need answers. I can't go through life not knowing who my real father is. It was bad enough not knowing where the man I thought was my dad was all these years."

God, my mom has ruined everyone's life: mine, Dad's, Robin's. Even Parker had to suffer because I couldn't get myself together behind the mess my mom caused. And through it all, I felt so isolated without my family. I can't let Robin go through that. Not alone.

"Okay. I'll go with you."

Chapter 39

The Fall of Us

Raven

It was after midnight by the time I left my sister's house. The next day, Parker and I spend the afternoon with Robin and Bram before flying home that evening.

Although my trip to see my sister was necessary, it put Parker and me behind at work, and we had to cram a week's worth of work into a few days, coupled with therapy and calls with Dad. I love that I can just pick up the phone and call Dad. Having him back in my life has alleviated my sleep terrors and calmed my angst. I didn't fully understand the impact of my family situation on my health and my life decisions until I went to therapy.

"Babe, are you making me one of those?" Parker walks up behind me at the kitchen counter, where I'm slicing a croissant in half. He wraps his arms around me, dips his head, and kisses me on the neck. I tip my neck to give him better access. He smells so good, and his body feels perfect pressed against my back. "I want meat and cheese in mine, too," he says, looking over my shoulder.

I continue making my croissant sandwich and also make one for him. Parker doesn't let me go. He remains draped over me the entire time, watching.

"Is this your new role as food inspector?"

"No. This is me being your doting man."

"Do you know how hard it is to make a sandwich with your fine self clinging to me like saran wrap?"

He laughs. He turns me around and pulls me into him. "I have an idea." He smirks, cupping my hips and pressing my body so it molds around his hard proof. He picks me up and sits me on the counter beside the sandwiches. He stands between my legs and presses his lips to mine. We kiss, enjoying each other's nearness in a moment full of love.

He pulls back. "I'm hungry."

"You would be. Here." I pick up one of the sandwiches and hold it to his mouth. He takes a bite. Then I do the same.

"So, what's our agenda today?" he asks.

"Remember those checks we cut to support Rose Ross' art foundation?"

"Yes."

"There's an exhibition to showcase the students' work that benefited from her foundation."

"I thought you wanted to donate the tickets."

"We need to go. I spent so much time volunteering and helping the students at her foundation that it will be the icing on the cake to see their work on exhibit. Besides, I hardly see her since she's been traveling back and forth to Ireland."

"Then it's settled. We'll go." He dips his head and kisses me again. It's heated and urgent. When he eases up, he licks across my lips. "Now, tell me how the charity event two weeks from now relates to today." The attorney in him doesn't miss a thing.

"I need heels to match my dress. You want to go shoe shopping with me?" I raise my eyebrows.

He groans. "Babe, you know how much I love you in heels. You're trying to kill me. No, you're trying to get—."

I interrupt. "Parker Page, if you don't stop saying I'm trying to get fucked." I can't stand that he knows me this well because even that's a turn-on.

"It's true."

"Let's finish eating, and then we'll go."

"You're not going in these." He pulls the waistband on my jeans.

"Why not?"

"If you're making me watch you try on heels, I'm getting something out of it. I want to see your legs. I want a show." He smiles wryly.

I roll my eyes. The things I do for this man.

"Knee high or thigh?"

"Thigh."

***

It's the end of summer, and soon, it'll be fall. Parents are fitting in the last of their family vacations, and the rest are lined up at the stores buying new outfits for children heading back to school. I think about Parker and me. Our child, had it lived, would be almost five years old and heading to kindergarten. I look down where my fingers are laced with his as I wait for the sales rep to bring my shoes.

"Where are you, honey?" Parker shakes my hand.

"Just thinking about kids going to school. That could have been us."

He lifts my fingers to his lips and kisses them. "It still can, babe. That's one of the things I wanted to talk to you about the night we flew out."

"About having children?"

"Yeah."

"Technically, we have to be doing certain things together to make that happen. And by things, I'm not talking shoe shopping."

"You're such a comedian. I'm talking about when we do. Would you want to try?"

"You're asking me to be your baby momma?"

"No, Rain. I'm only having kids with my wife. I'm asking if you want kids."

"With you, yes." I surprise myself by how quick the response rolls off my tongue.

The sales clerk returns with eight boxes of shoes. One by one, she sits them down, making two stacks. She opens the top boxes.

"I was able to find your size in all the shoes. Would you like me to help you with this?"

"Thanks, but I got it from here."

"Let me know if you need me," she says, then moves on to the next customer.

I remove the shoes from the box containing glitter and crystal pumps. I take off my black pumps and slide into the shoes.

"Okay, do your walk," Parker urges me.

I stand and pose in front of the mirror. "These are cute." I turn around and put one foot on the edge of the chair next to Parker. He slides his hand up my ankle, to the back of my leg, and up my thigh, past my skirt. I pull back. "You're naughty."

"Walk for me, babe." I walk up the shoe aisle and back down to Parker. "I like those."

"You would." I sit down, take them off, and try on the next pair. These have crystals, too, but the crystals wrap around my ankle instead of crossing the top of my foot. I walk up and down the aisle.

"I'm having you in those. Get them."

"I'm looking for shoes to pop with my black taffeta skirt. Not to have you-know-what in them."

"Doesn't matter. Those are coming home with us." I roll my eyes. Next, I try on a red four-inch pair of heels that look like shimmering lipstick. "Ah, babe, come here," Parker growls. I don't go to him. Instead, I walk to the mirror and look at the shoes on my feet. I pose with one foot pointed toward the mirror. Then, I point it outward. Parker walks up behind me. "I want you wearing these on that day."

"What day?"

"The day I sink into you. And I'm serious about having kids, Rain. I don't want to wait."

"What are you saying?" I turn and wrap my arms around his waist. His face is serious as he looks down at me.

"I want you to get off birth control. When you come back to me, we're not holding back. I want it all. I'm not waiting. We lost too much of our lives already."

"You're serious."

"I am. We've both come so far. Rain, honey. I want this to be the fall of *us*. But I don't want it to stop there. I don't just want to be a season in your life—I want to be there for all of them, for every season to be all about us, our love, our life. Let this fall be the beginning of forever."

Taking a deep breath, I process his words. Parker wants to start a family with me. Whenever I think about losing our child, I visualize how each year would have been different—celebrating our baby's first birthday, witnessing their first step, first tooth, and all the things that come with being a parent. We could have tried again. We wouldn't have lost all those years of me doing whatever I was doing with other men. Wasting my time. God, what was I thinking? It's always been Parker. I've never visualized my future with anyone but him. I want this. I want him.

"The fall of us," I affirm.

"Yes. This is about us. It's our time." He dips his head and kisses me in a display of affection that is too inappropriate to take place in the shoe section. "Babe. You got me riled up with all these shoes. Get them all. Let's go."

Parker signals the sales clerk, who happily rings up eight pairs of shoes."I want to look at the purses while we're here," I tell Parker, who is already a step ahead, calling the driver to come pick up the shoe bags.

"Okay, but no more shoes."

We leave instructions for the sales clerk, then head to the purse section. I immediately spot a purse that would match the red shoes.

"This one is perfect for those red shoes," I say, slipping my hand into the strap on the back of the shiny red clutch. "See." I flip my hand around a few times. "I can't lose it if it's stuck to my hand like this."

"Definitely a great buy," a familiar voice says. "I have a black one in Nubuck."

Tina. This woman is worse than a spam call interrupting to offer me something I don't need.

"Thanks for the endorsement, Tina," I say.

"Raven. How are you? Parker, how's it going?"

"Good," we say in unison.

"I see you two have moved beyond finishing each other's sentences."

"Don't let us interrupt your shopping, Tina," I say. I'm amiable but annoyed.

"It's fine. I'm about done for the day. I hope you bought shoes to go with that."

I'm surprised by the change in her demeanor since the last time I saw her. She appears genuinely friendly…almost.

"I did."

"You look happy, Parker," she says.

"With this woman at my side, how can I not be?" I look up at Parker. He pulls me to his side and smiles at me.

I remember the day at the Tavern bar when I met him with Tina over a year ago. Parker had asked me to come there. At the time, I didn't know he was planning to introduce her to me as his solution to what he later described as *"a pair of soft lips"* to solve a raging hard-on. Even then, he pulled me to his side. That day, Tina admitted she knew I was the love of his life.

"Raven, I'm sorry. I never doubted what Parker told me about you. I was being a bitch because the man I've wanted since high school wanted you. The light in his eyes whenever he looks at you is the light I wanted to see but never did. I knew what I was getting into and did so to spite you. I apologize. We, you, me, Parker…the others…we have a code to uphold. I ignored that in a quest to get what I wanted. I was wrong."

"Tina, you don't have to say this. I've always known where you were coming from. It wasn't my place to dictate Parker's actions. We weren't together then."

"She's right, Tina. We get it. We all make mistakes. Hopefully, we learn from them. I also played a role in what happened."

"But I want you to know that I want to be friends. I want to move on. The first time I met Raven, I knew she was your other half. I was jealous of that fact. I've been working on myself. I've learned from my mistakes. Tell me at least we can have a drink together, Raven, at the next event." As I stare at her, I'm met with sincerity in her eyes. She bites the side of her lip.

"Sure. I'll agree to that," I tell her, knowing this is another thing I need to move on from if I want to heal.

"Thank you. I mean it. You two are perfect together. I'll see you later," she says and walks off.

I look at Parker. "Well, I didn't expect that."

"Babe. We're all members of the same society. There are no weak links."

Chapter 40

I Want More

Noah

I TAKE A SIP of my whiskey. It goes down smoothly. I look around the high-top table at my brothers and cousins and realize how good we have it. We may be at a bar, but there's a lot of power between the five of us in the room. We thrive in a world where the odds are stacked against us. It was hard getting here, but we made it. Still, I want more.

"How come we're not at your house drinking, cuz?" Chase asks me.

"I haven't had a week of peace since the housewarming. I thought we'd get out for a change," I tell them.

"You shouldn't have bought such a beautiful place. It's addicting," Drew says.

"Your mistake for giving us the door code," Rok adds.

"You all need to call first. What if I'm busy?"

"Does that mean you've moved on from Rae?" Chase asks.

It's a legitimate question. Rain is the only woman I've brought to my house that wasn't family. Before her, I only had one-night stands with women. They never saw where I lived. I'd take them to the Four Seasons. When we were done, I'd put them in a car, send them home, and never see them again. Why would they be worried about walking in on me when they know the woman I want is unavailable? Or so she says.

The last time I saw Rain was when I held her in my arms in her office. She'll know I held her, but the woman with perfect recall will never remember how it felt. She was unconscious. He'll remember, though. Parker. He watched as I laid her on the couch. What she'll remember is him holding her that night. I felt my jaw tighten when he kissed her fingers. When he called her by her pet name, "babe," I wanted to punch him. That man gets under my skin in a way I've never felt before. I didn't even feel this way about Blake. Blake annoyed me. He didn't have a chance with Rain after he cheated on her. I wanted to crush him for what he did. She wouldn't let me. But, Parker...this is something else altogether. She has ties to him that, at the onset, seem unhealthy. They have a relationship I don't understand.

What I do know is that I want Rain. She felt something for me. She admitted as much. I want her to feel that again. I want to have her under me again. She wants to be friends. I want more.

"Rain and I are colleagues," I say, trying not to grit my teeth. Rok's eyes shift to me. I check myself. "Our project is estimated to go two years. She thinks we should stay professional."

"What do you think?" Drew asks, opening the can of worms I was hoping to avoid.

I look at Mak, then Rok. "I respect her wishes."

"Well then, there's a group of ladies over there checking us out," Drew says, like it's that easy to shut off what I feel for Rain.

"I'll leave that to Casanova and Chase," I tell them.

"Don't put me in this," Mak says.

"Since when?" We say in unison.

"Wow, what was that about?" Mak asks.

"You haven't met a pretty lady you didn't like. Does this mean you're settling down?" I ask.

He coughs. "What? No."

"Man, what's up? Is Melanie the real deal or what?" Chase asks.

"Melanie and I are figuring things out."

Rok shakes his head. He's not buying it. "That's what you always say. What's the deal, Baby Mak?"

"We were talking about Nik and Rae. How did this turn into the Me and Melanie show? Nik, how's our Sis?" Mak asks, redirecting.

"I'm going to get another drink. Anybody want anything?" I get a bunch of headshakes in response. I dodge their question about Rain and go to the bar.

"I'll have another whiskey, neat," I tell the bartender. He fixes my drink and slides it to me. I take a sip. "Thanks."

"Tired of your friends already?" a sweet, sultry voice asks.

I look to my side. It's one of the women from the group. She has heels on, but I place her around Rain's height. She has smooth brown skin and jet-black hair pressed with gentle waves barely touching her shoulders. She lifts a finger and sweeps her bangs from her brown eyes. Her full, kissable lips are painted in a rich burgundy color.

"It's my family. They're good people," I tell her. "What about you? It's kinda bold of you to approach me."

"I'm bold. I go after what I want. Nice accent. British?"

Bold, and sassy, like...Rain. But she's not her. When I look at this woman, as beautiful as she is, I don't feel what I do when Rain looks at me and smiles. When Rain laughs, my world lights up.

"Thanks. Yes."

"That's different." I know what she means. She didn't expect a man of color to speak with a British accent. I don't think about it unless someone points it out. Our family left London when I was twelve. Twenty years later, my accent is still there.

Rain used to point it out to me every once in a while. Like she did the last time I kissed her right before she left my house in the wee hours of the morning that fated Monday. *"I need to go before your sexy accent talks me out of my clothes," she whispered.* Her face was so close to mine. I remember wanting to take her back to bed and devour her. Letting her go was the hardest thing I'd ever done. If I have one regret—it's that.

"What are you drinking?" I ask the woman watching me intensely.

"A sidecar."

"Sidecar for the lady. Put it on my tab," I tell the bartender.

I look down into this woman's eyes. She's beautiful, fuckable. Those luscious lips would be incredible wrapped around my dick. But I'm not interested. There was a time when I had a different woman every week. Then I met Rain. I haven't been with a woman since. I told Rain she ruined me. Once I tasted her, I had to have more. I didn't want anyone else.

"Listen. You're a beautiful woman. I came here to shoot the breeze with my mates. Enjoy your drink," I say and walk away.

I go back to the table with our group.

"Shit, man. Tell me you didn't just walk away from that goddess," Mak says.

Fuck. He's right. I need to solve this thing with Rain. I can't get her out of my head. I have to work with her. What is this? I'm used to being in control, but I can't control wanting her. Fuck.

"She's not my type," I lie.

"Let it go, guys," Rok says. I lift my glass in silent thanks.

Thank the fuck. He understands how this is impacting me. I need to really get my shit together. We have a business to run and deal to do with Wade Wallace.

Chapter 41
Happy Birthday

Parker

The driver pulls into the back street that leads to our modern four-story home overlooking Baker Beach. For this party, instead of having it at the house where my parents reside, Mom wanted to add to the aesthetic of Hollywood glam by having it at our sea cliff house.

"You've got to be kidding me." Rain looks past me out the window. "That is not a red carpet going up the steps."

"It is."

"Your mom is over the top. Now I know why she wanted me in this." Rain touches her platinum dress. It molds to her body like molten liquid.

When she slipped into that, along with her matching platinum heels, I wanted to fuck her right in the closet. She looks that good. I turn to her, cup her cheek, and kiss her.

"You're so fine, babe. It's a good thing only our closes friends are attending. I don't want to destroy anyone for staring at you on my birthday. You ready?"

"Ready."

The driver opens the door, and I help Rain out. On instinct, I pull her into me again and kiss her.

"We need to go in," she whispers against my lips.

We turn and walk toward the steps leading to the front door. A photographer takes our picture. We step into the large entryway and make our way up a flight of stairs into the main part of the house. Neo soul music plays over the sound system. We head toward cheerful voices from the large living room overlooking the ocean. The deep reddish orange Golden Gate Bridge stands prominently displayed against a clear blue sky. My mom spots us as soon as we cross the threshold.

"Raven, darling. You look like a jewel." She kisses Rain on one cheek and then the other. "Parker, honey, I don't know what to say. I wish I could freeze this moment of you two. Happy birthday, honey," she says, pulling me into a hug.

My dad joins us. He pulls Rain into a hug and says, "You look beautiful. Welcome." She looks every ounce of Hollywood glam, with perfectly structured curls that fall in neat waves over her shoulders and red lipstick that pops against her honey-brown skin. "Son, happy birthday. You feel any older?"

"A bit," I admit. Because I do. The past five years have been hard. I've grown in ways I couldn't imagine. The hardest part was not having Rain. Of course, she's been there, but not as my woman. As much as watching her grow into herself has been beautiful, knowing another man was touching her was distressing.

"Well, get settled. Enjoy yourself. This is your day. The other kids are here," he says like we're little children. I know he's referring to Josh and Ethan. I look over his shoulder. They're talking with their parents and a handful of other friends across the room. Josh spots me, breaks away, and heads toward us. I already know he's coming to see his favorite person...Rain.

"Here she is. You look spectacular, Raven. May I?" Rain nods. He pulls her into a hug.

"Thanks, Josh. You look handsome as always." Rain rubs his shoulder. I love how they have their own special bond.

"Where's that photographer? I need a picture with you," he adds.

"Get your own girl," I tell him.

"Happy birthday, man. You look good, too. I don't care what you say. I'm getting a picture with Raven. You can be in it, too, if you ask nicely," he teases.

"I want in, too," Ethan says, joining us. "Raven, wow." He bends and kisses her cheek.

"Don't forget it's Parker's birthday." She looks between Josh and Ethan.

"We haven't forgotten," Josh says.

"Good to see you. Happy birthday, man," Ethan adds.

"Josh is right. We need a photo. Honey, grab the photographer," my mom tells my dad.

While my dad gets the photographer, other guests crowd around Rain and me, passing along their birthday wishes. I watch Rain as she talks to the guests like she's been a part of my world all her life. When Tina said we are all part of the same group and included Rain, she was right. Rain is an elite. She embodies all the qualities, goodness, and standards we live by.

My dad returns with the photographer. "Let's do this."

My mom ensures we're all arranged with me and Rain in the center. We take some with the two of us, then add more people: mom, dad, our friends, and their parents, until about twenty of us are in a picture. We're all dressed like Hollywood stars from the past. The women are wearing lovely gowns, and the guys are all dressed in tuxedos.

When we're done, we all gather in the room. Everyone has a glass of champagne and is ready for our toast. My dad kicks it off.

"Everyone, raise your glass," he says, and we all do. "Parker, son. We're all gathered today to celebrate you. There was a time when your mom and I weren't sure we could have children. The day you were born was the best day of our lives and the beginning of a beautiful life we never imagined. Every day with you has been a joy. Today, as we raise our glass, we wish you every loving moment you gave us a thousandfold. Cheers."

Everyone cheers in unison and clicks glasses. I hold Rain close and don't let her go. I want to experience every moment of this day with her at my side, and I want everyone to see how happy she makes me.

Like my dad said long ago, following an award dinner we attended, *"Sitting beside me were the most important people in my world," he said, talking about my mom and me. "People watch every move I make—to see what I do next. They want to know what interests me— what's important to me."* He taught me that because of our status, others have a sense of wonderment watching us. They want to know everything about us and what's important to us. For him, that was my mom and me. For me, it's Rain. Yes, I'm in a room full of mutuals. And at this moment, all eyes are on me, and my eyes are on Rain.

"Rain," I say, getting her attention. She looks up. I dip my head and kiss her. It's soft yet brief. She smiles at me, and it feels like heaven on earth.

"Happy birthday, love," she whispers.

Chapter 42

Symbols

Parker

We arrive back at my house. As I open the door, Rain leans into me, surrounding me with jasmine and honey. Her laugh is contagious as she talks about the party.

"Oh my god, that was a blast. I think it's one of the best birthday parties I've been to. Everyone looked so beautiful. Your mom knew what she was doing with her vintage Hollywood theme."

I remove Rain's coat and hang it in the foyer closet. She follows me into the kitchen and leans against the marble counter as I retrieve something to celebrate with from the refrigerator. I turn and look at her. It's been a while since I've seen her so relaxed. We were at this very counter wrestling over her phone almost three months ago. She was so stressed because the day before, she'd found out that Blake Wallace was cheating on her. She's come so far since then. Standing before me in her shimmering platinum bead and sequin dress that looks spectacular against her brown skin, she seems at peace and perfectly edible.

"Mom loves throwing parties. I'm glad you had fun. It was great seeing everyone enjoying the evening. Champagne?" I hold up two bottles. "Ruinart or Dom?"

"It's your birthday. You choose."

I open the Ruinart, pour two glasses, and hand one to Rain. I lift my glass. "To another trip around the sun. I'm glad you're here to celebrate with me."

"To another year. I wouldn't want to be anywhere else."

I clink my glass to hers, then drink. Rain drinks and then places her glass on the counter.

"You didn't open my gift."

I tuck a curl behind her ear. "We've been busy all day. Why don't you show me now?" I set my glass down and follow Rain into the living room.

The gift, which I'm almost certain is a painting, is wrapped in silver and propped against my oversized lounge chair. I sit across the room on the couch and stretch my arms across the back.

"What are you doing over there? Don't you want to unwrap it?" she asks.

I want to unwrap her, but I don't say that. "It's my birthday. I want to watch you in that beautiful dress while *you* unwrap my gift."

"So cheeky."

Rain picks up the package and holds it in front of her like a game show host. Slowly, she tears the wrapping from the back. The paper falls to the floor, revealing a watercolor painting of the Bay Bridge. The sparkle of the bridge lights and the way the piers span from one side of the bay to the other and disappear when they reach land are spectacular. My woman painted this. Sometimes, I wonder what her life would have been like had she become an artist instead of an attorney. Her work is that good.

"Rain, honey, it's spectacular. I know you love iconic structures, but what made you choose this one to paint?"

"I read that bridges symbolize communication, connection, union, and hope. All things that represent our lives these past years."

I stand and cross the room. I take the painting from her and hold it up. "It also symbolizes love," I say. I sit the painting on the chair. Snaking an arm around Rain's waist, I pull her into me and kiss her hard. Our tongues mingle as I lick into her and swallow her groans. She slides her hands up my chest and breaks the kiss.

"I think I should paint more often," she pants.

"You're so talented, babe. It's beautiful. Thank you."

"I never know what to get you."

"Whatever you give is heartfelt and perfect." I release her and take her hand. "Come sit with me." We go to the couch. "I'll hang it up in the morning. We had a long day. You've been standing in those shoes for hours."

Rain sits beside me and swings her legs over one of mine. This is her thing. She does it so she can see me when she talks. It's second nature. I wrap my arm around her waist and pull her closer.

"They don't hurt."

I grab her ankle and look at her shoe.

"This color's great, but I can't wait to see you in the red ones."

She laughs. "I knew you'd say that. Ever since we bought that pair you say the same thing."

"Well, it's true. I will have you in those."

"Anyway. Did you really have a good time tonight?"

"I did." I place my palm up in her lap. She puts her hand in mine. We lace our fingers.

"What was your favorite part of tonight?"

"You don't want to hear the answer to that."

She tips her head sideways and narrows her eyes at me like that will make me produce a better answer.

"Parker Page, Esquire, answer the question," she says in her courtroom voice.

"You."

"That's not possible. All those people, your parents, Josh, our friends. They were all there honoring your life and your family. It was amazing to watch. No one would miss me if I weren't there."

I cup Rain's face. "Don't say that."

"It's true."

"There's no truth in that statement. You are the icing on the cake. The entire day would have been a waste without you by my side. Don't you get it, Rain? You are the air I breathe."

"I'm struggling with that because I feel like I failed you."

"You haven't failed. You were finding your way. Have you forgotten our commitments?"

"I remember, and I'll accept what you say is true. But I don't want to talk about me. There had to have been something else you enjoyed."

"Watching you and Josh dance was pretty awesome. He seemed happy, and he loves you, too."

"He's just happy I'm working on finding him a woman."

"How's that going?"

"Good. I was thinking my friend, the artist who is a professor, might be a good match. He needs to bring on a board member with expertise in art history, amongst other things, to oversee hiring teachers for his private schools. With her experience, she'll fit the bill perfectly."

"Your friend Jade?"

"Yes. What do you think?"

"She's lovely, smart, and kind. Josh will lose his mind when he sees her. But can she handle his schedule? The man's on the road all the time."

"I'm not sure. We'll see."

"They need to meet somehow, and we'll have to see if she's attracted to him."

"That part should be easy. He's brilliant and the second most handsome man in the world," she says confidently.

"Okay, I know where this conversation is going. Time to get off my lap."

"Are you kicking me off because you still think I'm not ready?"

"I'm kicking you off because I need to."

Chapter 43

Ready For Love

Raven

Parker kisses my cheek and lifts my legs off his. Before I realize it, I'm sitting straight up on the couch, facing forward by myself as he heads toward the kitchen. He's avoiding me, and I want to know why.

"More champagne?" he calls over his shoulder.

I get up and follow him. He pours the room-temperature liquid down the drain and refills our glasses with chilled champagne.

I take a few sips and study Parker in silence. "Happy birthday, handsome. I hope I didn't do anything to spoil it for you."

"You're here, babe. That's all I can ask for."

I look up at him. It's hard to hold his gaze standing so close, even in my heels. "Put me on the counter so I can talk to you." He lifts me by the waist and sits me on the countertop. "I'm an attorney," I tell him in my mock attorney voice.

"So am I. What's your point, little lady?"

"You told me the truth but not the whole truth. What am I missing?"

"You're not missing a thing. In my eyes, you're perfect. You don't seem to believe me when I tell you that. That and this talk about whether you're ready—it's frustrating. We all have our faults, Rain. I realize I'm overly protective and obsessive over you. Everything I do is out of pure love. I even watched as you walked out the door because you asked me to. I don't know what else to do, Rain."

"I hurt you."

"We talked about this. You did what you had to. You found yourself. It makes me love you even more."

"Through it all, you never wavered. I hate what I did, but I'm glad I was able to find the pieces of myself that were missing. I wish I had been strong enough to find them while we were together."

"It's all in the past."

"It's your birthday. Like you said, I'm here—that makes you happy, but your eyes aren't reflecting that. What do you need?"

He holds my gaze a moment before responding. He's searching my eyes for answers. To what?

"I need you to come back to me," he says in a voice that's soft and full of love.

His words squeeze my heart. I can't even hold back the tears that stream down my face. I try wiping them away, but that only clears the way for more. The love emanating from him is so strong it envelops me like a warm blanket on a rainy day.

"To your bed?"

"You know that's not what I'm asking. I could have had you weeks ago if that's all I wanted. Don't you get it, Rain? I don't just want your body. And friendship isn't enough. I want you to be my wife. I told you that day, standing in the store. I want it all—no more waiting. We wasted too much time living separate lives. We were designed for each other."

Parker told me in London that he had planned to propose before we graduated. He didn't get the chance. I fell ill, our baby died, and soon after, I walked out of his life. I stare at his face, and I still see the lingering pain. Our entire world changed, and I can't put either of us through that again.

"You think I'm ready?"

"Only you can answer that question."

"You have my ring?"

"You know I do."

"Show me," I tell him. He helps me off the counter and we go to his walk-in closet.

Parker opens a drawer and takes out a box. The box has hinges on two sides, and the top splits in two. He parts it, revealing a brilliant five-carat round solitaire diamond ring. I gasp. He sits the box on the dresser, then lifts me so I'm sitting on the dresser, too. I pick up the box. He takes it from me and removes the ring.

"It feels like I've had this forever." He strokes his finger across the diamond.

"If memory serves me correctly, you've had it most of our relationship."

"Your perfect recall serves you."

I smile because it's lovely to hear him make a joke. He's been so serious lately. "Our first night together, you gave me this," I hold up my hand bearing the promise ring. "It was a promise of our commitment to each other—that I'd be your wife one day. You were so certain back then."

"I love you. It's that simple."

"Can I try it on?"

"No."

"No?" What in the world? This man. "It's me. You can't say no."

"I just did. I'm saving it for the love of my life. The woman who will be my wife. The one who'll have my children. This ring is for *her*."

Is he asking me to undo what I did? But how can I? I told him to let me go. To let me exist without him, and I'd find my way back to him…to love. That's what he wants…for me to say I'm back. This is what we've been working toward. Am I ready?

"Parker?"

"Hey, beautiful."

"Kiss me." He shakes his head. This man is going to be the death of me. "That's twice you've said no to me tonight."

"I'll give you whatever you want. I haven't broken that promise. I never will. The night's not over."

I smile to myself. God, do I dare marry an attorney? Discussions like this will be my life.

"Kiss me," I press. He dusts his lips on mine, and they're gone as quickly as they meet. I hold his arms so he can't pull away from me. Parker stares at me like he's trying to figure me out. We're on the precipice of something and both of us hold the power to tip this one way or the other.

Parker puts the diamond ring back in its case, closes it, and sets it on the dresser.

"I'm going to have my shower. You need help unzipping this?" He brushes his fingers across the silver sequins and beads on my dress. I feel electricity shoot throughout my body.

"It's your birthday. You can do what you want."

"No, I can't."

"Then, please tell me what you want."

"All I want is you. You are all I ever wanted, today and every day, for the rest of my life."

"What are you saying, Parker?"

"I want you in my bed tonight, Rain. Not just to cuddle up with me. I want you completely. I want to eat cake from your body. I want to hear you call out my name with me deep inside you. I want to watch you fall apart beneath me. You are what I want for my birthday and every day. There is nothing that I want more than you. But you need to decide whether that's what you want because those things are reserved for my wife."

"Parker."

"I told you never to ask a question you don't want the answer to."

I hold his gaze. "Help me down." He lifts me from the dresser and sets my feet on the floor. "Unzip this, please." I turn my back to him.

He unzips my dress, and the weight of the beads and sequins drags the sparkly fabric down my body until it pools around my feet on the floor. I turn around and stand in front of Parker in my underwear and heels. I step out of the dress, pick it up, and place it on the dresser in the center of the closet where I was previously sitting. I bend and take my heels off. I hear a slight groan come from Parker. He loves me in heels. He used to make love to me while I wore my heels when we came home from parties. That was our thing. But that was a long time ago. Not tonight.

I look up at Parker, whose six-foot-four frame dwarfs me in my bare feet. "I need to talk to you. You have a few options for where to talk: put me on the dresser, sit on your favorite chaise, or on the bed. The choice is yours."

"Here is fine." Parker loosens his tie and takes it off. Then, he slips off his shoes. "I'm waiting," he urges.

I cross my arms. He shakes his head, lifts me, and sits me back on the dresser. I pull him toward me and unbutton his shirt.

"You told me I didn't have to apologize, but I am. The week following our return from the hospital, I was beyond broken. I was a hot mess long before our loss, but it propelled me into this void that I couldn't see my way out of."

"We were both in a dark place."

"I'm sorry, Parker."

"You said you needed your distance from me. I gave it to you. I told you; I'll give you whatever you want."

"Except for the ring." He turns his wrist so I can take off his cufflinks. I flip the toggle into the post and remove his diamond-faced cufflink.

"Is that what you want? Do you want me to ask you, Rain?"

"Yes, Parker. I love you. I never stopped. I should have never walked away from our love. I realize fighting it made my life more difficult. I told you all those other relationships were a mistake. I want you to ask. I'm ready."

"I didn't doubt you when you returned from Seattle and told me that you wanted to make it work with me. But you were still working through other things. All the tender moments we shared where you wanted me to take you to bed—."

"You didn't."

"No, I didn't because those were moments when you wanted me in you, not with you. You were ready to come for me. But you weren't ready to come to me. To commit to forever."

"I didn't feel whole. I do now."

"You need to be clear with me, Rain." He's right. No more holding back.

I recall a quote from bell hooks' book *All About Love: New Visions: "Only love can heal the wounds of the past. However, the intensity of our woundedness often leads to a closing of the heart, making it impossible for us to give or receive the love that is given to us."* For so long, I've been wandering around like the walking dead, closed off to his love, afraid of facing my fears. I've faced them all—fought back from the brink of destruction. Now I'm ready to let him in. Parker loves me, and I want every ounce he has to offer. I love him.

"I'm coming back to you."

"Fully?"

"Completely. I heard you that day at the store. You told me to get off birth control because if I came back, we weren't going to waste any time. You said, when I return, we will begin building our lives, our family, our forever."

"I was serious."

"So am I. We want the same things, Parker. I'm off protection. So, are we going to make some babies or what?"

"I told you that's all reserved for my wife."

I show him the back of my hand. "I don't see a ring."

"Oh, is that what this is about?" A smug smile forms on his face, and I feel lighter knowing I put it there.

"No. It's about this." I pull Parker's face to mine and kiss him. He puts his thumb on my chin, forcing my mouth open, and he licks into me like he is starving. Our kiss is hot, messy, wet, and full of four years of longing. The kiss is so intense it makes me lightheaded. I can't breathe. Parker pulls back because even after all these years, he still knows my body. He presses his forehead to mine. Our breaths are heavy.

Parker retrieves the ring from the box beside me. I hold my hand out, but he lifts my other hand and removes the promise ring. He takes both rings and slides them on my wedding ring finger.

"Rain, I love you. Will you be my wife, the mother of my children? Will you let me give you the world? Let me show you how much I love you every day. Let us build a life together."

"Yes, Parker, to everything. I want to wake up to you every day. Experience everything life offers with you by my side as my friend, lover, and husband."

He kisses me again, and this time, I feel ready to receive his love.

Chapter 44
Inside My Love

Parker

Rain, the love of my life, has agreed to be my wife. This moment feels surreal. I knew she was special the day we locked eyes in class a lifetime ago. Without saying a word, it's as if I willed her to be mine. We silently held a whole conversation, using only body language as our professor ranted in the background. Once we were out of the class, we huddled outside the door and laughed about it. I recall thinking how lovely she was when I introduced myself. I saw forever in her eyes.

"I'm Parker." I held out my hand in between laughing about what happened in class.

"I'm Raven. People call me Rae."

"What's your full name, Raven?"

"Raven Rain Nichols."

"Rain. I love the sound of that. It reminds me how essential it is to all life. Can I call you Rain?"

"Yeah. You can call me Rain."

Our connection was instantaneous. That was over twelve years ago. Tonight, on my birthday, I got my woman back, and I couldn't be happier.

I break our kiss and bury my head in her neck, holding her tight, inhaling her essence. Surrounded by the scent of jasmine and honey, wrapped in her warmth, bathed in her beauty, I'm in love with all of her. I feel her delicate fingers in my hair. I trail kisses up her neck and behind her ear. *God, I love this woman.*

I whisper in her ear. "Remember what I told you at the store?"

"Everything. They're behind you."

I untangle myself from Rain. I take her hand and lower it down my body to the bulge in my pants. "This is several years of steel that's been waiting for you. I won't be able to take my time tonight, but we have all weekend for me to worship you. You okay with that?"

"I want it all."

I turn and grab her red heels from the shoe display. I walk back to where Rain sits in the center of the closet on the dresser, wearing a wry grin. I lift her foot and slide the red pump on, then lift the other foot, put the other shoe on, and lower her leg. I slide my hands along her thighs and around her body. I squeeze her hips and pull her towards me. I press my lips to hers, and she opens her mouth to take me in. She wraps her arms around my neck and legs around my body and deepens the kiss. I groan into her. I want this woman. *My woman.*

I break the kiss and whisper, "This is exactly how you were wrapped around me for our first time together."

"I'm a little older and wiser, but this time, I'm ready for everything you have to offer. Kiss me." I crash my lips to hers and lick into her like she's giving me life because she is.

I lift Rain, carry her into the bedroom, and lower her onto the bed without breaking the kiss. I suck her tongue like she's supplying life-saving love. Because she is. She is all I've ever wanted. The one thing I need.

I reach between us and cup her breast. Her nipple pebbles beneath the fabric. I push the bra up, squeeze, and pinch her breasts. She writhes beneath me. I lower my hand, pull her leg away from my back, and slide my hand beneath the fabric of her underwear. Her body is warm and waiting for me. I slide my fingers between her folds and coat them in her juices. She's slick and wet and ready. I rub her sweet spot, never breaking our kiss. I capture every cry and groan. I suck her mouth like I want to suck her body. She pushes against my hand, wanting me inside her. I nudge her leg with my knee and open her wider to put my fingers in her. Increasing the friction, I move my fingers in and out while my tongue mirrors the movement in her mouth. I feel the walls of her body squeeze my hand, and I know she is almost there. She moves her body in time with the rhythm of my fingers.

"Ah." She tries to express her pleasure. My mouth captures her groans as she comes around my hand while sucking my tongue. I lift my face, finally giving her space to call my name. "Parker. I need you," she cries out. I watch her as she unravels. She's perfect.

"I'm here, babe." I continue my movements until I pull her climax from her, and it's beautiful watching her fall.

Standing, I slide her panties down her legs. I strip my clothes, leaving them piled on the floor as I look down at the love of my life. She takes her bra off but leaves on her heels. She's so beautiful, splayed out like a feast before me. "I'm going to take you now. It might get rough," I tell her, because it's been fucking five years since I've been inside her.

She reaches her hands to me. I kneel over her, dip my head, and kiss her. I lift her leg over my shoulder, and then I rub my length through her release, coating me with her love. I position my tip at her entrance and slowly push in deeper and harder until I fill her. I close my eyes, feeling her walls squeezing me inside her. The sensation of her wanting me has me seeing stars. I pump in and out, chasing the feeling of finally having her again—finally being in heaven.

"Oh god," she screams. Tears stream down her cheeks.

"It's all right, babe. Come for me. Give it all to me. I love you." She quickens her movements in time with mine, squeezing me until she can't take it anymore, and her walls pulse violently as she comes around my length. I don't let up. I continue pumping through her climax.

"Oh. Parker," she screams as I continue. I can't let up. I'm chasing my own release as I pump in and out faster and faster. I look down at Rain and see the second she begins to fall again, and this time, I push harder, deeper, filling her as we come crashing together.

"God, Rain," I growl, filling my woman with my seed, with my love, with all of me. This is where I want to be, finally home inside my love.

Chapter 45

Tick Tock

Raven

Five. One for each year, he had to go without me. That's how many times Parker came inside me. I didn't believe him when he said that's what he wanted for his birthday. He's never lied to me. However, in the back of my mind, I underestimated his sexual prowess to pull it off in the amount of time he did.

Sitting across the tub from me, Parker smirks.

"What are you thinking about, babe?" He squeezes my toes.

Steam from the water rises between us; it's hot, soothing the ache between my thighs. Sex with Parker was always amazing. The others since him...paled in comparison. However, Nik, as insatiable as he was, came close. It's even better than I imagined with Parker now that we're older and now that I can fully embrace the magnitude of his love.

"I'm sore." He raises an eyebrow. "In the best way, though. I missed you." I smile at him. He returns the smile.

"I missed you too, in case you couldn't tell."

"I think I'm pregnant now," I deadpan. He laughs. It bounces off the bathroom walls and is the most beautiful sound. Seeing him happy without the shadow of ambiguity about our relationship is wonderful.

"It's about ten thirty. After breakfast, we can try again to be sure," he says.

I flick water at him with my foot. He grabs both my ankles and pulls me to him until I'm straddling him.

"Now you're just trying to get fucked. I thought you were sore." He takes the cloth from the side of the tub, dips it into the water, and then washes the suds from my shoulder.

"I am." He raises an eyebrow. "Sore, that is." I press my lips to his. He cups my cheek and licks into me. It's needy and urgent. Everything about him feels so good, so right. I miss this part. I pull back, breathless.

He reaches between us and strokes my sex. Even with all the water, I know I'm wet for him. My walls immediately contract around his fingers when he inserts them into me. He massages me, and the soreness subsides. "I need you inside me," I whisper, lifting my body. He positions himself at my entrance, and I sink down on him. "Ahh." I cry. I can't help it. It feels so good as he fills me.

"You feel so amazing, babe." He pushes up into me, and I rock into him in time with his rhythm. We continue like that until waves of water slosh around us in sync with our bodies' movements. "Come for me, Rain. Come with me." He pushes up. I squeeze my walls around his length, and we repeat the motion until our movement becomes erratic as we chase our release.

"I'm coming," I call out. He swallows my groans with a kiss, and we suck and lick into each other, and together we climax, and it's perfect.

"Rain," he grunts.

***

I watch Parker eat breakfast beside me at the kitchen counter. I reach over and take a piece of bacon from his plate.

"You didn't want this, did you?" I ask, taking a bite. "I'm eating for two, you know."

He wipes his mouth with a napkin, turns to me, and smiles. "You're enjoying this, aren't you?"

"I'm enjoying you. Can't you tell? I can't get enough. Seriously, though. We should call your parents and let them know we're—."

"What, having sex? Getting married? Having a baby?"

"All of the above. Just joking, not the sex part, but we are trying to have a baby. You know your mom is going to want to arrange everything for the wedding, engagement dinner, all that. Oh, and we have to talk to my dad. This might come as a surprise."

"He won't be surprised."

"Why not?"

"I asked him for your hand in marriage."

"You did? When?"

"Before we flew to Seattle. The baby part might surprise him, but I need to get you pregnant first."

"I'm pretty sure I am. We never had sex this intense."

"It's love." When he says that, I go to him and stand between his legs. He dips his head and kisses me. It's soft and loving. When he breaks the kiss, he smiles against my lips. "You're right. Let's call Mom and tell her we want to get married soon. She'll be thrilled."

"Okay."

Parker takes out his phone, pulls up his mom's contact information, and video calls her. She answers immediately.

"Hey, Mom," he says, pulling my back to his chest so we're both in the video.

"Hi, Raven, Parker. How are you? Recovered from the party, it seems. You two are radiating." His mom confirms what I feel.

"Rain has something to tell you."

"Darling, what can I help you with?" I raise the back of my hand to the phone and show my rings. "Oh, honey. Oh my god. Preston, come here. Look at our kids." Janis positions her husband on the screen. He smiles when he sees the ring.

"Congratulations. Son, this is certainly good news. Raven, I couldn't be happier to have you as part of our family."

"Thanks, Mom and Dad. We're happy. But there's more."

"More perfect than you two getting married?" his dad asks.

"We want to get married soon, likely within the next month or so. Also, we plan to start a family right away. We're ready to begin our lives together."

"Oh, honey," Janis says, immediately going into planning mode. "Okay. I have to start organizing things right away. Raven, darling, we'll get together. You tell me what you want and I'll make it happen."

"Thank you, Mrs. Page. I promise to schedule time with you. We wanted to share the good news."

"Have you told your dad?" Mr. Page asks.

"Not yet. We'll call him next," I say.

"I'm sure he'll be equally pleased. Well, we won't hold you. Thank you for sharing such lovely news with us. Truly, we couldn't have asked for anything more except for a house full of grandkids. I'll let you get started with that," Mrs. Page says with a wink.

The call ends and Parker turns me toward him. He wipes the tears from my cheek that I didn't realize had fallen.

"You heard Mom, babe. She wants a house full of kids."

"We can have one for now until I get through this project, then afterward—."

Parker pulls me close and kisses my forehead. I listen as he takes deep breaths and inhales me. Locked in his embrace, I savor the feeling of his closeness. I think about how many times he's held me like this, and I couldn't fully absorb the depth of his love. I feel it now deep in my soul. His love is pure and uncomplicated. This is what I've been missing. I pull back, lock eyes with my man, and smile.

"Rain, honey. The babies will come when they're ready. Right now, I need to ensure the seeds are planted." He wiggles his eyebrows.

I laugh. "You're so cheeky."

"You love it. Let's call your dad."

I turn back around in Parker's arms as he gets my dad on video. I lean into Parker. He rests his chin on my shoulder and extends his arm, so we're both on screen. My dad answers right away—he always does—like he's going to miss more of my life if he doesn't. I feel the same way. We lost so much time over the years. I don't want to miss any more moments with him.

"Baby girl. Parker. What are you two up to this morning?" my dad greets us. Judging from the grass and flowers alongside a pool, it looks like he's sitting in his yard. Although I haven't been to his house yet, I know he lives in the suburbs on the Peninsula. Sometimes, during our calls, I get glimpses of his lifestyle, like now.

"First of all, sir, thank you for the birthday gift. You have great taste in whiskey."

"I hope you had a wonderful birthday, Parker."

"I did. It was better than I could have dreamed. That's why we're calling. Rain?"

On cue, I hold up my hand, revealing my rings.

"Wow. When you two celebrate, you do it big. Congratulations. Parker, I guess I should refer to you as son from now on. Welcome to the family, Son. I'm happy for you two."

"Thank you, sir. We're thrilled."

"Dad, I'm giving you a heads-up. We plan to start a family right away. I want to make sure you don't miss out on my children growing up, so you'll have grandparent duties." I smile, and he smiles too.

"Whatever you need. I'm here for it all. You two mean the world to me. Thank you for accepting me into your lives. You have no idea how wonderful this news is to me."

"I know, Dad."

"We know, sir."

My dad touches his face. I think he's crying. "Oh, my allergies." He feigns irritation.

"Uhm, as I recall…you don't have allergies."

"Nothing gets past you, does it, baby girl?"

"Not a thing. But it's okay. I cried, too. Well, Dad, I'll let you get back to relaxing. We're still on for lunch next week?"

"I'll never miss a date with my baby girl. You two enjoy the rest of your day. Thank you for the good news. I love you both."

"Love you too," we say in unison and end the call.

"Group text?" Parker asks.

"Sure." I hold out my hand to display my ring. Parker pulls up the group chat with Josh, Ethan, and me. He takes a picture of my hand and taps send. His phone immediately begins buzzing with responses.

Josh: I'll be over in an hour. Let's celebrate.

Ethan: Did someone say party again? See you soon.

I pull out my phone to add my response to the thread. Parker watches me curiously as I type.

Me: My man omitted the part where we're supposed to make babies effective immediately.

Parker barks out a laugh. "Rain, babe. These two are not the ones to tell all our business. Ugh, I'm gonna get so much flak from this." He dips his head and kisses me. Our phones ping with responses.

Josh: Tick tock. You have one hour. After I leave, you can resume activities. For now, we celebrate.

Ethan: Give her a break, man. Josh and I are on the way.

"I see what you were doing, Rain. You're trying to get fucked."

"Me? You suggested we message them. Hey, like the man says, we have one hour. I'll race ya," I say and run upstairs.

Chapter 46

To the Next Generation

Parker

We managed to fit in one orgasm and a shower before the doorbell started ringing. It hasn't stopped since, with deliveries of flowers, cards, fruit baskets, and all sorts of well wishes. The doorbell rings again.

"I'll get it," I call to Rain, who's in the closet. She emerges wearing a black tank top with red embellished lips, black ankle jeans, and those damn red pumps I love. "Nix the heels. Put on some flip-flops, or go barefoot, babe. We're not leaving the house."

"You have on shoes," she protests.

"You can wear whatever you want as long as they're flat. I'm in love and in baby-making mode. Just looking at you makes me hard, honey. Add heels, and you're just trying—."

"Parker Page, Esquire. I told you to stop saying that."

"Don't Parker me. Take them off, or call the guys and tell them to stay home." I walk over to Rain and kiss her. "Please, babe. Anything but heels, thank you."

She closes her eyes and shakes her head. "All right, I'll put on my flats."

"I'll get the door."

I go downstairs to answer the door. It's food delivery. The delivery person has two bags in his hand and two at his feet. I place them all inside the house.

"Perfect timing," Josh says, coming up from behind the delivery person. "Thank you," he tells the man. "Can't have a party without food. Oh, and drink." He holds up a bag and then steps inside. He and I bring all the bags to the kitchen.

"What's in all these?"

I begin removing containers from the bags and lining them up on the counter. Rain joins us.

"Hey, handsome," she greets Josh.

"Hey, wife-to-be. Congratulations. May I?" Rain nods, and Josh hugs her. "I'm so happy for you," he says. "And this guy. Congratulations, man." He pats me on the shoulder.

Rain reaches into one of the bags Josh brought in and takes out several bottles of champagne. She reads the label. "Josh, these vintages are older than me. You and Parker really go all out when it comes to alcohol."

"We're celebrating love and family. Only the best will do," he says.

My phone buzzes. I look at the message.

Ethan: Tina caught me coming out of the bakery. She'd already heard the news and sends congrats. I mentioned I was headed over. She wants to know if she can join us.

"Babe, it's Ethan." I look at Rain and hand her my phone.

She reads the message and looks at me, then Josh. He has no idea what's going on.

"Okay. I'm assuming this is my first test," she announces.

"Test for what? I can say no."

"Tina said she wanted to be friends and share a drink the last time we saw her. She even welcomed me to your social group. This is my first test. What would a natural-born elite do in this situation?"

She asks the question aloud, but she's not expecting an answer. She's trying to figure out how to manage her role. She looks at Josh again. The bond they've developed over the years is sacred and caring. During times when I couldn't be by her side, Josh stepped in and helped her navigate the complexities of our world and our relationship. In turn, she helped him uncomplicate areas of his life. I wouldn't be who I am today without either of them. He winks at her.

"Let me know how you want me to respond to Ethan," I tell her.

She inhales. "Tell him yes. She can come."

I text a message to Ethan. His response is immediate.

Ethan: Done.

Rain's phone buzzes. She slides it from her pocket, reads the screen, and shows me.

Tina: Thank you.

It doesn't take long for Ethan and Tina to arrive. They were both in the vicinity. Ethan brings cake, and Tina comes with gifts and flowers. The house looks and smells like a florist, with arrangements of various sizes and colors lining the counters and buffet.

Tina pulls Rain into a hug. "Congratulations. This is wonderful news," she tells her. Rain doesn't quite lean fully into the hug, suggesting she's still slightly leery about Tina.

"Thank you."

"Raven, come here." Ethan opens his arms. Rain hugs him. "There's no turning back from here, little lady. You were one of us before. This makes it official."

"Thank you, Ethan." Rain returns to me, and I pull her to my side.

Josh opens a bottle of champagne and pours everyone a glass.

"Okay, everyone, raise your glass," he says, gesturing, and we all lift our glasses. "Parker, you've been like a brother to me for my entire life. Then, in college, you introduced me to a woman who became the sister I didn't know I needed, Raven. Raven, the first time I met you, I knew you were born to be among us. Your beauty, kindness, and grace are unmatched. With your guidance, you've helped me in ways I don't think you understand. I will be forever indebted to you for saving my crazy brother Parker from a life alone." We all laugh. "All jokes aside. As an only child, I never felt alone because throughout stages of my life I had you, Parker, Ethan, Tina, and Raven. Together, we stand strong as the next generation. We will never be alone because we have each other. And now, these two powerful people merge as one to build the future generation. Raven, Parker, those of us in this room vow to love and protect the children from your union. In this lifetime—they will want for nothing. We celebrate you and our future generation."

"To our future," Tina says.

"To the future," Ethan chimes in.

We tap our glasses together. I bend and kiss Rain. Everyone comes to us, and one by one, they hug us. Afterward, we all help ourselves to a plate of food and chat about how soon we think the wedding will be. Tina walks Rain through how weddings work within our world. There are no bachelorette or bachelor parties. Our group is tight-knit, so it's rare for outsiders to get a glimpse inside.

"So, are any initial celebrations kind of like this, just members of your inner circle?"

"That's right, but you can invite whomever you want to the wedding."

"Within reason," Rain clarifies.

"That's right."

"It makes sense. What's this?" Rain picks up one of the blue boxes Tina brought with her.

"Open it."

Rain opens one of the blue boxes. It contains a platinum spoon for a baby. She looks surprised.

"I never knew this was a real thing."

"I heard you want children right away. This is my contribution to sending signals to the universe. In our world, this is a real thing." Tina smiles. Rain reciprocates. It's good to see them working on their relationship. Josh was right. There's only a few of us. It's important we stick together.

"It's beautiful. Thank you. But just so you know, our children will work just as hard as we all do."

Ethan pats me on the shoulder. "Man, how's that coming along?" he teases.

"Give him a minute. He's just getting started," Josh chimes in.

"As I recall, Rain alerted you that we were *busy* working on that. Anyway, what's in this?" I ask, picking up a box and changing the subject. I open it. "Is this what I think it is?"

"It looks like it's for blowing bubbles," Rain says.

"It is," Tina interjects. "The baby has to have some fun."

"Okay, everyone. Thank you for celebrating Parker, me, and our future baby. We appreciate the sentiments, but we have to make one first."

"There's already a bun in the oven," Tina blurts out confidently.

"What are you talking about?" I ask.

"Look at her. Come on, guys. Tell me Raven isn't radiant like she's carrying our future generation."

"What she said," Ethan agrees.

"She's glowing. I'm going with the platinum spoon," Josh adds.

Rain shakes her head. "In that case. No more champagne for me."

"I haven't seen you take a sip," I say.

Rain touches her stomach and says, "Well, there you go. My body must know something I don't."

I look at Rain. All my life, I've only wanted what my parents had: love and family. Looking around the room at my friends and my future wife, I have exactly that. Rain smiles at me. She does look different; it's like part of me *is* growing within her. It's a beautiful thought that soon we'll be three.

Chapter 47

She Cast a Spell on Me

Noah

The gallery is already full of people—women in heels wearing couture outfits and men in fine-tailored suits—when the four of us arrive. It's not surprising since Rose Ross is one of the most admired CEOs in the country, and rightfully so. She took over the company from her father this year, rebranded it, and launched a new product estimated to generate billions of dollars. Our deal to head up their expansion has also helped Knight Development Corporation increase our revenue. I have one woman to thank for ensuring that the deal ran smoothly...Rain.

"Champagne?" A staff member walking with a tray of champagne glasses hands onc to Mclanic, Mak's datc. Shc takcs it, and then we each take one—Rok, Mak, and me.

"You think she'll be here?" Melanie asks Mak, whose arm is around her waist.

It's good to see him with a woman for once who's accomplished in her own right and not looking for someone with deep pockets. Rain knew what she was doing that night when she picked Melanie out of the crowd and introduced her to Mak. I hope Casanova doesn't do her like the rest and develops commitment issues when it gets too deep. That's usually when he runs, which is why we call him Casanova. He loves them and leaves them.

Somehow, I think what he has with Melanie is different. He seems genuinely invested in making her happy. He's still as confident as ever, but she keeps him on his toes, which no other woman has been able to do. That's how I felt about Rain—she cast a beautiful spell on me. One I'm not sure I can break.

"Yes, beautiful. I'm sure she'll be here," he assures her. Although I don't know how he's so sure. One thing I learned about Mak is that he's not only brilliant but also highly perceptive.

I'd been wondering when I would see Rain again in person. Our meetings over video or faceless conference calls only fuel my desire for her.

"We should mingle. There are some people I need to reconnect with," Rok says.

"Melanie, let's preview the art. We'll catch up with you two in a bit," Mak says, leading Melanie into the crowd.

Rok and I walk along the perimeter of bright white walls displaying vivid paintings.

"We should say hello to Rose. I expect there's already a crowd vying for her attention," Rok says.

"If my memory serves me correctly, she'd be in one of the rooms furthest from the door. She should be easy to spot with her centurion nearby. But you'll have no problem getting her attention," I tell my brother. Because he won't, he's the CEO of KDC, and our company is managing a multi-million-dollar, multi-year project for her company. She knows exactly who he is.

"Melanie seems excited about seeing Rae again. You sure you can handle all this?"

"I'm good. We're colleagues, remember. Our meetings have been going smoothly. She signed off on the new contracts with our third-party vendors."

"I'm not talking about that. I need you to have your emotions in check."

"They're checked," I say.

I lift my chin toward the beautiful woman with red lips in a black silk slip dress with her back to a black and white abstract painting. To her right is the tall Irishman I've seen her with previously. On her left, scanning the crowd is her bodyguard, who rarely leaves her side. There's no doubt in a room full of people, she's the main attraction. She's spectacular. She smiles graciously as people walk up to greet her and say whatever pleasantries one says to a woman like her. We head toward her. She spots us and smiles.

My brother steps close, extending his hand, which she shakes.

"Ms. Ross. Congratulations on another successful event."

"Roman. Thank you and your family for your generous contributions." My brother steps aside, and I extend my hand to her. "Noah, it's good to see you. My cousin has only good things to say about your work. Thank you for everything. June won't be here tonight, but I hope that won't stop you from enjoying the art."

"It's fine. I'm sure I'll see June soon enough."

"Let me introduce you to Niall, my fiancé. Niall, these are the Knight brothers who work with June. This is Roman, the CEO, and his brother Noah is the president of capital markets."

"I'm familiar with them. It's good to formally meet you. As you get closer to build-out, you'll have the opportunity to meet with my team members," he asserts, shaking my hand.

"His company manages security for our executive team," Rose says.

"We look forward to working with you," Rok says.

We briefly discuss the exhibition and next steps for the artists. Her commitment to youth in the San Francisco community is deep-rooted, on par with ours in Seattle. Rose's attention is diverted when her security guard takes one step forward. She looks at him. They share what looks like a secret code, a subtle gesture you had to be paying attention to catch. Her eyes shift over my shoulder. She smiles, and it's different than the one she gave us. Her eyes light up—this is personal, familiar. She is genuinely happy to see whoever has captured her attention. Curious, I turn. Other patrons milling around looking at the art and chatting are now watching as a couple enters. Then I see her...Rain.

She looks like a princess wearing a flowing black taffeta skirt that cinches at her tiny waist. The skirt barely sweeps the floor as she walks. My breath hitches seeing the smooth brown patch of skin exposed down her chest that I used to kiss. Her top is a white silk three-quarter sleeve shirt, which is open from her neck to just above her navel, where it tucks into her skirt. I want to trace my lips down that patch of skin again. Like Rose, she's wearing bright red lipstick. Watching her, I remember every touch, every kiss, and my body hardens thinking about it. She looks beautiful as she walks toward us, one hand in her skirt pocket and the other laced with...Parker's.

Chapter 48

Art and Other Conversations

Raven

The past few days feel like they've flown by. I'm working on multiple projects along with my volunteer work. But Parker and I are committed to dedicating time to building a strong relationship. We continue to attend therapy together, and when my fight or flight kicks in, which is rare nowadays, we talk things through. Rather, Parker says we'll fuck it out, then talk it out. It sounds weird, but it works for us. The important thing is we spend quality time together. That includes having date nights even though we decided that we would never live apart from now on. Which house we stay at overnight depends on our mood. However, we will eventually establish Parker's house as our full-time residence.

"Did you hear what I said? I'm worried about tonight," I tell Parker. His head is buried in the side of my neck while his hand is inside my silk shirt, cupping my bare breast. I knew I should have worn something else. Ever since I told him my boobs felt tender, he's been more than ready to oblige by massaging them. Of course, it's also a prelude to sex, so he's getting half the benefits. "Parker, we're almost there. You're insatiable."

"This is what happens when I don't get to have you before I leave the house. I told you not to wear the red heels."

"They match my lipstick."

"That's another thing. I can't kiss you in that stuff. So, I have to kiss you somewhere."

"Well, you get to have all of me following the event. Let me fix my shirt."

Parker sits up and removes his hand. He cups my face and kisses my cheek. "I told you this morning your boobs are sore because you're pregnant. Either way, you're getting it tonight so I can be sure. Now tell me what you're worried about." I shake my head at his response. I love this man.

"The Knight brothers will all be there. I haven't seen them all since...Seattle."

"Why does that bother you? They're your colleagues."

"The last time we were all together before the meeting was at a party. I felt like I got closer to them."

"We talked about this—set parameters. Your friendships don't have to end. You said they're good people. They'll likely have the same concerns about you. Except...Noah. I need to know if you need me to handle him."

"You're right. They're probably thinking the same thing. I promise I'll take care of Noah."

The car stops in front of the gallery. The driver rounds the car and opens the door near Parker.

"Are my boobs showing?"

"No, babe. You look perfect." He steps out of the car and then helps me.

He's so fine. It was hard not to give in to him before we left. I want him as much as he wants me. We have made love every day since his birthday. There's no way I'm not pregnant. Parker is so serious about having a child that he won't let me put my mouth on him. He said every seed is reserved for making our child. I cried when he told me, remembering how broken he was when we lost our baby years ago. We're doing this. We're ready.

I exit the car. Through the wall of windows, I can see the exhibition is full. Rose curates the best art shows, so she's sure to bring in a lot of donations. Her programming is phenomenal. My friend Jade and I volunteer to teach the students art classes regularly. It'll be exciting to see their work on display.

"Ready, babe?"

"Yes."

"Niall said they'll be in the back."

"Is that part of their security protocol?"

"It is. There may be times when we have to do the same, but I'll always let you know in advance. Tonight, people will be focused on Rose."

"I can't wait to see her. Her travel schedule has been insane lately," I tell him, holding his hand as we walk in.

When we began dating in college, Parker explained that he and his family wore trackers for security reasons. There were other reasons he couldn't go into. Technically, as his girlfriend, I should have been wearing one, too, but I resisted. However, I promised to always share my location with him. Parker programmed his GPS location to my phone, so I've always had access to his location. Soon, I'll have my own security detail provided by King Enterprise.

Stepping into his world, I've had to adjust to a new way of existing. The people, protocol, events—it was a lot to adapt to. He also told me that there would be times when we walk into a room and all eyes would be on us. That even though they don't know us—they know something is different. This is that moment.

Parker squeezes my hand. He's used to this. Although I've been through similar events, it always feels new, so I take his lead because it's become my life, too. These people have come to see a magnificent display of art and one of the most celebrated CEOs, and yet they're also curious about us. I smile at the patrons as we pass them. They may not be elites, but they have money; the minimum donation for this event was one million dollars.

"I see them," Parker says, leading us further into the gallery.

The crowd parts, and then I see Rose. She's smiling. I love this woman. She's so fun and smart and generous. Sometimes, if she's at the gallery when I'm volunteering, after the students leave, she, Jade, and I have a painting competition. We all write three subjects individually on a piece of paper. We put the nine pieces of paper in a bowl, and then one of us reaches in and picks one. We have twenty minutes to paint the scene. It's always a toss-up who wins. It's a way for us to relax, be creative, and have fun. I smile at the thought. As we near, my heart stops. Standing next to Rose are Rok and Nik.

Rose steps away from the painting and opens her arms. I let go of Parker's hand and embrace my friend.

"Raven, oh my god, you look amazing." She puts her lips to my ear and whispers, "I want to know everything about what you and Parker have been up to. We'll have you over before Niall and I leave for Belfast."

I kiss her cheek. "Of course."

I step back in time to see Parker in a man hug with Niall. Then we switch. Niall gives me a hug, and Parker hugs Rose.

"Troy, good to see you again, man." Troy and Parker bump fists. I smile up at Troy. How else am I supposed to address the striking six-foot-five man of steel guarding my friend?

"I was just telling your colleagues here that June is pleased with the project status." Rose tips her head toward Nik and Rok. I turn and greet them.

"Roman. It's so good to see you again." I extend a hand to Rok.

"You can call me Rok. It's always good to see you. We've missed you in Seattle," he says earnestly. "But we're glad to be on the same team."

"Noah. How are you?" I extend a hand to him. He shakes it, but I don't feel the same kinetic energy I feel whenever I touch Parker.

"Raven." His voice is powerful yet seductive. He's still struggling to rein in his emotions from our time together. I, on the other hand, have no option but to remember. "Always great to see you. You look lovely."

"Thank you." I look at Rok. "Roman, I don't believe you've met Parker. Parker, this is Roman Knight. And you've met Noah."

"Mr. Knight." Parker extends a hand to Rok. "Congratulations are in order. Knight Development has acquired a significant share of commercial development space. You're edging up on the competition."

"You seem to know a lot about my industry," Rok says.

"I have a vested interest," Parker says. I'm clueless as to where this conversation is headed, but I hope it remains amiable.

The soft sound of a woman's voice I haven't heard in three months says, "She's here."

Melanie.

I touch Rose's hand. "Give me a second."

"No problem."

I turn around. "Melanie. You look beautiful. And I see you have Mr. Knight on your arm."

"Can I call you Rae? We didn't get to talk much that night. But I want to thank you for introducing me to your brother Mak." I glance up at Parker, whose eyebrows are raised.

"Technically, he's not my brother, but you're welcome. You can call me Rae. I hope you two are doing well."

"I'm just going to say it. Sis. I'm doing great," Mak interjects and hugs me. "Thank you for finding this lovely lady for me."

"You're welcome."

Melanie looks toward Parker. I extend my hand. Parker fills it with his. "Melanie, Mark, this is Parker Page."

"Good to meet you, Parker," Mak greets him, masking any feeling he may have of seeing me with a man other than his brother. This is the hard part. Landing the Ross deal also changes the dynamics of my relationship with the brothers. They're part of Nik's package, just like Parker's part of mine.

"Nice to meet you," Melanie says.

"Everyone, it's great to see you again. But, if you'll excuse us a moment, I want to finish up with Rose before she leaves," I tell them all. They say their final words and then disperse. Rok places a hand on Nik's shoulder as they walk off. I know he's making him leave because Nik rarely leaves my side if we're in the same building.

I turn to Rose, who's conversing with her fiancé.

"Niall, I told Raven we have to get together before we fly out."

"How long are you here until?" Parker asks.

"Two days, then we head back to Ireland," Niall chimes in.

"We can make it work," I tell them.

"Mate. Are they going to be an issue?" Niall addresses Parker. His tone and a slight lift of his chin indicate he's referring to the brothers, making me wonder about their previous discussions. Why would they be an issue? Or is Noah the issue? Unlike his brothers, Noah looked dejected seeing me with Parker. It quickly became apparent in Seattle that he doesn't mask his feelings around me. I need to talk to him, but tonight is not the time. Tonight is about Rose and the Foundation.

"Everything's under control," Parker says.

"Brilliant. Let me know when you want me to restructure your team."

"Is that code word for putting together my security?" I narrow my eyes at Niall.

"I figured if you're like this one, you don't want to get involved in the details." He laces his fingers with Rose's.

Rose nods. "Let these guys handle it. We can use our brain power on something else. So, are we getting together?" she asks.

"Absolutely."

More patrons descend on Rose, competing for her attention. I hug her and Niall, then step aside, providing other patrons the opportunity to talk with her. Parker and I wander around the exhibition, looking at art. A gentleman I've never met recognizes Parker and comes to speak with him.

"Mr. Stein, good to see you again. This is Raven Nichols, Esquire."

"Good to meet you, Ms. Nichols," he greets me before carrying on with Parker. From their conversation, I gather he's someone Parker's worked with before since they discuss an old legal case.

"I need to step away for a second," I tell Parker. He kisses my cheek before I head to the restroom.

Once in the restroom, I look in the mirror. I just need to breathe. Being on constantly, combined with the pressure of seeing the Knight brothers, is a lot to deal with. Why does this have to be so complicated? This could be much easier if Nik agreed to work on our friendship. But with him, it's always all or nothing. Parker told me that I had already put in the time to get myself together and that others, including him, needed to earn a place in my life. Parker, my dad, and other elites have earned their spot. Nik hasn't. He needs to get himself together and work through whatever he needs to accept what I'm offering. We had our week. Beyond that, I don't owe him anything.

I close my eyes. So much has happened in my life. I've joined Parker's inner circle. Soon, I'll be Raven Page, Esquire. Regardless of my title, I have a critical position within society and my community. I open my eyes and head back to Parker.

"You have a minute?" I feel his hand latch onto mine before I see him.

"What are you doing, Noah? I need to get back," I say, feeling overly irritated at the intrusion. I need to dial myself back. Nik is not here to hurt me—he's working through his feelings.

"I didn't know you knew Rose that well."

"She's a friend."

"You have very powerful friends. I'm constantly learning new things about you." I pull my hand away from his. Briefly, he looks down to where they were joined. "There was a time you craved my touch."

"What's your point, Noah? We discussed this. You need to move on. I don't belong to you. I told you what the deal was." I hate that I have to be this way with him. But I need to stand my ground. He can't just claim me like I'm some possession.

"The deal is friends and colleagues or nothing. It's not enough. I want you completely."

"You—."

"I know, Rain. I can't have you. And I know you don't want me to call you Rain."

"Then don't, please."

"I can't help it. I miss everything about you. I'm not ready to move on." I hear the pain in his voice. He's staring at me so intensely. How do I get him to understand my position? To move on. I look over his shoulder and then back at him.

"We made a deal. One week. No strings. No names. No feelings. You promised not to come to claim me like you're my man, Noah."

"I remember."

"Then you know how this works. Your word is your worth. You say I have a lot of powerful friends. Noah, you are among the most powerful dealmakers I've met."

"It turns out you were better." I'm stunned, silent by his confession. He can't move on. He's breaking the deal.

I inhale and say, "Don't do this, Noah. No one can walk away better than me. When I leave, you end up with nothing. Don't make me do that."

"What do you suggest?"

"Take the deal. Be my friend. Move on. Go to therapy. Do whatever it takes to get over this...whatever you're feeling. I did."

"You say that like it's so easy."

I exhale. "It's not. It took me years to get to this point. However, in the process, I almost lost the love of my life because I was so stubborn, like you."

"What are you saying? You two are dating now?"

"No, Noah. That's not at all what I'm saying." I hold out my hand. Parker, who's been leaning against the wall watching the conversation unfold, walks over to me and laces his fingers in mine. "I'm marrying Parker." He lifts my fingers to his lips and kisses them.

"Hey, are you ready to go?" Parker asks. His tone is soft and low, immediately diffusing the angst I felt during the discussion with Noah.

"I'm ready."

Chapter 49

Protect Her

Parker

Rain and I kept our goodbyes brief as we left the exhibition. Usually following events, when we get in the car, she's full of chatter, rehashing conversations of the night and talking about how much fun she's had. Not tonight. Her head is on my shoulder, hand laced with mine, while she stares ahead into the dark vehicle.

"You okay?" She nods against me.

I squeeze her hand. To say watching her interact with Noah while holding my peace was difficult is an understatement. Not because I didn't think she could handle herself, but because it's hard to rein in my desire to protect her. She told me she'd handle him. She did. The poise with which she drove her point home was on target. Noah has a reputation he flaunts proudly as a man who negotiates multi-million-dollar deals for breakfast. She had to bring him back to that—to remind him of the person he initially revealed himself to be.

Our ride home is short. Inside, I hang Rain's coat in the foyer closet, grab a few water bottles from the refrigerator, and head upstairs. It's been a long day, and she still hasn't spoken since we left the venue. I follow Rain into the closet.

"Shower?" I ask, unzipping her skirt.

"Sure."

I undress, start the shower, and step in while Rain preps her hair. I like it when she allows it to get wet and it hangs down her back. Tonight, she has her shower cap on when she enters the shower. I step away from the water, allowing it to spray her skin. I fill my hands with her favorite bath soap and wash her shoulders and back. When she turns to face me, I wash her breasts and stomach. When we were in university, I learned that Rain loved when I bathed her. She said when I gently washed between her legs, it felt so sensual it made her come. I turn her so her back is to my front and let water flow over us both. It's warm. Having her near feels so right. She takes my hand and lowers it past her stomach. I know what she wants—to feel my touch washing her. Nothing more. Nothing less. Closeness.

When we're done and dry, Rain slips into a t-shirt, and I put on silk pajama bottoms. We don't go to bed. Sensing she wants to talk, I take Rain's hand and lead her to the couch near the window in our bedroom. I sit, and she sits astride me, knees on the couch, hips on my lap.

"Tonight was difficult." She places her hands on my forearms and strokes down them as she talks.

"Speaking the truth to people you care about usually is. You did great."

"Would you have done anything different?"

"You mean besides punching him in the nose?" I say with a grin.

She smiles. It's good to see her somber mood lift. "Parker," she chastises.

"No, babe. I wouldn't have done anything different if I were in your shoes."

"He may have been slightly stunned that you were nearby and he didn't know it."

"It served him right to corner you away from me. He needed to learn a lesson. How do you feel it went?"

"It felt like I was rehashing our previous conversation, but I needed to find a way to get through to him. To get him to see that what we had wasn't real."

"But it felt real to you."

"It didn't feel like us." She leans against me, pressing her chest to mine, and hugs me. I wrap my arms around her and squeeze.

"Because we were always meant to be," I whisper in her ear.

Rain sits back in my arms.

"It feels like my life over these past few months has been a culmination of difficult conversations."

"Ours wasn't difficult."

"No. Our baby-making conversation was easy. That was the best part. I'm talking about everything else. This stuff with Noah. And I still have to go with my sister tomorrow so she can confront Mom."

"Do you want me there?"

"I've been debating it. At a minimum, can you be nearby?"

"You don't have to ask. That's a given."

"I figured as much. You've been watching me like a hawk lately. No, that's the wrong word; it's more like treating me like fine China, as if I might break if you're not there."

"Because you're carrying my baby, Rain." Her eyes widen. I cup her chin and dust my lips against hers. I love this woman.

"It's only been a week. How do you know? Why did you say that?"

"Because it's true. You got pregnant on our first night together, just like you said. You thought you were joking."

"How do you know Parker? Is it because of my sore breasts?"

"Partially, but I've been seeing signs throughout the week."

"Signs like what?"

"When I sat in the tub the next morning watching you...you looked different. I remember how you looked the first time."

"When we were pregnant in college?"

"You glow. Your mannerisms are different. You respond to me differently. You get fiercely independent. You did back then. You're doing it now. And that's okay. But it also triggers my need to protect my family. I recognize the signs I missed before. I'm in love with you, Rain. We're getting married. You don't get to push me away this time."

Rain leans in and kisses me. It's sweet and gentle.

"Never. I'm all in. Is that why you came and found me tonight? To protect me? To protect what we have?"

"I will, tonight and every night from now on, you and our child." I touch her stomach. "You are my world, and I'll do everything within my power to protect you both. So, get used to me being around. If I have to take a break from the law to cater to you two, I'll do it."

"We can't get confirmation until after next week," she says.

"Then we'll get it then. The doctor will confirm what our hearts already know. And get ready, babe. You'll have regular doctor visits, and I'll be with you for each one."

"Does that mean you're not in baby-making mode?"

"I'll always be in baby-making mode."

I reach beneath her t-shirt and cup her breast. Her nipples harden in my hand. I lift her shirt over her head and toss it aside. I put my mouth on one breast and suck and lick, then move to the other and repeat. She feels so good. I reach my hand between her folds and stroke her sex. She's so wet.

"Lift up," I tell her. She lifts. I free my raging shaft and slide it along her entrance, coating myself. I position it, and she sinks down on me, and it feels so good. Her body sucks me in.

"Fuck. Babe."

"I know, it feels so good." She groans as our bodies move in a steady rhythm. Rain places a hand behind her on my knee and rocks her body against me. It's not enough. I stand, bring her with me, and lay her on the bed. I continue moving in and out of her. I feel her body contract, and I know she's close.

"Come for me, Rain. I'll be there with you." I cover her mouth with mine and suck and lick into it. It's wet. Sloppy. My thrust becomes more urgent as I chase my release. "Now, babe." I groan, and Rain comes around my dick, and I can't hold back and fill her with my love.

"Rain," I grunt, releasing streams of me into her body.

"Parker." She cries in pleasure.

"I know, babe." I roll on my back, pulling her over me. She is so full of my seed that it seeps out between us. But I don't care. This is love. This is us. This is our time—the fall of us.

Chapter 50

Witness Stand

Raven

My sister flew in late last night. Instead of staying at my mom's, where she typically does when in town, she opted for a hotel. I told her she could stay at my house or with me and Parker, but she refused. I think she needs time alone to get ready to face Mom.

I wait with Parker in the car until my sister arrives. This is not my battle to fight, but I'll support her through her journey. I don't want anything else to do with my mom. What she did was deplorable and almost ruined us all. Thank goodness Parker helped me find my dad, or I'd still be a hot mess.

"There she is." I squeeze Parker's hand. I'm nervous. I don't know what Parker feels, but I'm sure he can sense my nervous energy.

"The second you need me, let me know. I'll be here. You sure you don't want me to go in?"

"I promise I'll be okay. Robin is leading this discussion."

Parker helps me out of the car as my sister exits her car service. He kisses me briefly, then waves to my sister. I meet her on the doorstep. She rings the bell. We wait a few seconds. Bill answers the door, which is unusual because he never answers. My mom is already running from her lies.

"Hi, Bill," my sister says.

"Robin. Good to see you. Raven."

"Hi, Bill."

He steps aside. When I go in this time, I don't go to the kitchen. I don't help myself to water. I wait to see where Bill directs us.

"Have a seat." He gestures to the living room. "Your mom will be out in a second. I'll be in the back if you need me."

What the hell? This man, supposedly our father, although he's not mine, avoids us like bill collectors. *This is not my battle.* I repeat in my head. I catch Robin's gaze and raise my eyebrows in a "Are you going to say something?" look. I sit on an occasional chair close to the exit. Robin sits in the chair across from me, nearest the couch.

"Uh, Bill, you should stay. I have a question for you."

"Sure," he says nonchalantly, making me wonder whether he understands our intent in being here.

My mom appears behind him. "You two together. This must be serious. If you're coming to discuss who I think you are, you should leave now."

"You should sit. We're not going anywhere," Robin directs. The second they sit, she dives in: "I'm sure you both know by now about Rhett."

"Your sister said she planned to meet with him. That's all I know," Mom says. Bill raises an eyebrow.

"More than just meetings happened. We uncovered your secret." She surprises me by taking a page from my book and cutting straight to the chase. "You told him we weren't his children, then threatened to have him arrested for unmentionable things that weren't true. You did all that so you could be with this man." Robin points at Bill.

Bill looks at Mom, and I'm stunned he seems surprised. Oh my god. He doesn't know the whole story. Discreetly, I retrieve my phone. I type a text message to Parker.

Me: Bill doesn't know about the threat.

I hit send.

My mom looks agitated when she says, "You don't know what you're talking about."

"I beg to differ. We got the story straight from the man you told it to almost twenty years ago. You remember, your former husband?" Robin says.

"What is she talking about, Bernadette?" Bill asks.

"You should ask her," she redirects to Robin.

"This isn't my story to tell, but since you're still feigning ignorance, I'll spill the beans. Bill, she wanted to be with you so bad that she made up a lie that she thought was foolproof. She was wrong. We all took DNA tests. By we, I mean my sister and me and the man I thought was my father. Turns out he's not my father. Seems you're my daddy. Or is he, Mom? Is Bill my father, or did you have more than one man on the side? Because that's what you were, Bill, a side piece while she was married to our dad—the man who raised me. So, what's the real story, Mom? Who exactly is my father?"

"Answer her," Bill commands. He is fuming. I'm rarely around him, so I don't know how he behaves when mad.

I look at each of them, observing their body language. Mom is nervously biting her cheek, and Bill is on edge, glaring at Mom. My sister's knee is bouncing, anxiously waiting for a response. This is pathetic. I shouldn't be here. My mom is so stubborn. It's clear whose DNA I got that trait from. My mom stares blankly at Bill.

"Answer her," he screams. I jerk my head back, surprised by his sudden aggression.

I text Parker.

Me: He's livid.

Seconds later, the doorbell rings. I already know who it is. He doesn't wait for a response, not when it comes to my safety. The door flies open. Parker fills the doorframe.

"Parker?" my mom says in surprise.

"Bernadette, for Christ's sake, answer me," Bill yells, ignoring Parker's presence.

Parker holds a hand out. I go to him, and he positions me behind him.

"You need to calm down, sir," Parker says authoritatively. I've heard him speak this way in court. This is his *I'm not taking any prisoners when this is over* voice.

"I found out the woman I'm with threatened another man falsely and that potentially she had *my* baby. I want answers. You can leave," Bill strikes back. Wrong response. Parker steps forward.

"I will when Rain and Robin are ready. Robin, do you have what you need from these people?" He looks down at her.

"Mom, answer the question. Is Bill my biological father?" she presses.

My mom wrings her fingers, still defiant.

"Ma'am, you can answer the question or not. This is none of my business. But if you decide not to, I'll make it my business since my lady insists on staying here to support her sister. Once it becomes my business, it stops there. Both you and Bill lose the opportunity to control this narrative."

He looks at my mom like he's staring down a witness on the stand. This is the version of Parker that people should fear. This is the calm before the storm, the second before the point of no return. When he involves himself in a matter, the impact is irreversible. He can blow their lives up in ways they haven't imagined. As it stands now, I'm the one standing in the way of him taking action on what she did to my father and, subsequently, my life. She looks at me, then back to Parker. I see the moment in my mom's eyes when it registers—he means business.

"Bill is your father," she confesses.

My sister's eyes shut. Her hands grip the side of the chair. Bill pops up from his seat. I try to go to my sister but can't get past Parker.

"Parker," I whisper.

"No. We're leaving. This is done."

"Robin?" I call to her.

"I'm okay. Let's go."

Parker turns to face me. He places his hand in mine and walks me out the door. I'm surprised to see two tall men in black suits on either side of the door as we exit. He waits for Robin to exit. I turn and see the men go inside. Our driver stands by the car, waiting for us. Parker continues walking. I tug his hand.

"Who are those people, Parker? What's happening? What are they doing?"

Parker pauses. He looks at me. "They're there to ensure your mom is okay. They won't leave until they fully assess the situation and determine she's safe. It's time to go, babe." He walks me to the car. We all get in.

"We'll drop you off," he tells Robin.

Parker holds my hand the entire ride. The car is quiet until we reach the hotel.

"Thank you, both," Robin says when the car stops.

"Did you want to get dinner later?"

"No. I'm flying out tonight. I only came here for that. Whatever *that* was."

"Are you going to talk to Bill?" I ask.

"He needs to reach out to me. It seems he has more issues to deal with than learning about me."

"Let us know if you need anything," Parker says. The driver opens the door for Robin. We say our goodbyes; Robin gets out and disappears into the hotel.

Chapter 51
Family

Parker

It's been years since I felt like I was firing on all cylinders, but I feel that way now. A large piece of my world was missing without Rain, but now she's back, filling the gaping hole in my life formerly the size of the Grand Canyon. With her, I'm whole. Waking up each morning with her by my side, knowing that soon she'll be my wife, is my dream. It's so close.

The soft touch of Rain's fingers tracing my abs signals she's awake, counting my breaths. I open my eyes and look down at my woman—her body half on me and half on the bed.

"Hey, how are you feeling?" I ask.

It's been over a month since she's had a sleep terror. Confronting her family issues and attending therapy have worked wonders. I hope our being a couple again also contributed to her healing. I feel the weight of angst gone, knowing we're together. I stroke her back.

"Good."

"No nightmares?"

"Not for a while."

I turn to face her. "That's good to hear. You've been doing so well, hon."

"Everything between us feels right."

"I love you," I tell her. Rain lifts her head and bites my lip. "Hey, what was that for?"

"You better love me. I'm supposed to be having your baby." She's right. This woman and I plan to build a family together. I've been holding on to this dream for so long that I don't know what to do. I kiss Rain. She opens her mouth, and I devour her. My dick rises against her. I reach between us and lift her leg over my body. I take my raging shaft and move it along the slickness between her legs. She's ready. I roll her on her back and push in, filling her full. She moans in pleasure.

"Parker. You feel so good."

"So do you." I move in and out of her with urgent, needy thrusts, trying to quench my desire for her. She matches each thrust, clenching her walls against my length. She's about to come, and her movements signal she wants me to join her. Quickening my pace, I give in to the chase. "Come for me, babe." I push in again, and her walls contract around me faster and faster until she comes on me, milking me and releasing my climax. "Fuck, Rain, God." I explode, spilling into her in waves. I kiss her. It's urgent and wet—all the things it should be. "Ahh." My breathing is hard and unsteady. I roll on my back, bringing her with me.

"God, that was amazing. I can do this all day." She half laughs, trying to catch her breath.

"I don't know what we were thinking all those years. I swear I'm going have sex with you every day to make up for lost time."

"Are you saying I'm going to spend my life pregnant?"

"Whatever it takes. You feel amazing. But we need to get ready. We have a call with the doctor in a few hours to get our results. Are you excited?"

"I am."

"Does it bother you that we started trying before we get married?"

"No. Why would it? I've known you almost all my life. We took twelve years to discover who we were together, separately, and now this...." She kisses me gently. "We've proven that no matter what, we're destined to be together forever. Deep down in my heart, I wanted to try again after the last..."

"You don't have to say it. I know, hon."

"I need to say this." I nod. "Something inside me wanted to have your child—to try again, but I was so messed up back then. I didn't think I had the tools to provide a child with a better life than I had. I didn't know how to receive all the love you showed me when we were younger. As we got older, I didn't know how to forgive myself for how I responded to you. I didn't know how to love unconditionally. At least, I was afraid to. Now, the time is right. I'm ready. I know I'm worthy."

"You were always worthy."

"I was a hot mess back then. But now I'm a sticky mess. We should shower," she says. I pull her up my body. Evidence of my love spills from her, coating us both. I kiss her while lowering my hand between us. I stroke her sex. She groans into my mouth. I feel her body pulsing around my fingers.

"That's it, honey, feel me in you. Squeeze." Her walls grip my fingers inside her, and I feel more evidence of my love leave her body. She's ready again. I roll her on her back and, in one quick motion, slide my length into her. I push.

"Ahh." I love it when she falls apart beneath me. Her mouth falls open. I lick her lips.

She's so moist from our previous releases that I move easily in and out. Faster and faster, I pump. Harder and harder. "Rain. I'm coming." I continue pumping, chasing the sensation, and I feel her body pulse violently around me.

"Me too," she cries. I bury my head in her neck, pumping once more, and come inside her...again.

"Babe," I grunt before collapsing on her. "I love you."

***

Rain and I finally made it to a well-deserved shower before having breakfast. Our daily routine is similar to what it was in the past but with the addition of plenty of sex at night and in the morning. I think she finally understands that I'm serious about making up for lost time. It's the weekend. Rain and I alternate weeks to spend time in the community or fundraising for charity events. This is the first free weekend we've had in a while where it's just the two of us together.

I walk into the small sitting room where Rain sits by a window painting. Leaning against the wall, I watch her. The movement of her delicate hand is mesmerizing as she focuses on placing each brush stroke on the canvas, ensuring the paint is perfect. She's beautiful.

"Rain, it's almost time," I say. She turns to look at me and smiles.

"I have to wash these," she says, lifting her brushes.

I help put things away while she washes her brushes. When we're both done, we meet up in the home office. I sit on the chair behind my desk and place my phone on the holder facing me. I hold a hand to Rain. She walks over and sits on my lap.

"Ready, babe?"

"Yeah, I'm ready," she says. Rain puts an arm around my shoulder as we wait for the call. "Any second now," she adds.

The phone rings. I accept the video call.

"Hi, Dr. Nars," Rain greets.

"Hi Raven. Hi Parker. Good to see you both again," the doctor greets us.

"Good afternoon, Dr. Nars," I say.

"You're both anxious to hear the results, so I'll get to it. Your HCG shows you are pregnant."

The doctor continues talking, but everything after the results is a blur. This is incredible news. I tighten my arms around Rain. She looks at me, smiling, attempting to contain herself. Then she looks back at the phone, listening to the doctor.

"Thank you for the news. I expect you have further instructions for me."

"I do." The doctor then proceeds to outline the health program Rain should follow for the duration of her pregnancy.

Throughout the call, I do my best not to pull Rain's mouth to mine and kiss her. Weeks ago, she told me she was pregnant. She was right. We both were—just as we knew our connection was destined, we knew we'd created life. We are a family.

The doctor finishes, and Rain ends the call. She turns to me and crashes her lips into mine. Our kiss is full of love, and everything words can't express. Rain slides her fingers up my neck and into my hair, deepening the kiss. She groans into my mouth. I break the kiss.

"Babe, don't make me take you back to bed. Let me look at you." I brush the hair off her face. "There she is—the mother of my child. You're beautiful, Rain. Thank you for everything you're about to embark on. I love you."

"We have a lot of doctor visits ahead of us. You ready for that?"

"Ready for it all. We're in this together."

Chapter 52

The Plan

Raven

The past month has been a whirlwind. We haven't disclosed our pregnancy news yet, but Parker's mom, Janis, and I have spoken almost daily about wedding events. She has been a dream to work with—it's like she's been waiting for the past twelve years to prepare a wedding for me and Parker. We plan to keep things simple and beautiful, luxurious yet not showy. Janis said that when you see these multi-million-dollar weddings, it's usually people trying to show they have money and status.

I'm excited to have my first official event recognizing me as one of their own. Our dinner will be a private event for only the elites and, in my case, includes the parents, which is my dad. However, there is no way in hell I'm inviting my mother. I'm officially estranged from her. My sister, however, will attend the wedding the following month. Parker wasn't joking when he said he wanted this to be the fall of us. It's the fall we re-committed to our love, got pregnant, and will soon be married.

"Parker, Dad is going to be here any minute. Do I look okay? He won't be able to tell, will he?" I say, standing in front of the mirror and looking at myself. I haven't had many symptoms besides my initial breast tenderness and irritability early on. I'm seven weeks pregnant and have adjusted my wardrobe to loose-fitting clothes despite not showing. My featherweight oversized jeans, flower-embellished white tank, and platform flip-flops remind me of my college days when I dressed much more carefree.

Parker walks up behind me, snakes his arms around my waist, and places his hands on my stomach. "You and the baby look great." He kisses my neck. "You sure you don't want to tell your dad yet?"

I turn around in Parker's arms. "We'll tell everyone together next month. Now kiss me so we can go downstairs." He gives me a baby-making kiss, and although I don't want to, I break the kiss. "We'll finish this later," I tell him before we head downstairs.

"Babe, I reviewed our calendars. Between now and our wedding, we have two charity events, reoccurring doctor's visits, our group welcome dinner, and our meeting with the attorney."

I blow out a breath and sit at the kitchen counter. "Yeah, our schedules are full, especially with our work schedules."

Parker begins removing the plastic wrap from the dishes that our cook prepared. I grab a piece of prosciutto and pop it in my mouth.

"Ew. I think this is rancid," I say spitting it out.

"What?" Parker picks up a piece and eats it. "There's nothing wrong with this."

A tangy buttery salt smell wafts around me. "Cover it up. I don't want to smell it."

Parker returns the meat tray to the refrigerator. He throws out the piece I spit out. "Babe, tell me what else you smell." He lifts the cover from the remaining dishes.

I shake my head. "Nothing."

"That's your food trigger."

"Cured meat? What the hell?"

"It's okay babe. Now we know." Parker washes his hands, then he brings a wet rag and cleans my fingers. Afterwards he hugs me. "Yep, my woman is pregnant."

"I thought I'd be the type to throw up, but this is worse, not being able to eat foods l like."

"It's okay, you'll get through it. This is another reason we need to iron out your schedule. This is not going to be the last symptom you experience. I need you to take it easy. We'll be gone for three weeks for our honeymoon. I'm cutting back on new projects. Later in your pregnancy, I'm taking a sabbatical to be with you more. You mentioned you have additional support at work. How's that going?" Parker goes to the refrigerator and gets two bottles of sparkling water. He hands me one.

Parker and I have had numerous discussions about my in-office and travel schedule. He's concerned about my health and my history of fainting. I lost the argument, which really wasn't an argument per se. There are things I could have done differently in my last pregnancy that I still think about—like when I lost my balance carrying a load of groceries. That day, our lives changed forever. I hadn't received the optimal care because, for several weeks prior to my doctor's visit, I wasn't feeling good but didn't know I was pregnant. I don't want to repeat that. Yes, I agreed to work from home most days and will only travel with Parker on a private jet. My days of commercial flights are over. And if, on some rare occasion, Parker is unable to be with me, then a designated member of the security team will be.

"It's good. I have associates who can step in on all the projects while I'm out. It should be fine when we go to New Zealand for our honeymoon."

Work has been smooth. The Ross Enterprises project is in a lull, waiting for Knight Development to complete the next phase of its work. I have several other projects that are keeping me focused at my firm. That means Nik and I don't have a scheduled meeting this month. It also gives him more time to work on his response to being friends, which, as far as I'm concerned, is his only option. I'd hate to leave the project because he can't pull himself together. It could be worse if Parker stepped in to deal with him.

"You're going to love the house overlooking the ocean."

"How come we've never been before?"

"It's one of our newer properties. I've only seen pictures. We'll fly into the major airport, and from there, we'll take a helicopter to the house."

"So, this is my life. Hideaway homes, private jets, and a secret entourage."

Parker swivels my chair and stands between my legs. "This is our life—you and me. A few people will be around when we travel, but you won't notice, if that's what's bothering you. We only need to focus on what we're doing. And here..." He places a hand on my belly. "This child will have us both. That is until we make more babies who'll have each other as well."

"Seriously, let me work on baking this one." I laugh. The doorbell rings.

"I'll get it, babe." Parker gives me a chaste kiss, then goes to the door. The deep timbre of my dad's voice greets him.

"Yeah, that case may have been short, but it felt like it took a year out of my life." My dad pats Parker on the back as they enter the kitchen. "There's my baby girl," he says, then kisses my cheek.

"Hey, Dad. You two talking shop already?"

Taking a seat next to me, he says, "Briefly. I want to hear how planning for your big day is coming."

"Parker's mom has a team coordinating it. She and I meet weekly. So far, everything is going smoothly. You'll get a chance to meet Parker's family and our friends. You already know some."

"You mentioned it's a private dinner."

"I did. People from the elite society." I use air quotes when I say the word elite.

"Babe. Don't make it sound so secretive."

"Well, it is. I never heard anything about you all before I met you." Parker shakes his head and brings food that our cook has prepared from the stove to the counter alongside the rest of the dishes.

"Sir, it's not as strange as my wife-to-be makes it seem." When Parker says the word wife, it hits me. Soon, I'll be his wife. After all these years of knowing each other and finishing each other's sentences—when he inhales, I exhale. We are so interconnected that nothing, not even time, can separate us. We've proven the strength of our bond.

"He's right, dad. They're wonderful people who have welcomed me way before this year."

"And your sister...did she RSVP to your wedding?"

"Yeah. How'd your call go with her?"

"As good as could be expected. She was broken up about the results, and rightfully so. Your mother did a number on us all. I told Robin what I told you—that she'll always be my daughter."

"What about Bill?"

"What about him?"

"Do you think he'll embrace her?"

"According to her, he's yet to show it. She has us. We're her family no matter what."

"And you talked to her about the trust you established?"

"I did. It's hers to do whatever she wants. Like I said, she's my daughter, too."

"Thank you again for what you did. I plan to donate a portion to charity each year."

"I suppose you don't need to establish another one with the Page Foundation. Your family is doing great work, Parker."

"Thank you, sir. You ready to eat?"

"Ready when you are."

I stand and help Parker by getting the plates and cutlery.

"What would you like to drink, Dad?" I ask.

"You're a sparkling water fan. I'll have that."

"I'll get it, babe. You have a seat," Parker says, going to the refrigerator.

I return to my seat. We all plate our meal. When my dad visits, we eat family style, not formal. I like it this way. It helps us continue to build that bond we used to have when I was younger.

"So, Rain. When do you think you'll be ready to come over for dinner? Maira is dying to meet you."

Dad is right; it's time I met his wife. I've hesitated to meet her after all the drama my mom has caused. To this day, I've only bonded with Parker's parents and a few of the elite parents. It doesn't help that Mom's emotional immaturity, coupled with the lies that also caused Dad to leave, has scarred me. It's one of the things I'm working through in therapy.

"Let's schedule something next week. That way, I'll have met her before you come to our celebratory dinner."

"Are you sure? I realize you're still working through things. How's therapy?"

"Good. I'm glad Parker is there with me; otherwise, it would have been too difficult to manage on my own."

"Babe, you would have done fine on your own, but all the same—I'm glad I can be with you."

"I've never seen anything like what you two share."

"Trust me, Dad—I don't understand it, but it feels right. Just like I knew I had to have you back in my life. You two are my private bubble."

"But you'll add to that bubble as part of your plan."

I smile at him. He is my dad. I should have guessed he already knows.

"You're right, sir. That's the plan."

"Okay, baby girl. I'll talk to Maira, and we'll plan to have you and Parker over Tuesday or Wednesday."

"Sounds perfect," I say. And it is. Having Parker, my baby, and my dad and creating the life I dreamed of with a family I love...is perfect.

CHAPTER 53
The Mystery Bidder

Noah

THE PAST MONTH HAS been one of the most difficult. I'm used to negotiating multi-million-dollar deals. Lately, the greater the stakes, the harder the deal. I'm up for it, but following my week with Rain, thoughts of building a family linger in my head. I can't shake the thought that I might lose Rain to another man. When intrusive thoughts overcome me, that's usually when I do my best work. In those moments, I turn in on myself and focus on the art of the deal. Not now. Now, when she's not where I want her—in my arms.

"Earth to Noah." The lovely sound of Rain's voice pulls me out of my head and back to the conference room.

"Sorry. You were saying."

"After we finish up with these documents, I'm heading to lunch." Her phone, lying face up on the conference room table, buzzes. "Wallace" pops up on the screen. What the hell? It can't be that loser who cheated on her. As I recall, she listed his number under "The Coward"—that is, before she blocked him. If it's not him, which one is it? Jude? Jayden? She taps the screen.

"This is Raven. Hi. Give me a second to get back to my desk." She puts her phone on mute. "Noah, I need to take this. I'll be back to finish this up. Give me five minutes," she says, then leaves the room.

What the fuck? I'm busting my balls trying to close this deal with Wade Wallace. What if that's him? Is she the mystery bidder? How could she be? I don't recall Mak telling me the actual date the fourth bidder met with Wade. Rain was in Seattle with me the entire week. And the day I met Wade, she was in the air on a helicopter ride. I dial Mak. He answers right away.

"Man, I just saw you before you flew to San Francisco. What's up?"

"The fourth bidder. Do you know what day the person met Wade Wallace? Was it the week of my meeting with him? Did they meet before or after the rest of us?"

"What? Slow down, man. What's going on? I thought you and Wade were in sync and waiting for the final word," Mak says.

"Do you know the day?"

"It would have been that week. The press release from the report you sent me to review came out the previous Friday. You brought the proposal to our attention."

"I know, man. That means the bidder could have met Wade anywhere between the day of the press release and Wednesday of the following week."

"Who are you thinking is the bidder?"

"I don't know. But I think I know who does."

"Who?"

"Rain."

"Shit, man. What are you talking about? Why would Rae know?"

"She dated Blake. There's no telling how many more of his family members she knows. As you saw at the Ross Foundation charity event, she has some powerful friends. When I think about it, this is deeper than someone being well-connected."

"What do you mean?"

"Our girl is one of those power players. Did you see how Rose and her man immediately took the lead in greeting them versus the other way around? And the room, did you notice how all the attention shifted to Rain and her partner when they entered?"

"I did. It was as if the president walked in."

I tap my fingers on the table, thinking about how to handle this. "Her friend, Niall, would be part of that. He and Parker seem like best friends."

"They likely are. So, what are you thinking? Are you going to ask her about it?" Mak asks.

"We have an NDA. I can only mention that I saw his last name on her phone."

"Is she with you now?"

"Seriously, man?"

"I don't mean in the room with you."

"She took a call. The name on the phone came up, Wallace."

"That could be any of them."

"I expect, based on her track record, it can only be one person. Wade Wallace. Listen, man, I gotta go. She's coming back in."

"Fill me in later," Mak says. I end the call.

Chapter 54

Take It Or Leave It

Raven

Noah is on his phone when I pass the conference room window. I hesitate before stepping all the way into the room.

"Don't hang up on my account. I can come back."

Nik ends his call. "All good. I'm done. Let's wrap these up."

"Yeah. I don't want to be late for lunch. You know how that goes."

"I didn't realize until you fainted that day. My apologies for my lack of awareness. You would have thought after I spent a week—."

"Noah, don't. It's okay. My well-being is not your responsibility. I knew better."

"I understand, but I know you're intentional with everything you do. I should have picked up on your habits and the fact that your office always has fresh fruit and snacks. Even that week—."

"Noah."

"Let me finish, Raven. That week, you were diligent about eating every few hours. I should have picked up on that fact. It was more than just being hungry, and I should have known better. Forgive me."

I don't acknowledge his comments. I need him to move on from the conversation.

"Okay, so I made the final edits to these two documents," I say, sliding the papers in front of him.

Noah scans the page. "I reviewed this one. The supplier gave me a hard time with this one, but they agreed to your client's request." He signs the document and then hands it to me.

"Always the winning negotiator."

"Except when it comes to you. You've gotta know this past month has been gnawing at me."

"Noah. We need to finish this," I say, sliding another document to him. "Remember, there is no us, so don't go down that path."

"You're set on marrying this Parker dude. Seems sudden. I saw him in the office next to yours. Is he here today because of me?"

I close my eyes, take a deep breath, and reopen them. "Noah, remember I told you I liked you and thought we could be friends?"

"You've changed your mind?"

"I'm about to. You and I spent a week together. I ask you not to come claim me like I was yours."

"I told you I should have never agreed to that."

"But you did. I don't know what path we would have gone down if our agreement had been different. You might have learned more about me. You would have discovered I've known Parker all of my adult life. There's a history between us that you don't understand—one you and I don't have because we barely know each other. And before you say it—I'm not talking about the way we got to know each other in Seattle."

"My plan is to fix that."

"Your path to get to know me is as a friend. That's the deal. Take it or leave it."

"You didn't answer my question."

"Because some things don't deserve a response. For a man trying to convince me I should be with him instead of Parker—you're failing."

"That bad?"

"Yeah. That bad. Don't insult me any more than you have."

"Rain...Raven. I'm sorry. I'm not trying to insult you. I'm trying to get back what we had. I heard you when you said I need to do what I needed to get over it. I've been trying. I told you in Seattle, I don't know how to do this."

"It's evident."

"Raven, I feel like I'm fucking this up, but believe me its unintentional."

"We had a deal. One week. It ended. It's done. You have to move on."

"So you can be with Parker," he says with disdain.

"Did you ever stop to think that maybe Parker is in love with me? He knew how to handle me that day in the office. Does that seem random to you? He knew because he put in the work to learn everything about me. He cares that deeply; he knows me better than I know myself."

"I'll admit. He knew what he was doing—he knew what you needed. I get what you're telling me. He's here because of you."

"Bingo. He's here because he's seen and loves every side of me. He's here because his instincts draw him to me, like how he arrived early that day. His need to protect me is inherent. And my need to be with him is unbreakable. You and I don't have that. We'll never have that, at least not the way Parker and I have it. I told you. I'm marrying Parker. When you find the right woman, I'll embrace her. I don't expect you to do that with Parker, but I expect you to respect him. More importantly, if you want to continue to have me in your life, I expect we will work on our friendship. That's the deal."

"And if I don't take it?"

"We already discussed this. One of us walks away. I don't have a problem doing that. That part, you know."

"I'll take that under advisement. Are we done with this?" He signs the page in front of him and hands it back to me.

"We're done. I'm going to lunch."

"Are you two meeting Wade Wallace?" he asks unexpectedly. I tip my head and stare at him blankly. "I saw the name Wallace on your phone. I didn't expect you'd take a call from Blake after what he did. And based on your track record, your friends are in the upper echelon. The most prominent in that family is Wade. Tell me I'm wrong. If it's his nephew, let me know and I'll solve that problem for you once and for all."

I shake my head. "I'm not at liberty to respond to anything related to that call. But to be specific, Parker and I are having lunch. Moving forward, that'll likely be the case when I'm in the office." I gather the documents we reviewed, slide them into a folder, pick up my notebook, and stand. "Noah, it was good to see you. Think about the deal that's on the table. In a few weeks, I'll be married. There is no us. There's only work. I understand you're used to getting what you want. So is Parker. He wants me. I happen to want him, too."

***

At the restaurant, Parker and I are seated in a private room away from prying eyes. As usual, our meals were ordered in advance. I like it like that.

There's no lost time. Dishes begin arriving shortly after we're seated. I dip my bread in the tapenade.

"Hon, you seemed in a hurry to leave the office. Is everything okay? Do I need to handle Noah?"

"No, but he hasn't committed to making this work."

"You have other projects equally as large now. You're building a new team. You can put someone else on this project. Or—."

"I'm not ready to walk away from this project completely, or the law, for that matter."

"I'd never ask you to. We can start our own firm. You could be the Chief Counsel for the Foundation. There are numerous possibilities for someone with your talents."

"Real estate is my forte."

"Like I said. We can start our own thing. Bring your dad in. The three of us would be powerhouses together." He pulls me to him, cups my cheek, and kisses me. "We also have a house to fill with children. You tell me what you want—we'll make it happen."

"I love you. You know that?"

"I do. So, talk to me. What do I need to know about Noah?"

"He asked me something strange."

"What, babe?"

"A call came through, and I stepped out to take it."

"I saw you when you went to your office. What about it?"

"It was Wade Wallace."

Chapter 55

Connecting the Dots

Parker

When Rain says Wade called, my mind immediately goes to the real estate deal Noah is working on with Wade, which she doesn't know about. However, Rain's connection to Wade is through Blake. She is aware we own a majority state in the Wallace empire.

"Why was he concerned about Wade calling you?"

"Remember the party in Seattle where Blake showed up?"

"You said Noah's brother made him leave. I had Blake call and apologize to you. He hasn't bothered you since, right?"

"No. He hasn't."

"I told you when you left for Seattle that people like him always get what's coming to them. I saw the press release that Monday morning I flew out to..." I look at Rain. "Wait, that was you? You told me to let you handle him. Did you work out a deal with his uncle?"

"I did."

I don't know whether to kiss my woman or take her home and dive into her. "You beautiful creature," I say, grinning, recalling the press release.

"Blake Wallace, nephew to billionaire developer Wade Wallace, steps down as VP of Cost Associates, the media company where he's worked for the

past five years. Wallace cites personal reasons for his exit. He has not stated what his next move will be."

"You're not mad at me?"

"For what? Taking care of business?"

"Blake said some libelous things about you. I knew he wouldn't stop unless I took action."

"Babe. You didn't have to do that. I could have dealt with him, but thank you." I see relief in her eyes when she realizes it is okay to do what it takes to protect us. I press my forehead to hers. "You did amazing."

For years, I've been telling Rain that people will treat us however we allow them to. But putting them in their place sends a signal to them and others that you're not one to mess with. She witnessed this early on when I dealt with Kevin after he tried to forcibly take her away from the party she was at in college. She was confused as to why people were staring at her the next day in class after he was kicked out of Stanford, and those hosting the party were charged with several offenses. To see her leverage her network to handle a ruthless man like Blake shows how much she's grown since then.

"Thanks. But why is Noah so interested in Wade Wallace? At the party, their family seemed vested in what was happening with Blake. They all knew of him by reputation. That was months ago. Why is this important now?"

This is not the conversation I want to have with Rain in a restaurant, but we promised to tell each other everything. I can't predict how she'll react to my stepping in on one of Noah's development deals. I promised to stand down and let her handle Noah. So far, I have.

"What exactly did he ask you?"

"He assumed we were going to lunch with Wade."

"And what did you say?"

"I told him I wasn't at liberty to discuss anything related to the call."

"How would he know it was Wade? You don't list full names on your phone."

With her perfect recall, she doesn't need to. She lists them the way she wants—Wallace for Wade Wallace. Josh is listed as the second handsome man; my parents are Page One and Page Two, and so on. In London, I learned of her nickname for me. We were searching for her phone one evening before heading to dinner when she thought she lost her phone. She made me call it. I found it in a crevice on the couch. I learned that night she had changed my contact name to "Torn Page" following the incident in the park. I made her change it back to Parker. Recently, she changed it to "My Man." Rain does it to humor herself. Whenever a call comes through, and she smiles, I smile, too, because she's so cute.

"He connected the dots. He basically said my MO is having powerful friends. He said Wade is the most prominent in the Wallace family; therefore, it had to be him that called me."

He's right. Since I introduced Rain to my world, she's met many of the most influential people. Over our lifetime, she'll meet many more.

"What was his demeanor?"

"Curious. Wait. Wade is selling his business. Your family is the majority shareholder. Noah is all about making deals and expanding their square footage. Parker, what are you not telling me?"

She's good. I knew my woman was brilliant.

"I met with Wade when I learned Knight Development was a potential bidder."

"How would you know that? You're not tracking everything Wade does."

"I researched Noah. I wanted to know who was wooing you."

"Parker, what the hell? What have you done? I told you, let me handle him."

"I haven't done anything. Wade knows I'm vested in how the deal goes down."

"You mean you'll snatch the rug from under Noah's feet if he doesn't comply with my request? Don't you dare. I told you I'd take care of this."

"I'll only interfere if you give me the word to do so." Rain closes her eyes and shakes her head. She's upset with me. I brush my thumb along her cheek. "Look at me."

She opens her eyes, and we lock gazes. She's fighting her former instinct to run.

"It's a good thing we have two houses. Your bed is going to be cold tonight."

I smile. "Raven Rain Page, Esquire."

"That's not my name."

"Yeah, it is. We have the official documents."

"Well, we're not married yet."

"Another technicality."

"Argh."

I dust my lips against hers. She's cute when she gets like this, but she needs to calm down.

"We're never sleeping apart ever again. We're going home early today so that I can remind you how much we love each other. Then, after I make love to you, you're going to tell me what you're upset about."

"Parker Page, you're insufferable."

"And you're the love of my life and, in a few weeks—my wife. I mean it, babe. We're going home to fuck this out. I haven't done anything wrong. I told you I'd give you time to handle your business with him. My word is gold. Now let's go." I take her hand and place it on my lap to show I mean business. "You have me so hard."

Rain narrows her eyes at me, but I know she's not serious. We gather our things and leave. Due to the mid-day hour, getting home doesn't take long. I stop in the kitchen to grab our bottled water before heading to the bedroom with Rain. In the bedroom, I pull Rain to me and kiss her senselessly. Just like I knew she would, she tugs at my suit, trying to get me out of my clothes. I break the kiss and step back.

"Take off your clothes," I tell her. While she takes off hers, I do the same. When we're both naked, I lift her, lay her on the bed, and hover over her. "Now, remind me where you're sleeping tonight. I don't think I heard you correctly at the restaurant." I reach between us, between her folds, and massage her clit. "I'm waiting." Her legs fall wide open at the sensation of me rubbing her. She's so wet.

"At my house," she says breathlessly in mock defiance. I push my fingers inside her. I dip my head and kiss her hard, moving my tongue in and out of her mouth in time with my fingers fucking her. I feel her walls tighten against my fingers. She's on the verge of coming. "Ahh," she groans in my mouth.

I remove my fingers and position my shaft between her legs. Slowly, I push in. I want all her orgasms on me. I push in and out, matching her rhythm and knowing exactly what she needs to come. I push again, and she comes apart beneath me.

"Oh, Parker."

"That's it, honey," I tell her. Then I quicken my pace, chasing my own release. I rock into her over and over and over. She comes again hard, and this time, I come with her. "Rain," I grunt into her neck.

"God, I love you," she calls out.

I collapse on top of her and then roll over, bringing her with me. "Now you're home."

Chapter 56
The Introduction

Raven

The vibe at the Twelve Fifty-Six AM lounge in Oakland is luxurious and chill. The establishment is full, and we have to maneuver through the crowd as Parker and I make our way toward the back near the bar. Parker stands beside me as I sit. He's been in hyper-protection mode. I'm eight weeks pregnant. Most recently, I've been exhausted, but this evening I feel like I have my second wind. I'm sure he'll ease up a bit tonight since only his inner circle of friends are attending this get-together. Well, all except for my friend Jade, who's heading my way.

I invited her so she could meet Josh, and hopefully, he'll bring her on as a consultant to staff his private schools.

"She's here," I say gleefully, rubbing my hands together.

"I see."

"You think he'll like her?"

"What's not to like, babe? She's beautiful and smart. As long as she can handle his busy schedule."

"We'll know soon enough."

Jade joins us and gives me a hug.

"Girl, I love this place. And these people...are these the ones?" she says it like it's a secret.

"Yeah."

"Hey, Parker." He dips his head and kisses Jade's cheek.

"Hi, Jade. It's good to see you. Would you like some wine?"

She sits on the barstool beside me. "Sure."

Parker orders wine for him and Jade and sparkling water for me. He hands Jade and me our glasses. He looks over the crowd.

"Rain, honey, I need to catch up with Ethan for a second. Will you be okay for a few?"

"No worries, Parker. I'll be fine." He dips his head and lightly kisses me before moving to the other side of the room.

I turn to Jade. "So, are you ready for tonight?"

"You said he's looking for someone to help hire instructors for schools around the country."

"You'd be perfect for this. Besides, you said you wanted to travel. This will allow you to see the country and learn, meet new people, and discover new artists."

"And grow new artists, too. If I hire the right talent, think about how many new young artists they could establish."

"I think it's great. Follow your passion," I say, then take a sip of my water.

"What about you? How's it going with the big project?"

"You mean, am I planning to stay on since Nik is struggling with his newfound role as a colleague?"

"Well, where did you all land with that?"

I look around before responding to ensure no one is in earshot.

"I'm still working on it. I told him if he thinks it's hard for him, how does he think I feel?"

"Yeah," she sighs. "I don't know how you do it. I know when we were younger, I'd remember everything, because that's what happens when your mind is young and fresh. But now I have selective memory—I intentionally tune things out. But to have perfect recall and look at him and have every detail of the week flash in my head, including every sense—it's too much, Raven. How do you navigate something like that?"

"It's hard. I play tricks on my mind. Like when he's around, I tell myself that it wasn't real, that it was a movie I watched where the main character looked like Nik."

"That's insane."

"It's what I have to do. If I don't, I'll get wrapped up in old memories. When I do that, everything feels real, as if it just happened—not months ago, more like minutes ago."

"See, that's the part that would freak me out."

"It freaks me out too, Jade. That's why I limit my exposure to him. I only meet face-to-face when I need to."

"Then why do it at all? You can do anything you want. Start your own business. Take on other projects."

"And let him run me away from what saved me from my memories? Taking on this project helped me cross a huge hurdle to find my way back to me, to love, to Parker."

"Then use it for what it was—your way back to finding you. Now leverage it to move on or put your foot down with Noah."

"You're right. I have to pull the plug. I think I've been too easy with him." Jade looks around the room, studying the crowd. This must be wild to her, being amongst all these people she doesn't know after all I've told her. Soon, if I can work my magic, this will be her world, too. She grabs my leg. "What?"

"Tell me that's not him. Oh. My. God," she says, looking at the dark-haired, mysteriously brooding tall man who could be Parker's brother.

"That's him." I don't say *the second most handsome man in the world.* "Josh."

Josh looks around the room, and I know he's searching for me. When he spots me, he winks. Jade and I watch as he makes his way through the crowd to us. It's only seconds before he reaches us.

Josh looks at me. Then Jade. When I see the smile on his face, I know. She is the one. "May I?" he asks. I nod. Josh hugs me.

"Josh, this is Jade, my best friend. Jade, this is Josh, my soon-to-be brother."

"I've always been your brother." He's right. He's been with me as long as Parker has. I know now that he and Jade will be with me forever.

Jade holds her hand out to Josh and says, "Josh, you look familiar."

Chapter 57
Amongst Friends

Raven

When I went to Seattle four months ago, my life was the opposite of what it is now. Back then I was looking to recover from a breakup and reconnect with my sister the week before a career-defining meeting. All while running from my mess of a life and the man I love. Now, I'm so grateful to be in a better headspace, standing next to my future husband, carrying our child, living my dreams. It's nearing yearend. We're at yet another event and I'm tired. I'm not sure if its fatigue associated with being pregnant or I'm doing too much. All I know is I'm with Parker and he's all I need.

"This is it. This is the last business event I'll be attending for the year." I lean into Parker, who wraps his arms tight around my waist as we stand near the oversized fireplace.

I need to accept it. I'm addicted to this man. Always have been. We stole away to the den in the mansion Ross Enterprises rented to host this gathering. Since getting pregnant, I have tried my hardest to avoid large crowds. Sometimes, my brain goes into overdrive thinking about possible scenarios, and I have to get away to shut it all down. I suppose, like Parker, I've gone into protective mode.

"That's right, honey." He brushes my hair over my shoulders and stares down at me. "You're amazing. You know that?"

I step back and slide my hands along the sky-blue silk halter maxi dress. I chose it because it has a seam at the waist, making it look like a two-piece. It'll be the last dress, other than my wedding dress, that I'll have the waistline to fit in for a while. I added a crystal belt resembling a string of diamonds—like the diamond jewelry collection Parker gave me over the years. I touch the bracelet he gave me on our first dating anniversary. The belt coordinates with my crystal-embellished heels Parker bought during our shopping spree before his birthday. He says the red ones get him going—in reality, they all do.

"I know you're bound to tell me the truth. Thank you."

"And you have heels on. You know you're going to get it tonight." Case in point.

I laugh. "Uhm, I've gotten it every night since I got pregnant."

He smirks. "I'm just stating the facts."

"So, are we going to do this?"

"We are. You know, we don't have to stay all night, Rain. We can leave when you're ready."

This feels strange. Not only is this the last work event before I get married and go on my honeymoon, but it's nearing the end of the year, and we're entering the holiday season. Noah is likely here tonight, but the next time he sees me, I'll be married, and he'll know I'm carrying. That's why this evening I need him to pull himself together.

"I'm ready. Let's do this," I say. Parker gives me a chaste kiss. "You still got lipstick on you."

"I don't need to hide the fact I'm into you. Don't worry. I'll lick the rest of it off you when we get in the car." He smiles, and it is amazing to have this man loving me.

"Okay, handsome."

Parker and I leave the library and enter the large, bright, traditional ballroom. A pianist is playing pop covers. The dance floor is full of people. Around the perimeter are tables where staff from both Ross Enterprises and consultants working with Knight Development Corporation are seated. We head to our table, where we're seated with June and her entourage. Rose won't be attending as she's still in Ireland, but June and her siblings are here. It's rare to see their younger sister Jasmine. She's a more youthful, beautiful mixture of June and Jake. They all have beautiful brown skin like mine. Jasmine's hair is naturally thick and curly, like June's, and her dreamy brown almond-shaped eyes look more like Jake's. She's been doing her own thing, but they want her to join the family business.

"Hi, June," I say as she stands to greet me.

"You look spectacular. How are you?"

"I'm good."

Her brother Jake stands. "Hi Raven. Ready for the big day?"

"Yes. We are." I look at Parker.

"Hi, June, Jake, and this must be the lovely Jasmine." Parker shakes their hands one by one.

Jasmine stands. "Hi Raven. Hi Parker. It's nice to meet you finally. Raven talks about you all the time. Now I see why."

We all sit. Jake lifts his chin, and a server pours champagne for everyone. I place a hand over my glass.

"Sparkling water, please," Parker informs him.

Seven months...that's how long it will be until I can taste wine again. Well, if Parker doesn't fill me with more babies, which I know he's committed to doing.

"I can't wait to hear about your trip to New Zealand," Jasmine says.

"I don't think I've ever been," Jake adds.

"Neither have I," June says. "I guess we have to add it to the list. What do you think?" she asks her siblings.

It's lovely to see how close they are. My sister and I are getting closer, and I sense the wedge that used to be there over the years is mostly gone. It feels good to finally get my life and family status on track. Having my dad back and being able to fully love Parker are both dreams I never thought I'd obtain. Yet here we are, days away from Dad walking me down the aisle to Parker.

"I think we need to discuss it," a deep Irish-accented voice I recognize says. It's June's chief of security.

"Aedan, man. How's it going?" Parker greets him.

"Good, mate. Congrats to you and Raven."

"Thanks," Parker says.

"Thank you," I add.

Aedan sits next to June. In my usual modus operandi, I observe their body language. Something's different. I swear I see him wink at her. I turn to Parker and whisper, "Are they together now?"

As far as I knew, Aedan took over security for June when she joined Ross Enterprises. The Ross family is so brilliant that people with nefarious intent are gunning to get access to their technology. Aedan's team at King Enterprise runs point for Ross Enterprises' executives, including Jake, while his brother Niall keeps a watchful eye on his fiancé, my friend and employer, Rose Ross.

"That's none of our business." Parker gently squeezes my hand. I turn my nose up at him. He lifts my fingers to his lips and kisses them. Then he turns to the table and says, "You're welcome to use our place any time. It's in a remote area by the sea. You can access it via helicopter or jeep if you prefer that route."

"That's awesome," Jake says.

"Definitely cool," June adds.

As dinner is served, we talk about travel and then switch topics to discuss our work in our respective foundations. I'll split my efforts between the Page Foundation and the Rose Ross Foundation. Chatting with this group, I'm reminded why I've quickly become so close with Rose. Her cousins are as down-to-earth as she is, and Aedan is a more reserved version of his younger brother, Niall.

We've been sitting for a while. I don't want to dance, but I need to move around. I turn to Parker and ask, "Can we go for a walk?"

He stands and helps me up. "If you'll excuse us for a moment," he says, leading me out of the room and back to the den where we started.

"Are you okay, babe?" He searches my face for the alternative.

"Yeah, just getting antsy."

"You want to sit?"

"No. I want to do this." I put my arms around his neck. He lowers his face so I can kiss him. My man knows what I want. We kiss. It's gentle and loving—all the things I need it to be at this moment.

Parker pulls away. "Better?"

"Yeah."

"You ready to go home?"

"Not yet. I need to talk with Noah. I saw him come in while we were having dinner."

"Is that what's bothering you?"

"Not really. Being in crowds makes me anxious."

"Ah honey, what's going on? What can I do?"

"I don't think it's anything bad. I'm more aware of what I'm doing, where I am, and how I feel."

"Because of the baby?"

"I suppose. Yeah."

"We'll be fine, honey. I'll never be far from you. It won't be like the last time. Every moment of our lives, starting with the day you conceived, is the beginning of our lives together. I promise you and I are in this—tied at the hips."

"I believe you. But really, this was about stepping away for a moment. And if stepping away is with you—that's all the better. I love you."

"I love you too, babe." He kisses me again, and we hug until I am ready to go back into the main room to face the inevitable...Noah.

***

Parker and I walk down the hall, heading toward the main room. We don't get very far.

"Raven. Parker. Good evening. I trust you're well."

"Noah. We are. Thank you."

"Mr. Knight," Parker greets.

I look up at Parker. “Can you give us ten minutes? I’ll just step in here.” I gesture to the room we just left.

“I’ll be waiting right here.” Parker cups my cheek and brushes his thumb across my lip. Then he dips his head and gives me a chaste kiss. “Ten minutes,” he whispers against my lips. I nod.

“You good for ten?” I ask Noah.

“Yes.” He opens the door, and I step in. He closes it behind him. “You look lovely as always.”

“Thank you. Have you decided?”

“To be your friend or crash your wedding?”

I close my eyes and count to five in my head. This man is intentionally testing my patience. “You are a tough negotiator. What you are not is rude or ruthless.”

“Okay, so I wouldn’t crash your wedding. But I do want to know if I have a chance. Did I ever have one?”

“May I?” I reach my hand out to Noah.

“Touch me? Good god, woman. For the past four months, that’s all I’ve ever wanted. Yes, you can touch me.”

I smile. “Not like that. Like this.” I cup his cheek and trace my fingers along his face. He places his hand on mine and kisses the inside of my wrist. His eyes close briefly. “Noah, I need you to be my friend. Don’t taint our week by trying to make it more than it was. Let it stay beautiful.”

“I’ve been trying, Rain. You must know that. You open that door to something I—.”

“Your true self. I helped you reclaim something you forgot you had. Now, the door is open for the right person to walk through. That’s not me. It never was. I was just a catalyst.”

"A damn good one." He touches his forehead to mine. "You look happy with Parker."

"I told you. I'm in love with him. I have been for twelve years."

"Then I walked in."

"Yeah, you threw a wrench in my plans. Momentarily. I'm surprised you came to find me while I was with him."

"I've come to realize you're a package deal."

"Don't get any ideas."

"Trust me, I'm not. You're the only one I want." He smiles tentatively.

"Noah..."

"Could that have been me heading down the aisle?"

"You sure you're ready for the answer?"

"Always."

"Not with me."

"You sound so certain."

"Love will do that. That's how I know there's no us. You have to move on, Noah. I promise you'll find the right one. When you do, I'll personally hand her the key." He laughs. I know we're both remembering the day he gave me the charm bracelet with the key to his heart.

"And this one—The Space Needle for today. But what about this? I don't understand. It's a key. Do I get a car or something?" I teased him.

"Rain. This one is special. This is the key I lost a long time ago. I don't know where it's been all this time. All I know is you found it that day at the bar. It's the key to my heart, my home, my life. The key to a door I didn't know existed until I met you."

"Nik."

"Rain. I'm not ready to open that door, but I know you are the only woman who can. You found the key, so I'm giving it to you—it's yours. Clearly, it was meant to be found by you. I need you to take it and protect it because honestly, Rain, I've never met anyone like you, and I'm sure I never will again. Maybe one day, when I'm ready for it, it will find its way back to me—when I'm ready to open that door, we could do it together. But now is not the time. I made you a promise that day over eggs Benedict and coffee. I agreed I wouldn't come to claim you like I'm your man." He paused when I smiled at him, and he smiled tentatively before continuing. "I'm giving it away because I don't know anyone more deserving to have it than you. Remember how much I miss you every time you look at it. How much I wanted to be that man for you."

"Finders keepers." He kisses my forehead. "Seriously. It's yours."

"For a minute. Until you find her. Now, I need to hear the word from your mouth that you won't try to claim me as yours. You need to agree to be my friend and colleague. That's the deal."

"Have I ever told you why I was so closed off to women before I met you?"

"No, but I sense, like me, you've been fighting some demons."

"I have. You remind me of the girl who, in less than a week, got under my skin."

"Where is she now?"

"That's the thing. A drunk driver stole her from me a few days before our first date."

"Oh god, Noah. I had no idea. I'm so sorry."

"It was a long time ago. I shut down after that—that is, until I met you. You reopened that door. The possibility that I could feel that way again about someone seemed improbable. I don't want that door to close again."

"You don't have to. You've got to leave yourself open to the possibility of more with the right person. I'm sorry, Noah. I can't be that person. But I'm happy to have helped you discover that you can feel that way again."

"Have I thanked you for changing the course of my life? For showing me that I could be better?"

"Every conversation when you bare you soul to me, I hear your appreciation. It's the reason I allow these conversations. I know what it's like not to say the words that need to be said to the one you care about. I knew all along this would be difficult. Your words live in my soul."

"I feel like you're being stolen away from me."

"I was never yours. I've always been meant for someone else. You've got to try to move past me. Be my friend. Be my colleague. Be the man I know you can be."

"I'll agree to be your colleague. Whether you know it or not, I'm already your friend. I've proven that these past four months. You have to give me that, at least. But I'll never agree not to come to claim you like you're mine. I won't make the same mistake twice, Rain. If something happens and you leave him again, I'm claiming you. Full stop."

There's a tap at the door. Parker enters. I pull away from Noah. Parker holds his hand out. I walk over and lace my fingers with his. I turn and lock eyes with Noah.

"I won't make that mistake again," I say.

Chapter 58

Disclosures

Noah

"Let's lock this deal down," Rok says. I hear Mak agree in the background. He's been unusually quiet during most of our conversation. I'm not sure if it's because of what's happening with me, Rain, him and his girl, or whether it's something else. I do know this deal is important to all of us.

"I'm working on it. We're close. After the meeting, I'll let you know what disclosures he wants me to be aware of. If I can sign today, I will." The elevator dings, alerting me that I've reached Wade Wallace's executive floor. "I gotta go. Talk soon," I say and end the call.

"Right this way, Mr. Knight." Wade's executive assistant leads me down the hall to his office.

When I enter, Wade is looking out the window with one hand cupping the other behind his back.

"Mr. Knight, have a seat," he says, looking out the window.

I sit. He turns around and sits at the table with me.

"Good to see you again," I say. "You wanted to discuss the contract."

"You've been patiently waiting for the final word on whether you're the winning bidder."

"My proposal speaks for itself. My track record is solid. You're a family man. This is about legacy. I'm continuing my father's legacy."

"I'm sure he's proud of you."

Wade seems hesitant to make his point. My experience has shown me that when someone behaves this way, they might be pulling out of the deal or something has changed. That's not good, but I would rather know sooner than later.

"Sir, you mentioned disclosures. What exactly did you want to disclose?" I ask, getting to the point. I didn't get to be a great negotiator by idle chat.

"My team is drawing up the final agreement, but you have to agree to terms and conditions outlined by the majority stake holder."

"That's not you?"

"No. Everything you need will be in the agreement." He slides a sheet of paper across the table. "The date and time for your meeting is there." He points to the page.

"That's it. Show up, agree to the details, and it's ours?"

"That's right." He gets up, walks back to the window, and looks out. "Good luck, Mr. Knight."

Chapter 59

Get Together

Raven

My dad, Robin, and I decided to get together before the wedding. This will be the first time the three of us have been together since Dad was forced to leave. Forced to leave, not walked out on us. That is the new narrative I use to refer to how he left. Now that I know the truth, it's allowed me to think of that day differently. It helps me to understand my emotions better. I'm able to course-correct how I view things...relationships. Mostly, it's helped me to accept Parker's love.

"Are you ready for this baby, girl? You're taking a big step."

"Yeah. I'm ready. It's been a long time coming."

"Over twelve years," Dad adds.

"Truth be told, Dad, if I hadn't found you again, I don't know if I would be ready."

"I'm here. You're more than ready."

"It's good to have you and Robin."

Robin's eyes widen. "Me?"

"Yes, Robin. You and I have also missed out on so much of each other's lives," I tell her.

"Hopefully, we can leave all that behind and move forward," Dad says. "These past few months have been good for me."

"Me too, Dad," I concur.

"How are you doing with all this, Robin?" he asks.

"Still navigating it. You've been a great dad. On the other hand...I don't know how to move forward with Bill."

"Has he acknowledged he's your biological father?" I ask.

"Not to me. But I don't need that from him. I have all the acknowledgment I need in this room."

"I mean what I say. I raised you. I'm your father, Robin."

"I'm sorry Mom robbed you of our younger years."

"We get to make up for lost time. Your sister and I have already started."

"Yeah, Robin, we have regular father-daughter dates."

"And I'm waiting to have my grandchildren over, too."

"Don't rush it. Their wedding is in a few days," Robin says.

"Don't rush what?" Parker asks, returning to the kitchen after showing my dad's wife around the house.

Parker thought getting to know Maira while Robin and I had time with our dad would be a good idea. After several therapy sessions and discussions with my dad and Parker, I finally agreed to have dinner at Dad's a few weeks ago to meet his wife.

It was a beautiful day. Walking up to the front door of the sweeping ranch-style house in the mature tree-lined neighborhood, holding Parker's hand, gave me a sense of calm. I spent many of my college years visiting and living at Parker's Silicon Valley home; my dad's home was no less impressive. Both Dad and Maira greeted us upon arrival.

"Raven, Parker, this is my wife, Maira." My dad gestured to the beautiful, brown-skinned woman about my height with a short silk bob press wearing a casual patterned floral maxi dress cinched at the waist.

Stepping inside, I was surprised when Maira pulled me into a hug. Meeting the woman in his life after many years of wondering where my dad was felt strange. Until that moment, I envisioned she'd hold some animosity toward me for what my mom had done. With one warm embrace, my fear was alleviated.

"Raven. Wow, you're even more beautiful than Rhett described. It's so good to finally meet you," she said, then shook Parker's hand and greeted him. I knew then, everything would be okay.

It initially shocked me when Dad told me it took him over ten years to get serious with a woman. Then, when I thought about it, everyone in my mother's life has experienced collateral damage from her behavior. My dad waited to get married again. He chose not to have another family. I sabotaged the relationship with the love of my life. Robin withdrew from me. Now, we are all gathered at Parker and my home to rebuild our lives...together.

"Having children," Robin pipes in.

"Although I suspect something's up. Baby girl is glowing."

"What?" his wife exclaims.

"Can we discuss how often family dinners will be moving forward?" I ask.

"I'd like to note for the record that soon-to-be Mrs. Page is avoiding the question, your honor."

"Robin, give it up. There are no judges in here." I laugh.

It's nice to hear her make light of the fact that the three of us are in the same profession. I remember when Robin and I didn't see eye to eye on things. Now I understand our differences were more about traits she adopted from our mother and her biological father—the roll with the waves she gets from Bill, the unreliability she gets from our mom. My extreme recall ability is a heightened version of my dad's photographic memory.

"Well, isn't that what you say in court?"

"No," Parker, my dad, and I say in unison. Then, we all break into laughter.

"Raven, when the two of you return from your honeymoon, we'll coordinate our calendars. I love the idea of regular family dinners," Maira says.

"Same," Parker adds.

"That means we'll need to alternate between here and Seattle."

"I don't want you all to be on a plane constantly. How about once a quarter in Seattle?" Robin suggests.

My dad's wife agrees to take the lead in coordinating the schedule. We all enjoy our dinner and continue getting to know each other. For so many years, I dreamed of this day—getting my family back together. I look across the kitchen as Parker talks with Robin. She holds her hands in the air and spreads them the width of her body in her best attempt to show him the size of her new air fryer. Parker catches my gaze and winks. Dad is dishing more food onto his wife's plate.

"Rhett, that's fine," she tells him.

My dad turns to me. "You need more, baby girl. I know you're eating for two," he whispers. How does he know? I narrow my eyes at him. "I'm your father. Don't look at me like that."

"What?" I feign innocence.

"You haven't touched alcohol since before you two got back together."

"I plead the fifth."

"Yeah, you're definitely mine." He shakes his head and chuckles.

"You two keeping secrets over there?" his wife asks.

"Seems that way," he says. "Why don't we toast the couple."

Chapter 60

Terms and Conditions

Parker

Wade Wallace is a good guy with the highest level of moral standards. I've known his family for years. So, I didn't hesitate to agree when he said he wanted to disclose that I was the majority stakeholder in his corporation. Noah needs to know who he's dealing with. He thinks my wife is a tough negotiator. He hasn't dealt with me.

I look out the window and take in the view of San Francisco. I love this city. I love Rain more, which is why I'm holding this business meeting on our wedding day. She estimated that hair and makeup would take two hours. That gives me all the time I need to handle this deal.

I look down at my watch. One minute. I turn around just in time to see Noah Knight walk in the door.

"Right on time. Let's get to business," I say, gesturing for him to sit. I sit, too. I slide a document across the table. My eyes are locked on Noah's. His brows are furrowed. Good. The element of surprise. He's not as good as he thought. "You've read this all before. There are only two adjustments in the Terms and Conditions under the Morality Clause. Ethics and standards—that's your thing, right?"

"Interesting. Doing deals on your wedding day."

"You underestimate me. I accomplish more in an hour than most do in a year."

"When Wade mentioned a stakeholder, I never guessed it would be you. What do you want?"

"My wife says she asked you to walk away, and I quote, 'don't come to claim her like she's yours.'"

"What's that to you?"

He can't be serious.

"You missed the part about her being my wife. More importantly, she asked you to do something—you declined."

"Like I asked, what's that to you?"

"She says you're used to getting what you want. So am I. In this scenario, I want Rain to get exactly what she wants, or you leave here with nothing. That's the deal. You move on."

"She walked away from you once. She could do it again."

"She won't. Listen, you want a woman who doesn't feel the same about you. She told you as much. She gave you the option to be a friend or watch her leave. You say you care about her. Then don't make her walk away from her dreams. She worked hard to establish herself with Ross Enterprises. Rain is good at what she does, so good that even you couldn't negotiate her down before you knew her real identity. Let her go. Let her live the life she deserves."

"And if I don't?"

"The fact you asked reveals everything I need to know—that you don't care about her. How you handle the next few days determines your life. You either walk away as the winning bidder or leave with nothing. There's one thing I guarantee you won't walk away with ever...Rain. Walk away, Noah. Congratulate my wife and leave her alone."

"It's not my nature to give up what I want."

"You're looking at the only man she wants. Trust me, after twelve years, I know. This is your chance to walk away clean and live your life."

"Is this the reason she couldn't make her other relationships work? You stepped in and scared them all off? Was it you that made Blake resign?"

I laugh because this man has no clue what he's talking about.

"Normally, I wouldn't respond to such ignorance, but you need to hear this so you can make an informed decision. I didn't make Blake resign nor interfere in his relationship with Rain. Any relationship she had ended because that's what Rain wanted. Did I destroy them after they were done with her? Absolutely. That was *our* deal. They never had a chance with her because all this time, it was me that she loved."

"This is a game you play with her. That's not love."

"It's not a game. You don't know her like I do. Sure, you see her as a great negotiator. But did you notice how she despises conflict or how it makes her feel vulnerable? Did you notice it made her sick to her stomach to face off with Blake in public, so she let your family step in and handle him at the party? Were you aware of that, Noah? Or did you confuse her behavior with being meek? But she can't be meek—she crushed her development deal with *you*."

"Raven's a beautiful woman with a mind of her own. If not me, someone else will come for her or attract her attention."

"She is stunning. But do you notice how her eyes shift away when given a compliment or how she redirects the conversation? I do. I hold her face and look her in the eyes when I make a point. I make sure she can read in my eyes what I truly feel when I praise her. I'm not worried about how you or others look at her because I know her—I'm what she wants. She made her choice long ago."

"I'm sure there are some things you don't know about her."

"I doubt that," I tell him. Noah smirks. "Ah, I see where this is going—you think I don't know how you two spent your time together in Seattle. You don't know much about Rain, like why she left *your* bed every morning. Yeah, Noah, I know how you two spent your seven days together. She's an early riser. Did you know she does it to silence the continuous stream of thoughts in her head? She told you she had a condition. Did you know she sought me out every morning when she left your bed—that only the sound of my voice comforts her? Mine—not yours. So yes, I know how you spent your time and what she thought about it. The look on your face tells me that's news to you. Isn't it, Noah? Over the course of the week, you saw Rain as passionate. But did you know she has difficulty receiving love? Did you know that when she gets too close to people, she sabotages the relationship and walks away? But all that is her story to share, not mine. However, she did walk away from you. That's your signal to let her go."

"She may have walked away the first night but returned for the week. Who's to say she won't come back again? I obviously have something she wants. She walked away from you, too, once."

I bark out a laugh. "Don't fool yourself, Noah. I'm the only man that means anything to her. You witnessed that for yourself. When she was done with you, she ran straight to my arms. Do you know why she does that? Because she compares every man to me. You all failed on every point. I bet you didn't know that, Noah. Every time she touched you, she was analyzing you. How close could she get to finding someone like me? All this time, it's been me. That's why she couldn't make other relationships work; she loves me. You were a distraction. But you didn't know any of that, did you? You only know what you two shared for one week. You didn't recognize those moments were fleeting."

"She said those words to me. Sounds like words you put there."

"On the contrary, those *are* her words. You're the wake-up call that sent her back to my arms. You see, it's not a game. We love each other, and she's tired of others getting destroyed while she runs from our love. You think I was the one who destroyed Blake. That's a funny story. She asked me not to ruin him. That's how it is between us. Whatever Rain asks of me, I give it to her."

"Then, if not you, who?"

"Rain. She decided it was time to take matters into her own hands. She leveraged her resources to take him down." I smile, thinking about how I rewarded my woman for that. I lock eyes with Noah. I need this conversation to be over with. "I told you—you think she's meek. But the truth is she despises conflict. That's why I'm here. My woman asked you to do something. You didn't do it. She didn't have to tell me anything about your deal, but she did. She did because she was tired of asking you for something you wouldn't give her. So, what's it going to be?"

"What Raven and I had was real."

"No, it wasn't. You know why she never told you about me? Because she knew that when you were eventually done with her, after you figured out you couldn't handle her, I'd destroy you. She didn't want that for you. But if you knew all that—if you really knew Rain as I do—we wouldn't be having this conversation."

"There's nothing you can say or do to make me stop going after what I want."

"Are you sure of that? Something tells me you want to take Knight Development to number one. I understand men like you. It's your dream to dominate your field. You can't help it. It's part of your DNA. You crave power. So much so that you'll do anything to get it. You're one deal away from realizing your dream—one that I will snatch from you if you don't leave Rain alone."

"Raven would never condone this. She'll despise you for this."

"You're not as smart as I thought."

"You should go now. Don't you have a wedding to attend?"

"You're right. Rain was glowing this morning. But I digress. As I said, either way, you lose. Rain loves me. We're building a life together. You want to wait for her? Even when we grow old and pass on, we'll be together, and you'll be what? Pining? You were on the receiving end of a deal that's done. This is not a movie. Move on, Noah. Be the man you professed to be. Find your own woman. I'm only here because my woman asked for something...for you to get a life."

I check my watch. "I have somewhere to be, Noah. So, this is what's going to happen. I'll leave this document with you. Pay close attention to the terms and conditions. You'll find the clause about how you address my wife of particular interest. I expect an executed agreement to be emailed to me in forty-eight hours. Then, you get to live your dream, and if you still want to be friends with my wife—that's up to her. If you don't sign it. You lose everything. See, the thing that you fail to understand is that you can't win this negotiation. I know each plausible outcome. You think Rain or I have a lingering point of failure that will allow you to divide us? You did your best. It didn't make a dent. She tried to tell you."

"She's under your influence."

I smile. This is getting old. "Noah, when I wake up tomorrow, I'll make love to my wife like I do every day. I'll tell her about this conversation. Because that's how we are—we tell each other *everything*. She'll pretend she's upset for about a minute, maybe less—not because of the conversation but because it transpired on our wedding day. Then I'll show her how much I love her because that's what people who love each other do. We'll enjoy the rest of our honeymoon without another thought of you. But like you said, I have somewhere to be. Goodbye, Noah."

I leave and gesture to security to walk him out.

Chapter 61

You Are the Sun

Parker

When I woke up this morning my thoughts were consumed with Rain. It was hard to sleep knowing the day I dreamed about was finally here. I must have watched her for an hour while she slept tucked into my side with my hand resting on her stomach. It's hard to believe. We're having a baby…a family, everything I've ever desired.

When she woke, I showed her how much I love her. We finally got dressed, went to the kitchen, and I fed her breakfast. For so many years, it's been one of my favorite things to do. When we were attending university, I'd sit her at the counter and feed her. She wanted sex. I told her I'd give her whatever she wanted if she ate all her breakfast. She always ate her breakfast.

"Parker, what are you doing?" she asked.

"Worshiping you on our special day."

"You always do that. You have nothing to prove. I've felt nothing but love from you since I met you."

"Because you're all I've ever wanted. And our baby you're carrying is icing on the cake. I plan to dedicate my life to my family."

Rain cried at my admission, and I kissed her tears away. I tried to carry her back to bed to make love, but she said we didn't have time. We did.

I pulled her onto my lap right in the kitchen and we came together in a cacophony of cries and moans. God, I love her so much.

Later, I met with Noah while Rain was getting her makeup done. Afterward, I put on my black tuxedo, stand before our friends and family, and wait for Rain to join me at the altar.

When the first few bars of music to *How Do You Keep the Music Playing* cue, the hum of whispering voices goes silent. My eyes pool with water before I see my wife's face. When we chose the song sung by James Ingram and Patti Austin, we knew we couldn't maintain our composure. But it's our wedding. This song expresses the sum of our thirteen-year journey to today. That first day we locked eyes in class, every cell in my body gravitated to her. We were designed for each other. We didn't know how to explain it, but neither of us could deny it—we're inseparable. At the first lyric, I close my eyes. When I reopen them, the woman whose face fills my dreams walks in wearing a form-fitting white bustier wedding dress that pools at her feet. Beside her, with his arm lovingly locked with hers, is Rhett.

She takes my breath away. It takes all my energy not to cry like a baby at the sight of my beautiful wife walking toward me. *This is it,* I think to myself. My dream has come true...Rain. And within her, our child.

As she walks down the aisle, her eyes lock on mine. She smiles, and I smile back. When she reaches me, her father places her hand in mine. He takes a seat with our families. There are no sides across the aisle in our society—we are all one.

After the music plays out, the minister begins his script. The entire time, Rain and I stare at each other. Her eyes well with tears. I know she is reliving the scenes of our lives together. My eyes well up, too, and I let the tears fall. It's been a long time getting to this moment. When it is time to say my vows, I steady my breathing, place a ring on her finger, hold both her hands, and speak from my heart.

"Rain. The first day I met you I told you that rain was essential to all life. I know now that it's my life force because that is what you are, Rain. There is no me without you. You are the air I breathe, the sun that warms me to the core, the rhythm to my heartbeat, and breathing you, intaking your love, is the sustenance that keeps me alive. In turn, every day I'll show my thanks to you for saying yes to living an eternity with me. For today and forever more, I vow to love, honor, and protect you. Let this ring symbolize our unbreakable bond. I love you, Rain."

When the minister says I can kiss the bride, I feel like I am floating on air. I want to devour her, but I don't. When we break the kiss, she whispers against my lips, "I can't live without you. Thank you for waiting for me." I lose it and cry. We both do. I hold my wife in front of everyone until we can pull ourselves together. I don't think there is a dry eye in the room.

At the reception, when we cut the cake, and I feed her a piece, she starts to feed me, but I direct her hand to put it in her mouth. Then I touch my thumb to her bottom lip, open her mouth, and cover it with mine. That's how I eat my cake...from her mouth. It's how I've usually had my dessert ever since that day I was sick in college and she fed me honey on her body. I smile, thinking about it. I made love to her twice that afternoon. That was a lifetime ago. Yeah, I still eat sweets from her—even at our wedding. Everyone is watching. When I eat cake from her mouth, the room says, "Ahh" in unison. I want her so bad. I would take her here and now if we were alone.

The day is beautiful. Everything smells like jasmine, her favorite scent. Each table has a setting full of flowers. I can tell she's having a good time, but I notice she gets tired quickly. We need to be careful with this pregnancy. Josh notices, too, when he dances with her, and cuts it short. Our friends are so good to us, so observant. We're going to have such a great life together.

"What are you doing, Parker?" Rain asks as I hold her hand up.

"Admiring your delicate fingers dripping in diamonds."

"You put all this here. They're beautiful. Thank you."

I look past her out the window of our plane. "We'll be in the air for a while, babe. I think it's time for you to eat something." I pull a few grapes from the bunch on the table and add a few more items from the spread on the table to her plate—all her favorites.

Rain eats from the plate I prepared. I watch as she slowly chews each piece she puts in her mouth. I get to experience this every day. This...a life with her, and soon our child, is everything.

"Are you seriously taking off work until after our baby is born?" she asks.

"Maybe longer. We don't need to work, honey. I do it because I enjoy it. My priority is you and our child. So if you still want to work—you do that. But while you're carrying, I'll be focused on you. When our child is born, they will get the attention I had from my parents."

"You'll give up law?"

"Everything I've always wanted is right next to me...you, our child...the life we build. The sun will rise and set with you. You are the sun that circles my planet, warming me from the surface to my core. And you're all I can ever ask for. I love you."

Chapter 62

On This Day

Raven

Parker wasn't joking when he said we'll always wake up together. Other couples may have separate wedding day activities—not us. I woke up this morning wrapped in the protection of Parker's powerful arms. It's been that way since the day I returned from Seattle. Even before we recommitted to each other, the warmth of his body surrounded me daily. And on his birthday, when we finally recommitted our bodies to one another, and I told him I'd marry him, he told me he'd make love to me every day. He has. I truly feel loved.

On this day, I feel blessed to have my abilities. These are memories I'll layer over my life. The look on his face when I opened my eyes this morning to find him propped on his elbow, staring down at me—smiling.

"Hey, beautiful."

"Hey, handsome."

"Today is the first day of the rest of our lives...together. I love you," he said, placing his hand on my stomach, lowering his head, and kissing it. "I love you too," he told our unborn child.

Then he kissed me. It was soft initially, but then desire took over. I opened my mouth, and his tongue wrapped around mine. We sucked and licked until the need to have him in me was overwhelming. I reached for his hardened shaft. He rolled over me, nudging my leg with his knee. I positioned his length at my entrance. He bent my knee to gain better access and pushed into me. My body clenched around him, sucking all of him into me. God, I love this man.

Parker moved in and out of me, and I rocked in time with his rhythm on the verge of my climax. "I'm coming." I cried out. "Oh, God, Parker." He continued pumping in and out faster, harder. I watched his face as he chased his own release.

"Rain," he growled. He pushed harder and covered my mouth with his in a wet, wonderful kiss that captured our groans as we climaxed together. And when it was over, and my body pulsed around him, and his love seeped out between us, I saw stars. I listened as our breaths became one.

That's what I'll remember about this morning. And when I reflect on our wedding ceremony, I'll replay thoughts of my dad with his arm wrapped around mine, looking so proud as he walked me down the aisle. I'll see the smile on Parker's face as I approach him. I'll remember the vows we made to each other in front of our friends and family. I'll recall the moment we said, *"I do."* Two words that Parker could have asked me years ago. The two words I was finally ready to say. Two words that will forever seal our love. He always said we were destined for each other. We were. Nothing else can explain our journey or help explain the promise I made at a time when I was so broken that I thought I'd die. *"I promise to find my way back to you."* It took almost five years, but I made it.

"In the sight of God and these witnesses, I now pronounce you husband and wife! You may now kiss," the minister said. Parker kissed me, and we became

one. Then we celebrated with everyone. Yeah, I'll remember that this day was perfect.

"What are you thinking about, babe?" Parker squeezes my hand.

I press my head against the leather seat back and turn to Parker. "How much I love you." I smile at him.

"We can go in the back and get in bed if you want to show me before we land."

"You're so cheeky."

"You love it. Did you have a good time?"

"Yeah. It's a lot, you know...all the people, the well wishes, the...I don't know, all of it. It was somewhat overwhelming. But it was lovely."

"I know what you mean. Come here." He pulls me to him, and I sit in his lap. "Have I ever told you this is my dream? Marrying you, having children with you, loving you." He slides his hands under my beaded white top and links his fingers over my stomach. I can never get enough of his touch, his kisses, his...love.

"I had an idea. You certainly had a million opportunities to walk away."

"I'll never walk away from you. When I found you, I knew we were meant to be together. There is no lifetime or alternate universe where I wouldn't find you, Rain. There is no me without you. I love you."

"And I was born to love you, Parker. Thank you for allowing me the space to become the woman I am today."

Epilogue

It's Done

Noah

One week later.

The brief sound of the front door alarm is the only thing alerting me that someone entered the house. I slide the patio chair back, abandoning my view of the lake, and walk inside to find Rok pulling a beer out of the refrigerator.

"Help yourself," I tell him.

Ignoring my subtle attempt at humor, he flips the top off the bottle. "So, talk to me," he says.

"Always the CEO, even on the weekend. What do you want to know?" I go to the refrigerator and get myself a beer. "Are you making your famous charcuterie board today? I could go for a snack about now." I pull out a few food items that I know my brother likes to use to create his masterpiece: an assortment of cheese, vegetables, fruits, and cured meat.

Rok washes his hands and then gets to work preparing our snack. In the five months since I have lived here, a week hasn't passed without one of my relatives stopping in. This home is one of the best purchases I've made to date. Our family gatherings are the things I look forward to. One day, I'll have a family of my own. I thought that would be with Rain. I know better now.

"Give me the cliff notes on Wade and the dissertation on Rae." Wow, straight to the point.

"I signed the deal. It's done."

I signed. On Rain's wedding day, sitting across the room from Parker, I didn't want to admit how much this deal meant to me. Thinking back, I certainly wasn't going to admit I didn't want to back down because he had what I wanted...Rain. At the end of the day, he was right. If I truly cared about her, I would do whatever she asked. She'd never ask me to be her friend if she didn't want me in her life. I do care about her enough to want her to be happy—even if that's without me. But it hurts. For one week, she was mine.

"Congratulations are in order once again. You are knocking these deals out of the park, man."

The alarm sounds again. "What are we eating?" It's Mak.

"When you all get your own houses, I'm coming over every day. Shouldn't you be with your girl?" I ask Mak.

"Stop procrastinating," Rok presses.

"She's got a thing. What did I miss?"

"She's got a thing, or are things getting too serious? I know how you are," I say.

"Anyway, back to the point. Catch me up on what I missed," Mak persists.

"Nothing yet. The short story is we got the Wade Buildings," Rok says.

"Hell yeah," Mak exclaims.

"I'm still waiting for Nik to fill me in on what happened with Rae."

Mak helps himself to a beer and grabs an olive from the platter Rok made. "Thanks." He holds up his olive before popping it into his mouth. These two have made themselves entirely at home here.

"She's married," I tell them.

"I need something besides the obvious, Nik. I told you don't make Lil sis uncomfortable. You continued to pursue her."

"We were negotiating."

"You're telling me she was negotiating whether to maintain her life or start from scratch somewhere else? That's not my idea of negotiating. You were making her choose between her livelihood or you. All along, she should have felt she made the right decision taking the lead on the project."

"I wasn't looking at it that way. And before you say it, I should have. It took time, but I got there. I'm moving on."

"As in no longer pursuing her."

"She's in love with Parker. Their friendship spans more than a decade. I can't compete with that. They've built a life together, and their recent marriage solidified that."

"I'm sorry to hear what you're going through, but it's for the best. The right woman will come along, and when she does, snatch her up, man."

"Yeah, if there's one thing I learned, it's that." The next time I fall for a woman and know she feels the same, I'm not waiting. I'm going to commit myself to her. My heart told me that Rain was that woman. She could have been had I set aside my fears of having love snatched away. Yet the past few weeks, coupled with her wedding, felt more like the fall of us than the collapse of a deal.

Parker thinks I've completely walked away from what I want because I signed the agreement. I haven't. If anything happens and Rain needs me, I'm there. If she walks away from him again, I will stop at nothing to claim what's mine, even if breaching the terms and conditions impacts KDC.

"Well, at least you got one thing right—you brought the Knight Development Corporation to the top of our industry. Toast. To the Knight family legacy." Rok holds up his glass.

"To the Knights," we say in unison.

***

Parker

Two weeks following the wedding.

Leaning over the side of the pool, I take in the view of the bay, with its dark pebbled shores disappearing into azure waters. It's peaceful here in our home tucked away on the side of a mountain, hours away from the nearest neighbor. It feels like another world. I leave the pool and quickly shower outdoors before joining my wife. My wife. I love the sound of that.

"Enjoying the view?" Rain asks from her coveted spot on the outdoor chaise, where she's been lounging and reading for the past twenty minutes while I've been doing laps. I walk over, slide beside her, and pull her onto my lap.

"This is the best view." I kiss her. This is the first time we've just focused on us in years. Except for me checking to ensure I received the executed agreement from Noah, we haven't been interrupted by any work the past few weeks. Rain is amazing. Loving her is easy. We've both been consumed with each other—not that we weren't before our honeymoon. But something changed. I don't know whether it's because Rain's pregnant or we're married; a shift happened, and neither of us wants to miss a moment together. "Have I told you I love you today?"

"Several times. When we woke up. The first time you came inside me, the second—."

I laugh. "That many, huh?"

"Maybe more. It's all good. I love you, too. So, I'll be twelve weeks by the time we get back. Should we tell the family?"

I smooth my hands across her stomach. She's barely showing. No one would know looking at her, but I know. We've both known for a while, even before the doctor confirmed. We're going to have a baby. I take a deep breath and take in this moment. We created another life...together. I have a family—what I wanted most in life. Rain is the woman I will spend the rest of my life with.

"Yes. Let's arrange dinner at our house, and we can tell everyone then."

"This will be the first time we host them all."

"It'll be great. Your dad and my parents got along so well at the two dinners, like they've known each other forever."

"That was awesome. Your mom is the best at organizing events."

"This one has been her dream. Mine, too."

"You always say that."

"Because it's true. I have been fortunate all my life. However, there's always been this lingering desire to have what my parents had. Now, I do. You and our baby fulfill my wildest dreams. Thank you for creating a life with me. I'm so in love with you. I'm beyond blessed to spend the rest of my life with you."

"I'm here, forever."

I turn to my side, tucking Rain beneath me. I cup her chin. "I'm going to make love to you again. And afterward, I'll tell you I love you...again. I always will."

She smiles. "I love you, too."

***

Raven

Four weeks following the wedding.

"Darling, let me know if I can help with anything," Janis says as I leave the dining room and head into the kitchen.

"Parker can help. I'm just going to grab the dessert." I say, hoping no one sees through my half-truth.

In the kitchen, Parker bends down, lifts my shirt, and kisses my stomach. His breath is warm, and his lips are moist against my skin. I muss his hair like I do every time. That is his new routine: kiss the baby, then me. He rises and places his hands on the counter, caging me in.

"You're beautiful, hon. You ready for this?"

"Yeah, I'm ready." He dips his head and kisses me. It's heated like every kiss. I can't get enough of this man. He breaks the kiss and then adjusts himself.

"You bring the cake. I'll bring the gifts."

Parker retrieves the cake from the refrigerator. It's my favorite, red velvet. Instead of red decorations, I had the baker design icing flowers in the shape of a yellow baby shoe. "I'll walk in first and hand the gifts to Janis and my dad."

"Got it. I'll put the cake on the sideboard until they open the gifts. They won't be able to see the design from there."

Parker and I return to the dining room. I walk over to Dad, kiss him on the cheek, and place a yellow-wrapped gift in his hand. "For both of you," I say. Then I go to Janis and repeat the gesture. Preston rubs Janis' back. I can tell, like my dad, that he already knows what is coming. Parker stands behind me with his arms around my waist, waiting for them to open their gifts.

My dad unwraps the gift and then hands it to his wife to open the box. Across the table, Janis opens the box while Preston looks on. She gasps when she opens the hinged platinum picture frame. "Oh my god." She jumps up and hugs me. Her eyes well up with tears. I empathize with her; she's been waiting for this day for a long time. Besides Parker, she's been my biggest supporter. She has always wanted to see us together, happy, with a family.

"Baby girl, Parker, congratulations." My dad examines the ultrasound photo and the adjacent picture of Parker and me.

After Parker and I get our share of hugs from around the room, he places the cake in the center of the table. His mom takes over and plates a piece for everyone.

Looking at my dad, I say, "Well, Dad, you were right. I'm three months along now."

He winks and smiles. "I'm so happy for you two."

"Son, you continue to bless us with precious moments. You and Raven have made your mother and me truly happy. We couldn't want anything more."

"More babies," Janis throws in.

"Keep the children coming. Got it," Parker says.

I smile before saying, "I suppose Parker and I will have our hands full. In addition to building a family, we've decided to open our own law firm." I don't bother sharing that Alejandro offered me a partnership, which I respectfully turned down. After discussing it with Parker, we have decided to focus on building our family sans corporate travel. Instead of chasing the international route, establishing our firm focused on the local market will allow us the freedom and flexibility to build the type of life we want for our children.

When we received official word we were pregnant, Parker was willing to walk away from the law to be available to me and to ensure my safety as we build a family and cater to our children's needs. We're in this together. Owning our own firm, neither of us has to give up anything. We can work alongside each other. I'll have the career I want, and so will he, working alongside me—always my loving protector. Similar to Parker, our children will want for nothing. As his parents did, our children will sit between us at home or in the car. He'll stretch his hand across them to mine. He'll raise my fingers to his lips and kiss them. Then I'll use that hand to caress one child's cheek, and he'll do the same to the other or perhaps muss their hair—anointing our children in our love. This is *our* dream, designed in love.

"Oh, darling, that's great," Janis says, bringing my thoughts to the present.

"Rhett, we're hoping that one day you'll join us as a partner."

"I'd be honored."

"Okay, no more shop talk. Let's have cake," I say, looking around the room.

Parker looks at me curiously, eyebrows furrowed. "What are you looking for, babe?"

"Making sure Josh is nowhere to be found. You know how much he loves cake." We all laugh. And it's beautiful.

Parker, me, the baby, we're a family. Soon, we'll have more. Those around the table are the family I've always longed for...uncomplicated, loving, happy. My journey getting here has been long but lucrative. Sitting here laughing and sharing stories with my family is exactly where I want to be. I'm finally happy. I'm whole. I'm at peace. I am loved.

The End.

Enjoyed **The Fall of Us**? Please take a moment to leave an online review. Thank you!

Interested in whether the other characters from the series make love connections? Subscribe to my newsletter at www.ritaagordon.com/subscribe-page to stay updated.

Blurb

The Fall of Us

To what extent would you go to reclaim your life?

In the pulsating heart of a city where power reigns supreme and passion ignites, Raven Nichols finds herself torn between two magnetic forces: Parker Page, her constant friend and first love, and Noah Knight, a captivating stranger who challenges everything she thought she knew.

Grappling with her own demons, Raven is drawn back into Parker's sphere, his allure as potent as ever. But promises made in the heat of youthful passion may not withstand the weight of time and trials to transformation.

Enter Noah Knight, a man who thrives on the thrill of conquest and the rush of control. Like Parker, the command and confidence he conveys are Raven's catnip. Yet beneath his formidable exterior lies a vulnerability she can't resist. Their fleeting connection leaves her breathless, but the clash between her heart's desires and sense of duty leaves her reeling.

With each passing day, Raven's world grows more tangled as she navigates the treacherous terrain of love, loyalty, and self-discovery. In a landscape where power is currency and every choice has consequences, she must confront her own truth and decide which path to follow.

Will she honor her promise to Parker and reclaim their lost love, or will Noah's allure prove too powerful to resist?

The Fall of Us*, a second chance romance, is Book 3 and the highly anticipated conclusion to the "Let It Rain" series.*

Excerpts

Seven Days in Seattle

Book 1 of the *Let It Rain* series.

Blurb

One week. No strings. No names. No feelings. What could go wrong?

Rain

This Seattle meeting will change my life...just not the way I expected.

Instead of focusing on my presentation, I'm dealing with a cheating boyfriend and sister who bailed on me. The only good thing to happen is when a stranger at a bar offers a pretty distraction: a one-night stand, no strings attached, no questions asked. A distraction from my mess of a life is exactly what I need....

But our one-night stand turns into a week-long affair. He only wanted sex, no feelings, no last names, no talk about business, nothing personal. And I was fine with that. Until I wasn't.

Nik

I don't have time for relationships. I have a company to run, a legacy to uphold, a reputation to protect. I only care about power and success. I don't do dates and I don't do tomorrows. I only do one-night stands with women who know the rules and don't ask for more.

But then I met Rain at a bar. She's beautiful, smart, and sassy. And suddenly, I want more. The more time we spend together, the more I want from her. Her name. Her story. Her dreams. And I was fine with that. Until I wasn't.

Fate is about to punish us for staying anonymous...by throwing us into each other's lives in the worst possible way.

Seven Days in Seattle*, a contemporary romance, is Book 1 of the "Let It Rain" series.*

Seven Days in Seattle

Book 1 of the *Let It Rain* series.

Chapter 1

The Way We Were

Raven

Sometimes, there are moments when you have to laugh hysterically just to keep from crying. Then, there are moments when you just want to scream.

"Parker Page, I swear I'll kill you if you don't give that back to me," I yell across the kitchen counter, then dash to the other side where my soon-to-be ex-best friend Parker clutches my phone, scrolling through the contacts. When I'm directly behind him, he lifts his arm and holds my phone above his head. He's a six-foot-four-inch-tall wall of muscles. I'm a five-foot-six piece of brown paper and have to jump in my bare feet to try and reach it. "What are we, twelve? Give. Me. My. Phone." I jump up again and miss. When he extends his arm over the counter, I do the only thing I can in a moment of desperation. I jump on his back.

"Woman, if you don't get off my back. Let me handle this situation." He leans over the counter and turns to the side to get me off his back. Gravity takes over and I swing to his front, and like a koala, I cling to him, bringing him down to the counter, hovering over me. My shoulder shoves a fruit bowl that tips over. Oranges, apples, and lemons roll the length of the counter, and one after another, I hear them collide with the delivery bags containing our dinner. A wave of uncontrollable laughter washes over me when I think how ridiculous we must look. And it feels good to laugh after sulking the last two days. I pull Parker's arm forward until he's forced to lean over me on the counter. Still straddling him, I lick his face to distract him and manage to grab the phone from his hands.

"Got it," I say triumphantly, but it comes out more like a pant. Parker is still leaning over me, arms on either side of my head. "Now you back off *me*." I reach up and muss his curly dirty blond hair. Our faces are so close that I get a whiff of him. It's deep, woodsy, and sweet, and I'm tempted to dip my nose in his neck, but I don't dare. "This is sexy, but you really need a haircut. Now get off," I tell him.

The look Parker gives me is a mix of surprise and seduction. He touches his wet cheek. "What was that?" He straightens, grabs me by the waist, lifts me like I weigh nothing, and gently stands me back on the floor. I walk across the kitchen and sit on the opposite side of the counter.

"What?" My lips spread into a sly smile.

Parker retrieves a bottle of wine from his wine fridge, opens it, and fills two glasses. He hands me a drink across the marble counter. I lift it to my lips and sip. Parker always has the best wine. He must have been a sommelier in another life.

"The woman with perfect recall is asking me *what*."

He has a point. I don't forget anything. It's both a blessing and a curse that I can recall in detail what I've seen and heard. It helped in my profession as a lawyer, but unfortunately I could never utter the phrase, "I forgot." Only my closest family and friends and my boss, Alejandro, know about it. It's not something you talk about. People either pick up on its existence or don't. Parker picked up on it when he became my best friend at Stanford University. We had almost every class together since we both studied law. Parker knew everything about me and vice versa, so there was no pulling the wool over his eyes.

"That's me, using my feminine wiles to get what I want," I tell him.

"Be careful," he growls. "I may be your best friend, but I am all man."

"Yeah. That part I remember."

It's etched like glass in my memory because, for five years, Parker Page was my man in every biblical sense of the word. And he's right. He is all man. Just not mine. Well, not that way anymore. We're very much alike. Both stubborn. Both opinionated. Both passionate. And if I'm honest, we're both a little wild, which is how I ended up on his back on a Sunday night at the age of thirty.

As I watch Parker move seamlessly through the kitchen, I reflect on that time of our lives. In all appearances, we were the perfect match. Young, beautiful, intelligent, determined...unstoppable. And for a while, we were, in essence, perfect...for a while. We tried to make it work as a couple. We really did. But in life, there are obstacles you can't move on from. Well, mainly one I couldn't move on from. However, we found our rhythm as friends; it just works better this way—we're inseparable. And right now, my best friend, my confidant, my protector, has latched on to a bone named Blake Wallace, my ex. The man I discovered was cheating on me.

Parker opens the food delivery bags and plates our pasta. Then he carries both plates to my side of the counter and sits beside me.

"That's what I thought," he says and hands me a fork. "But seriously, let me deal with Blake."

"That's not necessary. I've already dealt with Blake." I twist the fork into my pasta until a large roll of noodles forms, and then lean in and eat the entire thing. "Hmm," I moan. "I swear pasta and wine are my love language."

"I know," Parker says, then picks up his napkin, puts a finger under my chin, and turns my head toward him. He wipes the corner of my lips. "You're such a mess."

"I know." It's the story of my life.

"So, tell me. Did you confront him before or after dinner?"

This is not a conversation I want to have. To stir up bad memories that lay rancid in my mind like the stench of sauce that's gone sour in Tupperware. It's a lid that's best left unopened. But I always tell Parker everything, so I prepare myself and down the rest of my wine in one gulp. I think about that moment in the restaurant as Parker refills my glass.

"Mr. Wallace, it's good to see you again so soon. I trust you and your lady friend had a good meal last night?"

"Yes. Everything was great. The ribeye was perfection."

"Will you be having the same this evening? I can go over the specialties if you like."

"Let's wait for my girlfriend to return. She's in the restroom," he said. I waited for the manager to leave before returning to the table. I don't know if I waited out of embarrassment or whether I was trying to help him save face. I should have outed him in front of the manager, but that's not how I operate.

When the manager left, I returned to the table.

After I was seated, Blake reached across the table to touch my hand. I pulled my hand away like his touch had burned me.

"Is everything okay?" he asked, and my blood began to boil. My mind started racing, and every disappointing interaction I'd had with Blake flashed through my head. I felt dizzy as the scenes played on repeat in my mind.

"Rae, is everything okay?" he repeated, pulling me out of the dumpster fire he'd started.

I took a deep breath. "Did I hear the manager correctly? Oh wait," I snapped my fingers. "We both know I can't misunderstand something I can recall verbatim. You lied."

"I—."

"I'm talking. You need to listen. You said you were with 'the boys' at the gym last night. Mr. Manager here says you were with a woman that wasn't me. So, I can assume three weeks ago, when I asked you to go with me after work to have drinks with Parker and our friend Josh, and you said you had to work late—you didn't really have to work. Two weeks ago, Thursday when you couldn't break away for lunch, when you, and I quote, 'never miss a lunch,' you really didn't miss lunch. You just didn't want to go with me."

"Rae, let me—."

"Explain? No, let me explain. Your actions speak louder than words, Blake. So, I'd say you've said enough. I'm not that woman. I don't need to settle for less. You should have said something four months ago at the charity event if you didn't know what you wanted. But you didn't. You know why, Blake? Because you are a pathetic excuse for a man and a colossal waste of my time. When I walk out of here, don't call me, don't text me, and as a matter of fact, lose my number. When you see me in public, pretend you don't know me because that's what I'm going to do. I don't have any more room in my brain for trash, Blake. Goodbye." I grabbed my purse and left the restaurant. I wandered into the bar next door, ordered a drink, and called Parker.

"Rain. Hey, babe."

"Parker, come get me."

Once again, Parker came to my rescue and I'm here walking him through another one of my failed relationships.

"I couldn't stomach the thought of sitting through dinner with him after overhearing his conversation with the manager. The fact that he didn't have the guts to tell me to my face that he didn't feel our relationship was working makes me feel cheap and unimportant."

"You're right. He should have been man enough to talk to you. He should have apologized."

"He should have, but he didn't. So, I confronted him before he could order, then left him sitting there. You know me, there is no retort once I lay out all the facts."

I eat more pasta. When I notice Parker isn't eating, I raise my chin toward his plate. He twirls his pasta and takes a bite. I scrunch my nose. He rolls his eyes. I put my fingers to my lips and blow him a kiss. It's silly, but we have a way of speaking without words. We've had that ever since we met in our contract law course at Stanford. One day, our professor was upset because some students did poorly on the test, and he admonished the entire class. His German accent was so heavy that he was almost unintelligible as he ranted, *"You're not going to get this by divine inspiration. If only I were a brain surgeon."* Our professor's voice boomed in the lecture hall. I had an urge to turn to my left, and Parker turned at that exact moment. Our eyes locked and I pursed my lips. He raised his eyebrows and he shook his head.

We held a whole conversation without saying a word, using only body language, as our professor continued ranting in the background. Once we were out of the class, we huddled outside the door and laughed like old friends.

"I'm Parker." He held his hand out to me between laughs.

"I'm Raven. People call me Rae."

"What's your full name, Raven?"

"Raven Rain Nichols."

"Rain. I love the sound of that. I'm reminded how essential it is to all life. Can I call you Rain?"

"Yeah. You can call me Rain."

That was twelve years ago, and although we're no longer a couple, we've been inseparable ever since. And now, the way Parker looks at me tells me how deeply he still cares. We've been through too much together. Whatever *this* is between us, it's good, it's precious, and I'll do everything within my power to protect it. Sometimes, I think that's why it was better that we stopped being a couple, to hold on to what we have—to conserve *us*.

"It wasn't your fault," Parker tells me. "I can't believe the audacity of that man. I hate that this happened to you, but I'm glad you weren't with him long."

He's right. One second is too long to be with anyone who doesn't treat you as you deserve. I was with Blake for four months. Early in the relationship, he was attentive and seemed interested in my work as a real estate attorney. But over the past few months, he became preoccupied. Thinking back, I feel so stupid. I should have read the signs. I've been focused on proving myself at work, and rightfully so, but it sucks how this went down. I never would have learned about him cheating if I hadn't stepped away to freshen up in the restroom before dinner. I was stunned to hear the restaurant manager mention seeing Blake the previous night with a woman. He had told me he was at the gym. That wasn't the truth. He was having dinner with another woman at that restaurant.

"I get it wasn't my fault, but you can't just call him up and give him a piece of your mind. I understand you're only protecting me, but you and I are attorneys. We have reputations to uphold. This could go sideways."

"You may as well hand over your phone because I'm calling him whether you like it or not. I can guarantee that he'll rethink doing this to anyone again."

"I'm not giving you my phone. If you want to call Blake, do it on your own." I shake my head, resigned that my best friend won't take no for an answer regarding something like this. Because even though we're no longer lovers, Parker is still protective of me. I get it. We're both invested in each other.

If I'm being honest, it goes much deeper than that for Parker. In the past, when my relationships went sideways, I ended them first. If I didn't, once Parker found out that they were heading downhill, he'd take matters into his own hands. He's not a mean guy, and he'd never hurt anyone unless they hurt me, but they undoubtedly wished they'd never met me when he was done. Parker Page is powerful, privileged, and used to getting his way. He comes from one of the most elite families in California. His family is part of a group you'll never hear about in the media—they're that rich. So, if he tells Blake to do something, then Blake would be wise to proceed with caution.

"Okay. I'll handle this. But not like I did the others. I'll talk to him. At a minimum, like you said, he owes you an apology, Rain."

"Fine. I'm done with this conversation, and I'm done with men. Anyway, I need to focus on my career. This meeting in Seattle could be my ticket to becoming a partner."

Being an ambitious overachiever has done wonders for my career, but it hasn't afforded me time to nurture relationships with men. That is, except for Parker. But I needed to break free of him to prove I don't need a powerful man in the room to validate or protect me. That despite everything, I can stand on my own merit. I've been so focused on this that I haven't put the time into getting to know the men I've dated. I would have noticed signs that Blake wasn't all in sooner if I had.

"You will, Rain. You have one of the most brilliant minds in real estate law. And don't be so jaded regarding men. I wasn't so bad, was I?"

"Oh my god, Parker. I didn't mean—." I don't finish. Instead, I hop off my stool, throw my arms around Parker's neck, and hug him dramatically. I kiss him on the cheek and muss his hair again. "The fact that you are still in my life says everything, and don't you forget that."

Parker untangles me from his body and glares at me, reading my face. After a second, his brows unfurrow, his expression softens, and he seems satisfied with what he sees. "You have everything you need for the week?" he asks. The mood lifts and I return to my seat.

"Yes. Thank you for volunteering to drop me off at SFO tomorrow. Car service is so impersonal—there's no one for me to hug before I leave. I think that could be awkward for the driver," I whine, and my admission gets a chuckle.

“Depends on the driver. Well, at least you get to see your sister. It’s been a while. Tell her hi for me.”

“Yeah. Let’s see how Robin is. You know she can be finicky at times.” Rather, all the time, I should have said. We’re so different that sometimes I wonder whether we’re even from the same parents.

“It’ll be fine, Rain.”

“It would have been better if you had some time off to go with me. This is my first break in a year.”

A year ago, Parker saw that the demands that I was putting on myself were taking their toll and suggested we drive down the coast for a three-day weekend in Carmel. He was right; I needed the break. It allowed me to momentarily clear my head of men, my memories, my work—it was the best weekend ever. I should have listened to him when he suggested I take a break from dating. If I had, I never would have given Blake a second look. I wouldn’t be in this position: scrubbing the recesses of my mind, remembering the time wasted on him. Ugh, stupid Blake Wallace.

I don’t need this mess in my head. I need to focus. Focus. Focus, Rain. I direct my eyes to Parker’s mouth as he speaks. I trace the curve of his lips with my gaze.

“My calendar is set for the next month, or I would fly out for a few days. And my parents need me to review some contracts for them.”

“They have people for that.”

“That’s what I told them. Anyway, I’m sorry I can’t be there. Hopefully you get time to see some sights before you dive in with your client meetings.”

“I have a list of things to see and do. Let’s see how far I get. It’s not all fun and games, in any case. I still plan to work a few hours after I arrive tomorrow. And of course, I have to check email throughout the week to stay on top of things. Also, Alejandro wants to brief me before I get into vacation mode. He says this could be the biggest deal of my career."

My boss, Alejandro Rodriguez, is the founding partner in the law firm. A top international attorney, he is outside counsel for some of the most prestigious corporations in the world, Ross Enterprises being one. A year and a half ago, he poached me from my firm to focus on building out his real estate division. Our client, Ross Enterprises, is expanding their company to more locations and needs an attorney who specializes in real estate development to review real estate contracts and advise their legal counsel. That's where I come in. Structuring real estate contracts to protect Ross Enterprises is right up my alley. If I nail my next few projects, I could potentially make partner, which makes next Monday's meeting a big deal.

Parker begins clearing the counter and putting away the food containers. I return the spilled fruit to the bowl, then wet a towel and wash down all the marble counter surfaces. That's another thing we share—we're both neat freaks. When the kitchen is clean, Parker goes to the sink to wash his hands. I stand beside him and wash mine, too. When I'm done, I hold them out with my palms up. Parker gives me the "you're something else" look, shakes his head, and dries my hands. I bump him with my hip.

"Thanks, Parker."

He pulls me to his side and kisses the top of my head. "I have to prepare for a brief. I'll be in my office for a while. You want to watch TV or something?"

"No, I'm good. I'll plop on the sofa in your office and catch up on my reading. But first, I'm changing into my PJs."

It doesn't take long for me to shower and change. I wander through the house, taking in the space that's become my second home. Parker and I share the same taste in modern design. His grey-toned walls, mahogany furnishings, and brass fixtures reflect our shared aesthetic. As I walk toward the office through the narrow hallway from the main bedroom suite, a photo on the wall catches my eye. It's a picture of me and Parker throwing our caps in the air on graduation day. Seeing the image brings back fond memories of our time together in college.

We were two people figuring out what it was like to be adults living on our own. First as classmates and friends, then as lovers. Even back then, we were inseparable. Like an addiction, the need to be near one another was all-consuming—we loved each other that much. Whenever Parker was near me it was as if the world fell away. I don't know if I was prepared for that kind of love, having come from a broken family. It scared me. It still does.

It wasn't until our third year of undergrad that we formally started dating. We continued dating while working on our juris doctorates, even though we went to separate schools. However, something shifted during our time away from each other. I used to think it was the stress of school, the distance, or the fact that we were getting older and growing into our own. But that was me playing tricks with my mind. Truth is, Parker and I were speeding down a path to becoming...more. Then, one night, our relationship took a terrible turn that threw us off track—if I'm being honest, me more so than Parker. I think I used the situation as a catalyst to refocus. To try and become my own person. By the time we received our JDs, we were no longer a couple, yet despite pushing past the passion and the pain, our friendship was preserved.

When people ask why we're so close that we seem like more than friends, we have a standard response. We say we've talked about it numerous times but can't explain our connection. We don't try anymore. We just know this is the way we are. At least that's what we say. But it's a lie. I know exactly why. I made a promise to Parker a long time ago. A commitment that became the ultimate tie that binds us, one I don't know if I can ever satisfy. When we broke up, I said the thing you say to someone who can't stop loving you no matter how bad you are for them. We all have our secrets, and the promise I made to Parker is mine. So yeah, if anyone asks, that's the way we are—inexplicably tied together.

When I reach the study, I find Parker on a call. I lean against the door frame, watch his beautiful face be all business-like, and pause before entering.

"Yes, I need that case cited. Don't forget all the corresponding notations. Right. Are you ready? Great, I'll see you tomorrow," Parker says to someone in an authoritative voice I seldom encounter.

After he ends the call, I walk into his study and stand beside him at his desk. He pulls me to his side. "Rain." My name slides off his tongue like silk, and I smile.

"Why haven't we created our own firm?" I ask. My hand instinctively slides up his neck and into his hair. It's soft. Silky.

Parker takes my wrist and flips it to check the time on my watch. I remember the day he brought it for my birthday, the year we started dating. He told me to wear it always as a reminder that our time together is precious. I thought walking around with a gold Rolex every day was silly, but I got used to it. He kisses my fingers and then releases me. He reaches across his desk, picks up my iPad, and hands it to me.

"Honestly, babe, I don't know. Don't we already spend so much of our lives together?"

He's right. Although we don't live together, we share meals at least four times a week, whether we meet for coffee before work, have lunch together, or have dinner. And when we don't see each other, we communicate by phone, typically via video call. We even use our friendship as a litmus test for people we date. If they can't accept that Parker and I are best friends, they're out.

Catching his hint, I take my iPad and move to the sofa facing his desk. I prop pillows on one end, lay back on them, and open my email. My eyes automatically shift to Parker when I feel him watching me, waiting for a response.

"I suppose you're right. Don't forget to set the alarm for six, and don't you dare leave me lying on this couch if I fall asleep. I swear I'll kill you if I wake up here."

I hear the crunch of a paper before I feel it bounce off my head. Then, as if on cue, we laugh.

Seven Days in Seattle

The Days With Rain

Book 2 of the *Let It Rain* series.

Blurb

Their love was supposed to last a lifetime. Fate had other plans.

What happens when you meet the love of your life, but you're not ready?

The moment Rain met Parker, they became inseparable. They shared everything, from their lawyer dreams to their deepest secrets.

Parker came from a wealthy, loving family and wanted to give Rain the world.

Rain came from a broken and distant family, and Parker was the only one who could calm her down and make her feel safe.

They fell in love and planned a future together, but life had other plans.

After twelve years of heartbreak, pain, and drifting apart, they finally decide to try and save their love. But is it too late?

The Days With Rain *is a contemporary romance and Book 2 of the "Let It Rain" series.*

The Days With Rain

Book 2 of the *Let It Rain* series.

Prologue

Heaven

Parker Page

Two weeks ago.

It's hard to focus with her around. Traces of jasmine and honey linger in the air like lust long after she leaves my arms. Although I informed her during dinner that I needed to retire to my study to prepare for tomorrow's brief, I anticipated her following me here. And despite the fact she has her own home and even though there are fifteen other rooms in my house, she's here. In a city the size of San Francisco, she should be somewhere else. She should be resting somewhere soft, not splayed sideways, sleeping on a sofa in my study. Still, somehow, she's here...with me.

I've resigned myself to the fact that this is how we are with each other, forever bound by a single thread, sending signals between us. This has been the soundtrack to our relationship for as long as I can remember. We've been apart, hanging by a thread on the fringes of each other's lives, separated by distance, and at other times together, tangled and messy, but always connected.

Now, I sit behind my desk and study her across the room, watching silently as she slumbers on the sofa. I sigh. She's beautiful. Her brown hair spills wildly across the pillow and falls in waves over the side of the couch. Light from the lamp casts a soft hue on her warm golden-brown skin. Her slender fingers curl and tug at the fur throw that covers her long, lean body. She won't sleep soundly until I put her to bed. I know that from experience. Because after twelve years of living and breathing in a world where she exists, there's not much I haven't learned about the woman who's become my best friend.

The click on my Rolex signifies it's midnight. Monday is here all too soon, and in a few hours, I must put her on a plane, and she'll be gone. I close my laptop, stand, and go to where she's lying on the sofa. I kneel before her, brush a curl from her face, and tuck it behind her ear.

"Hey," I say softly.

She stirs slightly, but her eyes stay closed. And like I've done a thousand times before, I scoop her into my arms. I carry her upstairs, through the house, down the hall, and place her in my bed. I step into my closet, remove my clothes, drop them in a basket, and then pull on a pair of silk pajama pants she got me. When I walk back to the bed, I slide in beside her, wrap my arms around her, and pull her into me. She could be anywhere in the world now, but she's not. She's here with me. And at this moment, holding her in my arms, inhaling her essence, *this* feels like heaven.

The Days With Rain

Love Letters

An Anthology

Book 4 of the *Let It Rain* series.

Blurb

Love is always enough.

Books from the *Let It Rain* series contain several passages that read like a love letter to the characters. Some made the final cut in the books, and others didn't. That doesn't make them less beautiful. You'll find both in *Love Letters.*

Love Letters is a curated collection of passages from the *Let it Rain* series, including deleted scenes, previously unpublished content, poems, and quotes.

***Love Letters**, Book 4 of the "Let It Rain" series, is an anthology and the final book.*

Coming soon. Only available in paperback.

Love Letters

Book 4 of the *Let It Rain* series.

Queen Bee

Mark "Mak" Knight

The first time I saw her was when my older brother Rok and I video-called Nik to razz him about canceling dinner with us. He never cancels. He did that night. We were more surprised when we discovered the reason he canceled. He pulled a woman close to him and positioned the phone for us to see her—she was stunning.

That was the first time in years that I'd seen something in my brother's eyes that resembled pure happiness. It was also the day I saw someone standing beside him who could be a sister, a friend, a future family member, someone who could be the solution to helping my brother be human again.

Yeah, that was the first time I saw her face. Rae.

"Rok. Was that you blowing up my phone? This better be good." Nik said before I took the phone away from Rok to see what was happening on the other end.

"We told you to take time away from work, not from us. What's the deal, man?" I asked as Nik pulled a woman to his side, angling his phone so they were both on the screen. I positioned the phone so Rok and I were on the screen together.

"Well, shit," I said. Rok took the phone from me.

"Hey, I'm Rok, with a K, Nik's older brother. And this one." He pointed his thumb at me. "The one with a potty mouth is our baby brother, Mak." I held my fingers up, forming the sign letter for K. Rok elbowed me in the side. "I see now why our brother canceled dinner plans with us," he said.

Nik turned and smiled at the woman still watching us on the phone screen—that's when we knew she was the one. His face relaxed as he briefly scanned hers—he had a gleam in his eyes like he had finally found what he was searching for. She turned to look at him briefly, then back at the screen.

"Hi, Rok, with a K, and Mak." She held up her delicate fingers, signing the letter K when she said my name, mirroring me. "I'm Rae, with an E. It's nice to meet you. Is Baby Mak potty trained?" she asked, and we couldn't suppress our laughter.

That was a week ago. Their story was only supposed to last one night. That's my brother's MO. But I discovered the next day that they were still together. Nik told me she wouldn't be in town for long. *"She's only going to be in Seattle for seven days,"* he said.

A lot can happen in one week. It was enough time for my older brother Rok and I to fall in love with her over brief calls with Nik and at our cousin Chase's birthday celebration. At the party, I ran off Rae's cheating ex, who happened to be in attendance, and she introduced me to a beautiful woman named Melanie. That's a story for another day. By the end of the week, we were all hooked. One week was enough to discover Rae's that special type of woman—the smart, sexy, sassy kind that would fit wonderfully into our world like the missing centerpiece of a thousand-piece puzzle you thought you'd never find.

That's what Rae is. The perfect find, the perfect fit—the woman who first captured our attention with her wit. The perfect woman for Nik.

Love Letters

30 Days In Belfast

Blurb

Just one distraction could lead to failure—several may spell ruin.

As the daughter of the wealthiest Black man in the country, Rose Ross struggles to make a name for herself as the COO of her father's tech company. She's even forced to let go of a promising relationship to focus on her career, but still cannot seem to escape her father's legacy. Rose fears that if she remains at Rick Ross Enterprises, she will never rise above the vast shadow his name casts.

When her ailing friend reaches out to her for help, Rose doesn't hesitate. She has just thirty days to curate the most important charity art exhibition in Europe and break into a field she is truly passionate about. However, just before she leaves for her flight to Belfast, her father informs her that she has only three weeks to decide whether she will succeed him as CEO.

With her concentration already split between one life-altering decision, Rose is stunned when she meets her friend's handsome and overprotective brothers. Right away, she recognizes an undeniable, yet different, attraction to both.

Her mind in turmoil, Rose's focus is now fractured among love and business. If she cannot make a decision—or if she makes the wrong one—she will lose everything she has worked for and, perhaps, more.

30 Days In Belfast *is a standalone contemporary romance.*

30 Days In Belfast

PROLOGUE

We Have Time

"If you love somebody, let them go, for if they return, they were always yours. If they don't, they never were."
– Kahlil Gibran, *A Tear and a Smile*

"I'll race ya," Shannon called as she ran past Rose toward the foam remnants of a forgotten wave on the shoreline.

Rose stopped scribing her initials in the sand heart drawing, a covert confession of love to her celebrity crush. She jumped up and headed toward the water. "Wait for me," she shouted to Shannon, who didn't see her. The glare from the sun dancing on the waves mimicking a million miniature mirrors distorted her view. Rose chased a wave and jumped in the water, pushing through the powerful current. When it subsided slightly, she popped up. "Shannon!" she called over the waves, but didn't see her friend. Rose continued to push through the currents, shoving the waves back with her arms that were growing sore by the minute. With each breath she took, she became more panicked, still unable to spot her friend.

Rose looked toward the shore to see if Shannon had made it back. "Shannon, where—" Rose called out before being sucked under by the current. Before it all became a faded memory.

Fifteen years later, the aftermath was fuzzy in her head. She remembered eventually getting herself to shore. The shock and overwhelming sense of loss she felt when she realized Shannon was not by her side finally came into focus as people crowded around her in the sand. An endless stream of questions rushed through her. The sudden end of a forever friendship stolen by sun, sand, and sneaker waves. Rose felt her face grow warm as memories of Shannon flooded her mind. Her heart started to race. Panic washed over her as she relived the day her friend died. All she wanted to do now was run.

"Rose, talk to me. I know it feels like it came out of left field. Tell me what you're thinking." The sound of Alejandro's voice sitting across the table pulled her out of her head. He was staring at her with a mix of concern and longing in his eyes. Shelved was the swoon-worthy smile that usually greeted her. The smile that made her melt after spending weeks away from her man. He reached his hand across the table.

Rose averted Alejandro's gaze and looked around his London flat, where they had just spent the last three evenings wrapped in each other's arms. Where they had made love for hours until they were both sore, satiated, and spent. Where they had shared rare stolen moments between their busy schedules. She was the one who convinced him to get the flat since he spent so much time traveling between New York and London. He was busy building his career as an international attorney, and Rose was recently promoted to COO. A reward for endless hours helping her father build his business and developing new technologies to innovate the company. Living on the west coast, paired with the busy travel schedule that came with her new position, meant they spent more time on video calls than in person.

Rose focused her attention on the modern, muted earth tones of the room. Her eyes were drawn to a painting she commissioned: A Black woman with a crown of flowers blooming from her head and partially covering her face. Rose remembered posing for the portrait with her chin turned toward her bare shoulder. "Think about your man," the artist had instructed her.

Now, she was sitting across the table from the man she thought she could build a life with. His words washed across her, pulling her down like the sneaker wave that snatched her childhood friend from her life forever. Stirring within her was the same sense of shock and sudden loss.

Rose sucked in a breath. "You sure about this?" she said, sounding as if negotiating a business deal—placing a wall around her heart and tamping the need to reach across the table to take his hand.

"No. But I do know we're both committed to our work. The time in between when we finally get together keeps growing. I'm torn between you and the job, and I don't want to ask you to bend for me. I respect that you're building your career, too. I want to make it work but can't see a way. You just got promoted and want to make a name for yourself away from your father's shadow. That's a tall order, and I'll use all my resources to support you in that effort. But trying to build something more between us is no small feat. Think about it. How many things did you and I have to shift to get these three nights together?"

"Quite a bit," she answered, hesitant to strengthen his argument.

"That's exactly the point. You and I know that you had to rearrange twice as much as me. I won't continue asking you to do that. Your father is my largest client. I know the demand he puts on me. I can only imagine how exponentially higher that is on you. I care about you, but I won't be the one to stifle your success. Let's take a step back and focus. Let's give ourselves a year." Alejandro leaned back in his chair and ran his hands through his hair.

Rose knew he was rethinking his words. But they were out, weighing heavy between them.

Was he right? Should they take a break, allowing time to establish themselves? Could they walk away and get back when the time was right? Would it ever be right?

The idea of them not being a couple made Rose feel like she did when she lost her best friend. The same emotions flowed through her all over again. She paused to think, unaware of what was keeping her from ending the conversation, putting her foot down, and refusing his suggestion.

Rose closed her eyes, inhaled, and opened them. Alejandro's gaze was still locked on her. "This isn't about something else. Or is it? You—" she started.

Alejandro stood, rounded the table, and pulled Rose to her feet and into a tight embrace. He planted kisses all over her face before touching his forehead to hers.

"Oh, Rose. Don't ever think that. I...I'd be hard-pressed to believe I could be with anyone other than you. You are the center of my universe, but I know I'm not yours. This is me setting you free—giving you time to do what you need to do. To be you without me interfering."

Rose listened intently, her breath becoming synchronized with his.

"I'm not saying it's just about you," he continued. "I also need to figure out why I haven't moved heaven and earth to be by your side. And for that, I'm at fault." Alejandro swallowed, then turned to look out the window. Rose held onto his hand, walked up behind him, and pressed her chin to his back.

"Okay." Rose paused. "We'll give it some time."

30 Days In Belfast

Acknowledgements

It's hard to believe I wrote a three-book series. It's a considerable achievement, but it could not have been done without the help of others. Thank you to my tribe—those who helped me navigate my writing journey and those who've built me up. Firstly, thank you, Cassandra, for editing the series. You've taught me so much this past year. To Bess, Deborah, and Vianna, thank you for all your constant support. To my BFF, Sandra, I'm channeling your spirit to push me past my fears. To my besties at The Smut Peddler Collective, thank you for your friendship and support and for helping get my book in front of new readers. Janil and Natasha, I'll forever be grateful to you. You are the best! To Jessel, thank you for building me up. Lastly, thank you, Kenya, for hosting the writing sprints that kept me focused on writing the "Let it Rain" series. And to those sitting silently in the wings, thank you.

Love you all,

Rita

Discussion Questions

1. Raven's parents play a pivotal role in her response to her environment, including relationships. How do her inherited genetics or learned behaviors show up? What about the effects of her parents' presence or lack thereof in her life?

2. Throughout the book, Noah is persistent in believing that Raven is his person. Do you believe that's truly how he feels? Is he still riding the sexual high? Or is this part of his possessive "take what's mine" persona? Why?

3. In *The Fall of Us*, Parker takes a big step back from his overly possessive, professing all my love, reclaiming my woman stance that we saw in *The Days With Rain*. Raven subtly offers herself to him several times, but he doesn't bite. What do you think contributes to the change we see in him?

4. We learn a lot of Raven's relationship woes were potentially avoidable. What do you think about her decision to seek out experiences with other men despite what her heart wanted?

5. Which scene stuck with you the most?

Interested in facilitating deeper book discussion? Subscribe to my newsletter and receive a link to my free resource, Romance Book Discussion Guide. https://bit.ly/ritasnews.

About the Author

Photo by Abigail Huller

Rita Gordon is an indie author and former corporate baddie who writes love stories where love always wins. As an emerging voice in the contemporary romance genre, she brings a fresh perspective to storytelling. Inspired by the power of love and the beauty of cultural exploration, her writing captures the essence of human emotions, leaving readers spellbound with each page turn. When she's not busy working through her TBRs and writing, she travels, draws flower designs for her coloring books, and volunteers in her community.

To learn more about the author, visit **ritaagordon.com**.

Connect With Rita

Let's stay in touch! You can find me here:

Subscribe to her newsletter:

www.ritaagordon.com/subscrib-page

Follow Rita on:

X | Instagram | Pinterest:

@rgordonshaw

TikTok:

@authorritagordon (ritagordonwrites)

Facebook:

www.facebook.com/authorritagordon

Goodreads:

www.goodreads.com/author/show/21524163.Rita_A_Gordon

Also by Rita A. Gordon

Standalone Novel

30 Days in Belfast

Let It Rain Series

Seven Days in Seattle (Book 1)

The Days with Rain (Book 2)

The Fall of Us (Book 3)

Love Notes: Anthology (Book 4, coming soon)

Coloring Books

Little Flower Garden

The Big Flower

Inspirational Books & Journals

The Book of Love

On a Positive Note

Grateful

www.ritaagordon.com

www.ingramcontent.com/pod-product-compliance
Lightning Source LLC
Chambersburg PA
CBHW020246030826
48979CB00030B/2631/J

* 9 7 9 8 9 8 9 9 4 2 9 1 6 *